MOUNTOLIVE

by Lawrence Durrell

MOUNTOLIVE

LAWRENCE DURRELL

A Dutton  *Paperback*

NEW YORK

E. P. DUTTON & CO., INC.

A

CLAUDE

ἄγαθου διάμονος

LAWRENCE DURRELL, a British citizen of Irish parentage, was born in the Himalaya region of India. His first ten years were spent in India. After schooling in England, he decided to become a writer. Throughout the 1930's Mr. Durrell devoted most of his talents to his poetry which has won much acclaim. His first novel, *The Black Book,* was published in Paris in 1938, and was cited by T. S. Eliot as being one of the great hopes for modern English fiction. *The Black Book* was published in the United States for the first time in 1960.

World War II temporarily interrupted Mr. Durrell's literary career. During the war years and for some time thereafter, he served Great Britain in various official and diplomatic capacities in Athens, Cairo, Rhodes and Belgrade.

The publication of *Justine* in 1957, and the subsequent appearance of *Balthazar* (1958), *Mountolive* (1959), and *Clea* (1960) as parts of the same magnificent series called *The Alexandria Quartet* devoted to an examination of the various aspects of love, immediately caused Mr. Durrell to be recognized as one of the greatest and most important writers of modern times.

NOTE

All the characters and situations described in this book (a sibling to JUSTINE *and* BALTHAZAR *and the third volume of a quartet) are purely imaginary. I have exercised a novelist's right in taking a few necessary liberties with modern Middle Eastern history and the staff-structure of the Diplomatic Service. I have also improved the beauty of Trafalgar Square by adding a few elms to soften its austerity. Honi soit qui mal y pense.*

The dream dissipated, were one to recover one's commonsense mood, the thing would be of but mediocre import—'tis the story of mental wrong-doing. Everyone knows very well and it offends no one. But alas! one sometimes carries the thing a little further. What, one dares wonder, what would not be the idea's realization if its mere abstract shape thus exalted has just so profoundly moved one? The accursed reverie is vivified and its existence is a crime.

Justine
D. A. F. DE SADE

I

As a junior of exceptional promise, he had been sent to Egypt for a year in order to improve his Arabic and found himself attached to the High Commission as a sort of scribe to await his first diplomatic posting; but he was already conducting himself as a young secretary of legation, fully aware of the responsibilities of future office. Only somehow today it was rather more difficult than usual to be reserved, so exciting had the fish-drive become.

He had in fact quite forgotten about his once-crisp tennis flannels and college blazer and the fact that the wash of bilge rising through the floor-boards had toe-capped his white plimsolls with a black stain. In Egypt one seemed to forget oneself continually like this. He blessed the chance letter of introduction which had brought him to the Hosnani lands, to the rambling old-fashioned house built upon a network of lakes and embankments near Alexandria. Yes.

The punt which now carried him, thrust by slow thrust across the turbid water, was turning slowly eastward to take up its position in the great semicircle of boats which was being gradually closed in upon a target-area marked out by the black reed spines of fish-pans. And as they closed in, stroke by stroke, the Egyptian night fell—the sudden reduction of all objects to bas-reliefs upon a screen of gold and violet. The land had become dense as tapestry in the lilac afterglow, quivering here and there with water-mirages from the rising damps, expanding and contracting horizons, until one thought of the world as being mirrored in a soap-bubble trembling on the edge of disappearance. Voices too across the water sounded now loud, now soft and clear. His own cough fled across the lake in sudden wing-beats. Dusk, yet it was still hot, his shirt stuck to his back. The spokes of darkness which reached out to them only outlined the shapes of the reed-fringed islands, which punctuated the water like great pin-cushions, like paws, like hassocks.

Slowly, at the pace of prayer or meditation, the great arc of boats was forming and closing in, but with the land and the water liquefying at this rate he kept having the illusion that they were travelling across the sky rather than across the alluvial waters of Mareotis. And out of sight he could hear the splatter of geese, and in one corner water and sky split apart as a flight rose, trailing its webs across the estuary like sea-planes, honking crassly. Mountolive sighed and stared down into the brown water, chin on his hands. He was unused to feeling so happy. Youth is the age of despairs.

Behind him he could hear the hare-lipped younger brother Narouz grunting at every thrust of the pole while the lurch of the boat echoed in his loins. The mud, thick as molasses, dripped back into the water with a slow *flob flob*, and the pole sucked lusciously. It was very beautiful, but it all stank so: yet to his surprise he found he rather enjoyed the rotting smells of the estuary. Draughts of wind from the far sea-line ebbed around them from time to time, refreshing the mind. Choirs of gnats whizzed up there like silver rain in the eye of the dying sun. The cobweb of changing light fired his mind. "Narouz," he said, "I am so happy," as he listened to his own unhurried heart-beats. The youth gave his shy hissing laugh and said: "Good, good," ducking his head. "But this is nothing. Wait. We are closing in." Mountolive smiled. "Egypt," he said to himself as one might repeat the name of a woman. "Egypt."

"Over there," said Narouz in his hoarse, melodious voice, "the ducks are not *rusés*, do you know?" (His English was imperfect and stilted.) "For the poaching of them, it is easy (you say 'poaching' don't you?) You dive under them and take them by the legs. Easier than shooting, eh? If you wish, tomorrow we will go." He grunted again at the pole and sighed.

12

"What about snakes?" said Mountolive. He had seen several large ones swimming about that afternoon.

Narouz squared his stout shoulders and chuckled. "No snakes," he said and laughed once more.

Mountolive turned sideways to rest his cheek on the wood of the prow. Out of the corner of his eye he could see his companion, standing up as he poled, and study the hairy arms and hands, the sturdy braced legs. "Shall I take a turn?" he asked in Arabic. He had already noticed how much pleasure it gave his hosts when he spoke to them in their native tongue. Their answers, smilingly given, were a sort of embrace. "Shall I?"

"Of course not" said Narouz, smiling his ugly smile which was only redeemed by magnificent eyes and a deep voice. Sweat dripped down from the curly black hair with its widow's peak. And then lest his refusal might seem impolite, he added: "The drive will start with darkness. I know what to do; and you must look and see the fish." The two little pink frills of flesh which edged his unbasted lip were wet with spittle. He winked lovingly at the English youth.

The darkness was racing towards them now and the light expiring. Narouz suddenly cried: "Now is the moment. Look there." He clapped his hands loudly and shouted across the water, startling his companion who followed his pointed finger with raised head. "What?" the dull report of a gun from the furtherest boat shook the air and suddenly the sky-line was sliced in half by a new flight, rising more slowly and dividing earth from air in a pink travelling wound; like the heart of a pomegranate staring through its skin. Then, turning from pink to scarlet, flushed back into white and fell to the lake-level like a shower of snow to melt as it touched the water—"Flamingo" they both cried and laughed, and the darkness snapped upon them, extinguishing the visible world.

For a long moment now they rested, breathing deeply, to let their eyes grow accustomed to it. Voices and laughter from the distant boats floating across their path. Someone cried "Ya

Narouz" and again "Ya Narouz". He only grunted. And now there came the short syncopated tapping of a finger-drum, music whose rhythms copied themselves instantly in Mountolive's mind so that he felt his own fingers begin to tap upon the boards. The lake was floorless now, the yellow mud had vanished—the soft cracked mud of prehistoric lake-faults, or the bituminous mud which the Nile drove down before it on its course to the sea. All the darkness still smelt of it. "Ya Narouz" came the cry again, and Mountolive recognized the voice of Nessim the elder brother borne upon a sea-breath as it spaced out the words. "Time . . . to . . . light . . . up." Narouz yelped an answer and grunted with satisfaction as he fumbled for matches. "Now you'll see" he said with pride.

The circle of boats had narrowed now to encompass the pans and in the hot dusk matches began to spark, while soon the carbide lamps attached to the prows blossomed into trembling yellow flowers, wobbling up into definition, enabling those who were out of line to correct their trim. Narouz bent over his guest with an apology and groped at the prow. Mountolive smelt the sweat of his strong body as he bent down to test the rubber tube and shake the old bakelite box of the lamp, full of rock-carbide. Then he turned a key, struck a match, and for a moment the dense fumes engulfed them both where they sat, breath held, only to clear swiftly while beneath them also flowered, like some immense coloured crystal, a semicircle of lake water, candent and faithful as a magic lantern to the startled images of fish scattering and reforming with movements of surprise, curiosity, perhaps even pleasure. Narouz expelled his breath sharply and retired to his place. "Look down" he urged, and added "But keep your head well down." And as Mountolive, who did not understand this last piece of advice, turned to question him, he said "Put a coat around your head. The kingfishers go mad with the fish and they are not night-sighted. Last time I had my cheek cut open; and Sobhi lost an eye. Face forwards and down."

Mountolive did as he was bidden and lay there floating over the nervous pool of lamplight whose floor was now peerless crystal not mud and alive with water-tortoises and frogs and sliding fish—a whole population disturbed by this intrusion from the overworld. The punt lurched again and moved while the cold bilge came up around his toes. Out of the corner of his eye he could see that now the great half-circle of light, the chain of blossoms, was closing more rapidly; and as if to give the boats orientation and measure, there arose a drumming and singing, subdued and melancholy, yet authoritative. He felt the tug of the turning boat echoed again in his backbone. His sensations recalled nothing he had ever known, were completely original.

The water had become dense now, and thick; like an oat-meal soup that is slowly stirred into thickness over a slow fire. But when he looked more closely he saw that the illusion was caused not by the water but by the multiplication of the fish themselves. They had begun to swarm, darting in schools, excited by the very consciousness of their own numbers, yet all sliding and skirmishing one way. The cordon too had tightened like a noose and only twenty feet now separated them from the next boat, the next pool of waxen light. The boatmen had begun to utter hoarse cries and pound the waters around them, themselves excited by the premonition of those fishy swarms which crowded the soft lake bottom, growing more and more excited as the shallows began and they recognized themselves trapped in the shining circle. There was something like delirium in their swarming and circling now. Vague shadows of men began to unwind hand-nets in the boats and the shouting thickened. Mountolive felt his blood beating faster with excitement. "In a moment" cried Narouz. "Lie still."

The waters thickened to glue and silver bodies began to leap into the darkness only to fall back, glittering like coinage, into the shallows. The circles of light touched, overlapped, and the whole ceinture was complete, and from all around it there came the smash and crash of dark bodies leaping into the shallows, furling out the long hand-nets which were joined end to end and whose dark loops were already bulging like Christmas stockings with the squirming bodies of fish. The leapers had taken fright too and their panic-stricken leaps ripped up the whole surface of the pan, flashing back cold water upon the stuttering lamps, falling into the boats, a shuddering harvest of cold scales and drumming tails. Their exciting death-struggles were as contagious as the drumming had been. Laughter shook the air as the nets closed. Mountolive could see Arabs with their long white robes tucked up to the waist pressing forwards with steadying hands held to the dark prows beside them, pushing their linked nets slowly forward. The light gleamed upon their dark thighs. The darkness was full of their barbaric blitheness.

And now came another unexpected phenomenon—for the sky itself began to thicken above them as the water had below. The darkness was suddenly swollen with unidentifiable shapes for the jumpers had alerted the sleepers from the shores of the lakes, and with shrill incoherent cries the new visitants from the sedge-lined outer estuary joined in the hunt—hundreds of pelican, flamingo, crane and kingfisher—coming in on irregular trajectories to careen and swoop and snap at the jumping fish. The waters and the air alike seethed with life as the fishermen aligned their nets and began to scoop the swarming catch into the boats, or turned out their nets to let the rippling cascades of silver pour over the gunwales until the helmsmen were sitting ankle-deep in the squirming bodies. There would be enough and to spare for men and birds, and while the larger waders of the lake folded and unfolded awkward wings like old-fashioned painted parasols, or hovered in ungainly parcels above the snapping, leaping water, the kingfishers and herring-gulls came in from every direction at the speed of thunderbolts, half mad with greed and excitement, flying on suicidal courses, some to break their necks outright upon the decks of

16

the boats, some to flash beak forward into the dark body of a fisherman to split open a cheek or a thigh in their terrifying cupidity. The splash of water, the hoarse cries, the snapping of beaks and wings, and the mad tattoo of the finger-drums gave the whole scene an unforgettable splendour, vaguely recalling to the mind of Mountolive forgotten Pharaonic frescoes of light and darkness.

Here and there too the men began to fight off the birds, striking at the dark air around them with sticks until amid the swarming scrolls of captured fish one could see surprisingly rainbow feathers of magical hue and broken beaks from which blood trickled upon the silver scales of the fish. For three-quarters of an hour the scene continued thus until the dark boats were brimming. Now Nessim was alongside, shouting to them in the darkness. "We must go back." He pointed to a lantern waving across the water, creating a warm cave of light in which they glimpsed the smooth turning flanks of a horse and the serrated edge of palm-leaves. "My mother is waiting for us" cried Nessim. His flawless head bent down to take the edge of a light-pool as he smiled. His was a Byzantine face such as one might find among the frescoes of Ravenna— almond-shaped, dark-eyed, clear-featured. But Mountolive was looking, so to speak, through the face of Nessim and into that of Leila who was so like him, his mother. "Narouz," he called hoarsely, for the younger brother had jumped into the water to fasten a net. "Narouz!" One could hardly make oneself heard in the commotion. "We must go back."

And so at last the two boats each with its Cyclops-eye of light turned back across the dark water to the far jetty where Leila waited patiently for them with the horses in the mos-quito-loud silence. A young moon was up now.

Her voice came laughingly across the variable airs of the lake, chiding them for being late, and Narouz chuckled. "We've brought lots of fish," cried Nessim. She stood, slightly darker than the darkness, and their hands met as if

17

guided by some perfected instinct which found no place in their conscious minds. Mountolive's heart shook as he stood up and climbed onto the jetty with her help. But no sooner were the two brothers ashore than Narouz cried: "Race you home, Nessim" and they dived for their horses which bucked and started at the laughing onslaught. "Careful," she cried sharply, but before a second had passed they were off, hooves drumming on the soft rides of the embankment, Narouz chuckling like a Mephistopheles. "What is one to do?" she said with mock resignation, and now the factor came forward with their own horses.

They mounted and set off for the house. Ordering the servant to ride on before with the lantern, Leila brought her horse close in so that they might ride knee-to-knee, solaced by the touch of each other's bodies. They had not been lovers for very long—barely ten days—though to the youthful Mountolive it seemed a century, an eternity of despair and delight. He had been formally educated in England, educated not to wish to feel. All the other valuable lessons he had already mastered, despite his youth—to confront the problems of the drawing-room and the street with sang-froid; but towards personal emotions he could only oppose the nervous silence of a national sensibility almost anaesthetized into clumsy taciturnity: an education in selected reticences and shames. Breeding and sensibility seldom march together, though the breach can be carefully disguised in codes of manners, forms of address towards the world. He had heard and read of passion, but had regarded it as something which would never impinge on him, and now here it was, bursting into the secret life which, like every overgrown schoolboy, lived on autonomously behind the indulgent screen of everyday manners and transactions, everyday talk and affections. The social man in him was overripe before the inner man had grown up. Leila had turned him out as one might turn out an old trunk, throwing everything into confusion. He suspected himself now to be only a mawkish and callow youth, his reserves depleted. With indignation almost, he realized that here at last there was something for which he might even be prepared to die—something whose very crudity carried with it a winged message which pierced to the quick of his mind. Even in the darkness he could feel himself wanting to blush. It was absurd. To *love* was absurd, like being knocked off the mantelpiece. He caught himself wondering what his mother would think if she could picture them riding among the spectres of these palm-trees by a lake which mirrored a young moon, knee touching knee. "Are you happy?" she whispered and he felt her lips brush his wrist. Lovers can find nothing to say to each other that has not been said and unsaid a thousand times over. Kisses were invented to translate such nothings into wounds. "Mountolive," she said again, "David darling."—"Yes."—"You are so quiet. I thought you must be asleep." Mountolive frowned, confronting his own dispersed inner nature. "I was thinking," he said. Once more he felt her lips on his wrist.

"Darling."

"Darling."

They rode on knee-to-knee until the old house came into view, built four-square upon the network of embankments which carved up the estuary and the sweet-water canals. The air was full of fruit-bats. The upper balconies of the house were brightly lit and here the invalid sat crookedly in his wheel-chair, staring jealously out at the night, waiting for them. Leila's husband was dying of some obscure disease of the musculature, a progressive atrophy which cruelly emphasized the already great difference in their ages—for while she was only in her forties, though she looked much younger, he was well past sixty. His infirmity had hollowed him out into a cadaverous shell composed of rugs and shawls from which protruded two long sensitive hands. Saturnine of feature and with an uncouthness of mien which was echoed in his younger son's face, his head was askew on his shoulders and in some lights resembled those carnival masks which are carried on poles. It only remains to be added that Leila loved him!

"*Leila loved him.*" In the silence of his own mind Mountolive could never think the words without mentally shrieking them like a parrot. How could she? He had asked himself over and over again. How could she?

As he heard the hooves of the horses on the cobbles of the courtyard, the husband urged his wheel-chair forward to the balcony's edge, calling testily: "Leila, is that you?" in the voice of an old child ready to be hurt by the warmth of her smile thrown upwards to him from the ground and the deep sweet contralto in which she answered him, mixing oriental submissiveness with the kind of comfort which only a child could understand. "Darling". And running up the long wooden flights of stairs to embrace him, calling out "We are all safely back." Mountolive slowly dismounted in the court-yard, hearing the sick man's sigh of relief. He busied himself with an unnecessary tightening of a girth rather than see them embrace. He was not jealous, but his incredulity pierced and wounded him. It was hateful to be young, to be maladroit, to feel carried out of one's depth. How had all this come about? He felt a million miles away from England; his past had sloughed from him like a skin. The warm night was fragrant with jasmine and roses. Later if she came to his room he would become as still as a needle, speechless and thoughtless, taking that strangely youthful body in his arms almost without desire or regrets; his eyes closed then, like a man standing under an icy waterfall. He climbed the stairs slowly; she had made him aware that he was tall, upright and handsome.

"Did you like it, Mountolive?" croaked the invalid, with a voice in which floated (like oil in water) pride and suspicion. A tall negro servant wheeled a small table forward on which the decanter of whisky stood—a world of anomalies: to drink "sundowners" like colonials in this old rambling house full of magnificent carpets, walls covered with assegais captured at

Omdurman, and weird Second Empire furniture of a Turkish cast. "Sit," he said, and Mountolive, smiling at him, sat, noticing that even here in the reception rooms there were books and periodicals lying about—symbols of the unsatisfied hunger for thought which Leila had never allowed to master her. Normally, she kept her books and papers in the *hareem*, but they always overflowed into the house. Her husband had no share of this world. She tried as far as possible not to make him conscious of it, dreading his jealousy which had become troublesome as his physical incapacity increased. His sons were washing—somewhere Mountolive heard the sound of running water. Soon he would excuse himself and retire to change into a white suit for dinner. He drank and talked to the crumpled man in the wheel-chair in his low melodious voice. It seemed to him terrifying and improper to be the lover of his wife; and yet he was always breathless with surprise to see how naturally and simply Leila carried off the whole deception. (Her cool honeyed voice, etc., etc.; he should try not to think of her too much.) He frowned and sipped his drink.

It had been quite difficult to find his way out to the lands to present his letter of introduction: the motor road still only ran as far as the ford, after which horses had to be used to reach the house among the canals. He had been marooned for nearly an hour before a kindly passer-by had offered him a horse on which he reached his destination. That day there had been nobody at home save the invalid. Mountolive noticed with some amusement that in reading the letter of introduction, couched in the flowery high style of Arabic, the invalid muttered aloud the conventional politenesses of reciprocity to the compliments he was reading just as if the writer of the letter had himself been present. Then at once he looked up tenderly into the face of the young Englishman and spoke, and Mountolive softly answered. "You will come and stay with us—it is the only way to improve your Arabic. For two months if you wish. My sons know English and will be delighted to converse with you; my wife also. It would be a blessing to them to have a new face, a stranger in the house. And my dear Nessim is in his last year at Oxford." Pride and pleasure glowed in his sunken eyes for a minute and flickered out to give place to the customary look of pain and chagrin. Illness invites contempt. A sick man knows it.

Mountolive had accepted, and by renouncing both home and local leave had obtained permission to stay for two months in the house of this Coptic squire. It was a complete departure from everything he had known to be thus included in the pattern of a family life based in and nourished by the unconscious pageantry of a feudalism which stretched back certainly as far as the Middle Ages, and perhaps beyond. The world of Burton, Beckford, Lady Hester. . . . Did they then still exist? But here, seen from the vantage point of someone inside the canvas his own imagination had painted, he had suddenly found the exotic becoming completely normal. Its poetry was irradiated by the unconsciousness with which it was lived. Mountolive who had already found the open sesame of language ready to hand, suddenly began to feel himself really penetrating a foreign country, foreign *moeurs*, for the first time. He felt as one always feels in such a case, namely the vertiginous pleasure of losing an old self and growing a new one to replace it. He felt he was slipping, losing so to speak the contours of himself. Is this the real meaning of education? He had begun transplanting a whole huge intact world from his imagination into the soil of his new life.

The Hosnani family itself was oddly assorted. The graceful Nessim and his mother were familiars of the spirit, belonging to the same intense world of intelligence and sensibility. He, the eldest son, was always on the watch to serve his mother, should she need a door opened or a handkerchief recovered from the ground. His English and French were perfect, impeccable as his manners, graceful and strong as his physique. Then, facing them across the candle-light, sat the other two:

the invalid in his rugs, and the younger son, tough and brutish as a mastiff and with an indefinable air of being ready at any moment to answer a call to arms. Heavily built and ugly, he was nevertheless gentle; but you could see from the loving way he drank in each word uttered by his father where his love-allegiance lay. His simplicity shone in his eyes, and he too was ready to be of service, and indeed, when the work of the lands did not take him from the house, was always quick to dismiss the silent body-servant who stood behind the wheel-chair and to serve his father with a glowing pride, glad even to pick him up bodily and take him tenderly, almost gloatingly, to the lavatory. He regarded his mother with something like the pride and childish sadness which shone in the eyes of the cripple. Yet, though the brothers were divided in this way like twigs of olive, there was no breach between them—they were of the same branch and felt it, and they loved one another dearly, for they were in truth complementaries, the one being strong where the other was weak. Nessim feared bloodshed, manual work and bad manners: Narouz rejoiced in them all. And Leila? Mountolive of course found her a beautiful enigma when he might, had he been more experienced, have recognized in her naturalness a perfect simplicity of spirit and in her extravagant nature a temperament which had been denied its true unfolding, had fallen back with good grace among com-promises. This marriage, for example, to a man so much older than herself had been one of arrangement—this was still Egypt. The fortunes of her family had been matched against the fortunes of the Hosnanis—it resembled, as all such unions do, a merger between two great companies. Whether she was happy or unhappy she herself had never thought to consider. She was hungry, that was all, hungry for the world of books and meetings which lay forever outside this old house and the heavy charges of the land which supported their fortunes. She was obedient and pliant, loyal as a finely-bred animal. Only a disorienting monotony beset her. When young she had completed her studies in Cairo brilliantly and for a few years nourished the hope of going to Europe to continue them. She had wanted to be a doctor. But at this time the women of Egypt were lucky if they could escape the black veil—let alone the narrow confines of Egyptian thought and society. Europe for the Egyptians was simply a shopping centre for the rich to visit. Naturally, she went several times to Paris with her parents and indeed fell in love with it as we all do, but when it came to attempting to breach the barriers of Egyptian habit and to escape the parental net altogether—escape into a life which might have nourished a clever brain—there she struck upon the rock of her parents' conservatism. She must marry and make Egypt her home, they said coldly, and selected for her among the rich men of their acquaintance the kindliest and the most able they could find. Standing upon the cliff-edge of these dreams, still beautiful and rich (and indeed, in Alexandrian society she was known as "the dark swallow") Leila found everything becoming shadowy and insubstantial. She must conform. Of course, nobody would mind her visiting Europe with her husband every few years to shop or have a holiday. . . . But her life must belong to Egypt.

She gave in, responding at first with despair, later with resignation, to the life they had designed for her. Her husband was kind and thoughtful, but mentally something of a dullard. The life sapped her will. Her loyalty was such that she immersed herself in his affairs, living because he wished it far from the only capital which bore the remotest traces of a European way of life—Alexandria. For years now she had surrendered herself to the blunting airs of the Delta, and the monotony of life on the Hosnani lands. She lived mostly through Nessim who was being educated largely abroad and whose rare visits brought some life to the house. But to allay her own active curiosity about the world, she subscribed to books and periodicals in the four languages which she knew as well as her own, perhaps better, for nobody can think or feel only in the dimensionless obsolescence of Arabic. So it had been for many years now, a battle of resignations in which the element of despair only arose in the form of nervous illnesss for which her husband prescribed a not unintelligent specific— a ten-day holiday in Alexandria which always brought the colour back into her cheeks. But even these visits became in time more rare: she had insensibly slipped out of society and found herself less and less practised in the small talk and small ideas upon which it is based. The life of the city bored her. It was shallow as the waters of the great lake itself, derived; her powers of introspection sharpened with the years, and as her friends fell away only a few names and faces remained—Balthazar the doctor, for example, and Amaril and a few others. But Alexandria was soon to belong more fully to Nessim than to herself. When his studies ended he was to be conscripted into the banking house with its rapidly ramifying ancillaries, roots pushing out into shipping and oil and tungsten, roots needing water. . . . But by this time she would have become virtually a hermit.

This lonely life had made her feel somewhat unprepared for Mountolive, for the arrival of a stranger in their midst. On that first day she came in late from a desert ride and slipped into her place between her husband and his guest with some pleasurable excitement. Mountolive hardly looked at her, for the thrilling voice alone set up odd little vibrations in his heart which he registered but did not wish to study. She wore white jodhpurs and a yellow shirt with a scarf. Her smooth small hands were white and ringless. Neither of her sons appeared at lunch that day, and after the meal it was she who elected to show him round the house and gardens, already pleasantly astonished by the youth's respectable Arabic and sound French. She treated him with the faintly apprehensive solicitude of a woman towards her only man-child. His genuine interest and desire to learn filled her with the emotions of a gratitude which surprised her. It was absurd; but then never

25

had a stranger shown any desire to study and assess them, their language, religion and habits. And Mountolive's manners were as perfect as his self-command was weak. They both walked about the rose-garden hearing each other's voices in a sort of dream. They felt short of breath, almost as if they were suffocating.

When he said good-bye that night and accepted her husband's invitation to return and stay with them, she was nowhere to be found. A servant brought a message to say that she was feeling indisposed with a headache and was lying down. But she waited for his return with a kind of obstinate and apprehensive attention.

He did, of course, meet both the brothers on the evening of that first day, for Nessim appeared in the afternoon from Alexandria and Mountolive instantly recognized in him a person of his own kind, a person whose life was a code. They responded to each other nervously, like a concord in music.

And Narouz. "Where is this old Narouz?" she asked her husband, as if the second son were his concern rather than hers, his stake in the world. "He has been locked in the incubators for forty days. To-morrow he will return." Leila looked faintly embarrassed. "He is to be the farmer of the family, and Nessim the banker" she explained to Mountolive, flushing slightly. Then, turning to her husband again, she said "May I take Mountolive to see Narouz at work?" "Of course." Mountolive was enchanted by her pronunciation of his name. She uttered it with a French intonation "Montolif", and it sounded to him a most romantic name. This thought also was new. She took his arm and they walked through the rose-gardens and across the palm-plantations to where the incubators were housed in a long low building of earth-brick, constructed well below ground-level. They knocked once or twice on a sunken door, but at last Leila impatiently pushed it open and they entered a narrow corridor with ten earthen ovens ranged along each side facing each other.

"Close the door" shouted a deep voice as Narouz rose from among a nest of cobwebs and came through the gloom to identify the intruders. Mountolive was somewhat intimidated by his scowl and hare-lip and the harshness of his shout; it was as if, despite his youth, they had intruded upon some tousled anchorite in a cliff-chapel. His skin was yellow and his eyes wrinkled from this long vigil. But when he saw them Narouz apologized and appeared delighted that they had troubled to visit him. He became at once proud and anxious to explain the workings of the incubators, and Leila tactfully left him a clear field. Mountolive already knew that the hatching of eggs by artificial heat was an art for which Egypt had been famous from the remotest antiquity and was delighted to be informed about the process. In this underground fairway full of ancient cobwebs and unswept dirt they talked techniques and temperatures with the equivocal dark eyes of the woman upon them, studying their contrasting physiques and manners, their voices. Narouz' beautiful eyes were now alive and brilliant with pleasure. His guest's lively interest seemed to thrill him too, and he explained everything in detail, even the strange technique by which egg-heats are judged in default of the thermometer, simply by placing the egg in the eye-socket.

Later, walking back through the rose-garden with Leila, Mountolive said: "How very nice your son is." And Leila, unexpectedly, blushed and hung her head. She answered in a low tone, with emotion: "It is so much on our conscience that we did not have his hare-lip sewn up in time. And afterwards the village children teased him, calling him a camel, and that hurt him. You know that a camel's lip is split in two? No? It is. Narouz has had much to contend with." The young man walking at her side felt a sudden pang of sympathy for her. But he remained tongue-tied. And then, that evening, she had disappeared.

At the outset his own feelings somewhat confused him, but he was unused to introspection, unfamiliar so to speak with the

27

entail of his own personality—in a word, as he was young, he successfully dismissed them. (All this he repeated in his own mind afterwards, recalling every detail gravely to himself as he shaved in the old-fashioned mirror or tied a tie. He went over the whole business obsessively time and again, as if vicariously to provoke and master the whole new range of emotions which Leila had liberated in him. At times he would utter the imprecation "Damn" under his breath, between set teeth, as if he were recalling in his own memory some fearful disaster. It was unpleasant to be forced to grow. It was thrilling to grow. He gravitated between fear and grotesque elation.)

They often rode together in the desert at her husband's suggestion, and there one night of the full moon, lying together in a dune dusted soft by the wind to the contours of snow or snuff, he found himself confronted by a new version of Leila. They had eaten their dinner and talked by ghost-light. "Wait" she said suddenly. "There is a crumb on your lip." And leaning forward she took it softly upon her own tongue. He felt the small warm tongue of an Egyptian cat upon his underlip for a moment. (This is where in his mind he always said the word "Damn".) At this he turned pale and felt as if he were about to faint. But she was there so close, harmlessly close, smiling and wrinkling up her nose, that he could only take her in his arms, stumbling forward like a man into a mirror. Their muttering images met now like reflections on a surface of lake-water. His mind dispersed into a thousand pieces, winging away into the desert around them. The act of becoming lovers was so easy and was completed with such apparent lack of premeditation, that for a while he hardly knew himself what had happened. When his mind caught up with him he showed at once how young he was, stammering: "But why me, Leila?" as if there was all the choice in the wide world before her, and was astonished when she lay back and repeated the words after him with what seemed like a musical contempt; the puerility of his question indeed annoyed her.

"Why you? Because." And then, to Mountolive's amazement, she recited in a low sweet voice a passage from one of her favourite authors.

"There is a destiny now possible to us—the highest ever set before a nation to be accepted or refused. We are still undegenerate in race; a race mingled of the best northern blood. We are not yet dissolute in temper, but still have the firmness to govern, and the grace to obey. We have been taught a religion of pure mercy which we must now finally betray or learn to defend by fulfilling. And we are rich in an inheritance of honour, bequeathed to us through a thousand years of noble history, which it should be our daily thirst to increase with splendid avarice, so that Englishmen, if it be a sin to covet honour, should be the most offending souls alive."

Mountolive listened to her voice with astonishment, pity and shame. It was clear that what she saw in him was something like a prototype of a nation which existed now only in her imagination. She was kissing and cherishing a painted image of England. It was for him the oddest experience in the world. He felt the tears come into his eyes as she continued the magnificent peroration, suiting her clear voice to the melody of the prose. "Or will you, youths of England, make your country again a royal throne of kings, a sceptred isle, for all the world a source of light, a centre of peace; mistress of learning and the arts; faithful guardian of great memories in the midst of irreverent and ephemeral visions; a faithful servant of time-tried principles, under temptation from fond experiments and licentious desires; and amidst the cruel and clamorous jealousies of the nations, worshipped in her strange valour, of goodwill towards men?" The words began to vibrate in his skull.

"Stop. Stop," he cried sharply. "We are not like that any longer, Leila." It was an absurd book-fed dream this Copt had discovered and translated. He felt as if all those magical embraces had been somehow won under false pretences—as if her absurd thoughts were reducing the whole thing, diminishing

29

the scale of it to something as shadowy and unreal as, say, a transaction with a woman of the streets. Can you fall in love with the stone effigy of a dead crusader?

"You asked me *why*," she said, still with contempt. "Because," with a sigh, "you are English, I suppose." (It surprised him each time he went over this scene in his mind and only an oath could express the astonishment of it. "Damn".)

And then, like all the inexperienced lovers since the world began, he was not content to let things be; he must explore and evaluate them in his conscious mind. None of the answers she gave him were expected. If he mentioned her husband she at once became angry, interrupting him with withering directness: "I *love* him. I will *not* have him lightly spoken of. He is a noble man and I would never do anything to wound him."

"But . . . but . . ." stammered the young Mountolive; and now, laughing at his perplexity, she once more put her arms about him, saying "Fool, David, *fool*! It is he who told me to take you for a lover. Think—is he not wise in his way? Fearing to lose me altogether by a mischance? Have you never starved for love? Don't you know how dangerous love is?" No, he did not know.

What on earth was an Englishman to make of these strange patterns of thought, these confused and contending loyalties? He was struck dumb. "Only I must not fall in love and I won't." Was this why she had elected to love Mountolive's England through him rather than Mountolive himself? He could find no answer to this. The limitations of his immaturity tongue-tied him. He closed his eyes and felt as if he were falling backwards into black space. And Leila, divining this, found in him an innocence which was itself endearing: in a way she set herself to make a man of him, using every feminine warmth, every candour. He was both a lover to her and a sort of hapless man-child who could be guided by her towards his own growth. Only (she must have made the reservation quite clearly in her own mind) she must beware of any possible resentment which he might feel at this tutelage. So she hid her own experience and became for him almost a companion of his own age, sharing a complicity which somehow seemed so innocent, so beyond reproach, that even his sense of guilt was almost lulled, and he began to drink in through her a new resolution and self-confidence. He told himself with equal resolution that he also must respect her reservations and not fall in love, but this kind of dissociation is impossible for the young. He could not distinguish between his own various emotional needs, between passion-love and the sort of romance fed on narcissism. His desire strangled him. He could not qualify it. And here his English education hampered him at every step. He could not even feel happy without feeling guilty. But all this he did not know very clearly: he only half-guessed that he had discovered more than a lover, more than an accomplice. Leila was not only more experienced; to his utter chagrin he found that she was even better read, in his own language, than he was, and better instructed. But, as a model companion and lover, she never let him feel it. There are so many resources open to a woman of experience. She took refuge always in a tenderness which expressed itself in teasing. She chided his ignorance and provoked his curiosity. And she was amused by the effect of her passion on him—those kisses which fell burning like spittle upon a hot iron. Through her eyes he began to see Egypt once more—but extended through a new dimension. To have a grasp of the language was nothing, he now realized; for Leila exposed the hollowness of the knowledge when pitted against understanding.

An inveterate note-taker by habit, he found his little pocket diary now swollen with the data which emerged from their long rides together, but it was always data which concerned the country, for he did not dare to put down a single word about his feelings or so much as record even Leila's name. In this manner:

"Sunday. Riding through a poor fly-blown village my companion

points to marks like cuneiform scratched on the walls of houses and asks if I can read them. Like a fool I say no, but perhaps they are Amharic? Laughter. Explanation is that a venerable pedlar who travels through here every six months carries a special henna from Medina, much esteemed here by virtue of its connection with the holy city. People are mostly too poor to pay, so he extends credit, but lest he or they forget, marks his tally on the clay wall with a sherd."

"Monday. Ali says that shooting stars are stones thrown by the angels in heaven to drive off evil djinns when they try to eavesdrop on the conversations in Paradise and learn the secrets of the future. All Arabs terrified of the desert, even Bedouin. Strange."

"Also, the pause in conversation which we call 'Angels Passing' is greeted another way. After a moment of silence one says: 'Wahed Dhu' or 'One is God' and then the whole company repeats fervently in response 'La Illah Illa Allah' or 'No God but one God' before normal conversation is resumed. These little habits are extremely taking."

"Also: my host uses a curious phrase when he speaks of retiring from business. He calls it 'making his soul'.

"Also: have never before tasted the Yemen coffee with a speck of ambergris to each cup. It is delicious.

"Also: Mohammed Shebab offered me on meeting a touch of jasmine-scent from a phial with a glass stopper—as we would offer a cigarette in Europe.

"Also: they love birds. In a tumbledown cemetery I saw graves with little drinking-wells cut in the marble for them which my companion told me were filled on Friday visits by women of the village.

"Also: Ali, the Negro factor, an immense eunuch, told me that they feared above all blue eyes and red hair as evil signs. Odd that the examining angels in the Koran as their most repulsive features have blue eyes."

So the young Mountolive noted and pondered upon the strange ways of the people among whom he had come to live, painstakingly as befitted a student of manners so remote from his own; yet also in a kind of ecstasy to find a sort of poetic correspondence between the reality and the dream-picture of the East which he had constructed from his reading. There was less of a disparity here than between the twin images which Leila appeared to nurse—a poetic image of England and its exemplar, the shy and in many ways callow youth she had taken for a lover. But he was not altogether a fool; he was learning the two most important lessons in life: to make love honestly and to reflect.

Yet there were other episodes and scenes which touched and excited him in a different way. One day they all rode out across the plantations to visit the old nurse Halima, now living in honourable retirement. She had been the boys' chief nurse and companion during their infancy. "She even suckled them when my milk dried up" explained Leila.

Narouz gave a hoarse chuckle. "She was our 'chewer' " he explained to Mountolive. "Do you know the word?" In Egypt at this time young children were fed by servants whose duty it was to chew the food up first before spoon-feeding them with it.

Halima was a freed black slave from the Sudan, and she too was "making her soul" now in a little wattle house among the fields of sugar-cane, happily surrounded by innumerable children and grandchildren. It was impossible to judge her age. She was delighted out of all measure at the sight of the Hosnani youths, and Mountolive was touched by the way they both dismounted and raced into her embrace. Nor was Leila less affectionate. And when the old negress had recovered herself she insisted on executing a short dance in honour of their visit; oddly it was not without grace. They all stood around her affectionately clapping their hands in time while she turned first upon one heel and then upon the other; and as she ended her song their embraces and laughter were renewed. This un-affected and spontaneous tenderness delighted Mountolive and he looked upon his mistress with shining eyes in which she could read not only his love but a new respect. He was dying now to be alone with her, to embrace her; but he listened patiently while old Halima told him of the family's qualities and how they had enabled her to visit the holy city twice as a recognition of her services. She kept one hand tenderly upon Narouz's sleeve as she spoke, gazing into his face from time to time with the affection of an animal. Then when he unpacked from the dusty old game-bag he always carried all the presents they had brought for her, the smiles and dismays played over her old face successively like eclipses of the moon. She wept.

But there were other scenes, less palatable perhaps, but nonetheless representative of the *moeurs* of Egypt. One morning early he had witnessed a short incident which took place in the courtyard under his window. A dark youth stood uneasily here before a different Narouz, scowling fiercely yet with ebbing courage into those blue eyes. Mountolive had heard the words "Master, it was no lie" spoken twice in a low clear voice as he lay reading; he rose and walked to the window in time to see Narouz, who was repeating in a low, obstinate voice, pressed between his teeth into a hiss, the words "You lied again", perform an act whose carnal brutality thrilled him; he was in time to see his host take out a knife from his belt and sever a portion of the boy's ear-lobe, but slowly, and indeed softly, as one might sever a grape from its stalk with a fruit-knife. A wave of blood flowed down the servant's neck but he stood still. "Now go," said Narouz in the same diabolical hiss, "and tell your father that for every lie I will cut a piece of your flesh until we come to the true part, the part which does not lie." The boy suddenly broke into a staggering run and disappeared with a gasp. Narouz wiped his knife-blade on his baggy trousers and walked up the stairs into the house, whistling. Mountolive was spellbound!

And then (the variety of these incidents was the most bewildering thing about them) that very afternoon while out riding with Narouz they had reached the boundaries of the property where the desert began, and had here come upon a huge sacred tree hung with every manner of *ex-voto* by the

34

childless or afflicted villagers; every twig seemed to have sprouted a hundred fluttering rags of cloth. Nearby was the shrine of some old hermit, long since dead, and whose name even had been forgotten except perhaps by a few aged villagers. The tumbledown tomb, however, was still a place of pilgrimage and intercession to Moslem and Copt alike; and it was here that, dismounting, Narouz said in the most natural manner in the world: "I always say a prayer here—let us pray together, eh?" Mountolive felt somewhat abashed, but he dismounted without a word and they stood side by side at the dusty little tomb of the lost saint, Narouz with his eyes raised to the sky and an expression of demonic meekness upon his face. Mountolive imitated his pose exactly, forming his hands into a cup-shape and placing them on his breast. Then they both bowed their heads and prayed for a long moment, after which Narouz expelled his breath in a long slow hiss, as if with relief, and made the gesture of drawing his fingers downwards across his face to absorb the blessing which flowed from the prayer. Mountolive imitated him, deeply touched.

"Good. We have prayed now" said Narouz with finality as they remounted and set off across the fields which lay silent under the sunlight save where the force-pumps sucked and wheezed as they pumped the lake-water into the irrigation channels. At the end of the long shady plantations, they encountered another, more familiar, sound, in the soughing of the wooden water-wheels, the *sakkia* of Egypt, and Narouz cocked an appreciative ear to the wind. "Listen," he said, "listen to the *sakkias*. Do you know their story? At least, what the villagers say? Alexander the Great had asses' ears though only one person knew his secret. That was his barber who was a Greek. Difficult to keep a secret if you are Greek! So the barber to relieve his soul went out into the fields and told it to a *sakkia*; ever since the *sakkias* are crying sadly to each other 'Alexander has asses' ears.' Is that not strange? Nessim says that in the museum at Alexandria there is a portrait of

35

Alexander wearing the horns of Ammon and perhaps this tale is a survival. Who can tell?"

They rode in silence for a while. "I hate to think I shall be leaving you next week," said Mountolive. "It has been a wonderful time." A curious expression appeared on Narouz' face, compounded of doubt and uneasy pleasure, and somewhere in between them a kind of animal resentment which Mountolive told himself was perhaps jealousy—jealousy of his mother? He watched the stern profile curiously, unsure quite how to interpret these matters to himself. After all, Leila's affairs were her own concern, were they not? Or perhaps their love-affair had somehow impinged upon the family feeling, so tightly were the duties and affections of the Hosnani family bound? He would have liked to speak freely to the brothers. Nessim at least would understand and sympathize with him, but thinking of Narouz he began to doubt. The younger brother—one could not quite trust him somehow. The early atmosphere of gratitude and delight in the visitor had subtly changed—though he could not trace an open hint of animosity or reserve. No, it was more subtle, less definable. Perhaps, thought Mountolive all at once, he had manufactured this feeling entirely out of his own sense of guilt? He wondered, watching the darkly bitter profile of Narouz. He rode beside him, deeply bemused by the thought.

He could not of course identify what it was that preoccupied the younger brother, for indeed it was a little scene which had taken place without his knowledge one night some weeks previously, while the household slept. At certain times the invalid took it into his head to stay up later than usual, to sit on the balcony in his wheel-chair and read late, usually some manual of estate management, or forestry, or whatnot. At such times the dutiful Narouz would settle himself upon a divan in the next room and wait, patiently as a dog, for the signal to help his father away to bed; he himself never read a book or paper if he could help it. But he enjoyed lying in the yellow lamplight, picking his teeth with a match and brooding until he heard the hoarse waspish voice of his father call his name.

On the night in question he must have dozed off, for when he woke he found to his surprise that all was dark. A brilliant moonlight flooded the room and the balcony, but the lights had been extinguished by an unknown hand. He started up. Astonishingly, the balcony was empty. For a moment, Narouz thought he must be dreaming, for never before had his father gone to bed alone. Yet standing there in the moonlight, battling with this sense of incomprehension and doubt, he thought he heard the sound of the wheel-chair's rubber tyres rolling upon the wooden boards of the invalid's bedroom. This was an astonishing departure from accepted routine. He crossed the balcony and tiptoed down the corridor in amazement. The door of his father's room was open. He peered inside. The room was full of moonlight. He heard the bump of the wheels upon the chest of drawers and a scrabble of fingers groping for a knob. Then he heard a drawer pulled open, and a sense of dismay filled him for he remembered that in it was kept the old Colt revolver which belonged to his father. He suddenly found himself unable to move or speak as he heard the breech snapped open and the unmistakable sound of paper rustling—a sound immediately interpreted by his memory. Then the small precise click of the shells slipping into the chambers. It was as if he were trapped in one of those dreams where one is running with all one's might and yet unable to move from the same spot. As the breech snapped home and the weapon was assembled, Narouz gathered himself together to walk boldly into the room but found that he could not move. His spine got pins and needles and he felt the hair bristle up on the back of his neck. Overcome by one of the horrifying inhibitions of early childhood he could do no more than take a single slow step forward and halt in the doorway, his teeth clenched to prevent them chattering.

The moonlight shone directly on to the mirror, and by its

reflected light he could see his father sitting upright in his chair, confronting his own image with an expression on his face which Narouz had never before seen. It was bleak and impassive, and in that ghostly derived light from the pier-glass it looked denuded of all human feeling, picked clean by the emotions which had been steadily sapping it. The younger son watched as if mesmerized. (Once, in early childhood, he had seen something like it—but not quite as stern, not quite as withdrawn as this: yet something like it. That was when his father was describing the death of the evil factor Mahmoud, when he said grimly: "So they came and tied him to a tree. *Et on lui a coupé les choses and stuffed them into his mouth.*" As a child it was enough just to repeat the words and recall the expression on his father's face to make Narouz feel on the point of faint-ing. Now this incident came back to him with redoubled terror as he saw the invalid confronting himself in a moonlit image, slowly raising the pistol to point it, not at his temple, but at the mirror, as he repeated in a hoarse croaking voice: "And now if she should fall in love, you know what you must do.")

Presently there was a silence and a single dry weary sob. Narouz felt tears of sympathy come into his eyes but still the spell held him; he could neither move nor speak nor even sob aloud. His father's head sank down on his breast, and his pistol-hand fell with it until Narouz heard the faint tap of the barrel on the floor. A long thrilling silence fell in the room, in the corridor, on the balcony, the gardens everywhere—the silence of a relief which once more let the imprisoned blood flow in his heart and veins. (Somewhere sighing in her sleep Leila must have turned, pressing her disputed white arms to a cool place among the pillows.) A single mosquito droned. The spell dissolved.

Narouz retired down the corridor to the balcony where he stood for a moment fighting with his tears before calling "Father"; his voice was squeaky and nervous—the voice of a

38

schoolboy. At once the light went on in his father's room, a drawer closed, and he heard the noise of rubber rolling on wood. He waited for a long second and presently came the familiar testy growl "Narouz" which told him that everything was well. He blew his nose in his sleeve and hurried into the bedroom. His father was sitting facing the door with a book upon his knees. "Lazy brute," he said, "I could not wake you."

"I'm sorry," said Narouz. He was all of a sudden delighted. So great was his relief that he suddenly wished to abase himself, to be sworn at, to be abused. "I am a lazy brute, a thoughtless swine, a grain of salt" he said eagerly, hoping to provoke his father into still more wounding reproaches. He was smiling. He wanted to bathe voluptuously in the sick man's fury.

"Get me to bed" said the invalid shortly, and his son stooped with lustful tenderness to gather up that wasted body from the wheel-chair, inexpressibly relieved that there was still breath in it. . . .

But how indeed was Mountolive to know all this? He only recognized a reserve in Narouz which was absent from the gently smiling Nessim. As for the father of Narouz, he was quite frankly disturbed by him, by his sick hanging head, and the self-pity which his voice exuded. Unhappily, too, there was another conflict which had to find an issue somehow, and this time Mountolive unwittingly provided an opening by committing one of those *gaffes* which diplomats, more than any other tribe, fear and dread; the memory of which can keep them awake at nights for years. It was an absurd enough slip, but it gave the sick man an excuse for an outburst which Mountolive recognized as characteristic. It all happened at table, during dinner one evening, and at first the company laughed easily enough over it—and in the expanding circle of their communal amusement there was no bitterness, only the smiling protest of Leila: "But my dear David, we are not

Moslems, but Christians *like yourself.*" Of course he had known this; how could his words have slipped out? It was one of those dreadful remarks which once uttered seem not only inexcusable but also impossible to repair. Nessim, however, appeared delighted rather than offended, and with his usual tact, did not permit himself to laugh aloud without touching his friend's wrist with his hand, lest by chance Mountolive might think the laughter directed at him rather than at his mistake. Yet, as the laughter itself fell away, he became consciously aware that a wound had been opened from the flinty features of the man in the wheel-chair who alone did not smile. "I see nothing to smile at." His fingers plucked at the shiny arms of the chair. "Nothing at all. The slip exactly expresses the British point of view—the view with which we Copts have always had to contend. There were never any differences between us and the Moslems in Egypt before they came. The British have taught the Moslems to hate the Copts and to discriminate against them. Yes, Mountolive, the British. Pay heed to my words."

"I am sorry" stammered Mountolive, still trying to atone for his *gaffe.*

"I am not," said the invalid. "It is good that we should mention these matters openly because we Copts feel them in here, in our deepest hearts. The British have made the Moslems oppress us. Study the Commission. Talk to your compatriots there about the Copts and you will hear their contempt and loathing of us. They have inoculated the Moslems with it."

"Oh, surely, Sir!" said Mountolive, in an agony of apology.

"Surely," asseverated the sick man, nodding his head upon that sprained stalk of neck. "We *know* the truth." Leila made some small involuntary gesture, almost a signal, as if to stop her husband before he was fully launched into a harangue, but he did not heed her. He sat back chewing a piece of bread and said indistinctly: "But then what do you, what does any Englishman know or care of the Copts? An obscure religious heresy, they think, a debased language with a liturgy hopelessly confused by Arabic and Greek. It has always been so. When the first Crusade captured Jerusalem it was expressly ruled that no Copt enter the city—*our Holy City*. So little could those Western Christians distinguish between Moslems who defeated them at Askelon and the Copts—the only branch of the Christian Church which was thoroughly integrated into the Orient! But then your good Bishop of Salisbury openly said he considered these Oriental Christians as worse than infidels, and your Crusaders massacred them joyfully." An expression of bitterness translated into a cruel smile lit up his features for a moment. Then, as his customary morose hangdog expression appeared, licking his lips he plunged once more into an argument the matter of which, Mountolive suddenly realized, had been preying upon his secret mind from the first day of his visit. He had indeed carried the whole of this conversation stacked up inside him, waiting for the moment to launch it. Narouz gazed at his father with sympathetic adoration, his features copying their expression from what was said—pride, at the words "Our Holy City", anger at the words "worse than infidels". Leila sat pale and absorbed, looking out towards the balcony; only Nessim looked serious yet easy in spirit. He watched his father sympathetically and respectfully but without visible emotion. He was still almost smiling.

"Do you know what they call us—the Moslems?" Once more his head wagged. "I will tell you. *Gins Pharoony*. Yes, we are *genus Pharaonicus*—the true descendants of the ancients, the true marrow of Egypt. We call ourselves *Gypt*—ancient Egyptians. Yet we are Christians like you, only of the oldest and purest strain. And all through we have been the brains of Egypt—even in the time of the Khedive. Despite persecutions we have held an honoured place here; our Christianity has always been respected. *Here* in Egypt, not *there* in Europe. Yes, the Moslems who have hated Greek and Jew have recognized in the Copt the true inheritor of the ancient Egyptian strain. When Mohammed Ali came to Egypt he put all the financial

41

affairs of the country into the hands of the Copts. So did Ismail his successor. Again and again you will find that Egypt was to all intents and purposes ruled by us, the despised Copts, because we had more brains and more integrity than the others. Indeed, when Mohammed Ali first arrived he found a Copt in charge of all state affairs and made him his Grand Vizier."

"Ibrahim El Gohari" said Narouz with the triumphant air of a schoolboy who can recite his lesson correctly.

"Exactly," echoed his father, no less triumphantly. "He was the only Egyptian permitted to smoke his pipe in the presence of the first of the Khedives. A *Copt!*"

Mountolive was cursing the slip which had led him to receive this curtain lecture, and yet at the same time listening with great attention. These grievances were obviously deeply felt. "And when Gohari died where did Mohammed Ali turn?"

"To Ghali Doss" said Narouz again, delightedly.

"Exactly. As Chancellor of the Exchequer he had full powers over revenue and taxation. A Copt. Another *Copt*. And *his* son Basileus was made a Bey and a member of the Privy Council. These men ruled Egypt with honour; and there were many of them given great appointments."

"Sedarous Takla in Esneh" said Narouz, "Shehata Hasaballah in Assiout, Girgis Yacoub in Beni Souef." His eyes shone as he spoke and he basked like a serpent in the warmth of his father's approbation. "Yes," cried the invalid, striking his chair-arm with his hand. "Yes. And even under Said and Ismail the Copts played their part. The public prosecutor in every province was a Copt. Do you realize what that means? The reposing of such a trust in a *Christian* minority? The Moslems knew us, they knew we were Egyptians first and Christians afterwards. *Christian Egyptians*—have you British with your romantic ideas about Moslems ever thought what the words mean? The only *Christian Orientals* fully integrated into a Moslem state? It would be the dream of Germans to discover such a key to Egypt, would it not? Everywhere Christians in positions of trust, in key positions as *mudirs*, Governors, and so on. Under Ismail a Copt held the Ministry of War."

"Ayad Bey Hanna" said Narouz with relish.

"Yes. Even under Arabi a Coptic Minister of Justice. And a Court Master of Ceremonies. Both Copts. And others, many others."

"How did all this change?" said Mountolive quietly, and the sick man levered himself up in his rugs to point a shaking finger at his guest and say: "The British changed it, with their hatred of the Copts. Gorst initiated a diplomatic friendship with Khedive Abbas, and as a result of his schemes not a single Copt was to be found in the entourage of the Court or even in the services of its departments. Indeed, if you spoke to the men who surrounded that corrupt and bestial man, supported by the British, you would have been led to think that the enemy was the Christian part of the nation. At this point, let me read you something." Here Narouz, swiftly as a well-rehearsed acolyte, slipped into the next room and returned with a book with a marker in it. He laid it open on the lap of his father and returned in a flash to his seat. Clearing his throat the sick man read harshly: " 'When the British took control of Egypt the Copts occupied a number of the highest positions in the State. In less than a quarter of a century almost all the Coptic Heads of Departments had disappeared. They were at first fully represented in the bench of judges, but gradually the number was reduced to *nil*; the process of removing them and shutting the door against fresh appointments has gone on until they have been reduced to a state of discouragement bordering on despair!' These are the words of an Englishman. It is to his honour that he has written them." He snapped the book shut and went on. "To-day, with British rule, the Copt is debarred from holding the position of Governor or even of *Mamur*—the administrative magistrate of a province. Even those who work for the Government are compelled to work on Sunday because,

43

in deference to the Moslems, Friday has been made a day of prayer. No provision has been made for the Copts to worship. They are not even properly represented on Government Councils and Committees. They pay large taxes for education—but no provision is made that such money goes towards Christian education. It is all Islamic. But I will not weary you with the rest of our grievances. Only that you should understand why we feel that Britain hates us and wishes to stamp us out."

"I don't think that that *can* be so," said Mountolive feebly, now rendered somewhat breathless by the forthrightness of the criticism but unaware how to deal with it. All this matter was entirely new to him for his studies had consisted only in reading the conventional study by Lane as the true Gospel on Egypt. The sick man nodded again, as if with each nod he drove his point home a little deeper. Narouz whose face like a mirror had reflected the various feelings of the conversation, nodded too. Then the father pointed at his eldest son. "Nessim," he said, "look at *him*. A true Copt. Brilliant, reserved. What an ornament he would make to the Egyptian diplomatic service. Eh? As a diplomat-to-be you should judge better than I. But no. He will be a businessman because we Copts know that it is useless, *useless*." He banged the arm of his wheel-chair again, and the spittle came up into his mouth.

But this was an opportunity for which Nessim had been waiting, for now he took his father's sleeve and kissed it submissively, saying at the same time with a smile: "But David will learn all this anyway. It is enough now." And smiling round at his mother sanctioned the relieved signal she made to the servants which called an end to the dinner.

They took their coffee in uncomfortable silence on the balcony where the invalid sat gloomily apart staring out at the darkness, and the few attempts at general conversation fell flat. To do him justice, the sick men himself was feeling ashamed of his outburst now. He had sworn to himself not to introduce the topic before his guest, and was conscious that he

44

had contravened the laws of hospitality in so doing. But he too could now see no way of repairing the conversation in which the good feeling they had reciprocated and enjoyed until now had temporarily foundered.

Here once more Nessim's tact came to the rescue; he took Leila and Mountolive out into the rose-garden where the three of them walked in silence for a while, their minds embalmed by the dense night-odour of the flowers. When they were out of earshot of the balcony the eldest son said lightly: "David, I hope you didn't mind my father's outburst at dinner. He feels very deeply about all this."

"I know."

"And you know," said Leila eagerly, anxious to dispose of the whole subject and return once more to the normal atmosphere of friendliness, "he really isn't wrong *factually*, however he expresses himself. Our position is an unenviable one, and it is due entirely to you, the British. We do live rather like a secret society—the most brilliant, indeed, once the key community in our own country."

"I cannot understand it" said Mountolive.

"It is not so difficult," said Nessim lightly. "The clue is the Church militant. It is odd, isn't it, that for us there was no real war between Cross and Crescent? That was entirely a Western European creation. So indeed was the idea of the cruel Moslem infidel. The Moslem was never a persecutor of the Copts on religious grounds. On the contrary, the Koran itself shows that Jesus is respected as a true Prophet, indeed a precursor of Mohammed. The other day Leila quoted you the little portrait of the child Jesus in one of the *suras*—remember? Breathing life into the clay models of birds he was making with other children. . . ."

"I remember."

"Why, even in Mohammed's tomb," said Leila, "there has always been that empty chamber which waits for the body of Jesus. According to the prophecy he is to be buried in Medina,

45

the fountain of Islam, remember? And here in Egypt no Moslem feels anything but respect and love for the Christian God. Even to-day. Ask anyone, ask any *muezzin*." (This was as if to say "Ask anyone who speaks the truth"—for no unclean person, drunkard, madman or woman is regarded as eligible for uttering the Moslem call to prayer.)

"You have remained Crusaders at heart," said Nessim softly, ironically but still with a smile on his lips. He turned and walked softly away between the roses, leaving them alone. At once Leila's hand sought his familiar clasp. "Never mind this," she said lightly, in a different voice. "One day we will find our way back to the centre with or without your help! We have long memories!"

They sat together for a while on a block of fallen marble, talking of other things, these larger issues forgotten now they were alone. "How dark it is to-night. I can only see one star. That means mist. Did you know that in Islam every man has his own star which appears when he is born and goes out when he dies? Perhaps is your star, David Mountolive."

"Or yours?"

"It is too bright for mine. They pale, you know, as one gets older. Mine must be quite pale, past middle age by now. And when you leave us, it will become paler still." They embraced.

They spoke of their plans to meet as often as possible; of his intention to return whenever he could get leave. "But you will not be long in Egypt," she said with her light fatalistic glance and smile. "You will be posted soon? Where to, I wonder? You will forget us—but no, the English are always faithful to old friends, are they not? Kiss me."

"Let us not think of that now," said Mountolive. Indeed, he felt quite deprived of any power to confront this parting coolly. "Let us talk of other things. Look, I went into Alexandria yesterday and hunted about until I found something suitable to give Ali and the other servants."

"What was it?"

In his suitcase upstairs he had some Mecca water in sealed blue bottles from the Holy Well of Zem Zem. These he proposed to give as *pourboires*. "Do you think it will be well taken coming from an infidel?" he asked anxiously, and Leila was delighted. "What a good idea, David. How typical and how tactful! O what are we going to do with ourselves when you have gone?" He felt quite absurdly pleased with himself. Was it possible to imagine a time when they might no longer embrace like this or sit hand in hand in the darkness to feel each other's pulses marking time quietly away into silence—the dead reaches of experience past? He averted his mind from the thought—feebly resisting the sharply-pointed truth. But now she said: "But fear nothing. I have already planned our relations for years ahead; don't smile—it may even be better when we have stopped making love and started . . . what ? I don't know—somehow thinking about each other from a neutral position; as lovers, I mean, who have been forced to separate; who perhaps never should have become lovers; I shall write to you often. A new sort of relationship will begin."

"Please stop," he said, feeling hopelessness steal over him.

"Why?" she said, and smiling now lightly kissed his temples. "I am more experienced than you are. We shall see." Underneath her lightness he recognized something strong, resistant and durable—the very character of an experience he lacked. She was a gallant creature, and it is only the gallant who can remain light-hearted in adversity. But the night before he left she did not, despite her promises, come to his room. She was woman enough to wish to sharpen the pangs of separation, to make them more durable. And his tired eyes and weary air at breakfast filled her with an undiminished pleasure at his obvious suffering.

She rode to the ferry with him when he left, but the presence of Narouz and Nessim made private conversation impossible, and once again she was almost glad of the fact. There was, in fact, nothing left for either to say. And she unconsciously wished to avoid the tiresome iteration which goes with all love-making and which in the end stales it. She wanted his image of her to remain sharply in focus, and stainless; for she alone recognized that this parting was the pattern, a sample so to speak, of a parting far more definitive and final, a parting which, if their communication was to remain only through the medium of words and paper, might altogether lose her Mount-olive. You cannot write more than a dozen love-letters without finding yourself gravelled for fresh matter. The richest of human experiences is also the most limited in its range of ex-pression. Words kill love as they kill everything else. She had already planned to turn their intercourse away upon another plane, a richer one; but Mountolive was still too young to take advantage of what she might have to offer him—the treasures of the imagination. She would have to give him time to grow. She realized quite clearly that she both loved him dearly, and could resign herself to never seeing him again. Her love had already encompassed and mastered the object's disappearance—its own death! This thought, defined so sharply in her own mind, gave her a stupendous advantage over him—for he was still wallowing in the choppy sea of his own illogical and entangled emotions, desire, self-regard, and all the other nur-sery troubles of a teething love, whereas she was already drawing strength and self-assurance from the very hopelessness of her own case. Her pride of spirit and intelligence lent her a new and unsuspected strength. And though she was sorry with one part of her mind to see him go so soon, though she was glad to see him suffer, and prepared never to see him return, yet she knew she already possessed him, and in a paradoxical way, to say good-bye to him was almost easy.

They said good-bye at the ferry and all four participated in the long farewell embrace. It was a fine, ringing morning, with low mists trammelling the outlines of the great lake. Nessim had ordered a car which stood under the further palm-tree, a black, trembling dot. Mountolive took one wild look around

48

him as he stepped into the boat—as if he wished to furnish his memory forever with details of this land, these three faces smiling and wishing him good luck in his own tongue and theirs. "I'll be back!" he shouted, but in his tone she could detect all his anxiety and pain. Narouz raised a crooked arm and smiled his crooked smile; while Nessim put his arm about Leila's shoulder as he waved, fully aware of what she felt, though he would have been unable to find words for feelings so equivocal and so true.

The boat pulled away. It was over. Ended.

o   o   o   o   o

II

Late that autumn his posting came through. He was somewhat surprised to find himself accredited to the Mission in Prague, as he had been given to understand that after his lengthy refresher in Arabic he might expect to find himself a lodgement somewhere in the Levant Consular where his special knowledge would prove of use. Yet despite an initial dismay he accepted his fate with good grace and joined in the elaborate game of musical chairs which the Foreign Office plays with such eloquent impersonality. The only consolation, a meagre one, was to find that everyone in his first mission knew as little as he did about the language and politics of the country. His Chancery consisted of two Japanese experts and three specialists in Latin American affairs. They all twisted their faces in melancholy unison over the vagaries of the Czech language and gazed out from their office windows on snow-lit landscapes full of a solemn Slav foreboding. He was in the Service now.

He had only managed to see Leila half a dozen times in Alexandria—meetings made more troubling and incoherent than thrilling by the enforced secrecy which surrounded them. He ought to have felt like a young dog—but in fact he felt rather a cad. He only returned to the Hosnani lands once, for a spell of three days' leave—and here at any rate the old spiteful magic of circumstance and place held him; but so briefly—like a fugitive afterglow from the conflagration of the previous spring. Leila appeared to be somehow fading, receding on the curvature of a world moving in time, detaching herself from his own memories of her. The foreground of his new life was becoming crowded with the expensive coloured toys of his professional life—banquets and anniversaries and forms of

50

behaviour new to him. His concentration was becoming dispersed.

For Leila, however, it was a different matter; she was already so intent upon the recreation of herself in the new role she had planned that she rehearsed it every day to herself, in her own private mind, and to her astonishment realized that she was waiting with actual impatience for the parting to become final, for the old links to snap. As an actor uncertain of a new part might wait in a fever of anxiety for his cue to be spoken. She longed for what she most dreaded, the word "Good-bye".

But with his first sad letter from Prague, she felt something like a new sense of elation rising in her, for now at last she would be free to possess Mountolive as she wished—greedily in her mind. The difference in their ages—widening like the chasms in floating pack-ice—were swiftly carrying their bodies out of reach of each other, out of touch. There was no permanence in any of the records to be made by the flesh with its language of promises and endearments, these were all already compromised by a beauty no longer in its first flower. But she calculated that her inner powers were strong enough to keep him to herself in the one special sense most dear to maturity, if only she could gain the courage to substitute mind for heart. Nor was she wrong in realizing that had they been free to indulge passion at will, their relationship could not have survived more than a twelvemonth. But the distance and the necessity to transfer their commerce to new ground had the effect of refreshing their images in one another. For him the image of Leila did not dissolve but suffered a new and thrilling mutation as it took shape on paper. She kept pace with his growth in those long, well-written, ardent letters which betrayed only the hunger which is as poignant as anything the flesh is called upon to cure: the hunger for friendship, the fear of being forgotten.

From Prague, Oslo, Berne, this correspondence flowed backwards and forwards, the letters swelling or diminishing in size but always remaining constant to the mind directing it—the lively, dedicated mind of Leila. Mountolive, growing, found these long letters in warm English or concise French an aid to the process, a provocation. She planted ideas beside him in the soft ground of a professional life which demanded little beyond charm and reserve—just as a gardener will plant sticks for a climbing sweet-pea. If the one love died, another grew up in its place. Leila became his only mentor and confidant, his only source of encouragement. It was to meet these demands of hers that he taught himself to write well in English and French. Taught himself to appreciate things which normally would have been outside the orbit of his interests—painting and music. He informed himself in order to inform her.

"You say you will be in Zagreb next month. Please visit and describe to me . . ." she would write, or "How lucky you will be in passing through Amsterdam; there is a retrospective Klee which has received tremendous notices in the French press. *Please* pay it a visit and describe your impressions honestly to me, even if unfavourable. I have never seen an original myself." This was Leila's parody of love, a flirtation of minds, in which the roles were now reversed; for she was deprived of the riches of Europe and she fed upon his long letters and parcels of books with the double gluttony. The young man strained every nerve to meet these demands, and suddenly found the hitherto padlocked worlds of paint, architecture, music and writing opening on every side of him. So she gave him almost a gratuitous education in the world which he would never have been able to compass by himself. And where the old dependence of his youth slowly foundered, the new one grew. Mountolive, in the strictest sense of the words, had now found a woman after his own heart.

The old love was slowly metamorphosed into admiration, just as his physical longing for her (so bitter at first) turned into a consuming and depersonalized tenderness which fed upon her absence instead of dying from it. In a few years she was able to confess: "I feel somehow nearer to you to-day, on paper, than I did before we parted. Why is this?" But she knew only too well. Yet she added at once, for honesty's sake: "Is this feeling a little unhealthy perhaps? To outsiders it might even seem a little pathetic or ludicrous—who can say? And these long long letters, David—are they the bitter-sweet of a Severina's commerce with her nephew Fabrizio? I often wonder if they were lovers—their intimacy is so hot and close? Stendhal never actually says so. I wish I knew Italy. Has your lover turned aunt in her old age? Don't answer even if you know the truth. Yet it is lucky in a way that we are both solitaries, with large blank unfilled areas of heart—like the early maps of Africa?— and need each other still. I mean, you as an only child with only your mother to think of, and I—of course, I have many cares, but live within a very narrow cage. Your description of the ballerina and your love-affair was amusing and touching; thank you for telling me. Have a care, dear friend, and do not wound yourself."

It was a measure of the understanding which had grown up between them that he was now able to confide in her without reserve details of the few personal histories which occupied him: the love-affair with Grishkin which almost entangled him in a premature marriage; his unhappy passion for an Ambassador's mistress which exposed him to a duel, and perhaps disgrace. If she felt any pangs, she concealed them, writing to advise and console him with the warmth of an apparent detachment. They were frank with each other, and sometimes her own deliberate exchanges all but shocked him, dwelling as they did upon the self-examinations which people transfer to paper only when there is no one to whom they can talk. As when she could write: "It was a shock, I mean, to suddenly see Nessim's naked body floating in the mirror, the slender white back so like yours and the loins. I sat down and, to my own surprise, burst into tears, because I wondered suddenly whether my attachment for you wasn't lodged here somehow among the feeble incestuous desires of the inner heart. I know so little about the penetralia of sex which they are exploring so laboriously, the doctors. Their findings fill me with misgivings. Then I also wondered whether there wasn't a touch of the vampire about me, clinging so close to you for so long, always dragging at your sleeve when by now you must have outgrown me quite. What do you think? Write and reassure me, David, even while you kiss little Grishkin, will you? Look, I am sending you a recent photo so you can judge how much I have aged. Show it to her, and tell her that I fear nothing so much as her unfounded jealousy. But one glance will set her heart at rest. I must not forget to thank you for the telegram on my birthday —it gave me a sudden image of you sitting on the balcony talking to Nessim. He is now so rich and independent that he hardly ever bothers to visit the land. He is too occupied with great affairs in the city. Yet . . . he feels the depth of my absence as I would wish you to; more strongly than if we were living in each other's laps. We write often and at length; our minds understudy each other, yet we leave our hearts free to love, to grow. Through him I hope that one day we Copts will regain our place in Egypt—but no more of this now. . . ."

Clear-headed, self-possessed and spirited the words ran on in that tall fluent hand upon different-coloured stationery, letters that he would open eagerly in some remote Legation garden, reading them with an answer half-formulated in his mind which must be written and sealed up in time to catch the outgoing bag. He had come to depend on this friendship which still dictated, as a form, the words "My dearest love" at the head of letters concerned solely with, say, art, or love (his love) or life (his life).

And for his part, he was scrupulously honest with her—as for instance in writing about his ballerina: "It is true that I even considered at one time marrying her. I was certainly very much in love. But she cured me in time. You see, her language

54

which I did not know, effectively hid her commonness from me. Fortunately she once or twice risked a public familiarity which froze me; once when the whole ballet was invited to a reception I got myself seated next to her believing that she would behave with discretion since none of my colleagues knew of our liaison. Imagine their amusement and my horror when all of a sudden while we were seated at supper she passed her hand up the back of my head to ruffle my hair in a gesture of coarse endearment! It served me right. But I realized the truth in time, and even her wretched pregnancy when it came seemed altogether too transparent a ruse. I was cured."

When at last they parted Grishkin taunted him saying: "You are only a diplomat. You have no politics and no religion!" But it was to Leila that he turned for an elucidation of this telling charge. And it was Leila who discussed it with him with the blithe disciplined tenderness of an old lover.

So in her skilful fashion she held him year by year until his youthful awkwardness gave place to a maturity which matched her own. Though it was only a dialect of love they spoke, it sufficed her and absorbed him; yet it remained for him impossible to classify or analyse.

And punctually now as the calendar years succeeded each other, as his posts changed, so the image of Leila was shot through with the colours and experiences of the countries which passed like fictions before his eyes: cherry-starred Japan, hook-nosed Lima, dull Portugal and snow-bound Helsinki. But never Egypt, despite all his entreaties for postings which he knew were falling or had fallen vacant. It seemed that the Foreign Office would never forgive him for having learned Arabic, and even deliberately selected posts from which leave taken in Egypt was difficult or impossible. Yet the link held. Twice he met Nessim in Paris, but that was all. They were delighted with each other, and with their own worldliness.

In time his annoyance gave place to resignation. His profession which valued only judgement, coolness and reserve, taught him the hardest lesson of all and the most crippling—never to utter the pejorative thought aloud. It offered him too something like a long Jesuitical training in self-deception which enabled him to present an ever more highly polished surface to the world without deepening his human experience. If his personality did not become completely diluted it was due to Leila; for he lived surrounded by his ambitious and sycophantic fellows who taught him only how to excel in forms of address, and the elaborate kindnesses which, in pleasing, pave the way to advancement. His real life became a buried stream, flowing on underground, seldom emerging into that artificial world in which the diplomat lives—slowly suffocating like a cat in an air-pump. Was he happy or unhappy? He hardly knew any longer. He was alone, that was all. And several times, encouraged by Leila, he thought to solace his solitary concentration (which was turning to selfishness) by marrying. But somehow, surrounded as he was by eligible young women, he found that his only attraction lay among those who were already married, or who were much older than himself. Foreigners were beyond consideration for even at that time mixed marriages were regarded as a serious bar to advancement in the service. In diplomacy as in everything else there is a right and a wrong kind of marriage. But as the years slipped by he found himself climbing the slow gyres—by expediency, compromise and hard work—towards the narrow anteroom of diplomatic power: the rank of councillor or minister. Then one day the whole bright mirage which lay buried and forgotten reawoke, re-emerged, substantial and shining from the past; in the fullness of his powers he woke one day to learn that the coveted "K" was his, and something else even more desirable—the long-denied Embassy to Egypt. . . .

But Leila would not have been a woman had she not been capable of one moment of weakness which all but prejudiced the whole unique pattern of their relationship. It came with her husband's death. But it was swiftly followed by a romantic punishment which drove her further back into the solitude which, for one wild moment, she dreamed of abandoning. It was perhaps as well, for everything might have been lost by it.

There was a long silence after her telegram announcing Faltaus' death; and then a letter unlike anything she had written before, so full of hesitations and ambiguities was it. "My indecision has become to my surprise such an agony. I am really quite distraught. I want you to think most carefully about the proposal I am about to make. Analyse it, and if the least trace of disgust arises in your mind, the least reservation, we will banish it and never speak of it again. David! To-day as I looked in my mirror, as critically and cruelly as I could, I found myself entertaining a thought which for years now I have rigorously excluded. The thought of *seeing you again*. Only I could not for the life of me see the terms and conditions of such a meeting. My vision of it was covered by a black cloud of doubt. Now that Faltaus is dead and buried the whole of *that* part of my life has snapped off short. I have no other except the one I shared with you—a paper life. Crudely, we have been like people drifting steadily apart in age as each year passed. Subconsciously I must have been waiting for Faltaus' death, though I never wished it, for how else should this hope, this delusion suddenly rise up in me now? It suddenly occurred to me last night that we might still have six months or a year left to spend together before the link snaps for good in the old sense. Is this rubbish? Yes! Would I in fact only encumber you, embarrass you by arriving in Paris as I plan to do in two months' time? For goodness' sake write back at once and dissuade me from my false hopes, from such folly—for I recognize deep within myself that it is a folly. But . . . to enjoy you for a few months before I return here to take up this life: how hard it is to abandon the hope. Scotch it, please, at once; so that when I do come I will be at peace, simply regarding you (as I have all these years) as something more than my closest friend."

She knew it was unfair to put him in such a position; but she could not help herself. Was it fortunate then that fate prevented him from having to make such an elaborate decision—for her letter arrived on his desk in the same post as Nessim's long telegram announcing the onset of her illness? And while he was still hesitating between a choice of answers there came her post-card, written in a new sprawling hand, which absolved him finally by the words: "Do not write again until I can read you; I am bandaged from head to foot. Something very bad, very definitive has happened."

During the whole of that hot summer the confluent small-pox—invented perhaps as the cruellest remedy for human vanity—dragged on, melting down what remained of her once celebrated beauty. It was useless to pretend even to herself that her whole life would not be altered by it. But how? Mountolive waited in an agony of indecision until their correspondence could be renewed, writing now to Nessim, now to Narouz. A void had suddenly opened at his feet.

Then: "It is an odd experience to look upon one's own features full of pot-holes and landslides—like a familiar landscape blown up. I fear that I must get used to the new sensation of being a hag. But by my own force. Of course, all this may strengthen other sides of my character—as acids can—I've lost the metaphor! Ach! what sophistry it is, for there is no way out. And how bitterly ashamed I am of the proposals contained in my last long letter. *This* is not the face to parade through Europe, nor would one dare to shame you by letting it claim your acquaintance at close range. To-day I ordered a dozen black veils such as the poor people of my religion still wear! But it seemed so painful an act that I ordered my jeweller to come and measure me afresh for some new bracelets and rings. I have become so thin of late. A reward for bravery too, as children are bribed with a sweet for facing a nasty medicine. Poor little Hakim. He wept bitterly as he showed me his wares. I felt his tears on my fingers. Yet somehow, I was able to laugh. My voice too has changed. I have been so sick of lying in darkened rooms. The veils will free me. Yes, and of *course* I have been debating suicide—who does not at such times? No, but if I live on it won't be to pity myself. Or perhaps woman's vanity is not, as we think, a mortal matter—a killing business? I must be confident and strong. Please don't turn solemn and pity me. When you write, let your letters be gay as always, will you?"

But thereafter came a long silence before their correspondence was fully resumed, and her letters now had a new quality—of bitter resignation. She had retired, she wrote, to the land once more, where she lived alone with Narouz. "His gentle savagery makes him an ideal companion. Besides, at times I am troubled in mind now, not quite *compos mentis*, and then I retire for days at a time to the little summer-house, remember? At the end of the garden. There I read and write with only my snake—the genius of the house these days is a great dusty cobra, tame as a cat. It is company enough. Besides, I have other cares now, other plans. Desert without and desert within!

> *The veil's a fine and private place:*
> *But none, I think, do there embrace.*

"If I should write nonsense to you during the times when the *afreet* has bewitched my mind (as the servants say) don't answer. These attacks only last a day or two at most."

And so the new epoch began. For years she sat, an eccentric and veiled recluse in Karm Abu Girg, writing those long marvellous letters, her mind still ranging freely about the lost worlds of Europe in which he still found himself a traveller. But there were fewer imperatives of the old eager kind. She seldom looked outward now towards new experiences, but mostly backwards into the past as one whose memory of small things needed to be refreshed. Could one hear the cicadas on the Tour Magne? Was the Seine corn-green at Bougival? At the

Pallio of Siena were the costumes of silk? The cherry-trees of Navarra. . . . She wanted to verify the past, to look back over her shoulder, and patiently Mountolive undertook these re-assurances on every journey. Rembrandt's little monkey—had she seen or only imagined it in his canvases? No, it existed, he told her sadly. Very occasionally a request touching the new came up. "My interest has been aroused by some singular poems in Values (Sept) signed Ludwig Pursewarden. Some-thing new and harsh here. As you are going to London next week, please enquire about him for me. Is he German? Is he the novelist who wrote those two strange novels about Africa? The name is the same."

It was this request which led directly to Mountolive's first meeting with the poet who later was to play a part of some importance in his life. Despite the almost French devotion he felt (copied from Leila) for artists, he found Pursewarden's name an awkward, almost comical one to write upon the post-card which he addressed to him care of his publishers. For a month he heard nothing; but as he was in London on a three-months' course of instruction he could afford to be patient. When his answer came it was, surprisingly enough, written upon the familiar Foreign Office notepaper; his post, it appeared, was that of a junior in the Cultural Department! He telephoned him at once and was agreeably surprised by the pleasant, collected voice. He had half-expected someone aggressively underbred, and was relieved to hear a civilized note of self-collected humour in Pursewarden's voice. They agreed to meet for a drink at the "Compasses" near Westminster Bridge that evening, and Mountolive looked forward to the meeting as much for Leila's sake as his own, for he intended to write her an account of it, carefully describing her artist for her.

It was snowing with light persistence, the snow melting as it touched the pavements, but lingering longer on coat-collars and hats. (A snowflake on the eyelash suddenly bursts the world asunder into the gleaming component colours of the prism.) Mountolive bent his head and came round the corner just in time to see a youthful-looking couple turn into the bar of the "Compasses". The girl, who turned to address a remark to her companion over her shoulder as the door opened, wore a brilliant tartan shawl with a great white brooch. The warm lamplight splashed upon her broad pale face with its helmet of dark curling hair. She was strikingly beautiful with a beauty whose somehow shocking placidity took Mountolive a full second to analyse. Then he saw that she was blind, her face slightly upcast to her companion's in the manner of those whose expressions never fully attain their target—the eyes of another. She stayed thus for a full second before her companion said something laughingly and pressed her onwards into the bar. Mountolive entered on their heels and found himself at once grasping the warm steady hand of Pursewarden. The blind girl, it seemed, was his sister. A few moments of awkwardness ensued while they disposed themselves by the blazing coke fire in the corner and ordered drinks.

Pursewarden, though in no way a striking person, seemed agreeably normal. He was of medium height and somewhat pale in colouring with a trimmed moustache which made a barely noticeable circumflex above a well-cut mouth. He was, however, so completely unlike his sister in colouring that Mountolive concluded that the magnificent dark hair of the sightless girl must perhaps be dyed, though it seemed natural enough, and her slender eyebrows were also dark. Only the eyes might have given one a clue to the secret of this Mediterranean pigmentation, and they, of course, were spectacularly missing. It was the head of a Medusa, its blindness was that of a Greek statue—a blindness perhaps brought about by intense concentration through centuries upon sunlight and blue water? Her expression, however, was not magistral but tender and appealing. Long silken fingers curled and softened at the butts like the fingers of a concert pianist moved softly upon the

oaken table between them, as if touching, confirming, certifying
—hesitating to ascribe qualities to his voice. At times her own
lips moved softly as if she were privately repeating the words
they spoke to herself in order to recapture their resonance and
meaning; then she was like someone following music with a
private score.

"Liza, my darling?" said the poet.

"Brandy and soda." She replied with her placid blankness in
a voice at once clear and melodious—a voice which might have
given some such overtone to the words "Honey and nectar".
They seated themselves somewhat awkwardly while the drinks
were dispensed. Brother and sister sat side by side, which gave
them a somewhat defensive air. The blind girl put one hand
in the brother's pocket. So began, in rather a halting fashion,
the conversation which lasted them far into the evening and
which he afterwards transcribed so accurately to Leila, thanks
to his formidable memory.

"He was somewhat shy at first and took refuge in a pleasant
diffidence. I found to my surprise that he was earmarked for a
Cairo posting next year and told him a little about my friends
there, offering to give him a few letters of introduction, notably
to Nessim. He may have been a little intimidated by my rank
but this soon wore off; he hasn't much of a head for drinks and
after the second began to talk in a most amusing and cutting
fashion. A rather different person now emerged—odd and
equivocal as one might expect an artist to be—but with pronounced views on a number of subjects, some of them not at
all to my taste. But they had an oddly personal ring. One felt
they were deduced from experience and not worked out simply
to *épater*. He is, for example, rather an old-fashioned reactionary
in his outlook, and is consequently rather *mal vu* by his brother
craftsmen who suspect him of Fascist sympathies; the prevailing distemper of left-wing thought, indeed all radicalism is
repugnant to him. But his views were expressed humorously
and without heat. I could not, for example, rouse him on the

Spanish issue. ('All those little *beige* people trooping off to die for the Left Book Club!')"

Mountolive had indeed been rather shocked by opinions as clear-cut as they were trenchant, for he at the time shared the prevailing egalitarian sympathies of the day—albeit in the anodyne liberalized form then current in The Office. Purse-warden's royal contempts made him rather a formidable person. "I confess," Mountolive wrote, "that I did not feel I had exactly placed him in any one category. But he expressed views rather than attitudes, and I must say he said a number of striking things which I memorized for you, as: 'The artist's work constitutes the only satisfactory relationship he can have with his fellow-men since he seeks his real friends among the dead and the unborn. That is why he can't dabble in politics, it isn't his job. He must concentrate on values rather than policies. To-day it all looks to me like a silly shadow-play, for ruling is an art, not a science, just as a society is an organism, not a system. Its smallest unit is the family and really royalism is the right structure for it—for a Royal Family is a mirror image of the human, a legitimate idolatry. I mean, for us, the British, with our essentially quixotic temperament and mental sloth. I don't know about the others. As for capitalism, its errors and injustices are all remediable, by fair taxation. We should be hunting not for an imaginary equality among men, but simply for a decent equity. But then Kings should be manufacturing a philosophy of sorts, as they did in China; an absolute Monarchy is hopeless for us to-day because the philosophy of kingship is at a low ebb. The same goes for a dictatorship.

" 'As for Communism, I can see that is hopeless too; the analysis of man in terms of economic behaviourism takes all the fun out of living, and to divest him of a personal psyche is madness.' And so on. He has visited Russia for a month with a cultural delegation and did not like what he felt there; other *boutades* like 'Sad Jews on whose faces one could see all the melancholia of a secret arithmetic; I asked an old man in Kiev

63

if Russia was a happy place. He drew his breath sharply and after looking around him furtively said: "We say that once Lucifer had good intentions, a change of heart. He decided to perform a good act for a change—just one. So hell was born on earth, and they named it Soviet Russia." '

"In all this, his sister played no part but sat in eloquent silence with her fingers softly touching the table, curling like tendrils of vine, smiling at his aphorisms as if at private wickednesses. Only once, when he had gone out for a second, she turned to me and said: 'He shouldn't concern himself with these matters really. His one job is to learn how to submit to despair.' I was very much struck by this oracular phrase which fell so naturally from her lips and did not know what to reply. When he returned he resumed his place and the conversation at one and the same time as if he had been thinking it over by himself. He said 'No, they are a biological necessity, Kings. Perhaps they mirror the very constitution of the psyche? We have compromised so admirably with the question of their divinity that I should hate to see them replaced by a dictator or a Workers' Council and a firing squad.' I had to protest at this preposterous view, but he was quite serious. 'I assure you that this is the way the left-wing tends; its object is civil war, though it does not realize it—thanks to the cunning with which the sapless puritans like Shaw and company have presented their case. Marxism is the revenge of the Irish and the Jews!' I had to laugh at this, and so—to do him justice— did he. 'But at least it will explain why I am *mal vu*,' he said, 'and why I am always glad to get out of England to countries where I feel no moral responsibility and no desire to work out such depressing formulations. After all, what the hell! I am a writer!''

"By this time he had had several drinks and was quite at his ease. 'Let us leave this barren field! O, how much I want to get away to the cities which were created by their women; a Paris or Rome built in response to the female lusts. I never see old

Nelson's soot-covered form in Trafalgar Square without thinking: poor Emma had to go all the way to Naples to assert the right to be pretty, feather-witted and *d'une splendeur* in bed. What am I, Pursewarden, doing here among people who live in a frenzy of propriety? Let me wander where people have come to terms with their own human obscenity, safe in the poet's cloak of invisibility. I want to learn to respect nothing while despising nothing—crooked is the path of the initiate!'

" 'My dear, you are tipsy!' cried Liza with delight.

" 'Tipsy and sad. Sad and tipsy. But joyful, joyful!'

"I must say this new and amusing vein in his character seemed to bring me much nearer to the man himself. 'Why the stylized emotions? Why the fear and trembling? All those gloomy lavatories with mackintoshed policewomen waiting to see if one pees straight or not? Think of all the passionate adjustment of dress that goes on in the kingdom! the keeping off the grass: is it any wonder that I absent-mindedly take the entrance marked Aliens Only whenever I return?'

" 'You are tipsy,' cried Liza again.

" 'No. I am happy.' He said it seriously. 'And happiness can't be induced. You must wait and ambush it like a quail or a girl with tired wings. Between art and contrivance there is a gulf fixed!'

"On he went in this new and headlong strain; and I must confess that I was much taken by the effortless play of a mind which was no longer conscious of itself. Of course, here and there I stumbled against a coarseness of expression which was boorish, and looked anxiously at his sister, but she only smiled her blind smile, indulgent and uncritical.

"It was late when we walked back together towards Trafalgar Square in the falling snow. There were few people about and the snowflakes deadened our footsteps. In the Square itself your poet stopped to apostrophize Nelson Stylites in true calf-killing fashion. I have forgotten exactly what he said, but it was sufficiently funny to make me laugh very heartily. And

65

then he suddenly changed his mood and turning to his sister said: 'Do you know what has been upsetting me all day, Liza? To-day is Blake's birthday. Think of it, the birthday of codger Blake. I felt I ought to see some signs of it on the national countenance, I looked about me eagerly all day. But there was nothing. Darling Liza, let *us* celebrate the old b . . .'s birthday, shall we? You and I and David Mountolive here— as if we were French or Italian, as if it meant something.' The snow was falling fast, the last sodden leaves lying in mounds, the pigeons uttering their guttural clotted noises. 'Shall we, Liza?' A spot of bright pink had appeared in each of her cheeks. Her lips were parted. Snowflakes like dissolving jewels in her dark hair. 'How?' she said, 'Just how?'

" 'We will dance for Blake' said Pursewarden, with a comical look of seriousness on his face, and taking her in his arms he started to waltz, humming the Blue Danube. Over his shoulder, through the falling snowflakes, he said: 'This is for Will and Kate Blake.' I don't know why I felt astonished and rather touched. They moved in perfect measure gradually increasing in speed until they were skimming across the square under the bronze lions, hardly heavier than the whiffs of spray from the fountains. Like pebbles skimming across a smooth lake or stones across an icebound pond. . . . It was a strange spectacle. I forgot my cold hands and the snow melting on my collar as I watched them. So they went, completing a long gradual ellipse across the open space, scattering the leaves and the pigeons, their breath steaming on the night-air. And then, gently, effortlessly spinning out the arc to bring them back to me—to where I stood now with a highly doubtful-looking policeman at my side. It was rather amusing. 'What's goin' on 'ere?' said the bobby, staring at them with a distrustful admiration. Their waltzing was so perfect that I think even he was stirred by it. On they went and on, magnificently in accord, the dark girl's hair flying behind her, her sightless face turned up towards the old admiral on his sooty perch. 'They are

66

celebrating Blake's birthday,' I explained in rather a shamefaced fashion, and the officer looked a shade more relieved as he followed them with an admiring eye. He coughed and said 'Well, he can't be drunk to dance like that, can he? The things people get up to on their birthdays!'

"At long last they were back, laughing and panting and kissing one another. Pursewarden's good humour seemed to be quite restored now, and he bade me the warmest of goodnights as I put them both in a taxi and sent them on their way. There! My dear Leila, I don't know what you will make of all this. I learned nothing of his private circumstances or background, but I shall be able to look him up; and you will be able to meet him next year when he comes to Egypt. I am sending you a small printed collection of his newest verses which he gave me. They have not appeared anywhere as yet."

In the warm central heating of the club bedroom, he turned the pages of the little book, more with a sense of duty than one of pleasure. It was not only modern poetry which bored him, but all poetry. He could never get the wave-length, so to speak, however hard he tried. He was forced to reduce the words to paraphrase in his own mind, so that they stopped their dance. This inadequacy in himself (Leila had taught him to regard it as such) irritated him. Yet as he turned the pages of the little book he was suddenly interested by a poem which impinged upon his memory, filling him with a sudden chill of misgiving. It was inscribed to the poet's sister and was unmistakably a love-poem to "a blind girl whose hair is painted black". At once he saw the white serene face of Liza Pursewarden rising up from the text.

> Greek statues with their bullet holes for eyes
> Blinded as Eros by surprise,
> The secrets of the foundling heart disguise,
> Lover and loved. . . .

It had a kind of savage deliberate awkwardness of surface;

67

but it was the sort of poem a modern Catullus might have written. It made Mountolive extremely thoughtful. Swallowing, he read it again. It had the simple beauty of shamelessness. He stared gravely at the wall for a long time before slipping the book into an envelope and addressing it to Leila.

There were no further meetings during that visit, though once or twice Mountolive tried to telephone to Pursewarden at his office. But each time he was either on leave or on some obscure mission in the north of England. Nevertheless he traced the sister and took her out to dinner on several occasions, finding her a delightful and somehow moving companion.

Leila wrote in due course to thank him for his information, adding characteristically: "The poems were splendid. But of course I would not wish to meet an artist I admired. The work has no connection with the man, I think. But I am glad he is coming to Egypt. Perhaps Nessim can help him—perhaps he can help Nessim? We shall see."

Mountolive did not know what the penultimate phrase meant.

The following summer, however, his leave coincided with a visit to Paris by Nessim, and the two friends met to enjoy the galleries and plan a painting holiday in Brittany. They had both recently started to try their hands at painting and were full of the fervour of amateurs in a new medium. It was here in Paris that they ran into Pursewarden who was enjoying a month's leave before taking up his post in Cairo. It was a happy accident, for he would be able to return with Nessim, and Mountolive was delighted at the chance of making his path smooth for him by this lucky introduction. Pursewarden himself was quite transfigured and in the happiest of moods, and Nessim seemed to like him immensely. For nearly three weeks they were inseparable, and when the time came to say good-bye, Mountolive had the genuine conviction that a friendship had been established and cemented over all this good food and blithe living. He saw them off at the station and that very evening reported to Leila on the notepaper of his favourite café: "It was a real regret to put them on the train and to think that next week I shall be back in Russia! My heart sinks at the thought. But I have grown to like P. very much, to understand him better. I am inclined to put down his robust scolding manners not to boorishness as I did, but to a profoundly hidden shyness, almost a feeling of guilt. His conversation this time was quite captivating. You must ask Nessim. I believe he liked him even more than I did. And so . . . what? An empty space, a long frozen journey, a soul-wearying three years ahead of me. Ah! my dear Leila, how much I miss you— what you stand for. When will we meet again, I wonder? If I have enough money on my next leave I may fly down to visit you. . . ."

He was unaware that before the three years were up he would once more find his way back to Egypt—the beloved country to which distance and exile lent a haunting brilliance as of tapestry. Could anything as rich as memory be a cheat? He never asked himself the question.

o   o   o   o   o

III

The central heating in the Embassy ballroom gave out a thick furry warmth which made the air taste twice-used; but the warmth itself was a welcome contrast to the frigid pine-starred landscapes outside the tall windows where the snow fell steadily, not only over Russia, it seemed, but over the whole world. It had been falling now for weeks on end. The numb drowsiness of the Soviet winter had engulfed them all. There seemed so little motion, so little sound in the world outside the walls which enclosed them. The tramp of soldier's boots between the shabby sentry-boxes outside the iron gates had died away now in the winter silence. In the gardens the branches of the trees bowed lower and lower under the freight of falling whiteness until one by one they sprang back, shedding their parcels of snow, in soundless explosions of glittering crystals; then the whole process began again, the soft white load of the tumbling snowflakes gathering upon them, pressing them down like springs until the weight became unendurable.

To-day it was Mountolive's turn to read the Lesson. Looking up from the lectern from time to time he saw the looming faces of his staff and fellow secretaries in the shadowy gloom of the ballroom as they followed his voice; faces gleaming white and sunless—he had a sudden image of them all floating belly upwards in a snowy lake, like bodies of trapped frogs gleaming upwards through the mirror of ice. He coughed behind his hand, and the contagion spread into a ripple of coughing which subsided once more into that spiritless silence, with only the susurrus of the pipes echoing through it. Everyone to-day looked morose and ill. The six Chancery guards looked absurdly pious, their best suits awkwardly worn, their jerks of hair pasted to their brows. All were ex-Marines and clearly showed traces of vodka hangovers. Mountolive sighed inwardly as he allowed his quiet melodious voice to enunciate the splendours—incomprehensible to them all—of the passage in the Gospel of St. John which he had found under the marker. The eagle smelt of camphor—why, he could not imagine. As usual, the Ambassador had stayed in bed; during the last year he had become very lax in his duties and was prepared to depend on Mountolive who was luckily always there to perform them with grace and lucidity. Sir Louis had given up even the pretence of caring about the welfare physical or spiritual of his little flock. Why should he not? In three months he would have retired for good.

It was arduous to replace him on these public occasions but it was also useful, thought Mountolive. It gave him a clear field in the exploitation of his own talents for administration. He was virtually running the whole Embassy now, it was in his hands. Nevertheless. . . .

He noticed that Cowdell, the Head of Chancery, was trying to catch his eye. He finished the lesson unfalteringly, replaced the markers, and made his way slowly back to his seat. The chaplain uttered a short catarrhal sentence and with a riffling of pages they found themselves confronting the banal text of "Onward Christian Soldiers" in the eleventh edition of the Foreign Service Hymnal. The harmonium in the corner suddenly began to pant like a fat man running for a bus; then it found its voice and gave out a slow nasal rendering of the first two phrases in tones whose harshness across the wintry hush was like the pulling out of entrails. Mountolive repressed a shudder, waiting for the instrument to subside on the dominant as it always did—as if about to burst into all-too-human sobs. Raggedly they raised their voices to attest to . . . to what? Mountolive found himself wondering. They were a Christian enclave in a hostile land, a country which had become like a great concentration camp owing to a simple failure of the human reason. Cowdell was nudging his elbow and he nudged back to indicate a willingness to receive any urgent communication not strictly upon religious matters. The Head of Chancery sang:

> *Someone's lucky ddy today*
> *Marching as to war* (fortissimo—with piety)
> *Ciphers have an urgent*
> *Going on before* (fortissimo, with piety).

Mountolive was annoyed. There was usually little to do on a Sunday, though the Cipher office remained open with a skeleton staff on duty. Why had they not, according to custom, telephoned to the villa and called him in? Perhaps it was something about the new liquidations? He started the next verse plaintively:

> *Someone should have told me*
> *How was I to know?*
> *Who's the duty cipherine?*

Cowdell shook his head and frowned as he added the rider: "*She is still at work-ork-ork.*"

They wheeled round the corner, so to speak, and drew collective breath while the music started to march down the aisle again. This respite enabled Cowdell to explain hoarsely: "No, it's an urgent *Personal*. Some groups corrupt still."

They smoothed their faces and consciences for the rest of the hymn while Mountolive grappled with his perplexity. As they knelt on the uncomfortable dusty hassocks and buried their faces in their hands, Cowdell continued from between his fingers: "You've been put up for a 'K' and a mission. Let me be the first to congratulate you, etc."

"Christ!" said Mountolive in a surprised whisper, to himself rather than to his Maker. He added "Thank you." His knees suddenly felt weak. For once he had to study to achieve his air of imperturbability. Surely he was still too young? The ramblings of the Chaplain, who resembled a swordfish, filled

72

him with more than the usual irritation. He clenched his teeth. Inside his mind he heard himself repeating the words: "To get out of Russia!" with ever-growing wonder. His heart leaped inside him.

At last the service ended and they trailed dolorously out of the ballroom and across the polished floors of the Residence, coughing and whispering. He managed to counterfeit a walk of slow piety, though it hardly matched his racing mind. But once in the Chancery, he closed the padded door slowly behind him, feeling it slowly suck up the air into its valve as it sealed, and then, drawing a sharp breath, clattered down the three flights of stairs to the wicket-gate which marked the entry to Archives. Here a duty-clerk dispensed tea to a couple of booted couriers who were banging the snow from their gloves and coats. The canvas bags were spread everywhere on the floor waiting to be loaded with the mail and chained up. Hoarse good-morning's followed him to the cipher-room door where he tapped sharply and waited for Miss Steele to let him in. She was smiling grimly. "I know what you want," she said. "It's in the tray—the Chancery copy. I've had it put in your tray and given a copy to the Secretary for H.E."

She bent her pale head once more to her codes. There it was, the flimsy pink membrane of paper with its neatly typed message. He sat down in a chair and read it over slowly twice. Lit a cigarette. Miss Steele raised her head. "May I congratulate you, sir?"—"Thank you" said Mountolive vaguely. He reached his hands to the electric fire for a moment to warm his fingers as he thought deeply. He was beginning to feel a vastly different person. The sensation bemused him.

After a while he walked slowly and thoughtfully upstairs to his own office, still deep in this new and voluptuous dream. The curtains had been drawn back—that meant that his secretary had come in; he stood for a while watching the sentries cross and recross the snowlit entrance to the main gate with its ironwork piled heavily with ice. While he stood there with his

73

dark eyes fixed upon an imagined world lying somewhere behind this huge snowscape, his secretary came in. She was smiling with jubilance. "It's come at last," she said. Mountolive smiled slowly back. "Yes. I wonder if H.E. will stand in my way?"

"Of course not," she said emphatically. "Why should he?"

Mountolive sat once more at his familiar desk and rubbed his chin. "He himself will be off in three months or so" said the girl. She looked at him curiously, almost angrily, for she could read no pleasure, no self-congratulation in his sober expression. Even good fortune could not pierce that carefully formulated reserve. "Well," he said slowly, for he was still swaddled by his own amazement, the voluptuous dream of an unmerited success. "We shall see." He had been possessed now by another new and even more vertiginous thought. He opened his eyes widely as he stared at the window. Surely now, he would at long last be free to *act*? At last the long discipline of self-effacement, of perpetual delegation, was at an end? This was frightening to contemplate, but also exciting. He felt as if now his true personality would be able to find a field of expression in acts; and still full of this engrossing delusion he stood up and smiled at the girl as he said: "At any rate, I must ask H.E.'s blessing before we answer. He is not on deck this morning, so lock up. To-morrow will do." She hovered disappointedly for a moment over him before gathering up his tray and taking out the key to his private safe. "Very well," she said.

"There's no hurry," said Mountolive. He felt that his real life now stretched before him; he was about to be reborn. "I don't see my *exequatur* coming through before, say, June. And so on." But his mind was already racing upon a parallel track, saying: "In July the whole Embassy moves up to Alexandria, to summer quarters. If I could time my arrival. . . ."

And then, side by side with this sense of exhilaration, came a twinge of characteristic meanness. Mountolive, like most

74

people who have nobody on whom to lavish affection, tended towards meanness in money matters. Unreasonable as it was, he suddenly felt a pang of depression at the thought of the costly dress uniform which his new position would demand. Only last week there had been a catalogue from Skinners showing a greatly increased scale for Foreign Service uniforms.

He got up and went into the room next door to see the private secretary. It was empty. An electric fire glowed. A lighted cigarette smoked in the ashtray beside the two bells marked respectively "His Ex." and "Her Ex.". On the pad beside them the Secretary had written in his round feminine hand "Not to be woken before eleven." This obviously referred to "His Ex.". As for "Her Ex.", she had only managed to last six months in Moscow before retiring to the amenities of Nice where she awaited her husband upon his retirement. Mountolive stubbed out the cigarette.

It would be useless to call on his Chief before midday, for the morning in Russia afflicted Sir Louis with a splenetic apathy which often made him unresponsive to ideas; and while he could not, in all conscience, do anything to qualify Mountolive's good fortune, he might easily show pique at not having been consulted according to custom by the Principal Private Secretary. Anyway. He retired to his now empty office and plunged into the latest copy of *The Times*, waiting with ill-concealed impatience for the Chancery clock to mark out midday with its jangling whirrs and gasps. Then he went downstairs and slipped into the Residence again through the padded door, walking with his swift limping walk across the polished floors with their soft archipelagoes of neutral rug. Everything smelt of disuse and Mansion polish; in the curtains a smell of cigar-smoke. At every window a screen of tossing snowflakes.

Merritt the valet was starting up the staircase with a tray containing a cocktail shaker full of Martini and a single glass. He was a pale heavily-built man who cultivated the gravity of a churchwarden while he moved about his tasks in the Residence. He stopped as Mountolive drew level and said hoarsely: "He's just up and dressing for a duty lunch, sir." Mountolive nodded and passed him, taking the stairs two at a time. The servant turned back to the buttery to add a second glass to his tray.

Sir Louis whistled dispiritedly at his own reflection in the great mirror as he dressed himself. "Ah, my boy," he said vaguely as Mountolive appeared behind him. "Just dressing. I know, I know. It's my unlucky day. Chancery rang me at eleven. So you have done it at last. Congratulations."

Mountolive sat down at the foot of the bed with relief to find the news taken so lightly. His Chief went on wrestling with a tie and a starched collar as he said: "I suppose you'll want to go off at once, eh? It's a loss to us."

"It would be convenient," admitted Mountolive slowly.

"A pity. I was hoping you'd see me out. But anyway," he made a flamboyant gesture with a disengaged hand, "you've done it. From tricorne and dirk to bicorne and sword—the final apotheosis." He groped for cuff-links and went on thoughtfully. "Of course, you could stay a bit; it'll take time to get *agrément*. Then you'll have to go to the Palace and kiss hands and all that sort of thing. Eh?"

"I have quite a lot of leave due" said Mountolive with the faintest trace of firmness underlying his diffident tone. Sir Louis retired to the bathroom and began scrubbing his false teeth under the tap. "And the next Honours List?" he shouted into the small mirror on the wall. "You'll wait for that?"

"I suppose." Merritt came in with the tray and the old man shouted "Put it anywhere. An extra glass?"

"Yes sir."

As the servant retired closing the door softly behind him, Mountolive got up to pour the cocktail. Sir Louis was talking to himself in a grumbling tone. "It's damn hard on the Mission. Well, anyway, David, I bet your first reaction to the news was: now I'm free to act, eh?" He chuckled like a fowl and returned

76

to his dressing-table in a high good humour. His junior paused in the act of pouring out, startled by such unusual insight. "How on earth did you know that?" he said frowning. Sir Louis gave another self-satisfied cluck.

"We all do. We all do. The final delusion. Have to go through it like the rest of us, you know. It's a tricky moment. You find yourself throwing your weight about—committing the sin against the Holy Ghost if you aren't careful."

"What would that be?"

"In diplomacy it means trying to build a policy on a minority view. Everyone's weak spot. Look how often we are tempted to build something on the Right here. Eh? Won't do. Minorities are no use unless they're prepared to *fight*. That's the thing." He accepted his drink in rosy old fingers, noting with approval the breath of dew upon the cold glasses. They toasted each other and smiled affectionately. In the last two years they had become the greatest of friends. "I shall miss you. But then, in another three months I shall be out of this . . . this place myself." He said the words with undisguised fervour. "No more nonsense about Objectivity. Eastern can find some nice impartial products of the London School of Economics to do their reporting." Recently the Foreign Office had complained that the Mission's despatches were lacking in balance. This had infuriated Sir Louis. He was fired even by the most fugitive memory of the slight. Putting down his empty glass he went on to himself in the mirror: "Balance! If the F.O. sent a mission to Polynesia they would expect their despatches to begin (he put on a cringing whining tone to enunciate it): 'While it is true that the inhabitants eat each other, nevertheless the food consumption per head is remarkably high.'" He broke off suddenly and sitting down to lace his shoes said: "Oh David, my boy, who the devil am I going to be able to talk to when you go? Eh? You'll be walking about in your ludicrous uniform with an osprey feather in your hat looking like the mating plumage of some rare Indian bird and I—I

77

shall be trotting backwards and forwards to the Kremlin to see those dull beasts."

The cocktails were rather strong. They embarked upon a second, and Mountolive said: "Actually, I came wondering if I could buy your old uniform, unless it's bespoke. I could get it altered."

"Uniform?" said Sir Louis, "I hadn't thought of that."

"They are so fearfully expensive."

"I know. And they've gone up. But you'd have to send mine back to the taxidermist for an overhaul. And they never fit around the neck, you know. All that braid stuff. I'm a frogging or two loose I think. Thank God this isn't a monarchy—one good thing. Frock coats in order, what? Well I don't know."

They sat pondering upon the question for a long moment. Then Sir Louis said: "What would you offer me?" His eye narrowed. Mountolive deliberated for a few moments before saying "Thirty pounds" in an unusually energetic and decisive tone. Sir Louis threw up his hands and simulated incoherence. "Only thirty? It cost me. . . ."

"I know," said Mountolive.

"Thirty pounds," meditated his Chief, hovering upon the fringes of outrage. "I think, dear boy——"

"The sword is a bit bent," said Mountolive obstinately.

"Not too badly," said Sir Louis. "The King of Siam pinched it in the door of his private motor-car. Honourable scar." He smiled once more and continued dressing, humming to himself. He took an absurd delight in this bargaining. Suddenly he turned round.

"Make it fifty" he said. Mountolive shook his head thoughtfully. "That is too much, sir."

"Forty-five."

Mountolive rose and took a turn up and down the room, amused by the old man's evident delight in this battle of wills. "I'll give you forty" he said at last and sat down once more with deliberation. Sir Louis brushed his silver hair furiously with his heavy tortoiseshell-backed brushes. "Have you any drink in your cellar?"

"As a matter of fact, yes, I have."

"Well then, you can have it for forty if you throw in a couple of cases of . . . what have you? Have you a respectable champagne?"

"Yes."

"Very well. Two—no, *three* cases of same."

They both laughed and Mountolive said "It's a hard bargain you drive." Sir Louis was delighted by the compliment. They shook hands upon it and the Ambassador was about to turn back to the cocktail tray when his junior said: "Forgive me, sir. Your third."

"Well?" said the old diplomat with a well-simulated start and a puzzled air. "What of it?" He knew perfectly well. Mountolive bit his lip. "You expressly asked me to warn you." He said it reproachfully. Sir Louis threw himself further back with more simulated surprise. "What's wrong with a final boneshaker before lunch, eh?"

"You'll only hum" said Mountolive sombrely.

"Oh Pouf, dear boy!" said Sir Louis.

"You will, sir."

Within the last year, and on the eve of retirement, the Ambassador had begun to drink rather too heavily—though never quite reaching the borders of incoherence. In the same period a new and somewhat surprising tic had developed. Enlivened by one cocktail too many he had formed the habit of uttering a low continuous humming noise at receptions which had earned him a rather questionable notoriety. But he himself had been unaware of this habit, and indeed at first indignantly denied its existence. He found to his surprise that he was in the habit of humming, over and over again, in *basso profundo*, a passage from the Dead March in Saul. It summed up, appropriately enough, a lifetime of acute boredom spent in the company of friendless officials and empty dignitaries. In a way, it was his response perhaps to a situation which he had subconsciously recognized as intolerable for a number of years; and he was grateful that Mountolive had had the courage to bring the habit to his notice and to help him overcome it. Nevertheless, he always felt bound to protest in spite of himself at his junior's reminder. "*Hum?*" he repeated now, indignantly pouting, "I never heard such nonsense." But he put down the glass and returned to the mirror for a final criticism of his toilet. "Well, anyway," he said, "time is up." He pressed a bell and Merritt appeared with a gardenia on a plate. Sir Louis was somewhat pedantic about flowers and always insisted on wearing his favourite one in his buttonhole when in *tenue de ville*. His wife flew him up boxes of them from Nice and Merritt kept them in the buttery refrigerator, to be rationed out religiously.

"Well David," he said, and patted Mountolive's arm with affection. "I owe you many a good turn. No humming today, however appropriate."

They walked slowly down the long curving staircase and into the hall where Mountolive saw his Chief gloved and coated before signalling the official car by house-telephone. "When do you want to go?" The old voice trembled with genuine regret.

"By the first of next month, sir. That leaves time to wind up and say good-bye."

"You won't stay and see me out?"

"If you order me to, sir."

"You know I wouldn't do that" said Sir Louis, shaking his white head, though in the past he had done worse things. "Never."

They shook hands warmly once more while Merritt walked past them to throw back the heavy front door, for his ears had caught the slither and scrape of tyre-chains on the frosty drive outside. A blast of snow and wind burst upon them. The carpets rose off the floor and subsided again. The Ambassador donned his great fur helmet and thrust his hands into the car-muff. Then, bowed double, he stalked out to the wintry grey-ness. Mountolive sighed and heard the Residence clock clear its dusty throat carefully before striking one.

Russia was behind him.

o   o   o   o   o

Berlin was also in the grip of snow, but here the sullen goaded helplessness of the Russias was replaced by a malig-nant euphoria hardly less dispiriting. The air was tonic with gloom and uncertainty. In the grey-green lamplight of the Embassy he listened thoughtfully to the latest evaluations of the new Attila, and a valuable summary of the measured pre-dictions which for months past had blackened the marbled minute-papers of German Department, and the columns of the P.E. printings—political evaluations. Was it really by now so obvious that this nation-wide exercise in political diabolism would end by plunging Europe into bloodshed? The case seemed overwhelming. But there was one hope—that Attila might turn eastwards and leave the cowering west to moulder away in peace. If the two dark angels which hovered over the European subconscious could only fight and destroy each other. . . . There was some real hope of this. "The *only* hope, sir" said the young attaché quietly, and not without a certain relish, so pleasing to a part of the mind is the prospect of total destruction, as the only cure for the classical *ennui* of modern man. "The only hope," he repeated. Extreme views, thought Mountolive, frowning. He had been taught to avoid them. It had become second nature to remain uncommitted in his mind.

That night he was dined somewhat extravagantly by the youthful Chargé d'Affaires, as the Ambassador was absent on duty, and after dinner was taken to the fashionable Tanzfest for the cabaret. The network of candle-lit cellars, whose walls were lined with blue damask, was filled with the glow of a hundred cigarettes, twinkling away like fireflies outside the radius of white lights where a huge hermaphrodite with the face of a narwhal conducted the measures of the "Fox Macabre Totentanz". Bathed in the pearly sweat of the nigger saxophonists the refrain ran on with its hysterical coda:

> *Berlin, dein Tanzer ist der Tod!*
> *Berlin, du wuhlst mit Lust im Kot!*
> *Halt ein! lass sein! und denk ein bischen nach:*
> *Du tanzt dir doch vom Leibe nicht die Schmach.*
> *denn du boxt, und du jazzt, und du foxt auf dem Pulverfass!*

It was an admirable commentary on the deliberations of the afternoon and underneath the frenetic licence and fervour of the singing he seemed to catch the drift of older undertones—passages from Tacitus, perhaps? Or the carousings of death-dedicated warriors heading for Valhalla? Somehow the heavy smell of the abattoir clung to it, despite the tinsel and the streamers. Thoughtfully Mountolive sat among the white whorls of cigar-smoke and watched the crude peristaltic movements of the Black Bottom. The words repeated themselves in his mind over and over again. "You won't dance the shame out of your belly," he repeated to himself as he watched the dancers break out and the lights change from green and gold to violet.

Then he suddenly sat up and said "My Goodness!" He had caught sight of a familiar face in a far corner of the cellar: that of Nessim. He was seated at a table among a group of elderly men in evening-dress, smoking a lean cheroot and nodding from time to time. They were taking scant notice of the cabaret. A magnum of champagne stood upon the table. It was too far to depend upon signals and Mountolive sent over a card, waiting until he saw Nessim follow the waiter's pointing finger before he smiled and raised a hand. They both stood up, and Nessim at once came over to his table with his warm shy smile to utter the conventional exclamations of surprise and delight. He was, he said, in Berlin on a two-day business visit. "Trying to market tungsten" he added quietly. He was flying back to Egypt at dawn next morning. Mountolive introduced him to his own host and persuaded him to spend a few moments at their table. "It is such a rare pleasure—and now." But Nessim had already heard the rumour of his impending appointment. "I know it isn't confirmed yet," he said, "but it leaked just the same—needless to say via Pursewarden. You can imagine our delight after so long."

They talked on for a while, Nessim smiling as he answered Mountolive's questions. Only Leila was at first not mentioned. After a while Nessim's face took on a curious expression—a sort of chaste cunning, and he said with hesitation: "I would like to make you a small confidence. I am hoping to be married." He sat back and drew slowly upon his cheroot. Mountolive uttered congratulations which could not disguise the faint tinge of anxious regret he felt—for one always fears the marriage of a friend since it involves the possible danger of being excluded from his friendship by the new domestic dispensation. "It is very good news indeed!" he repeated fervently, trying to still his doubt. At last then he could mention Leila. "Leila will be so delighted." Nessim gave him a swift upward glance from under his long lashes and then looked hastily away.

"That is not certain," he said, "as yet."

Mountolive put himself into a position of polite interrogation.

"The girl in question," said Nessim with a rabid coldness, "is first of all Jewish—and you know the absurd Coptic terror of Jews. We even have the proverb: 'If you let the Jewish fox into your vineyard it will eat your life'."

"I know," said Mountolive, "but surely the Hosnanis . . . ?"

"Then, she is not in society. Lastly, she is divorced."

Nessim enunciated these factors with increasing coldness.

83

He stubbed out his cheroot and gave Mountolive another equivocal glance.

"But if you love her?" said his friend quietly. And here, to his surprise, Nessim gave a short ugly smile which was intended to be self-deprecating, and rubbed his chin in his sleeve. "Love," he said, slowly and thoughtfully, as if to himself. "Yes, well, suppose I do then." But all at once he stood up and glanced anxiously back in the direction of his party at the far table. "I must go," he said. "Please treat the matter with absolute confidence, will you?"

They discussed plans for a possible meeting in England before Mountolive should fly out to his new appointment. Nessim was vague, unsure of his movements. They would have to wait upon the event. But now Mountolive's host had returned from the cloak-room, a fact which effectively prevented any further private exchanges. They said good-bye with good grace and Nessim walked slowly back to his table.

"Is your friend in armaments?" asked the Chargé d'Affaires as they were leaving. Mountolive shook his head. "He's a banker. Unless tungsten plays a part in armaments—I don't really know."

"It isn't important. Just idle curiosity. You see, the people at his table are all from Krupps, and so I wondered. That was all."

o   o   o   o   o

IV

To London he always returned with the tremulous eagerness of a lover who has been separated a long time from his mistress; he returned, so to speak, upon a note of interrogation. Had life altered? Had anything been changed? Perhaps the nation had, after all, woken up and begun to live? The thin black drizzle over Trafalgar Square, the soot-encrusted cornices of Whitehall, the slur of rubber tyres spinning upon macadam, the haunting conspiratorial voice of river traffic behind the veils of mist— they were both a reassurance and a threat. He loved it inarticulately, the melancholy of it, though he knew in his heart he could no longer live here permanently, for his profession had made an expatriate of him. He walked in the soft clinging rain towards Downing Street, muffled in his heavy overcoat, comparing himself from time to time, not without a certain complacence, to the histrionic Grand Duke who smiled at him from the occasional hoardings advertising De Reszke cigarettes.

He smiled to himself as he remembered some of Pursewarden's acid strictures on their native capital, repeating them in his own mind with pleasure, as compliments almost. Pursewarden transferring his sister's hand from one elbow to another in order to complete a vague gesture towards the charred-looking figure of Nelson under its swarming troops of pigeons befluffed against the brute cold. "Ah, Mountolive! Look at it all. Home of the eccentric and the sexually disabled. London! Thy food as appetizing as a barium meal, thy gloating discomforts, thy causes not lost but gone before." Mountolive had protested laughingly. "Never mind. It is *our own*—and it is greater than the sum of its defects." But his companion had found such sentiments uncongenial. He smiled now as he remembered the writer's wry criticisms of gloom, discomfort and the native barbarism. As for Mountolive, it nourished him, the gloom; he felt something like the fox's love for its earth. He listened with a comfortable smiling indulgence while his companion perorated with mock fury at the image of his native island, saying: "Ah, England! England where the members of the R.S.P.C.A. eat meat twice a day and the nudist devours imported fruit in the snow. The only country which is ashamed of poverty."

Big Ben struck its foundering plunging note. Lamps had begun to throw out their lines of prismatic light. Even in the rain there was the usual little cluster of tourists and loungers outside the gates of Number Ten. He turned sharply away and entered the silent archways of the Foreign Office, directing his alien steps to the bag-room, virtually deserted now, where he declared himself and gave instructions about the forwarding of his mail, and left an order for the printing of new and more resplendent invitation cards.

Then in a somewhat more thoughtful mood, and a warier walk to match it, he climbed the cold staircase smelling of cobwebs and reached the embrasures in the great hall patrolled by the uniformed janitors. It was late, and most of the inhabitants of what Pursewarden always called the "Central Dovecot" had surrendered their tagged keys and vanished. Here and there in the great building were small oases of light behind barred windows. The clink of teacups sounded somewhere out of sight. Someone fell over a pile of scarlet despatch boxes which had been stacked in a corridor against collection. Mountolive sighed with familiar pleasure. He had deliberately chosen the evening hours for his first few interviews because there was Kenilworth to be seen and . . . his ideas were not very precise upon the point; but he might atone for his dislike of the man by taking him to his club for a drink? For somewhere along the line he had made an enemy of him, he could not guess how, for it had never been marked by any open disagreement. Yet it was there, like a knot in wood.

86

They had been near-contemporaries at school and university, though never friends. But while he, Mountolive, had climbed smoothly and faultlessly up the ladder of promotion the other had been somehow faulted, had always missed his footing; had drifted about among the departments of little concern, collecting the routine honours, but never somehow catching a favourable current. The man's brilliance and industry were undeniable. Why had he never succeeded? Mountolive asked himself the question fretfully, indignantly. Luck? At any rate here was Kenilworth now heading the new department concerned with Personnel, innocuous enough, to be sure, but his failure embarrassed Mountolive. For a man of his endowment it was really a shame to be merely in charge of one of those blank administrative constructs which offered no openings into the worlds of policy. A dead end. And if he could not develop positively he would soon develop the negative powers of obstruction which always derive from a sense of failure.

As he was thinking this he was climbing slowly to the third floor to report his presence to Granier, moving through the violet crepuscule towards the tall cream doors behind which the Under-Secretary sat in a frozen bubble of green light, incising designs on his pink blotter with a paper-knife. Congratulations weighed something here, for they were spiced with professional envy. Granier was a clever, witty and good-tempered man with some of the mental agility and drive of a French grandmother. It was easy to like him. He spoke rapidly and confidently, marking his sentences with little motions of the ivory paper-weight. Mountolive fell in naturally with the charm of his language—the English of fine breeding and polish which carried those invisible diacritical marks, the expression of its caste.

"You looked in on the Berlin mission, I gather? Good. Anyway, if you've been following P.E. you will see the shape of things to come perhaps, and be able to judge the extent of our preoccupations with your own appointment. Eh?" He did not

87

like to use the word "war". It sounded theatrical. "If the worst comes to the worst we don't need to emphasize a concern for Suez—indeed, for the whole Arab complex of states. But since you've served out there I won't pretend to lecture you about it. But we'll look forward to your papers with interest. And moreover as you know Arabic."

"My Arabic has all gone, rusted away."

"Hush," said Granier, "not too loud. You owe your appointment in a very large measure to it. Can you get it back swiftly?"

"If I am allowed the leave I have accrued."

"Of course. Besides, now that the Commission is wound up, we shall have to get *agrément* and so on. And of course the Secretary of State will want to confer when he gets back from Washington. Then what about investiture, and kissing hands and all that? Though we regard every appointment of the sort as urgent . . . well, you know as well as I do the mandarin calm of F.O. movements." He smiled his clever and indulgent smile, lighting a Turkish cigarette. "I'm not so sure it isn't a good philosophy either," he went on. "At any rate, as a bias for policy. After all, we are always facing the inevitable, the irremediable; more haste, more muddle! More panic and less confidence. In diplomacy one can only propose, never dispose. That is up to God, don't you think?" Granier was one of those worldly Catholics who regard God as a congenial club-member whose motives are above question. He sighed and was silent for a moment before adding: "No, we'll have to set the chessboard up for you properly. It's not everyone who'd consider Egypt a plum. All the better for you."

Mountolive was mentally unrolling a map of Egypt with its green central spine bounded by deserts, the dusty anomalies of its peoples and creeds; and then watching it fade in three directions into incoherent desert and grassland; to the north Suez like a caesarian section through which the East was untimely ripped; then again the sinuous complex of mountains and dead granite, orchards and plains which were geographically

88

distributed about the map at hazard, boundaries marked by dots. ... The metaphor from chess was an apposite one. Cairo lay at the centre of this cobweb. He sighed and took his leave, preparing a new face with which to greet the unhappy Kenilworth.

As he walked thoughtfully back to the janitors on the first floor he noted with alarm that he was already ten minutes late for his second interview and prayed under his breath that this would not be regarded as a deliberate slight.

"Mr. Kenilworth has phoned down twice, sir. I told him where you were."

Mountolive breathed more freely and addressed himself once more to the staircase, only to turn right this time and wind down several cold but odourless corridors to where Kenilworth waited, tapping his rimless pince-nez against a large and shapely thumb. They greeted one another with a grotesque effusion which effectively masked a reciprocal distaste. "My *dear* David," ... Was it, Mountolive wondered, simply an antipathy to a physical type? Kenilworth was of a large and porcine aspect, over two hundred pounds of food-and-culture snob. He was prematurely grey. His fat, well-manicured fingers held a pen with a delicacy suggesting incipient crewel-work or crochet. "My *dear* David!" They embraced warmly. All the fat on Kenilworth's large body hung down when he stood up. His flesh was knitted in a heavy cable stitch. "My *dear* Kenny," said Mountolive with apprehension and self-disgust. "What splendid news. I flatter myself," Kenilworth put on an arch expression, "that I may have had something, quite small, quite insignificant, to do with it. Your Arabic weighed with the S. of S. and it was I who remembered it! A long memory. Paper work." He chuckled confusedly and sat down motioning Mountolive to a chair. They discussed commonplaces for a while and at last Kenilworth joined his fingers into a gesture reminiscent of a pout and said: "But to our *moutons*, dear boy. I've assembled all the personal papers for you to browse over. It is all in order. It's a well-found mission, you'll find, very well-found. I've every confidence in your Head of Chancery, Errol. Of course, your own recommendations will weigh. You will look into the staff structure, won't you, and let me know? Think about an A.D.C. too, eh? And I don't know how you feel about a P.A. unless you can rob the typists' pool. But as a bachelor, you'll need someone for the social side, won't you? I don't think your third secretary would be much good."

"Surely I can do all this on the spot?"

"Of course, of course. I was just anxious to see you settled in as comfortably as possible."

"Thank you."

"There is only one change I was contemplating on my own. That was Pursewarden as first political."

"Pursewarden?" said Mountolive with a start.

"I am transferring him. He has done statutory time, and he isn't really happy about it. Needs a change in my view."

"Has he said so?"

"Not in so many words."

Mountolive's heart sank. He took out the cigarette holder which he only used in moments of perplexity, charged it from the silver box on the desk, and sat back in the heavy old-fashioned chair. "Have you any other reasons?" he asked quietly. "Because I should personally like to keep him, at least for a time." Kenilworth's small eyes narrowed. His heavy neck became contused by the blush of annoyance which was trying to find its way up to his face. "To be frank with you, yes," he said shortly.

"Do tell me."

"You will find a long report on him by Errol in the papers I've assembled. I don't think he is altogether suitable. But then contract officers have never been as dependable as officers of the career. It's a generality, I know. I won't say that our friend isn't faithful to the firm—far from it. But I can say that he is opinionated and difficult. Well, *soit!* He's a writer, isn't he?" Kenilworth ingratiated himself with the image of Pursewarden

90

by a brief smile of unconscious contempt. "There has been endless friction with Errol. You see, since the gradual break-up of the High Commission after the signing of the Treaty, there has been a huge gap created, a hiatus; all the agencies which have grown up there since 1918 and which worked to the Commission have been cut adrift now that the parent body is giving place to an Embassy. There will be some thorough-going decisions for you to make. Everything is at sixes and sevens. Suspended animation has been the keynote of the last year and a half—and unsuspended hostilities between an Embassy lacking a Chief, and all these parentless bodies struggling against their own demise. Do you see? Now Pursewarden may be brilliant but he has put a lot of backs up—not only in the mission; people like Maskelyne, for example, who runs the War Office I.C. Branch and has this past five years. They are at each other's throats."

"But what has an I. Branch to do with us?"

"Exactly, nothing. But the High Commissioner's Political Section depended on Maskelyne's Intelligence reports. I.C. Intelligence Collation was the central agency for the Middle East Central Archives and all that sort of thing."

"Where's the quarrel?"

"Pursewarden as political feels that the Embassy has also in a way inherited Maskelyne's department from the Commission. Maskelyne refuses to countenance this. He demands parity or even complete freedom for his show. It is military after all."

"Then set it under a military attaché for the time being."

"Good, but Maskelyne refuses to agree to become part of your mission as his seniority is greater than your attaché designate's."

"What rubbish all this is. What is his rank?"

"Brigadier. You see, since the end of the '18 show, Cairo has been the senior post office of of the intelligence network and all intelligence was funnelled through Maskelyne. Now Purse-warden is trying to appropriate him, bring him to heel. Battle royal, of course. Poor Errol, who I admit is rather weak in some ways, is flapping between them like a loose sail. That is why I thought your task would be easier if you shed Pursewarden."

"Or Maskelyne."

"Good, but he's a War Office body. You couldn't. At any rate, he is most eager for you to arrive and arbitrate. He feels sure you will establish his complete autonomy."

"I can't tolerate an autonomous War Office Agency in a territory to which I am accredited, can I?"

"I agree. I agree, my dear fellow."

"What does the War Office say?"

"You know the military! They will stand by any decision you choose to make. They'll have to. But they have been dug in there for years now. Own staff branches and their transmitter up in Alexandria. I think they would like to stay."

"Not independently. How could I?"

"Exactly. That is what Pursewarden maintains. Good, but someone will have to go in the interests of equity. We can't have all this pin-pricking."

"What pin-pricking?"

"Well, Maskelyne withholding reports and being forced to disgorge them to Political Branch. Then Pursewarden criticizing their accuracy and questioning the value of I.C. Branch. I tell you, real fireworks. No joke. Better shed the fellow, besides you know, he's something of a . . . , keeps odd company. Errol is troubled about his security. Mind you, there is nothing *against* Pursewarden. It's simply that's he's, well . . . a bit of a vulgarian, would you say? I don't know how to qualify it. It's Errol's paper."

Mountolive sighed. "It's surely only the difference between, say, Eton and Worthing, isn't it?" They stared at one another. Neither thought the remark was funny. Kenilworth shrugged his shoulders with obvious pique. "My dear chap," he said, "if you propose to make an issue of it with the S. of S. I can't help it; you will get my proposals overruled. But my views have gone on record now. You'll forgive me if I let them stay like that, as a comment upon Errol's reports. After all, he has been running the show."

"I know."

"It is hardly fair on him."

Stirring vaguely in his subconscious Mountolive felt once more the intimations of power now available to him—a power to take decisions in factors like these which had hitherto been left to fate, or the haphazard dictation of mediating wills; factors which had been unworth the resentments and doubts which their summary resolution by an act of thought would have bred. But if he was ever to claim the world of action as his true inheritance he must begin somewhere. A Head of Mission had the right to propose and sponsor the staff of his choice. Why should Pursewarden suffer through these small administrative troubles, endure the discomfort of a new posting to some uncongenial place?

"I'm afraid the F.O. will lose him altogether if we play about with him," he said unconvincingly; and then, as if to atone for a proposition so circuitous, added crisply: "At any rate, I propose to keep him for a while."

The smile on Kenilworth's face was one in which his eyes played no part. Mountolive felt the silence close upon them like the door of a vault. There was nothing to be done about it. He rose with an exaggerated purposefulness and extruded his cigarette-end into the ugly ashtray as he said: "At any rate, those are my views; and I can always send him packing if he is no use to me."

Kenilworth swallowed quietly, like a toad under a stone, his expressionless eyes fixed upon the neutral wall-paper. The quiet susurrus of the London traffic came welling up between them. "I must go," said Mountolive, by now beginning to feel annoyed with himself. "I am collecting all the files to take down to the country to-morrow evening. To-day and to-morrow I'll clear off routine interviews, and then . . . some leave I hope. Good-bye, Kenny."

"Good-bye." But he did not move from his desk. He only nodded smilingly at the door as Mountolive closed it; then he turned back with a sigh to Errol's neatly-typed memoranda which had been assembled in the grey file marked *Attention of Ambassador Designate*. He read a few lines, and then looked up wearily at the dark window before crossing the room to draw the curtains and pick up the phone. " Give me Archives, please."

It would be wiser for the moment not to press his view.

This trifling estrangement, however, had the effect of making Mountolive set aside his plan to take Kenilworth back to his club with him. It was in its way a relief. He rang up Liza Pursewarden instead and took her out to dinner.

It was only two hours down to Dewford Mallows but once they were outside London it was clear that the whole country-side was deeply under snow. They had to slow down to a crawl which delighted Mountolive but infuriated the driver of the duty-car. "We'll be there for Christmas, sir," he said, "if at all!"

Ice-Age villages, their thatched barns and cottages perfected by the floury whiteness of snow, glistening as if from the tray of an expert confectioner; curving white meadows printed in cuneiform with the small footmarks of birds or otters, or the thawing blotches of cattle. The car windows sealing up steadily, gummed by the frost. They had no chains and no heater. Three miles from the village they came upon a wrecked lorry with a couple of villagers and an A.A. man standing idly about it, blowing on their perished fingers. The telegraph poles were down hereabouts. There was a dead bird lying on the glittering grey ice of Newton's Pond—a hawk. They would never get over Parson's Ridge, and Mountolive took pity on his driver and turned him back summarily on to the main road by the foot-bridge. "I live just over the hill," he said. "It'll take me just twenty-five minutes to walk it." The man was glad to turn back and unwilling to accept the tip Mountolive offered. Then he reversed slowly and turned the car away northward, while his passenger stepped forward into the brilliance, his condensing breath rising before him in a column.

He followed the familiar footpath across fields which tilted ever more steeply away towards an invisible sky-line, describing (his memory had to do duty for his eyesight) something as perfected in its simplicity as Cavendish's first plane. A ritual landscape made now overwhelmingly mysterious by the light of an invisible sun, moving somewhere up there behind the opaque screens of low mist which shifted before him, withdrawing and closing. It was a walk full of memories—but in default of visibility he was forced to imagine the two small hamlets on the hill-crown, the intent groves of beeches, the ruins of a Norman castle. His shoes cut a trembling mass of raindrops from the lush grass at every scythe-like step, until the bottoms of his trousers were soaked and his ankles turned to ice.

Out of the invisible marched shadowy oaks, and suddenly there came a rattling and splattering—as if their teeth were chattering with the cold; the thawing snow was dripping down upon the carpet of dead leaves from the upper branches.

Once over the crown all space was cut off. Rabbits lobbed softly away on all sides. The tall plumed grass had been starched into spikes by frost. Here and there came glimpses of a pale sun, its furred brilliance shining through the mist like a gas mantle burning brightly but without heat. And now he heard the click of his own shoes upon the macadam of the second-class road as he hastened his pace towards the tall gates of the house. Hereabouts the oaks were studded with brilliants; as he passed two fat pigeons rushed out of them and disappeared with the sharp wingflap of a thousand closing books. He was startled and then amused. There was the "form" of a hare in the paddock, quite near the house. Fingers of ice tumbled about the trees with a ragged clatter—a thousand broken wineglasses. He groped for the cold Yale key and smiled again as he felt it turn, admitting him to an unforgotten warmth which smelt of apricots and old books, polish and flowers; all the memories which led him back unerringly towards Piers Plowman, the pony, the fishing-rod, the stamp album. He stood in the hall and called her name softly.

His mother was sitting by the fire, just as he had last left her, with a book open upon her knees, smiling. It had become a convention between them to disregard his disappearances and returns: to behave as if he had simply absented himself for a few moments from this companionable room where she spent her life, reading or painting or knitting before the great fire-place. She was smiling now with the same smile—designed to cement space and time, and to anneal the loneliness which beset her while he was away. Mountolive put down his heavy brief-case and made a funny little involuntary gesture as he stepped towards her. "Oh dear," he said, "I can see from your face that you've heard. I was so hoping to surprise you with my news!"

They were both heartbroken by the fact; and as she kissed him she said: "The Garniers came to tea last week. Oh, David, I'm so sorry. I did so want you to have your surprise. But I pretend so badly."

Mountolive felt an absurd disposition towards tears of sheer vexation: he had invented the whole scene in his mind, had made up question and answer. It was like tearing up a play into which one had put a lot of imagination and hard work. "Damn," he said, "how thoughtless of them!"

"They were trying to please me—and of course it did. You can imagine how much, can't you?"

But from this point he stepped once more, lightly and effortlessly back into the current of memories which the house evoked around her and which led back almost to his eleventh birthday, the sense of well-being and plenitude as the warmth of the fire came out to greet him.

"Your father will be pleased," she said later, in a new voice, sharper for being full of an unrealized jealousy—tidemarks of a passion which had long since refunded itself into an unwilling acquiescence. "I put all your mail in his study for you." "His" study—the study which his father had never seen, never inhabited. The defection of his father stood always between them as their closest bond, seldom discussed yet somehow always there—the invisible weight of his private existence, apart from them both, in another corner of the world: happy or unhappy, who can say? "For those of us who stand upon the margins of the world, as yet unsolicited by any God, the only truth is that work itself is Love." An odd, a striking phrase for the old man to embed in a scholarly preface to a Pali text! Mountolive had turned the green volume over and over in his hands, debating the meaning of the words and measuring them against the memory of his father—the lean brown figure with the spare bone-structure of a famished sea-bird: dressed in an incongruous pith-helmet. Now apparently he wore the robes of an Indian *fakir!* Was one to smile? He had not seen his father since his departure from India on his eleventh birthday; he had become like someone condemned *in absentia* for a crime . . . which could not be formulated. A friendly withdrawal into the world of Eastern scholarship on which his heart had been set for many years. It was perplexing.

Mountolive senior had belonged to the vanished India, to the company of its rulers whose common devotion to their charge had made them a caste; but a caste which was prouder of a hostage given to Buddhist scholarship than of one given to an Honours List. Such disinterested devotions usually ended by a passionate self-identification with the subject of them—this sprawling sub-continent with its castes and creeds, its monuments and faiths and ruins. At first he had been simply a judge in the service, but within a few years he had become pre-eminent in Indian scholarship, an editor and interpreter of rare and neglected texts. The young Mountolive and his mother

97

had been comfortably settled in England on the understanding that he would join them on retirement; to this end had this pleasant house been furnished with the trophies, books and pictures of a long working career. If it now had something of the air of a museum, it was because it had been deserted by its real author who had decided to stay on in India to complete the studies which (they both now recognized) would last him the rest of his life. This was not an uncommon phenomenon among the officials of the now vanished and disbanded corps. But it had come gradually. He had deliberated upon it for years before arriving at the decision, so that the letter he wrote announcing it all had the air of a document long-meditated. It was in fact the last letter either of them received from him. From time to time, however, a passer-by who had visited him in the Buddhist Lodge near Madras to which he had retired, brought a kindly message from him. And of course the books themselves arrived punctually, one after the other, resplendent in their rich uniforms and bearing the grandiose imprints of University Presses. The books were, in a way, both his excuse and his apology.

Mountolive's mother had respected this decision; and nowadays hardly ever spoke of it. Only now and again the invisible author of their joint lives here in this snowy island emerged thus in a reference to "his" study; or in some other remark like it which, uncommented upon, evaporated back into the mystery (for them) of a life which represented an unknown, an unresolved factor. Mountolive could never see below the surface of his mother's pride in order to judge how much this defection might have injured her. Yet a common passionate shyness had grown up between them on the subject, for each secretly believed the other wounded.

Before dressing for dinner that evening, Mountolive went into the book-lined study, which was also a gun-room, and took formal possession of "his father's" desk which he used whenever he was at home. He locked his files away carefully and sorted out his mail. Among the letters and postcards was a bulky envelope with a Cyprus stamp addressed to him in the unmistakable hand of Pursewarden. It suggested a manuscript at first and he cracked the seal with his finger in some perplexity. "My dear David," it read. "You will be astonished to get a letter of such length from me, I don't doubt. But the news of your appointment only reached me lately in rumoured form, and there is much you should know about the state of affairs here which I could not address to you formally as Ambassador Designate (Confidential: Under Flying Seal) ahem!"

There would be time enough, thought Mountolive with a sigh, to study all this accumulation of memoranda, and he unlocked the desk again to place it with his other papers.

He sat at the great desk for a while in the quietness, soothed by the associations of the room with its *bric-à-brac*; the mandala paintings from some Burmese shrine, the Lepcha flags, the framed drawings for the first edition of the Jungle Book, the case of Emperor moths, the votive objects left at some abandoned temple. Then the rare books and pamphlets—early Kipling bearing the imprint of Thacker and Spink, Calcutta, Edwards Thompson's fascicules, Younghusband, Mallows, Derby. . . . Some museum would be glad of them one day. Under a pressmark they would revert back to anonymity.

He picked up the old Tibetan prayer-wheel which lay on the desk and twirled it once or twice, hearing the faint scrape of the revolving drum, still stuffed with the yellowing fragments of paper on which devout pens had long ago scribbled the classical invocation *Om Mani Padme Hum*. This had been an accidental parting gift. Before the boat left he had pestered his father for a celluloid aeroplane and together they had combed the bazaar for one without avail. Then his father had suddenly stopped at a pedlar's stall and bought the wheel for a few rupees, thrusting it into his unwilling fingers as a substitute. It was late. They had to rush. Their good-byes had been perfunctory.

Then after that, what? A tawny river-mouth under a brazen sun, the iridescent shimmer of heat blurring the faces, the smoke from the burning ghats, the dead bodies of men, blue and swollen, floating down the estuary. . . . That was as far as his memory went. He put down the heavy wheel and sighed. The wind shook the windows, whirling the snow against them, as if to remind him where he was. He took out his bundle of Arabic primers and the great dictionary. These· must live beside his bed for the next few months.

That night he was once more visited by the unaccountable affliction with which he always celebrated his return home—a crushing ear-ache which rapidly reduced him to a shivering pain-racked ghost of himself. It was a mystery, for no doctor had so far managed to allay—or even satisfactorily to diagnose—this onslaught of the Petit Mal. It never attacked him save when he was at home. As always, his mother overheard his groans and knew from old experience what they meant; she materialized out of the darkness by his bed bringing the comfort of ancient familiarity and the one specific which, since childhood, she had used to combat his distress. She always kept it handy now, in the cupboard beside her bed. Salad oil, warmed in a teaspoon over a candle-flame. He felt the warmth of the oil penetrate and embalm his brain, while his mother's voice upon the darkness soothed him with its promises of relief. In a little while the tide of agony receded to leave him, washed up so to speak, on the shores of sleep—a sleep stirred vaguely by those comforting memories of childhood illnesses which his mother had always shared—they fell ill together, as if by sympathy. Was it so that they might lie in adjoining rooms talking to each other, reading to each other, sharing the luxury of a common convalescence? He did not know.

He slept. It was a week before he addressed himself to his official papers and read the letter from Pursewarden.

o   o   o   o   o

V

My dear David,

You will be astonished to get a letter of such length from me, I don't doubt. But the news of your appointment only reached me lately in rumoured form, and there is much you should know about the state of affairs here which I could not address to you formally as Ambassador Designate (Confidential: Under Flying Seal) ahem!

Ouf! What a bore! I hate writing letters as you well know. And yet . . . I myself shall almost certainly be gone by the time you arrive, for I have taken steps to get myself transferred. After a long series of calculated wickednesses I have at *last* managed to persuade poor Errol that I am unsuitable for the Mission which I have adorned these past two years. Two years! A lifetime! And Errol himself is so good, so honest, so worthy; a curious goat-like creature who nevertheless conveys the impression of being a breech-delivery! He has put in his paper against me with the greatest reluctance. *Please do nothing to countermand the transfer which will result from it*, as it squares with my own private wishes. I implore you.

The deciding factor has been my desertion of my post for the past five weeks which has caused grave annoyance and finally decided Errol. I will explain everything. Do you remember, I wonder, the fat young French diplomat of the Rue du Bac? Nessim took us round once for drinks? Pombal by name? Well, I have taken refuge with him—he is serving here. It is really quite gay *chez lui*. The summer over, the headless Embassy retired with the Court to winter in Cairo, but this time without Yours Truly. I went underground. Nowadays we rise at eleven, turn out the girls, and after having a hot bath play backgammon until lunch-time; then an *arak* at the Café al

Akhtar with Balthazar and Amaril (who send their love) and lunch at the Union Bar. Then perhaps we call on Clea to see what she is painting, or go to a cinema. Pombal is doing all this legitimately; he is on local leave. I am *en retraite*. Occasionally the exasperated Errol rings up long distance in an attempt to trace me and I answer him in the voice of a *poule* from the Midi. It rattles him badly because he guesses it is me, but isn't quite sure. (The point about a Wykehamist is that he cannot *risk* giving offence.) We have lovely, lovely conversations. Yesterday I told him that I, Pursewarden, was under treatment for a glandular condition chez Professor Pombal but was now out of danger. Poor Errol! One day I shall apologize to him for all the trouble I have caused him. Not now. Not until I get my transfer to Siam or Santos.

All this is very wicked of me, I know, but . . . the tedium of this Chancery with all these un-grown-up people! The Errols are formidably Britannic. They are, for example, *both* economists. Why *both*, I ask myself? One of them must feel permanently redundant. They make love to two places of decimals only. Their children have all the air of vulgar fractions!

Well. The only nice ones are the Donkins; he clever and high-spirited, she rather common and fast-looking with too much rouge. But . . . poor dear, she is over-compensating for the fact that her little husband has grown a beard and turned Moslem! She sits with a hard aggressive air on his desk, swinging her leg and smoking swiftly. Mouth too red. Not quite a lady and hence insecure? Her husband is a clever youth but far too serious. I do not dare to ask if he intends to put in for the extra allowance of wives to which he is entitled.

But let me tell you in my laboured fashion what lies behind all this nonsense. I was sent here, as you know, under contract, and I fulfilled my original task faithfully—as witness the giant roll of paper headed (in a lettering usually reserved for tombstones) *Instruments for a Cultural Pact Between the Governments of His Britannic Majesty etc.* Blunt instruments indeed—for what can a Christian culture have in common with a Moslem or a Marxist? Our premises are hopelessly opposed. Never mind! I was told to do it and I done it. And much as I love what they've got here I don't understand the words in relation to an educational system based on the abacus and a theology which got left behind with Augustine and Aquinas. Personally I think we both have made a mess of it, and I have no *parti-pris* in the matter. And so on. I just don't see what D. H. Lawrence has to offer a pacha with seventeen wives, though I believe I know which one of them is happiest. . . . However, I done it, the Pact I mean.

This done I found myself rapidly sent to the top of the form as a Political and this enabled me to study papers and evaluate the whole Middle Eastern complex as a coherent whole, as a policy venture. Well, let me say that after prolonged study I have come to the reluctant conclusion that it is neither coherent nor even a policy—at any rate a policy capable of withstanding the pressures which are being built up here.

These rotten states, backward and venal as they are, must be seriously thought about; they cannot be held together just by encouraging just what is weakest and most corrupt in them, as we appear to be doing. This approach would presuppose another fifty years of peace and no radical element in the electorate at home: that given, the *status quo* might be maintained. But given this prevailing trend, can England be as short-sighted as this? Perhaps. I don't know. It is not my job to know these things, *as an artist*; as a political I am filled with misgiving. To encourage Arab unity while at the same time losing the power to use the poison-cup seems to me to be a very dubious thing: not policy but lunacy. And to add Arab unity to all the other currents which are running against us seems to me to be an engaging folly. Are we still beset by the doleful dream of the Arabian Nights, fathered on us by three generations of sexually disoriented Victorians whose subconscious reacted wholeheartedly to the thought of more than one legal wife? Or the romantic Bedouin-fever of the Bells and Lawrences? Perhaps. But the Victorians who fathered this dream on us were people who believed in *fighting* for the value of their currency; they knew that the world of politics was a jungle. To-day the Foreign Office appears to believe that the best way to deal with the jungle is to turn Nudist and conquer the wild beast by the sight of one's nakedness. I can hear you sigh. "Why can't Pursewarden be *more precise*. All these *boutades!*"

Very well. I spoke of the pressures. Let us divide them into internal and external, shall we, in the manner of Errol? My views may seem somewhat heretical, but here they are.

Well then, first, the abyss which separates the rich from the poor—it is positively Indian. In Egypt to-day, for example, six per cent of the people own over three-quarters of the land, thus leaving under a *feddan* a head for the rest to live on. Good! Then the population is doubling itself every second generation —or is it third? But I suppose any economic survey will tell you this. Meanwhile there is the steady growth of a vocal and literate middle-class whose sons are trained at Oxford among our comfy liberalisms—and who find no jobs waiting for them when they come back here. The *babu* is growing in power, and the dull story is being repeated here as elsewhere. "Intellectual coolies of the world unite."

To these internal pressures we are gracefully adding by direct encouragement, the rigour of a nationalism based in a fanatical religion. I personally admire it, but never forget that it is a fighting religion with no metaphysics, only an ethic. The Arab Union, etc. . . . My dear chap, why are we thinking up these absurd constructs to add to our own discomfiture— specially as it is clear to me that we have lost the basic power to act which alone would ensure that our influence remained paramount here? These tottering backward-looking feudalisms could only be supported by arms against these disintegrating elements inherent in the very nature of things to-day; but to use arms, "to preach with the sword" in the words of Lawrence, one must have a belief in one's own ethos, one's own mystique of life. What does the Foreign Office believe? I just don't know. In Egypt, for example, very little has been done beyond keeping the peace; the High Commission is vanishing after a rule of—since 1888?—and will not leave behind even the vestiges of a trained civil service to stabilize this rabble-ridden grotesque which we now apparently regard as a sovereign state. How long will fair words and courtly sentiments prevail against the massive discontents these people feel? One can trust a treaty king only as long as he can trust his people. How long remains before a flashpoint is reached? I don't know —and to be frank I don't much *care*. But I should say that some unforeseen outside pressure like a war would tumble over these scarecrow principalities at a breath. Anyway, these are my general reasons for wanting a change. I believe we should re-orient policy and build Jewry into the power behind the scenes here. And quick.

Now for the particular. Very early in my political life I ran up against a department of the War Office specializing in general intelligence, run by a Brigadier who resented the idea that his office should bow the knee to us. A question of rank, or allowances, or some such rot; under the Commission he had been allowed more or less a free hand. Incidentally, this is the remains of the old Arab Bureau left over from 1918 which has been living on quietly like a toad buried under a stone! Obviously in the general re-alignment, his show must (it seemed to me) integrate with somebody. And now there was only an embryonic Embassy in Egypt. As he had worked formerly to the High Commission's Political Branch, I thought he should work to me—and indeed, after a series of sharp battles, bent if not broke him—Maskelyne is the creature's name. He is so typical as to be rather interesting and I have made extensive notes on him for a book in my usual fashion. (One writes to recover a lost innocence!)

Well, since the Army discovered that imagination is a major

factor in producing cowardice they have trained the Maskelyne breed in the virtues of counter-imagination: a sort of amnesia which is almost Turkish. The contempt for death has been turned into a contempt for life and this type of man accepts life only on his own terms. A frozen brain alone enables him to keep up a routine of exceptional boredom. He is very thin, very tall, and his skin has been tanned by Indian service to the colour of smoked snakeskin, or a scab painted with iodine. His perfect teeth rest as lightly as a feather upon his pipestem. There is a peculiar gesture he has—I wish I could describe it, it interests me so much—of removing his pipe slowly before speaking, levelling his small dark eyes at one, and almost whispering: "Oh, do you really think so?" The vowels drawing themselves out infinitely into the lassitude, the boredom of the silence which surrounds him. He is gnawed by the circumscribed perfection of a breeding which makes him uncomfortable in civilian clothes, and indeed he walks about in his well-cut cavalry coat with a *Noli me tangere* air. (Breed for type and you always get anomalies of behaviour.) He is followed everywhere by his magnificent red pointer Nell (named after his wife?) who sleeps on his feet while he works at his files, and on his bed at night. He occupies a room in a hotel in which there is nothing personal—no books, no photographs, no papers. Only a set of silver-backed brushes, a bottle of whisky and a newspaper. (I imagine him sometimes brushing the silent fury out of his own scalp, furiously brushing his dark shiny hair back from the temples, faster and faster. Ah, that's better—that's better!)

He reaches his office at eight having bought his day-late copy of the *Daily Telegraph*. I have never seen him read anything else. He sits at his huge desk, consumed with a slow dark contempt for the venality of the human beings around him, perhaps the human race as a whole; imperturbably he examines and assorts their differing corruptions, their maladies, and outlines them upon marble minute-paper which he always signs with his little silver pen in a small awkward fly's handwriting. The current of his loathing flows through his veins slowly, heavily, like the Nile at flood. Well, you can see what a *numéro* he is. He lives purely in the military imagination for he never sees or meets the subjects of most of his papers; the information he collates comes in from suborned clerks, or discontented valets, or pent-up servants. It does not much matter. He prides himself on his readings of it, his I.A. (intelligence appreciation), just like an astrologer working upon charts belonging to unseen, unknown subjects. He is judicial, proud as the Calif, unswerving. I admire him very much. Honestly I do.

Maskelyne has set up two marks between which (as between degree-signs on a calibrated thermometer) the temperatures of his approval and disapproval are allowed to move, expressed in the phrases: "A good show for the Raj" and "Not such a good show for the Raj". He is too single-minded of course, ever to be able to imagine a really Bad Show for the Bloody Raj. Such a man seems unable to see the world around him on open sights; but then his profession and the need for reserve make him a complete recluse, make him inexperienced in the ways of the world upon which he sits in judgement. . . . Well, I am tempted to go on and frame the portrait of our spy-catcher, but I will desist. Read my next novel but four, it should also include a sketch of Telford, who is Maskelyne's Number Two—a large blotchy ingratiating civilian with ill-fitting dentures who manages to call one "old fruit" a hundred times a second between nervous guffaws. His worship of the cold snaky soldier is marvellous to behold. "Yes, Brigadier," "No, Brigadier," falling over a chair in his haste to serve; you would say he was completely in love with his boss. Maskelyne sits and watches his confusion coldly, his brown chin, cleft by a dark dimple, jutting like an arrow. Or he will lean back in his swivel-chair and tap softly on the door of the huge safe behind him with the faintly satisfied air of a gourmet patting his paunch as he says: "You don't believe me? I have it all in here, all in here." Those files, you think, watching this superlative, all-comprehending gesture, must contain material enough to indict the world! Perhaps they do.

Well, this is what happened: one day I found a characteristic document from Maskelyne on my desk headed *Nessim Hosnani*, and sub-titled *A Conspiracy Among the Copts* which alarmed me somewhat. According to the paper, our Nessim was busy working up a large and complicated plot against the Egyptian Royal House. Most of the data were rather questionable I thought, knowing Nessim, but the whole paper put me in a quandary for it carried the bland recommendation that the details should be transmitted by the Embassy to the Egyptian Ministry of Foreign Affairs! I can hear you draw your breath sharply. Even supposing this were true, such a course would put Nessim's life in the greatest danger. Have I explained that one of the major characteristics of Egyptian nationalism is the gradually growing envy and hate of the "foreigners"—the half-million or so of non-Moslems here? And that the moment full Egyptian sovereignty was declared the Moslems started in to bully and expropriate them? The brains of Egypt, as you know, is its foreign community. The capital which flowed into the land while it was safe under our suzerainty, is now at the mercy of these paunchy pachas. The Armenians, Greeks, Copts, Jews—they are all feeling the sharpening edge of this hate; many are wisely leaving, but most cannot. These huge capital investments in cotton, etc., cannot be abandoned overnight. The foreign communities are living from prayer to prayer and from bribe to bribe. They are trying to save their industries, their life-work from the gradual encroachment of the pashas. We have literally thrown them to the lions!

Well, I read and re-read this document, as I say, in a state of considerable anxiety. I knew that if I gave it to Errol he would run bleating with it to the King. So I went into action myself to test the weak points in it—mercifully it was not one of Maskelyne's best papers—and succeeded in throwing doubt upon many of his contentions. But what infuriated him was that I actually *suspended* the paper—I had to in order to keep it out of Chancery's hands! My sense of duty was sorely strained, but then there was no alternative; what would those silly young schoolboys next door have done? If Nessim was really guilty of the sort of plot Maskelyne envisaged, well and good; one could deal with him later according to his lights. But . . . you know Nessim. I felt that I owed it to him to be sure before passing such a paper upwards.

But of course Maskelyne was furious, though he had the grace not to show it. We sat in his office with the conversational temperature well below zero and still falling while he showed me his accumulated evidence and his agents' reports. For the most part they were not as solid as I had feared. "I have this man Selim suborned" Maskelyne kept croaking, "and I'm convinced his own secretary can't be wrong about it. There is this small secret society with the regular meetings—Selim has to wait with the car and drive them home. Then there is this curious cryptogram which goes out all over the Middle East from Balthazar's clinic, and then the visits to arms manufacturers in Sweden and Germany. . . ." I tell you, my brain was swimming! I could see all our friends neatly laid out on a slab by the Egyptian Secret Police, being measured for shrouds.

I must say too, that *circumstantially* the inferences which Maskelyne drew appeared to hold water. It all looked rather sinister; but luckily a few of the basic points would not yield to analysis—things like the so-called cipher which friend Balthazar shot out once every two months to chosen recipients in the big towns of the Middle East. Maskelyne was still trying to follow these up. But the data were far from complete and I stressed this as strongly as I could, much to the discomfort of Telford, though Maskelyne is too cool a bird of prey to be easily discountenanced. Nevertheless I got him to agree to pend the paper until something more substantial was forthcoming to broaden the basis of the doctrine. He hated me but he swallowed it, and so I felt that I had gained at least a temporary respite. The problem was what to do next—how to use the time to advantage? I was of course convinced that Nessim was innocent of these grotesque charges. But I could not, I admit, supply explanations as convincing as those of Maskelyne. What, I could not help wondering, were they really up to? If I was to deflate Maskelyne, I must find out for myself. Very annoying, and indeed professionally improper—but *que faire?* Little Ludwig must turn himself into a private investigator, a Sexton Blake, in order to do the job! But where to begin?

Maskelyne's only direct lead on Nessim was through the suborned secretary, Selim; through him he had accumulated quite a lot of interesting though not intrinsically alarming data about the Hosnani holdings in various fields—the land bank, shipping line, ginning mills, and so on. The rest was largely gossip and rumour, some of it damaging, but none of it more than circumstantial. But piled up in a heap it did make our gentle Nessim sound somewhat sinister. I felt that I must take it all apart somehow. Specially as a lot of it concerned and surrounded his marriage—the acid gossip of the lazy and envious, so typical of Alexandria—or anywhere else for that matter. In this, of course, the unconscious moral judgements of the Anglo-Saxon were well to the fore—I mean in the value-judgements of Maskelyne. As for Justine—well, I know her a bit, and I must confess I rather admired her surly magnificence. Nessim haunted her for some time before getting her to consent, I am told; I cannot say I had misgivings about it all exactly, but . . . even to-day their marriage feels in some curious way uncemented. They make a perfect pair, but never seem to touch each other; indeed, once I saw her very slightly shrink as he picked a thread from her fur. Probably imagination. Is there perhaps a thundercloud brooding there behind the dark satin-eyed wife? Plenty nerves, certainly. Plenty hysteria. Plenty Judaic melancholy. One recognizes her vaguely as the girl-friend of the man whose head was presented on a charger. . . . What do I mean?

Well, Maskelyne says with his dry empty contempt: "No sooner does she marry than she starts an affair with another man, and a foreigner to boot." This is course is Darley, the vaguely amiable bespectacled creature who inhabits Pombal's box-room at certain times. He teaches for a living and writes novels. He has that nice round babyish back to the head which one sees in cultural types; slight stoop, fair hair, and the shyness that goes with Great Emotions imperfectly kept under control. A fellow-romantic quotha! Looked at hard, he starts to stammer. But he's a good fellow, gentle and resigned . . . I confess that he seems unlikely material for someone as dashing as Nessim's wife to work upon. Can it be benevolence in her, or simply a perverse taste for innocence? There is a small mystery here. Anyway, it was Darley and Pombal who introduced me to the current Alexandrian *livre de chevet* which is a French novel called *Moeurs* (a swashing study in the grand manner of nymphomania and psychic impotence) written by Justine's last husband. Having written it he wisely divorced her and decamped but she is popularly supposed to be the central subject of the book and is regarded with grave sympathy by society. I must say, when you think that everyone is both polymorph and perverse here, it seems hard luck to be singled out like this as the main character in a *roman vache*. Anyway, this lies in the past, and now Nessim has carried her into the ranks of *le monde* where she acquits herself with a sharply defined grace and savagery. They suit her looks and the dark but simple splendours of Nessim himself. Is he happy? But wait, let me put the question another way. Was he ever happy? Is he unhappier now than he was? Hum! I think he could do a lot worse, for the girl is neither too innocent nor too unintelligent. She plays the piano really well, albeit with a sulky emphasis, and reads widely. Indeed, the novels of Yours Truly are much admired— with a disarming wholeheartedness. (Caught! Yes, this is why I am disposed to like her.)

On the other hand, what she sees in Darley I cannot credit.

The poor fellow flutters on a slab like a skate at her approach; he and Nessim are, however, great frequenters of each other, great friends. These modest British types—do they all turn out to be Turks secretly? Darley at any rate must have some appeal because he has also got himself regally entangled with a rather nice little cabaret dancer called Melissa. You would never think, to look at him, that he was capable of running a tandem, so little self-possession does he appear to have. A victim of his own fine sentiment? He wrings his hands, his spectacles steam up, when he mentions either name. Poor Darley! I always enjoy irritating him by quoting the poem by his minor namesake to him:

> O blest unfabled Incense Tree
> That burns in glorious Araby,
> With red scent chalicing the air,
> Till earth-life grows Elysian there.

He pleads with me blushingly to desist, though I cannot tell which Darley he is blushing for; I continue in magistral fashion:

> Half-buried in her flaming breast
> In this bright tree she makes her nest
> Hundred-sunned Phoenix! When she must
> Crumble at length to hoary dust!

It is not a bad conceit for Justine herself. "Stop" he always cries.

> Her gorgeous death-bed! Her rich pyre
> Burn up with aromatic fire!
> Her urn, sight-high from spoiler men!
> Her birth-place when self-born again!

"Please. Enough."

"What's wrong with it? It's not such a bad poem, is it?"

And I conclude with Melissa, disguised as an 18th Century Dresden China shepherdess.

The mountainless green wilds among,
Here ends she her unechoing song
With amber tears and odorous sighs
Mourned by the desert where she dies!

So much for Darley! But as for Justine's part in the matter I can find no rhyme, no reason, unless we accept one of Pombal's epigrams at its face value. He says, with fat seriousness: *"Les femmes sont fidèles au fond, tu sais? Elles ne trompent que les autres femmes!"* But it seems to me to offer no really concrete reason for Justine wishing to *tromper* the pallid rival Melissa. This would be *infra dig* for a woman with her position in society. See what I mean?

Well, then, it is upon Darley that our Maskelyne keeps his baleful ferret's eyes fixed; apparently Selim tells us that all the real information on Nessim is kept in a little wall-safe at the house and not in the office. There is only one key to this safe which Nessim always carries on his person. The private safe, says Selim, is full of papers. But he is vague as to what the papers can be. Love letters? Hum. At any rate, Selim has made one or two attempts to get at the safe, but without any luck. One day the bold Maskelyne himself decided to examine it at close range and take, if necessary, a wax squeeze. Selim let him in and he climbed the back stairs—and nearly ran into Darley, our cicisbeo, and Justine in the bedroom! He just heard their voices in time. Never tell me after this that the English are puritans. Some time later I saw a short story Darley published in which a character exclaims: "In his arms I felt mauled, chewed up, my fur coated with saliva, as if between the paws of some great excited cat." I reeled. "Crumbs!" I thought. "This is what Justine is doing to the poor bugger— eating him alive!"

I must say, it gave me a good laugh. Darley is so typical of my compatriots—snobbish and parochial in one. And so *good!* He lacks devil. (Thank God for the Irishman and the Jew who spat in my blood.) Well, why should I take this high and mighty line? Justine must be awfully good to sleep with, must kiss like a rainbow and squeeze out great sparks—yes. But out of Darley? It doesn't hold water. Nevertheless "this rotten creature" as Maskelyne calls her is certainly engaging his whole attention, or was when I was last there. Why?

All these factors were tumbling over and over in my mind as I drove up to Alexandria, having secured myself a long duty week-end which even the good Errol found unexceptionable. I never dreamed then, that within a year you might find yourself engaged by these mysteries. I only knew that I wanted, if possible, to demolish the Maskelyne thesis and stay the Chancery's hand in the matter of Nessim. But apart from this I was somewhat at a loss. I am no spy, after all; was I to creep about Alexandria dressed in a pudding-basin wig with concealed earphones, trying to clear the name of our friend? Nor could I very well present myself to Nessim and, clearing my throat, say nonchalantly: "Now about this spy-net you've got here. . . ." However, I drove steadily and thoughtfully on. Egypt, flat and unbosomed, flowed back and away from me on either side of the car. The green changed to blue, the blue to peacock's eye, to gazelle-brown, to panther-black. The desert was like a dry kiss, a flutter of eyelashes against the mind. Ahem! The night became horned with stars like branches of almond-blossom. I gibbered into the city after a drink or two under a new moon which felt as if it were drawing half its brilliance from the open sea. Everything smelt good again. The iron band that Cairo puts round one's head (the consciousness of being completely surrounded by burning desert?) dissolved, relaxed—gave place to the expectation of an open sea, an open road leading one's mind back to Europe. . . . Sorry. Off the point.

I telephoned the house, but they were both out at a reception; feeling somewhat relieved I betook myself to the Café Al Akhtar in the hope of finding congenial company and found: only our friend Darley. I like him. I like particularly the way he sits on his hands with excitement when he discusses art, which he insists on doing with Yours Truly—why? I answer as best I can and drink my *arak*. But this generalized sort of conversation puts me out of humour. For the artist, I think, as for the public, no such thing as art exists; it only exists for the critics and those who live in the forebrain. Artist and public simply register, like a seismograph, an electromagnetic charge which can't be rationalized. One only knows that a transmission of sorts goes on, true or false, successful or unsuccessful, according to chance. But to try to break down the elements and nose them over—one gets nowhere. (I suspect this approach to art is common to all those who cannot surrender themselves to it!) Paradox. Anyway.

Darley is in fine voice this eve, and I listen to him with grudging pleasure. He really *is* a good chap, and a sensitive one. But it is with relief that I hear Pombal is due to appear shortly after a visit to the cinema with a young woman he is besieging. I am hoping he will offer to put me up as hotels are expensive and I can then spend my travel allowance on drink. Well, at last old P. turns up, having had his face smacked by the girl's mother who caught them in the foyer. We have a splendid evening and I stay *chez* him as I had hoped.

The next morning I was up betimes though I had decided on nothing, was still bedevilled in mind about the whole issue. However, I thought I could at least visit Nessim in his office as I had so often done, to pass the time of day and cadge a coffee. Whispering up in the huge glass lift, so like a Byzantine sarcophagus, I felt confused. I had prepared no conversation for the event. The clerks and typists were all delighted and showed me straight through into the great domed room where he sat. . . . Now here is the curious thing. He not only seemed to be expecting me, but to have divined my reasons for calling! He seemed delighted, relieved and full of an impish sort of serenity. "I've been waiting months," he said with dancing eyes, "wondering when you were finally going to come and beard me, to ask me questions. At last! What a relief!" Everything melted between us after this and I felt I could take him on open sights. Nothing could exceed the warmth and candour of his answers. They carried immediate conviction with me.

The so-called secret society, he told me, was a student lodge of the Cabala devoted to the customary mumbo-jumbo of parlour mysticism. God knows, this is the capital of superstition. Even Clea has her horoscope cast afresh every morning. Sects abound. Was there anything odd in Balthazar running such a small band of would-be hermetics—a study group? As for the cryptogram it was a sort of mystical calculus—the old *boustro-phedon* no less—with the help of which the lodge-masters all over the Middle East could keep in touch. Surely no more mysterious than a stock-report or a polite exchange between mathematicians working on the same problem? Nessim drew one for me and explained roughly how it was used. He added that all this could be effectively checked by consulting Darley who had taken to visiting these meetings with Justine to suck up hermetical lore. *He* would be able to say just how subversive they were! So far so good. "But I can't disguise from you," he went on, "the existence of another movement, purely political, with which I am directly concerned. This is purely Coptic and is designed simply to rally the Copts—not to revolt against anyone (how could we?) but simply to band themselves together; to strengthen religious and political ties in order that the community can find its way back to a place in the sun. Now that Egypt is free from the Copt-hating British, we feel freer to seek high offices for our people, to get some Members of Parliament elected and so on. There is nothing in all this which should make an intelligent Moslem tremble. We seek nothing illegitimate or harmful; simply our rightful place in our own land as the most intelligent and able community in Egypt."

There was a good deal more about the back history of the Coptic community and its grievances—I won't bore you with it as you probably know it all. But he spoke it all with a tender shy fury which interested me as being so out of keeping with the placid Nessim we both knew. Later, when I met the mother, I understood; she is the driving force behind this particular minority-dream, or so I believe. Nessim went on: "Nor need France and Britain fear anything from us. We love them both. Such modern culture as we have is modelled on both. We ask for no aid, no money. We think of ourselves as Egyptian patriots, but knowing how stupid and backward the Arab National element is, and how fanatical, we do not think it can be long before there are violent differences between the Egyptians and yourselves. They are already flirting with Hitler. In the case of a war . . . who can tell? The Middle East is slipping out of the grasp of England and France day by day. We minorities see ourselves in peril as the process goes on. Our only hope is that there is some respite, like a war, which will enable you to come back and retake the lost ground. Otherwise, we will be expropriated, enslaved. But we still place our faith in you both. Now, from this point of view, a compact and extremely rich little group of Coptic bankers and businessmen could exercise an influence out of all proportion to its numbers. *We are your fifth column in Egypt, fellow Christians.* In another year or two, when the movement is perfected, we could bring immediate pressure to bear on the economic and industrial life of the country—if it served to push through a policy which you felt to be necessary. That is why I have been dying to tell you about us, for England should see in us a bridgehead to the East, a friendly enclave in an area which daily becomes more hostile, to you." He lay back, quite exhausted, but smiling.

"But of course I realize", he said, "that this concerns you as an official. Please treat the matter as a secret, for friendship's sake. The Egyptians would welcome any chance to expropriate us Copts—confiscate the millions which we control: perhaps even kill some of us. They must not know about us. That is why we meet secretly, have been building up the movement so slowly, with such circumspection. There must be no slips, you see. Now my dear Pursewarden, I fully realize that you cannot be expected to take all I tell you on trust, without proof. So I am going to take a rather unusual step. Day after to-morrow is Sitna Damiana and we are having a meeting in the desert. I would like you to come with me so that you can see everything, hear the proceedings and have your mind quite clear about our composition and our intentions. Later we may be of the greatest service to Britain here; I want to drive the fact home. Will you come?"

Would I come!

I went. It was really a great experience which made me realize that I had hardly seen Egypt—the true Egypt underlying the fly-tormented airless towns, the drawing-rooms of commerce, the bankers' sea-splashed villas, the Bourse, the Yacht Club, the Mosque. . . . But wait.

We set off in a cold mauve dawn and drove a little way down the Aboukir road before turning inland; thence across dust roads and deserted causeways, along canals and abandoned trails which the pashas of old had constructed to reach their hunting-boxes on the lake. At last we had to abandon the car, and here the other brother was waiting with horses—the troglodyte with the *gueule cassée*, Narouz of the broken face. What a contrast, this black peasant, compared to Nessim! And what power! I was much taken by him. He was caressing a swashing great hippo's backbone made into a whip—the classical *kurbash*. Saw him pick dragon-flies off the flowers at fifteen paces with it; later in the desert he ran down a wild dog and cut it up with a couple of strokes. The poor creature was virtually dismembered in a couple of blows, by this toy! Well, we rode sombrely along to the house. You went there ages ago, didn't you? I had a long session with the mother, an odd imperious bundle of a woman in black, heavily veiled, who spoke arresting English in a parched voice which had the edge of hysteria in it. Nice, somehow, but queer and somewhat on edge—voice of a desert father or desert sister? I don't know. Apparently the two sons were to take me across to the monastery in the desert. Apparently Narouz was due to speak. It was his maiden over—his first try at it. I must say, I couldn't see this hirsute savage being able to. Jaws working all the time pressing the muscles around his temples! He must, I reflected, grind his teeth in sleep. But somehow also the shy blue eyes of a girl. Nessim was devoted to him. And God what a rider!

Next morning we set off with a bundle of Arab horses which they rode sweetly and a train of shuffle-footed camels which were a present for the populace from Narouz—they were to be cut up and devoured. It was a long exhausting trek with the heat mirages playing havoc with concentration and eyesight and the water tepid and horrible in the skins, and yours truly feeling baleful and fatigued. The sun upon one's brainpan! My brains were sizzling in my skull by the time we came upon the first outcrop of palms—the jumping and buzzing image of the desert monastery where poor Damiana had her Diocletian head struck from her shoulders for the glory of our Lord.

By the time we reached it dusk had fallen, and here one entered a brilliantly-coloured engraving which could have illustrated . . . what? *Vathek!* A huge encampment of booths and houses had grown up for the festival. There must have been six thousand pilgrims camped around in houses of wattle and paper, of cloth and carpet. A whole township had grown up with its own lighting and primitive drainage—but a complete town, comprising even a small but choice brothel quarter. Camels pounded everywhere in the dusk, lanterns and cressets flapped and smoked. Our people pitched us a tent under a ruined arch where two grave bearded dervishes talked, under gonfalons folded like the brilliant wings of birds, and by the light of a great paper lantern covered in inscriptions. Dense darkness now, but brilliantly lit sideshows with all the fun of the fair. I was itching to have a look round and this suited them very well as they had things to arrange within the church, so Nessim gave me a rendezvous at the home tent in an hour and a half. He nearly lost me altogether, I was so enraptured by this freak town with its mud streets, and long avenues of sparkling stalls—food of every sort, melons, eggs, bananas, sweets, all displayed in that unearthly light. Every itinerant pedlar from Alexandria must have trekked out across the sand to sell to the pilgrims. In the dark corners were the children playing and squeaking like mice, while their elders cooked food in huts and tents, lit by tiny puffing candles. The sideshows were going full blast with their games of chance. In one booth a lovely prostitute sang heart-breakingly, chipped quartertones and plangent head-notes as she turned in her sheath of spiral sequins. She had her price on the door. It was not excessive, I thought, being a feeble-minded man, and I rather began to curse my social obligations. In another corner a story-teller was moaning out the sing-song romance of El Zahur. Drinkers of sherbet, of cinnamon, were spread at ease on the seats of makeshift cafés in these beflagged and lighted thoroughfares. From within the walls of the monastery came the sound of priests chanting. From without the unmistakable clatter of men playing at single-stick with the roar of the crowd acclaiming every stylish manœuvre. Tombs full of *flowers*, water-melons shedding a buttery light, trays of meat perfuming the air—sausages and cutlets and entrails buzzing on spits. The whole thing welded into one sharply fused picture of light and sound in my brain. The moon was coming up hand over fist.

In the Ringa-booths there were groups of glistening mauve abstracted Sudanese dancing to the odd music of the wobbling little harmonium with vertical keys and painted gourds for pipes; but they took their step from a black buck who banged it out with a steel rod upon a section of railway line hanging from the tent-pole. Here I ran into one of Cervoni's servants who was delighted to see me and pressed upon me some of the curious Sudanese beer they call *merissa*. I sat and watched this intent, almost maniacal form of dance—the slow revolutions about a centre and the queer cockroach-crushing steps, plunging the toe down and turning it in the earth. Until I was woken by the ripple of drums and saw a dervish pass holding one of the big camel-drums—a glowing hemisphere of copper. He was black—a Rifiya—and as I had never seen them do their fire-walking, scorpion-eating act, I thought I might follow him and see it to-night. (It was touching to hear Moslems singing religious songs to Damiana, a Christian saint; I heard voices ululating the words *"Ya Sitt Ya Bint El Wali"* over and over again. Isn't that odd? "O Lady, Lady of the Viceroy".) Across the darkness I tracked down a group of dervishes in a lighted corner between two great embrasures. It was the end of a dance and they were turning one of their number into a human chandelier, covered in burning candles, the hot wax dripping all over him. His eyes were vague and tranced. Last of all comes an old boy and drives a huge dagger through both cheeks. On each end of the dagger he hoists a candlestick with a branch of lighted candles in each. Transfixed thus the boy rises slowly to his toes and revolves in a dance—like a tree on fire. After the dance, they simply whipped the sword out of his jaw and the old man touched his wounds with a finger moistened with spittle. Within a second there was the boy standing there smiling again with nothing to show for his pains. But he looked awake now.

Outside all this—the white desert was turning under the moon to a great field of skulls and mill-stones. Trumpets and drums sounded and there came a rush of horsemen in conical hats waving wooden swords and shrieking in high voices, like women. The camel-and-horse races were due to start. Good, thought I, I shall have a look at that; but treading unwarily I came upon a grotesque scene which I would gladly have avoided if I had been able. The camels of Narouz were being cut up for the feast. Poor things, they knelt there peacefully with their forelegs folded under them like cats while a horde of men attacked them with axes in the moonlight. My blood ran cold, yet I could not tear myself away from this extraordinary spectacle. The animals made no move to avoid the blows, uttered no cries as they were dismembered. The axes bit into them, as if their great bodies were made of cork, sinking deep under every thrust. Whole members were being hacked off as painlessly, it seemed, as when a tree is pruned. The children were dancing about in the moonlight picking up the fragments and running off with them into the lighted town, great gobbets of bloody meat. The camels stared hard at the moon and said nothing. Off came the legs, out came the entrails; lastly the heads would topple under the axe like statuary and lie there in the sand with open eyes. The men doing the axeing were shouting and bantering as they worked. A huge soft carpet of black blood spread into the dunes around the group and the barefoot boys carried the print of it back with them into the township. I felt frightfully ill of a sudden and retired back to the lighted quarter for a drink; and sitting on a bench watched the passing show for a while to recover my nerve. Here at last Nessim found me and together we walked inside the walls, past the grouped cells called "combs". (Did you know that all early religions were built up on a cell pattern, imitating who-knows-what biological law? . . .) So we came at last to the church.

Wonderfully painted sanctuary screen, and ancient candles with waxen beards burning on the gold lectern, the light now soft and confused by incense to the colour of pollen; and the deep voices running like a river over the gravel-bottomed Liturgy of St. Basil. Moving softly from gear to gear, pausing and resuming, starting lower down the scale only to be pressed upwards into the throats and minds of these black shining people. The choir passed across us like swans, breath-catching in their high scarlet helmets and white robes with scarlet cross-bands. The light on their glossy black curls and sweating faces! Enormous frescoed eyes with whites gleaming. It was pre-Christian, this; each of these young men in his scarlet biretta had become Rameses the Second. The great chandeliers twinkled and fumed, puffs of smoky incense rose. Outside you could hear the noises of the camel-racing crew, inside only the grumble of the Word. The long hanging lamps had ostrich-eggs suspended under them. (This has always struck me as being worth investigating.)

I thought that this was our destination but we skirted the crowd and went down some stairs into a crypt. And this was it at last. A series of large beehive rooms, lime-washed white and spotless. In one, by candlelight, a group of about a hundred people sat upon rickety wooden benches waiting for us. Nessim pressed my arm and pushed me to a seat at the very back among a group of elderly men who gave me place. "First I will talk to them," he whispered, "and then Narouz is to speak to them—for the first time." There was no sign of the other brother as yet. The men next to me were wearing robes but some of them had European suits on underneath. Some had their heads wrapped in wimples. To judge by their well-kept hands and nails, none were workmen. They spoke Arabic but in low tones. No smoking.

Now the good Nessim rose and addressed them with the cool efficiency of someone taking a routine board meeting. He spoke quietly and as far as I could gather contented himself with giving them details about recent events, the election of certain people to various committees, the arrangements for trust funds and so on. He might have been addressing shareholders. They listened gravely. A few quiet questions were asked which he answered concisely. Then he said: "But this is not all, these details. You will wish to hear something about our nation and our faith, something that even our priests cannot tell you. My brother Narouz, who is known to you, will speak a little now."

What on earth could the baboon Narouz have to tell them, I wondered? It was most interesting. And now, from the outer darkness of the cell next door came Narouz, dressed in a white robe and looking pale as ashes. His hair had been smeared down on his forehead in an oiled quiff, like a collier on his day off. No, he looked like a terrified curate in a badly-ironed sur-plice; huge hands joined on his chest with the knuckles squeezed white. He took his place at a sort of wooden lectern with a candle burning on it, and stared with obvious wild terror at his audience, squeezing the muscles out all over his arms and shoulders. I thought he was going to fall down. He opened his clenched jaws but nothing came. He appeared to be paralysed.

There came a stir and a whisper, and I saw Nessim looking somewhat anxiously at him, as if he might need help. But Narouz stood stiff as a javelin, staring right through us as if at some terrifying scene taking place behind the white walls at our backs. The suspense was making us all uncomfortable. Then he made a queer motion with his mouth, as if his tongue were swollen, or as if he was surreptitiously swallowing a soft palate, and a hoarse cry escaped him. *"Meded! Meded!"* It was the invocation for divine strength you sometimes hear desert preachers utter before they fall into a trance—the dervishes. His face worked. And then came a change—all of a sudden it was as if an electric current had begun to pour into his body, into his muscles, his loins. He relaxed his grip on himself and slowly, pantingly began to speak, rolling those amazing eyes as if the power of speech itself was half-involuntary and causing him physical pain to support. . . . It was a terrifying perfor-mance, and for a moment or two I could not understand any-thing, he was articulating so badly. Then all of a sudden he broke through the veil and his voice gathered power, vibrating in the candle-light like a musical instrument.

"Our Egypt, our beloved country," drawing out the words like toffee, almost crooning them. It was clear that he had nothing prepared to say—it was not a speech, it was an invoca-tion uttered extempore such as one has sometimes heard—the brilliant spontaneous flights of drunkards, ballad singers, or those professional mourners who follow burial processions with their shrieks of death-divining poetry. The power and the ten-sion flooded out of him into the room; all of us were electrified, even myself whose Arabic was so bad! The tone, the range and the bottled ferocity and tenderness his words conveyed hit us, sent us sprawling, like music. It didn't seem to matter whether we understood them or not. It does not even now. Indeed, it would have been impossible to paraphrase the matter. "The Nile . . . the green river flowing in our hearts hears its children. They will return to her. Descendants of the Pharaohs, children of Ra, offspring of St. Mark. They will find the birthplace of light." And so on. At times the speaker closed his eyes, letting the torrent of words pour on unhindered. Once he set his head back, smiling like a dog, still with eyes closed, until the light shone upon his back teeth. That voice! It went on autonomously, rising to a roar, sinking to a whisper, trembling and crooning and wailing. Suddenly snapping out words like chain-shot, or rolling them softly about like honey. We were absolutely captured— the whole lot of us. But it was something comical to see Nessim's concern and wonder. He had expected nothing like this apparently for he was trembling like a leaf and quite white. Occasionally he was swept away himself by the flood of rhetoric and I saw him dash away a tear from his eye almost impatiently.

It went on like this for about three-quarters of an hour and suddenly, inexplicably, the current was cut off, the speaker was snuffed out. Narouz stood there gasping like a fish before us— as if thrown up by the tides of inner music onto a foreign shore. It was as abrupt as a metal shutter coming down—a silence impossible to repair again. His hands knotted again. He gave a startled groan and rushed out of the place with his funny scrambling motion. A tremendous silence fell—the silence which follows some great performance by an actor or orchestra —the germinal silence in which you can hear the very seeds in the human psyche stirring, trying to move towards the light of self-recognition. I was deeply moved and utterly exhausted. Fecundated!

At last Nessim rose and made an indefinite gesture. He too

125

was exhausted and walked like an old man; took my hand and led me up into the church again, where a wild hullabaloo of cymbals and bells had broken out. We walked through the great puffs of incense which now seemed to blow up at us from the centre of the earth—the angel and demon-haunted spaces below the world of men. In the moonlight he kept repeating: "I never knew, I never guessed this of Narouz. He is a *preacher*. I asked him only to talk of our history—but he made it . . ." He was at a loss for words. Nobody had apparently suspected the existence of this spell-binder in their midst—the man with the whip! "He could lead a great religious movement," I thought to myself. Nessim walked wearily and thoughtfully by my side among the palms. "He is a *preacher*, really" he said with amazement. "That is *why* he goes to see Taor." He explained that Narouz often rode into the desert to visit a famous woman saint (alleged by the way to have three breasts) who lives in a tiny cave near Wadi Natrun; she is famous for her wonder-working cures, but won't emerge from obscurity. "When he is away," said Nessim, "he has either gone to the island to fish with his new gun or to see Taor. Always one or the other."

When we got back to the tent the new preacher was lying wrapped in his blanket sobbing in a harsh voice like a wounded she-camel. He stopped when we entered, though he went on shaking for a while. Embarrassed, we said nothing and turned in that night in a heavy silence. A momentous experience indeed!

I couldn't sleep for quite a while, going over it all in my mind. The next morning we were up at dawn (bloody cold for May—the tent stiff with frost) and in the saddle by the earliest light. Narouz had completely come to himself. He twirled his whip and played tricks on the factors in a high good humour. Nessim was rather thoughtful and withdrawn, I thought. The long ride galled our minds and it was a relief to see the crested palms grow up again. We rested and spent the night again at Karm Abu Girg. The mother was not available at first and we were told to see her in the evening. Here an odd scene took place for which Nessim appeared as little prepared as I. As the three of us advanced through the rose-garden towards her little summerhouse, she came to the door with a lantern in her hand and said: "Well, my sons, how did it go?" At this Narouz fell upon his knees, reached out his arms to her. Nessim and I were covered with confusion. She came forward and put her arms round this snorting and sobbing peasant, at the same time motioning us to leave. I must say I was relieved when Nessim sneaked off into the rose-garden and was glad to follow him. "This is a new Narouz," he kept repeating softly, with genuine mystification. "I did not know of these powers."

Later Narouz came back to the house in the highest of spirits and we all played cards and drank *arak*. He showed me, with immense pride, a gun he had had made for him in Munich. It fires a heavy javelin under water and is worked by compressed air. He told me a good deal of this new method of fishing under water. It sounded a thrilling game and I was invited to visit his fishing island with him one week-end to have a pot. The preacher had vanished altogether by now; the simple-minded second son had returned.

Ouf! I am trying to get all the salient detail down as it may be of use to you later when I am gone. Sorry if it is a bore. On the way back to the town I talked at length to Nessim and got all the facts clear in my head. It did seem to me that from the policy point of view the Coptic group might be of the greatest use to us; and I was certain that this interpretation of things would be swallowed if properly explained to Maskelyne. High hopes!

So I rode back happily to Cairo to rearrange the chess-board accordingly. I went to see Maskelyne and tell him the good news. To my surprise he turned absolutely white with rage, the corners of his nose pinched in, his ears moving back about an inch like a greyhound. His voice and eyes remained the same. "Do you mean to tell me that you have tried to supplement a secret intelligence paper by consulting the subject of it? It goes against every elementary rule of intelligence. And how can you believe a word of so obvious a cover story? I have never heard of such a thing. You deliberately suspend a War Office paper, throw my fact-finding organization into disrepute, pretend we don't know our jobs, etc. . . ." You can gather the rest of the tirade. I began to get angry. He repeated dryly: "I have been doing this for fifteen years. I tell you it smells of arms, of subversion. You won't believe my I.A. and I think yours is ridiculous. Why not pass the paper to the *Egyptians* and let them find out for themselves?" Of course I could not afford to do this, and he knew it. He next said that he had asked the War Office to protest in London and was writing to Errol to ask for "redress". All this, of course, was to be expected. But then I tackled him upon another vector. "Look here," I said. "I have seen all your sources. They are all Arabs and as such unworthy of confidence. How about a gentlemen's agreement? There is no hurry—we can investigate the Hosnanis at leisure—but how about choosing a new set of sources—English sources? If the interpretations still match, I promise you I'll resign and make a full recantation. Otherwise I shall fight this thing right through."

"What sort of sources do you have in mind?"

"Well, there are a number of Englishmen in the Egyptian Police who speak Arabic and who know the people concerned. Why not use some of them?"

He looked at me for a long time. "But they are as corrupt as the Arabs. Nimrod *sells* his information to the press. The Globe pay him a retainer of twenty pounds a month for confidential information."

"There must be others."

"By God there are. You should see them!"

"And then there's Darley who apparently goes to these meetings which worry you so much. Why not ask him to help?"

"I won't compromise my net by introducing characters like that. It is not worth it. It is not secure."

"Then why not make a separate net—let Telford build it up. Specially for this group, for no other. And having no access to your main organization. Surely you could do that?"

He stared at me slowly, drop by drop. "I could if I chose to," he admitted. "And if I thought it would get us anywhere. But it won't."

"At any rate, why not try? Your own position here is rather equivocal until an Ambassador comes to define it and arbitrate between us. Suppose I do pass this paper out and this whole group gets swept up?"

"Well, what?"

"Supposing it is, as I believe it to be, something which could help British policy in this area, you'll get no thanks for having allowed the Egyptians to nip it in the bud. And indeed, if that did prove to be the case, you would find. . . ."

"I'll think about it." He had no intention of doing so, I could see, but he must have. He changed his mind; next day he rang up and said he was doing as I suggested, though "without prejudice"; the war was still on between us. Perhaps he had heard of your appointment and knew we were friends. I don't know.

Ouf! that is about as much as I can tell you; for the rest, the country is still here—everything that is heteroclyte, devious, polymorph, anfractuous, equivocal, opaque, ambiguous, many-branched, or just plain dotty. I wish you joy of it when I am far away! I know you will make your first mission a resounding success. Perhaps you won't regret these tags of information from

Yours sincerely,

Earwig van Beetfield.

o   o   o   o   o

Mountolive studied this document with great care. He found the tone annoying and the information mildly disturbing. But then, every mission was riven with faction; personal annoyances, divergent opinions, they were always coming to the fore. For a moment he wondered whether it would not be wiser to allow Pursewarden the transfer he desired; but he restrained the thought by allowing another to overlap it. If he was to act, he should not at this stage show irresolution—even with Kenilworth. He walked about in that wintry landscape waiting for events to take definite shape around his future. Finally, he composed a tardy note to Pursewarden, the fruit of much rewriting and thought, which he despatched through the bag room.

My dear P.,

I must thank you for your letter with the interesting data. I feel I cannot make any decisions before my own arrival. I don't wish to prejudge issues. I have however decided to keep you attached to the Mission for another year. I shall ask for a greater attention to discipline than your Chancery appears to do; and I know you won't fail me however disagreeable the prospect of staying seems to you. There is much to do this end, and much to decide before I leave.

Yours sincerely,

David Mountolive.

It conveyed, he hoped, the right mixture of encouragement and censure. But of course, Pursewarden would not have written flippantly had he visualized serving under him. Nevertheless, if his career was to take the right shape he must start at the beginning?

But in his own mind he had already planned upon getting Maskelyne transferred and Pursewarden elevated in rank as his chief political adviser. Nevertheless a hint of uneasiness remained. But he could not help smiling when he received a postcard from the incorrigible. "My dear Ambassador," it read. "Your news has worried me. You have so many great big bushy Etonians to choose from. . . . Nevertheless. At your service."

o   o   o   o   o

VI

The airplane stooped and began to slant slowly downwards, earthwards into the violet evening. The brown desert with its monotony of wind-carved dunes had given place now to a remembered relief-map of the delta. The slow loops and tangents of the brown river lay directly below, with small craft drifting about upon it like seeds. Deserted estuaries and sand-bars—the empty unpopulated areas of the hinterland where the fish and birds congregated in secret. Here and there the river split like a bamboo, to bend and coil round an island with fig-trees, a minaret, some dying palms—the feather-softness of the palms furrowing the flat exhausted landscape with its hot airs and mirages and humid silences. Squares of cultivation laboriously darned it here and there like a worn tweed plaid; between segments of bituminous swamp embraced by slow contours of the brown water. Here and there too rose knuckles of rosy limestone.

It was frightfully hot in the little cabin of the airplane. Mountolive wrestled in a desultory tormented fashion with his uniform. Skinners had done wonders with it—it fitted like a glove; but the *weight* of it. It was like being dressed in a boxing-glove. He would be parboiled. He felt the sweat pouring down his chest, tickling him. His mixed elation and alarm translated itself into queasiness. Was he going to be air-sick—and for the first time in his life? He hoped not. It would be awful to be sick into this impressive refurbished hat. "Five minutes to touchdown"; words scribbled on a page torn from an operations pad. Good. Good. He nodded mechanically and found himself fanning his face with this musical-comedy object. At any rate, it became him. He was quite surprised to see how handsome he looked in a mirror.

They circled softly down and the mauve dusk rose to meet them. It was as if the whole of Egypt were settling softly into an inkwell. Then flowering out of the golden whirls sent up by stray dust-devils he glimpsed the nippled minarets and towers of the famous tombs; the Moquattam hills were pink and nacreous as a finger-nail.

On the airfield were grouped the dignitaries who had been detailed to receive him officially. They were flanked by the members of his own staff with their wives—all wearing garden-party hats and gloves as if they were in the paddock at Longchamps. Everyone was nevertheless perspiring freely, indeed in streams. Mountolive felt *terra firma* under his polished dress shoes and drew a sigh of relief. The ground was almost hotter than the plane; but his nausea had vanished. He stepped forward tentatively to shake hands and realized that with the donning of his uniform everything had changed. A sudden loneliness smote him—for he realized that now, as an Ambassador, he must forever renounce the friendship of ordinary human beings in exchange for their *deference*. His uniform encased him like a suit of chain-armour. It shut him off from the ordinary world of human exchanges. "God!" he thought, "I shall be forever soliciting a normal human reaction from people who are bound to defer to my *rank!* I shall become like that dreadful parson in Sussex who always feebly swears in order to prove that he is really quite an ordinary human being despite the dog-collar!"

But the momentary spasm of loneliness passed in the joys of a new self-possession. There was nothing to do now but to exploit his charm to the full; to be handsome, to be capable, surely one had the right to enjoy the consciousness of these things without self-reproach? He proved himself upon the outer circle of Egyptian officials whom he greeted in excellent Arabic. Smiles broke out everywhere, at once merging into a confluence of self-congratulatory looks. He knew also how to present himself in half-profile to the sudden stare of flashbulbs as he made his first speech—a tissue of heart-warming platitudes pronounced with charming diffidence in Arabic which won murmurs of delight and excitement from the raffish circle of journalists.

A band suddenly struck up raggedly, playing woefully out of key; and under the plaintive iterations of a European melody played somehow in quartertones he recognized his own National Anthem. It was startling, and he had difficulty in not smiling. The police mission had been diligently training the Egyptian force in the uses of the slide-trombone. But the whole performance had a desultory and impromptu air, as if some rare form of ancient music (Palestrina?) were being interpreted on a set of fire-irons. He stood stiffly to attention. An aged Bimbashi with a glass eye stood before the band, also at attention—albeit rather shakily. Then it was over. "I'm sorry about the band" said Nimrod Pasha under his breath. "You see, sir, it was a scratch team. Most of the musicians are ill." Mountolive nodded gravely, sympathetically, and addressed himself to the next task. He walked with profuse keenness up and down a guard of honour to inspect their bearing; the men smelt strongly of sesame oil and sweat and one or two smiled affably. This was delightful. He restrained the impulse to grin back. Then, turning, he completed his devoirs to the Protocol section, warm and smelly too in its brilliant red flower-pot hats. Here the smiles rolled about, scattered all over the place like slices of unripe water-melon. An Ambassador who spoke Arabic! He put on the air of smiling diffidence which he knew best charmed. He had learned this. His crooked smile was appealing—even his own staff was visibly much taken with him, he noted with pride; but particularly the wives. They relaxed and turned their faces towards him like flower-traps. He had a few words for each of the secretaries.

Then at last the great car bore him smoothly away to the Residence on the banks of the Nile. Errol came with him to show him around and make the necessary introductions to the house-staff. The size and elegance of the building were exciting, and also rather intimidating. To have all these rooms at one's disposal was enough to deter any bachelor. "Still, for entertaining," he said almost sorrowfully, "I suppose they are necessary." But the place echoed around him as he walked about the magnificent ball-room, across the conservatories, the terraces, peering out on the grassy lawns which went right down to the bank of the cocoa-coloured Nile water. Outside, goose-necked sprinklers whirled and hissed night and day, keeping the coarse emerald grass fresh with moisture. He heard their sighing as he undressed and had a cold shower in the beautiful bathroom with its vitreous glass baubles; Errol was soon dismissed with an invitation to return after dinner and discuss plans and projects. "I'm tired," said Mountolive truthfully, "I want to have a quiet dinner alone. This heat—I should remember it; but I'd forgotten."

The Nile was rising, filling the air with the dank summer moisture of its yearly inundations, climbing the stone wall at the bottom of the Embassy garden inch by slimy inch. He lay on his bed for half an hour and listened to the cars drawing up at the Chancery entrance and the sound of voices and footsteps in the hall. His staff were busily autographing the handsome red visitors' book, bound in expensive morocco. Only Pursewarden had not put in an appearance. He was presumably still in hiding? Mountolive planned to give him a shaking-up at the first opportunity; he could not now afford absurdities which might put him in a difficult position with the rest of the staff. He hoped that his friend would not force him to become authoritative and unpleasant—he shrank from the thought. Nevertheless . . .

After a rest he dined alone on a corner of the long terrace, dressed only in trousers and a shirt, his feet clad in sandals. Then he shed the latter and walked barefoot across the floodlit lawns down to the river, feeling the brilliant grass spiky under his bare feet. But it was of a coarse, African variety and its roots were dusty, even under the sprays, as if it were suffering from dandruff. There were three peacocks wandering in the shadows with their brilliant Argus-eyed tails. The black soft sky was powdered with stars. Well, he had arrived—in every sense of the word. He remembered a phrase from one of Purse-warden's books: "The writer, most solitary of animals. . . ." The glass of whisky in his hand was icy-cold. He lay down in that airless darkness on the grass and gazed straight upwards into the sky, hardly thinking any more, but letting the drowsi-ness gradually creep up over him, inch by inch, like the rising tide of the river-waters at the garden's end. Why should he feel a sadness at the heart of things when he was so confident of powers, so full of resolution? He did not know.

Errol duly returned after a hastily eaten dinner and was charmed to find his chief spread out like a starfish on the elegant lawn, almost asleep. These informalities were excellent signs. "Ring for drink" said Mountolive benevolently, "and come and sit out here: it is more or less cool. There's a breath of wind off the river." Errol obeyed and came to seat himself diffidently on the grass. They talked about the general design of things. "I know", said Mountolive, "that the whole staff is trembling with anticipation about the summer move to Alex-andria. I used to when I was a junior in the Commission. Well, we'll move out of this swelter just as soon as I've presented my credentials. The King will be in Divan three days hence? Yes, I gathered from Abdel Latif at the airport. Good. Then to-morrow I want to bid all Chancery secretaries and wives to tea; and in the evening the junior staff for a coc'-tail. Everything else can wait until you fix the special train and load up the despatch boxes. How about Alexandria?"

Errol smiled mistily. "It is all in order, sir. There has been the usual scramble with incoming missions; but the Egyptians have been very good. Protocol has found an excellent residence with a good summer Chancery and other offices we could use. Everything is splendid. You'll only need a couple of Chancery staff apart from the house; I've fixed a duty roster so that we all get a chance to spend three weeks up there in rotation. The house staff can go ahead. You'll be doing some entertaining I expect. The Court will leave in about another fortnight. No problems."

No problems! It was a cheering phrase. Mountolive sighed and fell silent. On the darkness across the expanse of river-water, a faint noise broke out, as with a patter like a swarm of bees; laughter and singing mingled with the harsh thrilling rattle of the sistrum. "I had forgotten," he said with a pang. "The tears of Isis! It is the Night of the Drop, isn't it?" Errol nodded wisely. "Yes, sir." The river would be alive with slender feluccas with their lovely shapes, loud with guitars and voices. Isis-Diana would be bright in the heavens, but here the floodlit lawns created a cone of white light which dimmed the night-sky outside it. He gazed vaguely round, searching for the constellations. "Then that is all" he said, and Errol stood up. He cleared his throat and said: "Pursewarden didn't appear because he had 'flu." Mountolive thought this kind of loyalty a good sign. "No" he said smiling, "I know he is giving you trouble. I'm going to see he stops it." Errol looked at him with delighted surprise. "Thank you, sir." Mountolive walked him slowly to the house. "I also want to dine Maskelyne. To-morrow night, if convenient."

Errol nodded slowly. "He was at the airport, sir." "I didn't notice. Please get my secretary to make out a card for to-morrow night. But ring him first and tell him if it is incon-venient to let me know. For eight-fifteen, black tie."

"I will, sir."

"I want particularly to talk to him as we are taking up some new dispositions and I want his co-operation. He is a brilliant officer, I have been told."

Errol looked doubtful. "He has had some rather fierce ex-changes with Pursewarden. Indeed, this last week he has more or less besieged the Embassy. He is clever, but . . . somewhat hard-headed?" Errol was tentative, appeared unwilling to go too far. "Well," said Mountolive, "let me talk to him and see for myself. I think the new arrangement will suit everyone, even Master Pursewarden."

They said good-night.

The next day was full of familiar routines for Mountolive, but conducted, so to speak, from a new angle—the unfamiliar angle of a position which brought people immediately to their feet. It was exciting and also disturbing; even up to the rank of councillor he had managed to have a comfortably-based relationship with the junior staff at every level. Even the hulking Marines who staffed the section of Chancery Guards were friendly and equable towards him in the happiest of colloquial manners. Now they shrank into postures of reserve, almost of self-defence. These were the bitter fruits of power, he reflected, accepting his new role with resignation.

However, the opening moves were smoothly played; and even his staff party of the evening went off so well that people seemed reluctant to leave. He was late in changing for his dinner-party and Maskelyne had already been shown into the anodyne drawing-room when he finally appeared, bathed and changed. "Ah, Mountolive!" said the soldier, standing up and extending his hand with a dry expressionless calm. "I have been waiting for your arrival with some anxiety." Mountolive felt a sudden sting of pique after all the deference shown to him during the day to be left thus untitled by this personage. ("Heavens," he thought, "am I really a provincial at heart?")

"My dear Brigadier," his opening remarks carried a small but perceptible coolness as a result. Perhaps the soldier simply wished to make it clear that he was a War Office body, and not a Foreign Office one? It was a clumsy way to do it. Nevertheless, and somewhat to his own annoyance, Mountolive felt himself rather drawn to this lean and solitary-looking figure with its tired eyes and lustreless voice. His ugliness had a certain determined elegance. His ancient dinner-clothes were not very carefully pressed and brushed, but the quality of the material and cut were both excellent. Maskelyne sipped his drink slowly and calmly, lowering his greyhound's muzzle towards his glass circumspectly. He scrutinized Mountolive with the utmost coolness. They exchanged the formal politeness of host and guest for a while, and somewhat to his own annoyance, Mountolive found himself liking him despite the dry precarious manner. He suddenly seemed to see in him one who, like himself, had hesitated to ascribe any particular meaning to life.

The presence of servants excluded any but the most general exchanges during the dinner they shared, seated out upon the lawn, and Maskelyne seemed content to bide his time. Only once the name of Pursewarden came up and he said with his offhand air: "Yes. I hardly know him, of course, except officially. The odd thing is that his father—surely the name is too uncommon for me to be wrong?—his father was in my company during the first world war. He picked up an M.C. Indeed, I actually composed the citation which put him up for it: and of course, I had the disagreeable next-of-kin jobs. The son must have been a mere child then, I suppose. Of course, I may be wrong—not that it matters."

Mountolive was intrigued. "As a matter of fact," he said, "I think you *are* right—he mentioned something of the kind to me once. Have you ever talked to him about it?"

"Good Heavens, no! Why should I?" Maskelyne seemed very faintly shocked. "The son isn't really . . . my kind of person" he said quietly but without animus, simply as a statement of fact. "He . . . I . . . well, I read a book of his once." He stopped abruptly as if everything had been said; as if the subject had been disposed of for all time.

"He must have been a brave man" said Mountolive after an interval.

"Yes—or perhaps not" said his guest slowly, thoughtfully. He paused. "One wonders. He wasn't a real soldier. One saw it quite often at the front. Sometimes acts of gallantry come as much out of cowardice as bravery—that is the queer thing. His act, particularly, I mean, was really an unsoldierly one. Oddly enough."

"But——" protested Mountolive.

"Let me make myself clear. There is a difference between a necessary act of bravery and an unnecessary one. If he had remembered his training as a soldier, he would not have done what he did. It may sound like a quibble. He lost his head, quite literally, and acted without thinking. I admire him enormously as a man, but not as a soldier. Our life is a good deal more exacting—it is a science, you know, or should be."

He spoke thoughtfully in his dry, clearly enunciated way. It was clear that the topic was one which he had often debated in his own mind.

"I wonder," said Mountolive.

"I may be wrong," admitted the soldier.

The soft-footed servants had withdrawn at last, leaving them to their wine and cigars, and Maskelyne felt free to touch upon the real subject of his visit. "I expect you've studied all the differences which have arisen between ourselves and your political branch. They have been extremely sharp; and we are all waiting for you to resolve them."

Mountolive nodded. "They have all been resolved as far as I am concerned" he said with the faintest tinge of annoyance (he disliked being hurried). "I had a conference with your General on Tuesday and set out a new grouping which I am sure will please you. You will get a confirming signal this week ordering you to transfer your show to Jerusalem, which is to become the senior post and headquarters. This will obviate questions of rank and precedence; you can leave a staging post here under Telford, who is a civilian, but it will of course be a junior post. For convenience it can work to us and liaise with our Service Departments."

A silence fell. Maskelyne studied the ash of his cigar while the faintest trace of a smile hovered at the edges of his mouth.

"So Pursewarden wins," he said quietly. "Well, well!"

Mountolive was both surprised and insulted by his smile, though in truth it seemed entirely without malice.

"Pursewarden", he said quietly, "has been reprimanded for suppressing a War Office paper; on the other hand, I happen to know the subject of the paper rather well and I agree that you should supplement it more fully before asking us to take action."

"We are trying, as a matter of fact; Telford is putting down a grid about this Hosnani man—but some of the candidates put forward by Pursewarden seem to be rather . . . well, prejudicial, to put it mildly. However, Telford is trying to humour him by engaging them. But . . . well, there's one who sells information to the Press, and one who is at present consoling the Hosnani lady. Then there's another, Scobie, who spends his time dressed as a woman walking about the harbour at Alexandria—it would be a charity to suppose him in quest of police information. Altogether, I shall be quite glad to confide the net to Telford and tackle something a bit more serious. What people!"

"As I don't know the circumstances yet" said Mountolive quietly, "I can't comment. But I shall look into it."

"I'll give you an example" said Maskelyne, "of their general efficiency. Last week Telford detailed this policeman called Scobie to do a routine job. When the Syrians want to be clever, they don't use a diplomatic courier; they confide their pouch to a lady, the vice-consul's niece, who takes it down to Cairo by train. We wanted to see the contents of one particular pouch—details of arms shipments, we thought. Gave Scobie some doped chocolates—with the doped one clearly marked. His job was to send the lady to sleep for a couple of hours and walk off with her pouch. Do you know what happened? He was found doped in the train when it got to Cairo and couldn't be wakened for nearly twenty-four hours. We had to put him into the American hospital. Apparently as he sat down in the lady's compartment, the train gave a sudden jolt and all the chocolates turned over in their wrappers. The one we had so carefully marked was now upside down; he could not remember which it was. In his panic, he ate it himself. Now I ask you. . . ." Maskelyne's humourless eye flashed as he retailed this story. "Such people are not to be trusted," he added, acidly.

"I promise you I'll investigate the suitability of anyone proposed by Pursewarden; I also promise that if you mark papers to me there will be no hitch, and no repetition of this unauthorized behaviour."

"Thank you." He seemed genuinely grateful as he rose to take his leave. He waved away the beflagged duty car at the front door, muttering something about "an evening constitutional", and walked off down the drive, putting on a light overcoat to hide his dinner-jacket. Mountolive stood at the front door and watched his tall, lean figure moving in and out of the yellow pools of lamplight, absurdly elongated by distance. He sighed with relief and weariness. It had been a heavy day. "So much for Maskelyne."

He returned to the deserted lawns to have one last drink in the silence before he retired to bed. Altogether, the work completed that day had not been unsatisfactory. He had disposed of a dozen disagreeable duties of which telling Maskelyne about his future had been perhaps the hardest. Now he could relax.

Yet before climbing the staircase, he walked about for a while in the silent house, going from room to room, thinking; hugging the knowledge of his accession to power with all the secret pride of a woman who has discovered that she is pregnant.

o   o   o   o   o

141

VII

Once his official duties in the capital had been performed to his private satisfaction, Mountolive felt free to anticipate the Court by transferring his headquarters to the second capital, Alexandria. So far everything had gone quite smoothly. The King himself had praised his fluency in Arabic, and he had won the unusual distinction of press popularity by his judicious public use of the language. From every newspaper these days pictures of himself stared out, always with that crooked, diffident smile. Sorting out the little mound of press cuttings he found himself wondering: "My God, am I slowly becoming irresistible to myself?" They were excellent pictures; he was undeniably handsome with his greying temples and crisply cut features. "But the mere habit of culture is not enough to defend one from one's own charm. I shall be buried alive among these soft, easy aridities of a social practice which I do not even enjoy." He thought with his chin upon his wrist: "Why does not Leila write? Perhaps when I am in Alexandria next week I shall have word?" But he could at least leave Cairo with a good following wind. The other foreign missions were mad with envy at his success!

The move itself was completed with exemplary despatch by the diligent Errol and the Residence staff. He himself could afford to saunter down late when the special train had been loaded with all the diplomatic impedimenta which would enable them to make a show of working while they were away . . . suitcases and crates and scarlet despatch-boxes with their gold monograms. Cairo had by this time become unbearably hot. Yet their hearts were light as the train rasped out across the desert to the coast.

It was the best time of the year to remove, for the ugly spring khamseens were over and the town had put on its summer wear—coloured awnings along the Grande Corniche, and the ranks of coloured island craft which lay in shelves below the black turrets of the battleships and framed the blue Yacht Club harbour, atwinkle with sails. The season of summer parties had also begun and Nessim was able to give his long-promised reception for his returning friend. It was a barbaric spread and all Alexandria turned out to do Mountolive honour, for all the world as if he were a prodigal son returning, though in fact he knew few people apart from Nessim and his family. But he was glad to renew his acquaintance with Balthazar and Amaril, the two doctors who were always together, always chaffing each other; and with Clea whom he had once met in Europe. The sunlight, fading over the evening sea, blazed in upon the great brass-framed windows, turning them to molten diamonds before it melted and softened once more into the aquamarine twilight of Egypt. The curtains were drawn and now a hundred candles' breathing shone softly upon the white napery of the long tables, winking among the slender stems of the glasses. It was the season of ease, for the balls and rides and swimming-parties had started or were about to be planned. The cool sea-winds kept the temperature low, the air was fresh and invigorating.

Mountolive sank back into the accustomed pattern of things with a sense of sureness, almost of beatitude. Nessim had, so to speak, gone back into place like a picture into an alcove built for it, and the companionship of Justine—this dark-browed, queenly beauty at his side—enhanced rather than disturbed his relations with the outer world. Mountolive liked her, liked to feel her dark appraising eyes upon him lit with a sort of compassionate curiosity mixed with admiration. They made a splendid couple, he thought, with almost a touch of envy: like people trained to work together from childhood, instinctively responding to each other's unspoken needs and desires, moving

143

up unhesitatingly to support one another with their smiles. Though she was handsome and reserved and appeared to speak little, Mountolive thought he detected an endearing candour cropping up the whole time among her sentences—as if from some hidden spring of secret warmth. Was she pleased to find someone who valued her husband as deeply as she herself did? The cool, guileless pressure of her fingers suggested that, as did her thrilling voice when she said "I have known you so long from hearsay as David that it will be hard to call you anything else." As for Nessim, he had lost nothing during the time of separation, had preserved all his graces, adding to them only the weight of a worldly judgement which made him seem strikingly European in such provincial surroundings. His tact, for example, in never mentioning any subject which might have an official bearing to Mountolive was deeply endearing—and this despite the fact that they rode and shot together frequently, swam, sailed and painted. Such information upon political affairs as he had to put forward was always scrupulously re-layed through Pursewarden. He never compromised their friendship by mixing work with pleasure, or forcing Mount-olive to struggle between affection and duty.

Best of all, Pursewarden himself had reacted most favourably to his new position of eminence and was wearing what he called "his new leaf". A couple of brusque minutes in the terrible red ink—the use of which is the prerogative only of Heads of Mission—had quelled him and drawn from him a promise to "turn over a new fig-leaf", which he had dutifully done. His response had indeed been wholehearted and Mount-olive was both grateful and relieved to feel that at last he could rely upon a judgement which was determined not to overrun itself, or allow itself to founder among easy dependences and doubts. What else? Yes, the new Summer Residence was de-lightful and set in a cool garden full of pines above Roushdi. There were two excellent hard courts which rang all day to the pang of racquets. The staff seemed happy with their new head of mission. Only . . . Leila's silence was still an enigma. Then one evening Nessim handed him an envelope on which he recognized her familiar hand. Mountolive put it in his pocket to read when he was alone.

"Your reappearance in Egypt—you perhaps have guessed?—has upset me somehow: upset my apple-cart. I am all over the place and cannot pick up the pieces as yet. It puzzles me, I admit. I have been living with you so long in my imagination—quite *alone* there—that now I must almost reinvent you to bring you back to life. Perhaps I have been traducing you all these years, painting your picture to myself? You may be now simply a figment instead of a flesh and blood dignitary, moving among people and lights and policies. I can't find the courage to compare the truth to reality as yet; I'm scared. Be patient with a silly headstrong woman who never seems to know her own mind. Of course, we should have met long since—but I shrank like a snail. Be patient. Somewhere inside me I must wait for a tide to turn. I was so angry when I heard you were coming that I cried with sheer rage. Or was it panic? I suppose that really I had managed to forget . . . my own face, all these years. Suddenly it came back over me like an Iron Mask. Bah! soon my courage will come back, never fear. Sooner or later we must meet and shock one another. When? I don't know as yet. I don't know."

Disconsolately reading the words as he sat upon the terraces at dusk he thought: "I cannot assemble my feelings coherently enough to respond to her intelligently. What should I say or do? Nothing." But the word had a hollow ring. "Patience," he said softly to himself, turning the word this way and that in his mind, the better to examine it. Later, at the Cervonis' ball among the blue lights and the snapping of paper streamers, it seemed easy once more to be patient. He moved once more in a glad world in which he no longer felt cut off from his fellows—a world full of friends in which he could enjoy the memory of the long rides with Nessim, conversations with Amaril, or the troubling pleasure of dancing with the blonde Clea. Yes, he could be patient here, so close at hand. The time, place and circumstances were all of them rewards for patience. He felt no omens rising from the unclouded future, while even the premonitions of the slowly approaching war were things which he could share publicly with the others. "Can they really raze whole capitals, these bombers?" asked Clea quietly. "I've always believed that our inventions mirror our secret wishes, and we wish for the end of the city-man, don't we? All of us? Yes, but how hard to surrender London and Paris. What do you think?"

What did he think? Mountolive wrinkled his fine brows and shook his head. He was thinking of Leila draped in a black veil like a nun, sitting in her dusty summerhouse at Karm Abu Girg, among the splendid roses, with only a snake for company. . . .

So the untroubled, unhurried summer moved steadily onwards—August and September and Mountolive found little to daunt him professionally in a city so eager for friendship, so vulnerable to the least politeness, so expert in taking pleasure. Day after day the coloured sails fluttered and loitered in the harbour mirror among the steel fortresses, the magical white waves moved in perfect punctuation over desert beaches burnt white as calx by the African suns. By night, sitting above a garden resplendent with fireflies, he heard the deep booming tread of screws as the Eastern-bound liners coasted the deeper waters outside the harbour, heading for the ports on the other side of the world. In the desert they explored oases of greenness made trembling and insubstantial as dreams by the water mirages, or stalked the bronze knuckles of the sandstone ridges around the city on horses, which, for all their fleetness, carried food and drink to assuage their talkative riders.

He visited Petra and the strange coral delta along the Red Sea coast with its swarming population of rainbow-coloured tropical fish. The long cool balconies of the summer residence echoed night after night to the clink of ice in tall glasses, the clink of platitudes and commonplaces made thrilling to him by their position in place and time, by their appositeness to a city which knew that pleasure was the only thing that made industry worth while; on these balconies, hanging out over the blue littoral of the historic coast, warmly lit by candle-light, these fragmentary friendships flowered and took shape in new affections whose candour made him no longer feel separated from his fellow-men by the powers he wielded. He was popular and soon might be well-beloved. Even the morbid spiritual lassitude and self-indulgence of the city was delightful to one who, secure in income, could afford to live outside it. Alexandria seemed to him a very desirable summer cantonment, accessible to every affection and stranger-loving in the sense of the Greek word. But why should he not feel at home?

The Alexandrians themselves were strangers and exiles to the Egypt which existed below the glittering surface of their dreams, ringed by the hot deserts and fanned by the bleakness of a faith which renounced worldly pleasure: the Egypt of rags and sores, of beauty and desperation. Alexandria was still Europe—the capital of Asiatic Europe, if such a thing could exist. It could never be like Cairo where his whole life had an Egyptian cast, where he spoke ample Arabic; here French, Italian and Greek dominated the scene. The ambience, the social manner, everything was different, was cast in a European mould where somehow the camels and palm-trees and cloaked natives existed only as a brilliantly coloured frieze, a back-cloth to a life divided in its origins.

Then the autumn came and his duties drew him back once more to the winter capital, albeit puzzled and indeed a little aggrieved by the silence of Leila; but back to the consuming interests of a professional life which he found far from displeasing. There were papers to be constructed, miscellaneous reports, economic-social and military, to be made. His staff had shaken down well now, and worked with diligence and a will; even Pursewarden gave of his best. The enmity of Errol, never very deep, had been successfully neutralized, converted into a long-term truce. He had reason to feel pleased with himself.

Then at carnival time there came a message to say that Leila had at last signified her intention of meeting him—but both of them, it was understood, were to wear the conventional black domino of the season—the mask in which the Alexandrians revelled. He understood her anxiety. Nevertheless he was delighted by the thought and spoke warmly to Nessim on the telephone as he accepted the invitation, planning to remove his whole Chancery up to Alexandria for the carnival, so that his secretaries might enjoy the occasion with him. Remove he did, to find the city now basking under crisp winter skies as blue as a bird's egg and hardly touched at night by the desert frosts.

But here another disappointment awaited him; for when in the midst of the hubbub at the Cervoni ball Justine took his arm and piloted him through the garden to the place of rendezvous among the tall hedges, all they found was an empty marble seat with a silk handbag on it containing a note scrawled in lipstick. "At the last moment my nerve fails me. Forgive." He tried to hide his chagrin and discomfiture from Justine. She herself seemed almost incredulous, repeating: "But she came in from Karm Abu Girg specially for the meeting. I cannot understand it. She has been with Nessim all day." He felt a sympathy in the warm pressure of her hand upon his elbow as they returned, downcast, from the scene, brushing impatiently past the laughing masked figures in the garden.

By the pool he caught a glimpse of Amaril, sitting uncowled before a slender masked figure, talking in low, pleading tones, and leaning forward from time to time to embrace her. A pang of envy smote him, though God knew there was nothing he recognized as passional now in his desire to see Leila. It was, in a paradoxical way, that Egypt itself could not fully come alive for him until he had seen her—for she represented something like a second, almost mythical image of the reality which he was experiencing, expropriating day by day. He was like a

148

man seeking to marry the twin images in a camera periscope in order to lay his lens in true focus. Without having gone through the experience of having seen her once more, he felt vaguely helpless, unable either to confirm his own memories of this magical landscape, or fully assess his newest impressions of it. Yet he accepted his fate with philosophical calm. There was, after all, no real cause for alarm. Patience—there was ample room for patience now, to wait upon her courage.

Besides, other friendships had ripened now to fill the gap—friendships with Balthazar (who often came to dine and play chess), friendships with Amaril, Pierre Balbz, the Cervoni family. Clea too had begun her slow portrait of him at this time. His mother had been begging him to have a portrait in oils made for her; now he was able to pose in the resplendent uniform which Sir Louis had so obligingly sold him. The picture would make a surprise gift for Christmas, he thought, and was glad to let Clea dawdle over it, reconstructing the portions which displeased her. Through her (for she talked as she worked in order to keep her subjects' faces alive) he learned much during that summer about the lives and pre-occupations of the Alexandrians—the fantastic poetry and gro-tesque drama of life as these exiles of circumstance lived it; tales of the modern lake-dwellers, inhabitants of the stone skyscrapers which stared out over the ruins of the Pharos towards Europe.

One such tale struck his fancy—the love-story of Amaril (the elegant, much beloved doctor) for whom he had come to feel a particular affection. The very name on Clea's lips sounded with a common affection for this diffident and graceful man, who had so often sworn that he would never have the luck to be loved by a woman. "Poor Amaril," sighing and smiling as she painted she said: "Shall I tell you his story? It is somehow typical. It has made all his friends happy, for we were always apt to think that he had left the matter of love in this world until too late—had missed the bus."

"But Amaril is going abroad to England," said Mountolive.

"He has asked us for a visa. Am I to assume that his heart is broken? And who is Semira? Please tell me."

"The virtuous Semira!" Clea smiled again tenderly, and pausing in her work, put a portfolio into his hands. He turned the pages. "All noses," he said with surprise, and she nodded. "Yes, noses. Amaril has kept me busy for nearly three months, travelling about and collecting noses for her to choose from; noses of the living and the dead. Noses from the Yacht Club, the Etoile, from frescoes in the Museum, from coins. . . . It has been hard work assembling them all for comparative study. Finally, they have chosen the nose of a soldier in a Theban fresco."

Mountolive was puzzled. "Please, Clea, tell me the story."

"Will you promise to sit still, not to move?"

"I promise."

"Very well, then. You know Amaril quite well now; well, this romantic, endearing creature—so true a friend and so wise a doctor—has been our despair for years. It seemed that he could never, would never fall in love. We were sad for him— you know that despite our hardness of surface we Alexandrians are sentimental people, and wish our friends to enjoy life. Not that he was unhappy—and he has had lovers from time to time: but never *une amie* in our special sense. He himself bemoaned the fact frequently—I think not entirely to provoke pity or amusement, but to reassure himself that there was nothing wrong: that he was sympathetic and attractive to the race of women. Then last year at the Carnival, the miracle happened. He met a slender masked domino. They fell madly in love— indeed went farther than is customary for so cautious a lover as Amaril. He was completely transformed by the experience, but . . . the girl disappeared, still masked, without leaving her name. A pair of white hands and a ring with a yellow stone was all he knew of her—for despite their passion she had refused to unmask so that oddly enough, he had been denied so much as a kiss, though granted . . . other favours. Heavens, I am gossiping! Never mind.

"From then on Amaril became insupportable. The romantic frenzy, I admit, suited him very well—for he is a romantic to his finger-tips. He hunted through the city all year long for those hands, sought them everywhere, beseeched his friends to help him, neglected his practice, became almost a laughing-stock. We were amused and touched by his distress, but what could we do? How could we trace her? He waited for Carnival this year with burning impatience for she had promised to return to the place of rendezvous. Now comes the fun. She did reappear, and once more they renewed their vows of devotion; but this time Amaril was determined not to be given the slip—for she was somewhat evasive about names and addresses. He became desperate and bold, and refused to be parted from her which frightened her very much indeed. (All this he told me himself—for he appeared at my flat in the early morning, walking like a drunkard and with his hair standing on end, elated and rather frightened.)

"The girl made several attempts to give him the slip but he stuck to her and insisted on taking her home in one of those old horse-drawn cabs. She was almost beside herself, indeed, and when they reached the eastern end of the city, somewhat shabby and unfrequented, with large abandoned properties and decaying gardens, she made a run for it. Demented with romantic frenzy, Amaril chased the nymph and caught her up as she was slipping into a dark courtyard. In his eagerness he snatched at her cowl when the creature, her face at last bared, sank to the doorstep in tears. Amaril's description of the scene was rather terrifying. She sat there, shaken by a sort of snickering and whimpering and covering her face with her hands. *She had no nose.* For a moment he got a tremendous fright for he is the most superstitious of mortals, and knows all the beliefs about vampires appearing during carnival. But he made the sign of the cross and touched the clove of garlic in his pocket—but she didn't disappear. And then the doctor in him came to the fore, and taking her into the courtyard (she was half-

151

fainting with mortification and fear) he examined her closely. He tells me he heard his own brain ticking out possible diagnoses clearly and watchfully, while at the same time he felt that his heart had stopped beating and that he was suffocating. . . . In a flash he reviewed the possible causes of such a feature, repeating with terror words like syphilis, leprosy, lupus, and turning her small distorted face this way and that. He cried angrily: 'What is your name?' And she blurted out 'Semira— the virtuous Semira.' He was so unnerved that he roared with laughter.

"Now this is an oddity. Semira is the daughter of a very old deaf father. The family was once rich and famous, under the Khedives, and is of Ottoman extraction. But it was plagued by misfortunes and the progressive insanity of the sons, and has so far to-day decayed as to be virtually forgotten. It is also poverty-stricken. The old half-mad father locked Semira away in this rambling house, keeping her veiled for the most part. Vaguely, in society, one had heard tales of her—of a daughter who had taken the veil and spent her life in prayer, who had never been outside the gates of the house, who was a mystic; or who was deaf, dumb and bedridden. Vague tales, distorted as tales always are in Alexandria. But while the faint echo remained of the so-called virtuous Semira—she was really completely unknown to us and her family forgotten. Now it seemed that at carnival-time her curiosity about the outer world overcame her and she gate-crashed parties in a domino!

"But I am forgetting Amaril. Their footsteps had brought down an old manservant with a candle. Amaril demanded to see the master of the house. He had already come to a decision. The old father lay asleep in an old-fashioned four-poster bed, in a room covered in bat-droppings, at the top of the house. Semira was by now practically insensible. But Amaril had come to a great decision. Taking the candle in one hand and the small Semira in the crook of his arm, he walked the whole way up to the top and kicked open the door of the father's room. It must have been a strange and unfamiliar scene for the old man to witness as he sat up in bed—and Amaril describes it with all the touching flamboyance of the romantic, even moving himself in the recital so that he is in tears as he recalls it. He is touched by the magnificence of his own fancy, I think; I must say, loving him as much as I do, I felt tears coming into my own eyes as he told me how he put down the candle beside the bed, and kneeling down with Semira, said 'I wish to marry your daughter and take her back into the world.' The terror and incomprehension of the old man at this unexpected visit took some time to wear off, and for a while it was hard to make him understand. Then he began to tremble and wonder at this handsome apparition kneeling beside his bed holding up his noseless daughter with his arm and proposing the impossible with so much pride and passion.

" 'But,' the old man protested, 'no-one will take her, for she has no nose.' He got out of bed in a stained nightshirt and walked right round Amaril, who remained kneeling, studying him as one might an entomological specimen. (I am quoting.) Then he touched him with his bare foot—as if to see whether he was made of flesh and blood—and repeated: 'Who are you to take a woman without a nose?' Amaril replied: 'I am a doctor from Europe and I will give her a new nose,' for the idea, the fantastic idea, had been slowly becoming clear in his own mind. At the words, Semira gave a sob and turned her beautiful, horrible face to his, and Amaril thundered out: 'Semira, will you be my wife?' She could hardly articulate her response and seemed little less doubtful of the whole issue than was her father. Amaril stayed and talked to them, convincing them.

"The next day when he went back, he was received with a message that Semira was not to be seen and that what he proposed was impossible. But Amaril was not to be put off, and once more he forced his way in and bullied the father.

"This, then, is the fantasy in which he has been living. For Semira, as loving and eager as ever, cannot leave her house for the open world until he fulfils his promise. Amaril offered to marry her at once, but the suspicious old man wants to make sure of the nose. But what nose? First Balthazar was called in and together they examined Semira, and assured themselves that the illness was due neither to leprosy nor syphilis but to a rare form of lupus—a peculiar skin T.B. of rare kind of which many cases have been recorded from the Damietta region. It had been left untreated over the years and had finally collapsed the nose. I must say, it is horrible—just a slit like the gills of a fish. For I too have been sharing the deliberations of the doctors and have been going regularly to read to Semira in the darkened rooms where she has spent most of her life. She has wonderful dark eyes like an odalisque and a shapely mouth and well-modelled chin: and then the gills of a fish! It is too unfair. And it has taken her ages to actually believe that surgery can restore the defect. Here again Amaril has been brilliant, in getting her interested in her restoration, conquering her self-disgust, allowing her to choose the nose from that portfolio, discuss the whole project with him. He has let her choose her nose as one might let one's mistress choose a valuable bracelet from Pierantoni. It was just the right approach, for she is beginning to conquer her shame, and feel amost proud of being free to choose this valuable gift—the most treasured feature of a woman's face which aligns every glance and alters every meaning: and without which good eyes and teeth and hair become useless treasures.

"But now they have run into other difficulties, for the restoration of the nose itself requires techniques of surgery which are still very new; and Amaril, though a surgeon, does not wish there to be any mistake about the results. You see, he is after all building a woman of his own fancy, a face to a husband's own specifications; only Pygmalion had such a chance before! He is working on the project as if his life depended on it—which in a way I suppose it does.

"The operation itself will have to be done in stages, and

will take ages to complete. I have heard them discussing it over and over again in such detail that I feel I could almost perform it myself. First you cut off a strip of the costal cartilage, here, where the rib joins the breastbone, and make a graft from it. Then you cut out a triangular flap of skin from the forehead and pull downwards to cover the nose—the Indian technique, Balthazar calls it; but they are still debating the removal of a section of flesh and skin from inside the thigh. . . . You can imagine how fascinating this is for a painter and sculptor to think about. But meanwhile Amaril is going to England to perfect the operative technique under the best masters. Hence his demand for a visa. How many months he will be away we don't know yet, but he is setting out with all the air of a Knight in search of the Holy Grail. For he intends to complete the operation himself. Meanwhile, Semira will wait for him here, and I have promised to visit her frequently and keep her interested and amused if I can. It is not difficult, for the real world outside the four walls of her house sounds to her strange and cruel and romantic. Apart from a brief glimpse of it at carnival-time, she knows little of our lives. For her, Alexandria is as brilliantly coloured as a fairy-story. It will be some time before she sees it as it really is—with its harsh, circumscribed contours and its wicked, pleasure-loving and unromantic inhabitants. But you have moved!"

Mountolive apologized and said: "Your use of the word 'unromantic' startled me, for I was just thinking how romantic it all seems to a newcomer."

"Amaril is an exception, though a beloved one. Few are as generous, as unmercenary as he. As for Semira—I cannot at present see what the future holds for her beyond romance." Clea sighed and smiled and lit a cigarette.

"*Espérons*," she said quietly.

o   o   o   o   o

155

VIII

"A hundred times I've asked you not to use my razor," said Pombal plaintively, "and you do so again. You *know* I am afraid of syphilis. Who knows what spots, when you cut them, begin to leak?"

"*Mon cher collègue*," said Pursewarden stiffly (he was shaving his lip), and with a grimace which was somehow intended to express injured dignity, "what can you mean? I am British. *Hein?*"

He paused, and marking time with Pombal's cut-throat declaimed solemnly:

> "*The British who perfected the horseless carriage*
> *Are now working hard on the sexless marriage.*
> *Soon the only permissible communion*
> *Will be by agreement with one's Trade Union.*"

"Your blood may be infected," said his friend between grunts as he ministered to a broken suspender with one fat calf exposed upon the *bidet*. "You never know, after all."

"I am a writer" said Pursewarden with further and deeper dignity. "And therefore I *do* know. There is no blood in my veins. Plasma," he said darkly, wiping his ear-tip, "That is what flows in my veins. How else would I do all the work I do? Think of it. On the *Spectator* I am *Ubique*, on the *New Statesman* I am *Mens Sana*. On the *Daily Worker* I sign myself as *Corpore Sano*. I am also *Paralysis Agitans* on *The Times* and *Ejaculatio Praecox* in *New Verse*. I am . . ." But here his invention failed him.

"I never see you working," said Pombal.

"Working little, I earn less. If my work earned more than one hundred pounds a year I should not be able to take refuge in being misunderstood." He gave a strangled sob.

"*Compris*. You have been drinking. I saw the bottle on the hall table as I came in. Why so early?"

"I wished to be quite honest about it. It is your wine, after all. I wished to hide nothing. I *have* drunk a tot or so."

"Celebration?"

"Yes. To-night, my dear Georges, I am going to do something rather unworthy of myself. I have disposed of a dangerous enemy and advanced my own position by a large notch. In our service, this would be regarded as something to crow about. I am going to offer myself a dinner of self-congratulation."

"Who will pay it?"

"I will order, eat and pay for it myself."

"That is not much good."

Pursewarden made an impatient face in the mirror.

"On the contrary," he said. "A quiet evening is what I most need. I shall compose a few more fragments of my autobiography over the good oysters at Diamandakis."

"What is the title?"

"*Beating about the Bush*. The opening words are 'I first met Henry James in a brothel in Algiers. He had a naked houri on each knee.'"

"Henry James was a pussy, I think."

Pursewarden turned the shower on full and stepped into it crying: "No more literary criticism from the French please."

Pombal drove a comb through his dark hair with a laborious impatience and then consulted his watch. "*Merde*," he said, "I am going to be retarded again."

Pursewarden gave a shriek of delight. They adventured freely in each other's languages, rejoicing like schoolboys in the mistakes which cropped up among their conversations. Each blunder was greeted with a shout, was turned into a war-cry. Pursewarden hopped with pleasure and shouted happily above the hissing of the water: "Why not stay in and enjoy a nice little *nocturnal emission* on the short hairs?" (Pombal had described a radio broadcast thus the day before and had not been allowed to forget it.) He made a round face now to express mock annoyance. "I did *not* say it" he said.

"You bloody well did."

"I did not say 'the short hairs' but the 'short undulations'— *des ondes courtes.*"

"Equally dreadful. You Quai d'Orsay people shock me. Now my French may not be perfect, but I have never made a——'

"If I begin with your mistakes—ha! ha!"

Pursewarden danced up and down in the bath, shouting "Nocturnal emissions on the short hairs". Pombal threw a rolled towel at him and lumbered out of the bathroom before he could retaliate effectively.

Their abusive conversation was continued while the Frenchman made some further adjustments to his dress in the bedroom mirror. "Will you go down to Etoile later for the floor-show?"

"I certainly will," said Pursewarden. "I shall dance a Fox-Macabre with Darley's girl-friend or Sveva. Several Fox-Macabres, in fact. Then, later on, like an explorer who has run out of pemmican, purely for body-warmth, I shall select someone and conduct her to Mount Vulture. There to sharpen my talons on her flesh." He made what he imagined to be the noise a vulture makes as it feeds upon flesh—a soft, throaty croaking. Pombal shuddered.

"Monster," he cried. "I go—good-bye."

"Good-bye. *Toujours la maladresse!*"

"*Toujours.*" It was their war-cry.

Left alone, Pursewarden whistled softly as he dried himself in the torn bath-towel and completed his toilet. The irregularities in the water system of the Mount Vulture Hotel often drove him across the square to Pombal's flat in search of a leisurely bath and a shave. From time to time too, when Pombal went on leave, he would actually rent the place and share it, somewhat uneasily, with Darley who lived a furtive life of his own in the far corner of it. It was good from time to time to escape from the isolation of his hotel-room, and the vast muddle of paper which was growing up around his next novel. To escape—always to escape. . . . The desire of a writer to be alone with himself—"the writer, most solitary of human animals"; "I am quoting from the great Pursewarden himself" he told his reflection in the mirror as he wrestled with his tie. To-night he would dine quietly, self-indulgently, alone! He had gracefully refused a halting dinner invitation from Errol which he knew would involve him in one of those gauche, haunting evenings spent in playing imbecile paper-games or bridge. "My God" Pombal had said, "your compatriots' methods of passing the time! Those rooms which they fill with their sense of guilt! To express *one* idea is to stop a dinner-party dead in its tracks and provoke an *awkwardness*, a *silence*. . . . I try my best, but always feel I've put my foot in it. So I always automatically send flowers the next morning to my hostess. . . . What a nation you are! How intriguing for us French because how *repellent* is the way you live!"

Poor David Mountolive! Pursewarden thought of him with compassion and affection. What a price the career diplomat had to pay for the fruits of power! "His dreams must forever be awash with the memories of fatuities endured—deliberately endured in the name of what was most holy in the profession, namely the desire to please, the determination to captivate in order to influence. Well! It takes all sorts to unmake a world."

Combing his hair back he found himself thinking of Maskelyne, who must at this moment be sitting in the Jerusalem express, jogging stiffly, sedately down among the sand-dunes and orange-groves, sucking at a long pipe; in a hot carriage, fly-tormented without and roasted within by the corporate pride of a tradition which was dying. . . . Why should it be allowed to die? Maskelyne, full of the failure, the ignomy of a new post which carried *advancement* with it. The final cruel thrust. (The idea gave him a twinge of remorse for he did not underestimate the character of the unself-seeking soldier.) Narrow, acid, desiccated as a human being, nevertheless the writer somewhere treasured him while the man condemned him. (Indeed, he had made extensive notes upon him—a fact which would certainly have surprised Maskelyne had he known.) His way of holding his pipe, of carrying his nose high, his reserves. . . . It was simply that he might want to use him one day. "Are real human beings becoming simply extended humours capable of use, and does this cut one off from them a bit? Yes. For observation throws down a field about the observed person or object. Yes. Makes the unconditional response more difficult— the response to the common ties, affections, love and so on. But this is not only the writer's problem—it is everyone's problem. Growing up means separation in the interests of a better, more lucid joining up. . . . Bah!" He was able to console himself against his furtive sympathy with Maskelyne by recalling a few of the man's stupidities. His arrogance! "My dear fellow, when you've been in 'I' as long as I have you develop *intuition*. You can see things a mile off." The idea of anyone like Maskelyne developing intuition was delightful. Pursewarden gave a long crowing laugh and reached for his coat.

He slipped lightly downstairs into the dusky street, counting his money and smiling. It was the best hour of the day in Alexandria—the streets turning slowly to the metallic blue of carbon paper but still giving off the heat of the sun. Not all the lights were on in the town, and the large mauve parcels of dusk moved here and there, blurring the outlines of everything, repainting the hard outlines of buildings and human beings in smoke. Sleepy cafés woke to the whine of mandolines which merged in the shrilling of heated tyres on the tarmac of streets now crowded with life, with white-robed figures and the scarlet dots of *tarbushes*. The window-boxes gave off a piercing smell of slaked earth and urine. The great limousines soared away from the Bourse with softly crying horns, like polished flights of special geese. To be half-blinded by the mauve dusk, to move lightly, brushing shoulders with the throng, at peace, in that dry inspiriting air . . . these were the rare moments of happiness upon which he stumbled by chance, by accident. The pavements still retained their heat just as water-melons did when you cut them open at dusk; a damp heat slowly leaking up through the thin soles of one's shoes. The sea-winds were moving in to invest the upper town with their damp coolness, but as yet one only felt them spasmodically. One moved through the dry air, so full of static electricity (the crackle of the comb in his hair), as one might swim through a tepid summer sea full of creeping cold currents. He walked towards Baudrot slowly through little isolated patches of smell—a perfume shed by a passing woman, or the reek of jasmine from a dark archway—knowing that the damp sea air would soon blot them all out. It was the perfect moment for an *apéritif* in the half-light.

The long wooden outer balconies, lined with potted plants which exhaled the twilight smell of watered earth, were crowded now with human beings, half melted by the mirage into fugitive cartoons of gestures swallowed as soon as made. The coloured awnings trembled faintly above the blue veils which shifted uneasily in the darkening alleys, like the very nerves of the lovers themselves who hovered here, busy on the assignations, their gestures twinkling like butterflies full of the evening promises of Alexandria. Soon the mist would vanish and the lights would blaze up on cutlery and white cloth, on ear-rings and flashing jewellery, on sleek oiled heads and smiles made brilliant by their darkness, brown skins slashed by white teeth. Then the cars would begin once more to slide down from the upper town with their elegant precarious freight of diners and dancers. . . . This was the best moment of the day. Sitting here, with his back against a wooden trellis, he could gaze sleepily into the open street, unrecognized and ungreeted. Even the figures at the next table were unrecognizable, the merest outline of human beings. Their voices came lazily to him in the dusk, the mauve-veiled evening voices of Alexandrians uttering stockyard quotations or the lazy verses from Arabic love-poems—who could tell?

How good the taste of Dubonnet with a *zeste de citron*, with its concrete memory of a Europe long-since abandoned yet living on unforgotten below the surface of this unsubstantial life in Alexander's shabby capital! Tasting it he thought enviously of Pombal, of the farmhouse in Normandy to which his friend hoped one day to return heart-whole. How marvellous it would be to feel the same assured relations with his own country, the same certainty of return! But his gorge rose at the mere thought of it; and at the same time the pain and regret that it should be so. (She said: "I have read the books so slowly —not because I cannot read fast as yet in Braille; but because I wanted to surrender to the power of each word, even the cruelties and the weaknesses, to arrive at the grain of the thought.") The *grain!* It was a phrase which rang in one's ear like the whimper of a bullet which passes too close. He saw her—the marble whiteness of the sea-goddess' face, hair combed back upon her shoulders, staring out across the park where the dead autumn leaves and branches flared and smoked; a Medusa among the snows, dressed in her old tartan shawl. The blind spent all day in that gloomy subterranean library with its pools of shadow and light, their fingers moving like ants across the perforated surfaces of books engraved for them by a machine. ("I so much wanted to understand, but I could not.") Good, this is where you break into a cold sweat; this is where you turn through three hundred and sixty-five degrees, a human earth, to bury your face in your pillow with a groan! (The lights were coming on now, the veils were being driven upwards into the night, evaporating. The faces of human beings. . . .) He watched them intently, almost lustfully, as if to surprise their most inward intentions, their basic designs in moving here, idle as fireflies, walking in and out of the bars of yellow light; a finger atwinkle with rings, a flashing ear, a gold tooth set firmly in the middle of an amorous smile. "Waiter, *kam wahed*, another please." And the half-formulated thoughts began to float once more across his mind (innocent, purged by the darkness and the alcohol): thoughts which might later dress up, masquerade as verses. . . . Visitants from other lives.

Yes, he would do another year—one more whole year, simply out of affection for Mountolive. He would make it a good one, too. Then a transfer—but he averted his mind from this, for it might result in disaster. Ceylon? Santos? Something about this Egypt, with its burning airless spaces and its unrealized vastness—the grotesque granite monuments to dead Pharaohs, the tombs which became cities—something in all this suffocated him. It was no place for memory—and the strident curt reality of the day-world was almost more than a human being could bear. Open sores, sex, perfumes, and money.

They were crying the evening papers in a soup-language which was deeply thrilling—Greek, Arabic, French were the basic ingredients. The boys ran howling through the thoroughfares like winged messengers from the underworld, proclaiming . . . the fall of Byzantium? Their white robes were tucked up about their knees. They shouted plaintively, as if dying of hunger. He leaned from his wooden porch and bought an evening paper to read over his solitary meal. Reading at meals was another self-indulgence which he could not refuse himself.

Then he walked quietly along the arcades and through the street of the cafés, past a mauve mosque (sky-floating), a library, a temple (grilled: "Here once lay the body of the great Alexander"); and so down the long curving inclines of the street which took one to the seashore. The cool currents were still nosing about hereabouts, tantalizing to the cheek.

He suddenly collided with a figure in a mackintosh and belatedly recognized Darley. They exchanged confused pleasantries, weighed down by a mutual awkwardness. Their politenesses got them, so to speak, suddenly stuck to each other, suddenly stuck to the street as if it had turned to flypaper. Then at last Darley managed to break himself free and turn back down the dark street, saying: "Well, I mustn't keep you. I'm dead tired myself. Going home for a wash." Pursewarden stood still for a moment looking after him, deeply puzzled by his own confusion and smitten by the memory of the damp bedraggled towels which he had left lying about Pombal's bathroom, and the rim of shaving-soap grey with hairs around the washbasin. . . . Poor Darley! But how was it that, liking and respecting the man, he could not feel natural in his presence? He at once took on a hearty, unnatural tone with him purely out of nervousness. This must seem rude and contemptuous. The brisk hearty tone of some country medico rallying a patient . . . damn! He must some time take him back to the hotel for a solitary drink and try to get to know him a little. And yet, he had tried to get to know him on several occasions on those winter walks together. He rationalized his dissatisfaction by saying to himself "But the poor bastard is still interested in *literature*."

But his good humour returned when he reached the little Greek oyster-tavern by the sea whose walls were lined with butts and barrels of all sizes, and from whose kitchens came great gusts of smoke and smell of whitebait and octopus frying in olive oil. Here he sat, among the ragged boatmen and schooner-crews of the Levant, to eat his oysters and dip into the newspaper, while the evening began to compose itself comfortably around him, untroubled by thought or the demands of conversation with its wicked quotidian platitudes. Later he might be able to relate his ideas once more to the book which he was trying to complete so slowly, painfully, in these hard-won secret moments stolen from an empty professional life, stolen even from the circumstances which he built around himself by virtue of laziness, of gregariousness. ("Care for a drink?"—"Don't mind if I do." How many evenings had been lost like this?)

And the newspapers? He dwelt mostly upon the *Faits Divers*—those little oddities of human conduct which mirrored the true estate of man, which lived on behind the wordier abstractions, pleading for the comic and miraculous in lives made insensitive by drabness, by the authority of bald reason. Beside a banner headline which he would have to interpret in a draft despatch for Mountolive the next day—ARAB UNION APPEALS AGAIN—he could find the enduring human frailties in GREAT RELIGIOUS LEADER TRAPPED IN LIFT or LUNATIC BREAKS MONTE CARLO BANK which reflected the macabre unreason of fate and circumstance.

Later, under the influence of the excellent food at the *Coin de France* he began to smoke his evening more enjoyably still—like a pipe of opium. The inner world with its tensions unwound its spools inside him, flowing out and away in lines of thought which flickered intermittently into his consciousness like morse. As if he had become a real receiving apparatus—these rare moments of good dictation!

At ten he noted on the back of a letter from his bank a few of the gnomic phrases which belonged to his book. As "Ten. No attacks by the hippogriff this week. Some speeches for Old Parr?" And then, below it, disjointedly, words which, condensing now in the mind like dew, might later be polished and refashioned into the armature of his characters' acts.

(a) With every advance from the known to the unknown, the mystery increases.

(b) Here I am, walking about on two legs with a name—the whole intellectual history of Europe from Rabelais to de Sade.

(c) Man will be happy when his Gods perfect themselves.

(d) Even the Saint dies with all his imperfections on his head.

(e) Such a one as might be above divine reproach, beneath human contempt.

(f) Possession of a human heart—disease without remedy.

165

(g) All great books are excursions into pity.

(h) The yellow millet dream is everyman's way.

Later these oracular thoughts would all be brushed softly into the character of Old Parr, the sensualist Tiresias of his novel, though erupting thus, at haphazard, they offered no clue as to the order in which they would really be placed finally.

He yawned. He was pleasantly tipsy after his second Armagnac. Outside the grey awnings, the city had once more assumed the true pigmentation of night. Black faces now melted into blackness; one saw apparently empty garments walking about, as in *The Invisible Man*. Red pill-boxes mounted upon cancelled faces, the darkness of darkness. Whistling softly, he paid his bill and walked lightly down to the Corniche again to where, at the end of a narrow street, the green bubble of the Etoile flared and beckoned; he dived into the narrow bottleneck staircase to emerge into a airless ballroom, half-blinded now by the incandescent butcher's light and pausing only to let Zoltan take his mackintosh away to the cloakroom. For once he was not irked by the fear of his unpaid drink-chits —for he had drawn a substantial advance upon his new salary. "Two new girls" said the little waiter hoarsely in his ear," both from Hungary." He licked his lips and grinned. He looked as if he had been fried very slowly in olive oil to a rich dark brown.

The place was crowded, the floor-show nearly over. There were no familiar faces to be seen around, thank God. The lights went down, turned blue, black—and then with a shiver of tambourines and the roll of drums threw up the last performer into a blinding silver spot. Her sequins caught fire as she turned, blazing like a Viking ship, to jingle down the smelly corridor to the dressing-rooms.

He had seldom spoken to Melissa since their initial meeting months before, and her visits to Pombal's flat now rarely if ever coincided with his. Darley too was painstakingly secretive —perhaps from jealousy, or shame? Who could tell? They smiled and greeted one another in the street when their paths crossed, that was all. He watched her reflectively now as he drank a couple of whiskies and slowly felt the lights beginning to burn more brightly inside him, his feet respond to the dull sugared beat of the nigger jazz. He enjoyed dancing, enjoyed the comfortable shuffle of the four-beat bar, the rhythms that soaked into the floor under one's toes. Should he dance?

But he was too good a dancer to be adventurous, and holding Melissa in his arms thus he hardly bothered to do more than move softly, lightly round the floor, humming to himself the tune of *Jamais de la Vie*. She smiled at him and seemed glad to see a familiar face from the outer world. He felt her narrow hand with its slender wrist resting upon his shoulder, fingers clutching his coat like the claw of a sparrow. "You are *en forme*," she said. "I am *en forme*," he replied. They exchanged the meaningless pleasantries suitable to the time and place. He was interested and attracted by her execrable French. Later she came across to his table and he stood her a couple of *coups de champagne*—the statutory fee exacted by the management for private conversations. She was on duty that night, and each dance cost the dancer a fee; therefore this interlude won her gratitude, for her feet were hurting her. She talked gravely, chin on hand, and watching her he found her rather beautiful in an etiolated way. Her eyes were good—full of small timidities which recorded perhaps the shocks which too great an honesty exacts from life? But she looked, and clearly was, ill. He jotted down the words: "The soft bloom of phthisis." The whisky had improved his sulky good humour, and his few jests were rewarded by an unforced laughter which, to his surprise, he found delightful. He began to comprehend dimly what Darley must see in her—the *gamine* appeal of the city, of slenderness and neatness: the ready street-arab response to a hard world. Dancing again he said to her, but with drunken irony: "*Melissa, comment vous défendez-vous contre la solitude?*" Her response, for some queer reason, cut him to the heart. She turned upon him an eye replete with all the candour of experience and replied softly: "*Monsieur, je suis devenue la solitude même.*" The melancholy of the smiling face was completely untouched by self-pity. She made a little gesture, as if indicating a total world, and said "Look"—the shabby wills and desires of the Etoile's patrons, clothed in bodily forms, spread around them in that airless cellar. He understood and suddenly felt apologetic for never having treated her seriously. He was furious at his own complacency. On an impulse, he pressed his cheek to hers, affectionately as a brother. She was completely *natural!*

A human barrier dissolved now and they found that they could talk freely to each other, like old friends. As the evening wore on he found himself dancing with her more and more often. She seemed to welcome this, even though on the dance-floor itself he danced silently now, relaxed and happy. He made no gestures of intimacy, yet he felt somehow accepted by her. Then towards midnight a fat and expensive Syrian banker arrived and began to compete seriously for her company. Much to his annoyance, Pursewarden felt his anxiety rise, form itself almost into a proprietary jealousy. This made him swear under his breath! But he moved to a table near the floor the better to be able to claim her as soon as the music started. Melissa herself seemed oblivious to this fierce competition. She was tired. At last he asked her "What will you do when you leave here? Will you go back to Darley to-night?" She smiled at the name, but shook her head wearily. "I need some money for—never mind," she said softly, and then abruptly burst out, as if afraid of not being taken for sincere, with "For my winter coat. We have so little money. In this business, one has to dress. You understand?" Pursewarden said: "Not with that horrible Syrian?" Money! He thought of it with a pang. Melissa looked at him with an air of amused resignation. She said in a low voice, but without emphasis, without shame: "He has offered me 500 piastres to go home with him. I say no now, but later—I expect I shall have to." She shrugged her shoulders.

Pursewarden swore quietly. "No," he said. "Come with me. I shall give you 1,000 if you need it."

Her eyes grew round at the mention of so great a sum of money. He could see her telling it over coin by coin, fingering it, as if on an abacus, dividing it up into food, rent and clothes. "I mean it," he said sharply. And added almost at once: "Does Darley know?"

"Oh yes," she said quietly. "You know, he is very good. Our life is a struggle, but he knows me. He *trusts* me. He never asks for any details. He knows that one day when we have enough money to go away I will stop all this. It is not important for us." It sounded quaint, like some fearful blasphemy in the mouth of a child. Pursewarden laughed. "Come now," he said suddenly; he was dying to possess her, to cradle and annihilate her with the disgusting kisses of a false compassion. "Come now, Melissa darling," he said, but she winced and turned pale at the word, and he saw that he had made a mistake, for any sexual transaction must be made strictly outside the bounds of her personal affection for Darley. He was disgusted by himself and yet rendered powerless to act otherwise; "I tell you what," he said, "I shall give Darley a lot of money later this month—enough to take you away." She did not seem to be listening. "I'll get my coat" she said in a small mechanical voice, "and meet you in the hall." She went to make her peace with the manager, and Pursewarden waited for her in an agony of impatience. He had hit upon the perfect way to cure these twinges of a puritan conscience which lurked on underneath the carefree surface of an amoral life.

Several weeks before, he had received through Nessim a short note from Leila, written in an exquisite hand, which read as follows:

Dear Mr. Pursewarden,

I am writing to ask you to perform an unusual service for me. A favourite uncle of mine has just died. He was a great lover of England and the English language which he knew almost better than his own; in his will he left instructions that an epitaph in English should be placed upon his tomb, in prose or verse, and if possible original. I am anxious to honour his memory in this most suitable way and to carry out his last wishes, and this is why I write: to ask you if you would consider such an undertaking, a common one for poets to perform in ancient China, but uncommon to-day. I would be happy to commission you in the sum of £500 for such a work.

The epitaph had been duly delivered and the money deposited in his bank, but to his surprise he found himself unable to touch it. Some queer superstition clung to him. He had never written poetry to order before, and never an epitaph. He smelt something unlucky almost about so large a sum. It had stayed there in his bank, untouched. Now he was suddenly visited by the conviction that he must give it away to Darley! It would, among other things, atone for his habitual neglect of his qualities, his clumsy awkwardness.

She walked back to the hotel with him, pressed as close as a scabbard to his thigh—the professional walk of a woman of the streets. They hardly spoke. The streets were empty.

The old dirty lift, its seats trimmed with dusty brown braid and its mirrors with rotting lace curtains, jerked them slowly upwards into the cobwebbed gloom. Soon, he thought to himself, he would drop through the trap-door feet first, arms pinioned by arms, lips by lips, until he felt the noose tighten about his throat and the stars explode behind his eyeballs. Surcease, forgetfulness, what else should one seek from an unknown woman's body?

Outside the door he kissed her slowly and deliberately, pressing into the soft cone of her pursed lips until their teeth met with a slight click and a jar. She neither responded to him nor withdrew, presenting her small expressionless face to him (sightless in the gloom) like a pane of frosted glass. There was no excitement in her, only a profound and consuming world-weariness. Her hands were cold. He took them in his own, and a tremendous melancholy beset him. Was he to be left once more alone with himself? At once he took refuge in a comic drunkenness which he well knew how to simulate, and which would erect a scaffolding of words about reality, to disorder and distemper it. *"Viens, viens!"* he cried sharply, reverting almost to the false jocularity he assumed with Darley, and now beginning to feel really rather drunk again. *"Le maître vous invite."* Unsmiling, trustful as a lamb, she crossed the threshold into the room, looking about her. He groped for the bed-lamp. It did not work. He lit a candle which stood in a saucer on the night-table and turned to her with the dark shadows dancing in his nostrils and in the orbits of his eyes. They looked at one another while he conducted a furious mercenary patter to disguise his own unease. Then he stopped, for she was too tired to smile. Then, still unspeaking and unsmiling, she began to undress, item by item, dropping her clothes about her on the ragged carpet.

For a long moment he lay, simply exploring her slender body with its slanting ribs (structure of ferns) and the small, immature but firm breasts. Troubled by his silence, she sighed and said something inaudible. *"Laissez. Laissez parler les doigts . . . comme ça,"* he whispered to silence her. He would have liked to say some simple and concrete word. In the silence he felt her beginning to struggle against the luxurious darkness and the growing powers of his lust, struggling to compartment her feelings, to keep them away from her proper life among the bare transactions of existence. "A separate compartment," he thought, and "Is it marked Death?" He was determined to exploit her weakness, the tenderness he felt ebbing and flowing in her veins, but his own moral strength ebbed now and guttered. He turned pale and lay with his bright feverish eyes turned to the shabby ceiling, seeing backwards into time. A clock struck coarsely somewhere, and the sound of the hours woke Melissa, driving away her lassitude, replacing it once more with anxiety, with a desire to be done, to be poured back into the sleep with which she struggled.

They played with each other, counterfeiting a desultory passion which mocked its own origins, could neither ignite nor extinguish itself. (You can lie with lips apart, legs apart, for numberless eternities, telling yourself it is something you have forgotten, it is on the tip of your tongue, the edge of your mind. For the life of you you cannot remember what it is, the name, the town, the day, the hour . . . the biological memory fails.) She gave a small sniff, as if she were crying, holding him in those pale, reflective fingers, tenderly as one might hold a fledgling fallen from the nest. Expressions of doubt and anxiety flitted across her face—as if she were herself guilty for the failure of the current, the broken communication. Then she groaned—and he knew that she was thinking of the money. Such a large sum! His improvidence could never be repeated by other men! And now her crude solicitude, her roughness began to make him angry.

"*Chéri*," Their embraces were like the dry conjunction of waxworks, of figures modelled in *gesso* for some classical tomb. Her hands moved now charmlessly upon the barrel-vaulting of his ribs, his loins, his throat, his cheek; her fingers pressing here and there in darkness, finger of the blind seeking a secret panel in a wall, a forgotten switch which would slide back, illuminate another world, out of time. It was useless, it seemed. She gazed wildly around her. They lay under a nightmarish window full of sea-light, against which a single curtain moved softly like a sail, reminding her of Darley's bed. The room was full of the smell of stale joss, decomposing manuscripts, and the apples he ate while he worked. The sheets were dirty.

As usual, at a level far below the probings of self-disgust or humiliation, he was writing, swiftly and smoothly in his clear mind. He was covering sheet upon sheet of paper. For so many years now he had taken to writing out his life in his own mind —the living and the writing were simultaneous. He transferred the moment bodily to paper as it was lived, warm from the oven, naked and exposed. . . .

"Now" she said angrily, determined not to lose the piastres which in her imagination she had already spent, already owed, "now I will make you *La Veuve*" and he drew his breath in an exultant literary thrill to hear once more this wonderful slang expression stolen from the old nicknames of the French guillotine, with its fearful suggestion of teeth reflected in the concealed metaphor for the castration complex. *La Veuve!* The shark-infested seas of love which closed over the doomed sailor's head in a voiceless paralysis of the dream, the deep-sea dream which dragged one slowly downwards, dismembered and dismembering . . . until with a vulgar snick the steel fell, the clumsy thinking head ("use your loaf") smacked dully into the basket to spurt and wriggle like a fish. . . . *"Mon coeur,"* he said hoarsely, *"mon ange"*; simply to taste the commonest of metaphors, hunting through them a tenderness lost, torn up, cast aside among the snows. *"Mon ange."* A sea-widow into something rich and strange!

Suddenly she cried out in exasperation: "Ah God! But what is it? You do not want to?" her voice ending almost in a wail. She took his soft rather womanish hand upon her knee and spread it out like a book, bending over it a despairing curious face. She moved the candle the better to study the lines, drawing up her thin legs. Her hair fell about her face. He touched the rosy light on her shoulder and said mockingly "You tell fortunes." But she did not look up. She answered shortly "Everyone in the city tells fortunes." They stayed like this, like a tableau, for a long moment. "The *caput mortuum* of a love-scene" he thought to himself. Then Melissa sighed, as if with relief, and raised her head. "I see now," she said quietly. "You are all closed in, your heart is closed in, completely so." She joined index finger to index finger, thumb to thumb in a gesture such as one might use to throttle a rabbit. Her eyes flashed with sympathy. "Your life is dead, closed up. Not like Darley's. His is wide . . . very wide . . . open." She spread her arms out for a moment before dropping them to her knee once more. She added with the tremendous unconscious force of veracity: "*He* can still love." He felt as if he had been hit across the mouth. The candle flickered. "Look again," he said angrily. "Tell me some more." But she completely missed the anger and the chagrin in his voice and bent once more to that enigmatic white hand. "Shall I tell you everything?" she whispered, and for a minute his breath stopped. "Yes," he said curtly. Melissa smiled a stranger, private smile.

"I am not very good," she said softly, "I'll tell you only what I see." Then she turned her candid eyes to him and added: "I see death very close." Pursewarden smiled grimly. "Good" he said. Melissa drew her hair back to her ear with a finger and bent to his hand once more. "Yes, very close. You will hear about it in a matter of hours. What rubbish!" She gave a little laugh. And then, to his complete surprise she went on to describe his sister. "The blind one—*not* your wife." She closed her eyes and spread her repellent arms out before her like a sleep-walker. "Yes," said Pursewarden, "that is her. That is my sister." "Your sister?" Melissa was astounded. She dropped his hand. She had never in playing this game made an accurate prediction before. Pursewarden told her gravely: "She and I were lovers. We shall never be able to love other people." And now, with the recital begun he suddenly found it easy to tell the rest, to tell her everything. He was completely master of himself and she gazed at him with pity and tenderness. Was it easy because they spoke French? In French the truth of passion stood up coldly and cruelly to the scrutiny of human experience. In his own curious phrase he had always qualified it as "an unsniggerable language". Or was it simply that the fugitive sympathy of Melissa made these events easy to speak of? She herself did not judge, everything was known, had been experienced. She nodded gravely as he spoke of his love and his deliberate abandoning of it, of his attempt at marriage, of its failure.

Between pity and admiration they kissed, but passionately now, united by the ties of recorded human experience, by the sensation of having shared something. "I saw it in the hand," she said, "in your hand." She was somewhat frightened by the unwonted accuracy of her own powers. And he? He had always wanted someone to whom he could speak freely—*but it must be someone who could not fully understand!* The candle flickered. On the mirror with shaving soap he had written the mocking verses for Justine which began:

> Oh Dreadful is the check!
> Intense the agony.
> When the ear begins to hear
> And the eye begins to see!

He repeated them softly to himself, in the privacy of his own mind, as he thought of the dark composed features which he had seen here, by candle-light—the dark body seated in precisely the pose which Melissa now adopted, watching him with her chin on her knee, holding his hand with sympathy. And as he went on in his quiet voice to speak of his sister, of his perpetual quest for satisfactions which might be better than those he could remember, and which he had deliberately abandoned, other verses floated through his mind; the chaotic commentaries thrown up by his reading no less than by his experiences. Even as he saw once again the white marble face with its curling black hair thrown back about the nape of a slender neck, the ear-points, chin cleft by a dimple—a face which led him back always to those huge empty eye-sockets—he heard his inner mind repeating:

> *Amors par force vos demeine!*
> *Combien durra vostre folie?*
> *Trop avez mene ceste vie.*

He heard himself saying things which belonged elsewhere. With a bitter laugh, for example, "The Anglo-Saxons invented the word 'fornication' because they could not believe in the variety of love." And Melissa, nodding so gravely and sympathetically, began to look more important—for here was a man at last confiding in her things she could not understand, treasures of that mysterious male world which oscillated always between sottish sentimentality and brutish violence! "In my country almost all the really delicious things you can do to a woman are criminal offences, grounds for divorce." She was frightened by his sharp, cracked laugh. Of a sudden he looked so ugly. Then he dropped his voice again and continued pressing her hand to his cheek softly, as one presses upon a bruise; and inside the inaudible commentary continued:

> *"What meaneth Heaven by these diverse laws?*
> *Eros, Agape—self-division's cause?"*

Locked up there in the enchanted castle, between the terrified kisses and intimacies which would never now be recovered, they had studied La Lioba! What madness! Would they ever dare to enter the lists against other lovers? *Jurata fornicatio*—those verses dribbling away in the mind; and her body, after Rudel, *"gras, delgat et gen"*. He sighed, brushing away the memories like a cobweb and saying to himself: "Later, in search of an *askesis* he followed the desert fathers to Alexandria, to a place between two deserts, between the two breasts of Melissa. *O morosa delectatio.* And he buried his face there among the dunes, covered by her quick hair."

Then he was silent, staring at her with his clear eyes, his trembling lips closing for the first time about endearments which were now alight, now truly passionate. She shivered suddenly, aware that she would not escape him now, that she would have to submit to him fully.

"Melissa" he said triumphantly.

They enjoyed each other now, wisely and tenderly, like

friends long sought for and found among the commonplace crowds which thronged the echoing city. And here was a Melissa he had planned to find—eyes closed, warm open breathing mouth, torn from sleep with a kiss by the rosy candle-light. "It is time to go." But she pressed nearer and nearer to his body, whimpering with weariness. He gazed down fondly at her as she lay in the crook of his arm. "And the rest of your prophecy?" he said gaily. "Rubbish, all rubbish," she answered sleepily. "I can sometimes learn a character from a hand—but the future! I am not so clever."

The dawn was breaking behind the window. On a sudden impulse he went to the bathroom and turned on the bath-water. It flowed boiling hot, gushing into the bath with a swish of steam! How typical of the Mount Vulture Hotel, to have hot bath-water at such an hour and at no other. Excited as a schoolboy he called her. "Melissa, come and soak the weariness out of your bones or I'll never get you back to your home." He thought of ways and means of delivering the five hundred pounds to Darley in such a way as to disguise the source of the gift. He must never know that it came from a rival's epitaph on a dead Copt! "Melissa," he called again, but she was asleep.

He picked her up bodily and carried her into the bathroom. Lying snugly in the warm bath, she woke up, uncurled from sleep like one of those marvellous Japanese paper-flowers which open in water. She paddled the warmth luxuriously over her shallow pectorals and glowed, her thighs beginning to turn pink. Pursewarden sat upon the *bidet* with one hand in the warm water and talked to her as she woke from sleep. "You mustn't take too long," he said, "or Darley will be angry."

"Darley! Bah! He was out with Justine again last night." She sat up and began to soap her breasts, breathing in the luxury of soap and water like someone tasting a rare wine. She pronounced her rival's name with a small cringing loathing that seemed out of character. Pursewarden was surprised. "Such people—the Hosnanis" she said with contempt. "And poor Darley believes in them, in her. She is only using him. He is too good, too simple."

"*Using him?*"

She turned on the shower and revelling in the clouds of steam nodded a small pinched-up face at him. "I know all about *them*."

"What do you know?"

He felt inside himself the sudden stirring of a discomfort so pronounced that it had no name. She was about to overturn his world as one inadvertently knocks over an inkpot or a goldfish-bowl. Smiling a loving smile all the time. Standing there in the clouds of steam like an angel emerging from heaven in some seventeenth-century engraving.

"What do you know?" he repeated.

Melissa examined the cavities in her teeth with a hand-mirror, her body still wet and glistening. "I'll tell you. I used to be the mistress of a very important man, Cohen, very important and very rich." There was something pathetic about such boasting. "He was working with Nessim Hosnani and told me things. He also talked in his sleep. He is dead now. I think he was poisoned because he knew so much. He was helping to take arms into the Middle East, into Palestine, for Nessim Hosnani. Great quantities. He used to say '*Pour faire sauter les Anglais!*' " She ripped out the words vindictively, and all of a sudden, after a moment's thought added: "He used to do this." It was grotesque, her imitation of Cohen bunching up his fingers to kiss them and then waving them in a gesture as he said "*Tout à toi, John Bull!*" Her face crumpled and screwed up into an imitation of the dead man's malice.

"Dress now" said Pursewarden in a small voice. He went into the other room and stood for a moment gazing distractedly at the wall above the bookshelf. It was as if the whole city had crashed down about his ears.

"*That* is why I don't like the Hosnanis" cried Melissa from the bathroom in a new, brassy fishwife's voice. "They secretly hate the British."

"Dress" he called sharply, as if he were speaking to a horse. "And get a move on."

Suddenly chastened she dried herself and tiptoed out of the bathroom saying "I am ready immediately." Pursewarden stood quite still staring at the wall with a fixed, dazed expression. He might have fallen there from some other planet. He was so still that his body might have been a statue cast in some heavy metal. Melissa shot small glances at him as she dressed. "What is it?" she said. He did not answer. He was thinking furiously.

When she was dressed he took her arm and together they walked in silence down the staircase and into the street. The dawn was beginning to break. There were still street-lamps alight and they still cast shadows. She looked at his face from time to time, but it was expressionless. Punctually as they approached each light their shadows lengthened, grew narrower and more contorted, only to disappear into the half-light before renewing their shape. Pursewarden walked slowly, with a tired, deliberate trudge, still holding her arm. In each of these elongated capering shadows he saw now quite clearly the silhouette of the defeated Maskelyne.

At the corner by the square he stopped and with the same abstracted expression on his face said: "*Tiens!* I forgot. Here is the thousand I promised you."

He kissed her upon her cheek and turned back towards the hotel without a word.

o   o   o   o   o

IX

Mountolive was away on an official tour of the cotton-ginning plants in the Delta when the news was phoned through to him by Telford. Between incredulity and shock, he could hardly believe his ears. Telford spoke self-importantly in the curious slushy voice which his ill-fitting dentures conferred upon him; death was a matter of some importance in his trade. But the death of an enemy! He had to work hard to keep his tone sombre, grave, sympathetic, to keep the self-congratulation out of it. He spoke like a county coroner. "I thought you'd like to know, sir, so I took the liberty of interrupting your visit. Nimrod Pasha phoned me in the middle of the night and I went along. The police had already sealed up the place for the Parquet inquiry; Dr. Balthazar was there. I had a look around while he issued the certificate of death. I was allowed to bring away a lot of personal papers belonging to the . . . the deceased. Nothing of much interest. Manuscript of a novel. The whole business came as a complete surprise. He had been drinking very heavily—as usual, I'm afraid. Yes."

"But . . ." said Mountolive feebly, the rage and incredulity mixing in his mind like oil and water. "What on earth. . . ." His legs felt weak. He drew up a chair and sat down at the telephone crying peevishly: "Yes, yes, Telford—go on. Tell me what you can."

Telford cleared his throat, aware of the interest his news was creating, and tried to marshal the facts in his fuddled brain. "Well, sir, we have traced his movements. He came up here, very unshaven and haggard (Errol tells me) and asked for you. But you had just left. Your secretary says that he sat down at your desk and wrote something—it took him some time—

which he said was to be delivered to you personally. He insisted on her franking it 'Secret' and sealing it up with wax. It is in your safe now. Then he appears to have gone off on a . . . well, a binge. He spent all day at a small tavern on the sea-shore near Montaza which he often visited. It's just a shack down by the sea—a few timbers with a palm-leaf roof, run by a Greek. He spent the whole day there writing and drinking. He drank quite a lot of *zibib* according to the proprietor. He had a table set right down by the sea-shore in the sand. It was windy and the man suggested he would be better off in the shelter. But no. He sat there by the sea. In the late afternoon he ate a sandwich and took a tram back to town. He called on me.''

''Good: well.''

Telford hesitated and gasped. ''He came to the office. I must say that although unshaven he seemed in very good spirits. He made a few jokes. But he asked me for a cyanide tablet—you know the kind. I won't say any more. This line isn't really secure. You will understand, sir.''

''Yes, yes,'' cried Mountolive. ''Go on, man.''

Reassured Telford continued breathlessly: ''He said he wanted to poison a sick dog. It seemed reasonable enough, so I gave him one. That is probably what he used according to Dr. Balthazar. I hope you don't feel, sir, that I was in any way. . . .''

Mountolive felt nothing except a mounting indignation that anyone in his mission should confer such annoyance by a public act so flagrant! No, this was silly. ''It is stupid,'' he whispered to himself. But he could not help feeling that Pursewarden had been guilty of something. Damn it, it was inconsiderate and underbred—as well as being mysterious. Kenilworth's face floated before him for a moment. He joggled the receiver to get a clear contact, and shouted: ''But what does it all mean?''

''I don't know,'' said Telford, helplessly. ''It's rather mysterious.''

A pale Mountolive turned and made some muttered apologies to the little group of pashas who stood about the telephone in that dreary outhouse. Immediately they spread self-deprecating hands like a flock of doves taking flight. There was no inconvenience. An Ambassador was expected to be entrained in great events. They could wait.

"Telford," said Mountolive, sharply and angrily.

"Yes, sir."

"Tell me what else you know."

Telford cleared his throat and went on in his slushy voice:

"Well, there isn't anything of exceptional importance from my point of view. The last person to see him alive was that man Darley, the school-teacher. You probably don't know him, sir. Well, he met him on the way back to the hotel. He invited Darley in for a drink and they stayed talking for some considerable time and drinking gin. In the Hotel. The deceased said nothing of any special interest—and certainly nothing to suggest that he was planning to take his own life. On the contrary, he said he was going to take the night-train to Gaza for a holiday. He showed Darley the proofs of his latest novel, all wrapped up and addressed, and a mackintosh full of things he might need for the journey—pyjamas, toothpaste. What made him change his mind? I don't know, sir, but the answer may be in your safe. That is why I rang you."

"I see," said Mountolive. It was strange, but already he was beginning to get used to the idea of Pursewarden's disappearance from the scene. The shock was abating, diminishing: only the mystery remained. Telford still spluttered on the line. "Yes," he said, recovering mastery of himself. "Yes."

It was only a matter of moments before Mountolive recovered his demure official pose and reoriented himself to take a benign interest in the mills and their thumping machinery. He worked hard not to seem too abstracted and to seem suitably impressed by what was shown to him. He tried too to analyse the absurdity of his anger against Pursewarden having committed an act which seemed . . . a gross solecism! How absurd. Yet, as an act, it was somehow typical because so in-

182

considerate: perhaps he should have anticipated it? Profound depression alternated with his feelings of anger.

He motored back in the afternoon, full of an urgent expectancy, an unease. It was almost as if he were going to take Pursewarden to task, demand an explanation of him, administer a well-earned reproof. He arrived in a splendid evening's light to find that the Chancery was just closing, though the industrious Errol was still busy upon State papers in his office. Everyone down to the cipher clerks seemed to be afflicted by the air of gravid depression which sudden death always confers upon the uncomfortably living. He deliberately forced himself to walk slowly, talk slowly, not to hurry. Haste, like emotion, was always deplorable because it suggested that impulse or feeling was master where only reason should rule. His secretary had already left but he obtained the keys to his safe from Archives and sedately walked up the two short flights to his office. Heartbeats are mercifully inaudible to anyone but oneself.

The dead man's "effects" (the poetry of causality could not be better expressed than by the word) were stacked on his desk, looking curiously disembodied. A bundle of papers and manuscript, a parcel addressed to a publisher, a mackintosh and various odds and ends conscripted by the painstaking Telford in the interests of truth (though they had little beauty for Mountolive). He got a tremendous start when he saw Pursewarden's bloodless features staring up at him from his blotter —a death-mask in plaster of Paris with a note from Balthazar saying "I took the liberty of making an impression of the face after death. I trust this will seem sensible." Pursewarden's face! From some angles death can look like a fit of the sulks. Mountolive touched the effigy with reluctance, superstitiously, moving it this way and that. His flesh crept with a small sense of loathing; he realized suddenly that he was afraid of death.

Then to the safe with its envelope whose clumsy seals he cracked with a trembling thumb as he sat at his desk. Here at

183

least he should fine some sort of rational exegesis for this gross default of good manners! He drew a deep breath.

My dear David,

I have torn up half a dozen other attempts to explain this in detail. I found I was only making literature. There is quite enough about. My decision has to do with life. Paradox! I am terribly sorry, old man.

Quite by accident, in an unexpected quarter, I stumbled upon something which told me that Maskelyne's theories about Nessim were right, mine wrong. I do not give you my sources, and will not. But I now realize that Nessim is smuggling arms into Palestine and has been for some time. He is obviously the unknown source, deeply implicated in the operations which were described in Paper Seven—you will remember. (Secret Mandate File 341. Intelligence.)

But I simply am not equal to facing the simpler moral implications raised by this discovery. I know what has to be done about it. But the man happens to be my friend. Therefore . . . a *quietus*. (This will solve other deeper problems too.) Ach! what a boring world we have created around us. The slime of plot and counter-plot. I have just recognized that it is not my world at all. (I can hear you swearing as you read.)

I feel in a way a cad to shelve my own responsibilities like this, and yet, in truth, I know that they are not really mine, never have been mine. *But they are yours!* And jolly bitter you will find them. But . . . you are of the career . . . and you must act where I cannot bring myself to!

I know I am wanting in a sense of duty, but I have let Nessim know obliquely that his game has been spotted and the information passed on. Of course, in this vague form you could also be right in suppressing it altogether, forgetting it. I don't envy you your temptations. Mine, however, not to reason why. I'm tired, my dear chap; sick unto death, as the living say.

And so . . .

Will you give my sister my love and say that my thoughts were with her? Thank you.

Affectionately yours,

L. P.

Mountolive was aghast. He felt himself turning pale as he read. Then he sat for a long time staring at the expression on the face of the death-mask—the characteristic air of solitary impertinence which Pursewarden's profile always wore in repose; and still obstinately struggling with the absurd sense of diplomatic outrage which played about his mind, flickering like stabs of sheet-lightning.

"It is folly!" he cried aloud with vexation, as he banged the desk with the flat of his hand. "Utter folly! Nobody kills himself for an official reason!" He cursed the stupidity of the words as he uttered them. For the first time complete confusion overtook his mind.

In order to calm it he forced himself to read Telford's typed report slowly and carefully, spelling out the words to himself with moving lips, as if it were an exercise. It was an account of Pursewarden's movements during the twenty-four hours before his death with depositions by the various people who had seen him. Some of the reports were interesting, notably that of Balthazar who had seen him during the morning in the Café Al Aktar where Pursewarden was drinking *arak* and eating a *croissant*. He had apparently received a letter from his sister that morning and was reading it with an air of grave preoccupation. He put it in his pocket abruptly when Balthazar arrived. He was extremely unshaven and haggard. There seemed little enough of interest in the conversation which ensued save for one remark (probably a jest?) which stayed in Balthazar's memory. Pursewarden had been dancing with Melissa the evening before and said something about her being a desirable person to marry. ("This must have been a joke" added Balthazar.) He also said

that he had started another book "all about Love". Mountolive sighed as he slowly ran his eye down the typed page.
Love! Then came an odd thing. He had bought a printed Will
form and filled it in, making his sister his literary executor, and
bequeathing five hundred pounds to the schoolteacher Darley
and his mistress. This, for some reason, he had antedated by a
couple of months—perhaps he forgot the date? He had asked
two cipher clerks to witness it.

The letter from his sister was there also, but Telford had
tactfully put it into a separate envelope and sealed it. Mountolive read it, shaking his bewildered head, and then thrust it
into his pocket shamefacedly. He licked his lips and frowned
heavily at the wall. Liza!

Errol put his head timidly round the door and was shocked to
surprise tears upon the cheek of his Chief. He ducked back
tactfully and retreated hastily to his office, deeply shaken by a
sense of diplomatic inappropriateness somewhat similar to the
feelings which Mountolive himself had encountered when Telford telephoned him. Errol sat at his desk with attentive nervousness thinking: "A good diplomat should never show feeling." Then he lit a cigarette with sombre deliberation. For the
first time he realized that his Ambassador had feet of clay.
This increased his sense of self-respect somewhat. Mountolive
was, after all, only a man. . . . Nevertheless, the experience had
been disorienting.

Upstairs Mountolive too had lighted a cigarette in order to
calm his nerves. The accent of his apprehension was slowly
transferring itself from the bare *act* of Pursewarden (this incon-
venient plunge into anonymity)—was transferring itself to the
central meaning of the act—to the tidings it brought with it.
Nessim! And here he felt his own soul shrink and contract and
a deeper, more inarticulate anger beset him. He had trusted
Nessim! ("Why?" said the inner voice. "There was no need to
do so.") And then, by this wicked somersault, Pursewarden
had, in effect, transferred the whole weight of the moral prob-

186

lem to Mountolive's own shoulders. He had started up the hornets' nest: the old conflict between duty, reason and personal affection which every political man knows is his cross, the central weakness of his life! What a swine, he thought (almost admiringly), Pursewarden had been to transfer it all so easily— the enticing *ease* of such a decision: withdrawal! He added sadly: "I trusted Nessim because of Leila!" Vexation upon vexation. He smoked and stared now, seeing in the dead white plaster face (which the loving hands of Clea had printed from Balthazar's clumsy negative) the warm living face of Leila's son: the dark abstract features from a Ravenna fresco! The face of his friend. And then, his very thoughts uttered themselves in whispers: "Perhaps after all Leila is at the bottom of everything."

("Diplomats have no real friends," Grishkin had said bitterly, trying to wound him, to rouse him. "They use everyone." He had used, she was implying, her body and her beauty: and now that she was pregnant. . . .)

He exhaled slowly and deeply, invigorated by the nicotine-laden oxygen which gave his nerves time to settle, his brain time to clear. As the mist lifted he discerned something like a new landscape opening before him; for here was something which could not help but alter all the dispositions of chance and friendship, alter every date on the affectionate calendar his mind had compiled about his stay in Egypt: the tennis and swimming and riding. Even these simple motions of joining with the ordinary world of social habit and pleasure, of relieving the *taedium vitae* of his isolation, were all infected by the new knowledge. Moreover, what was to be done with the information which Pursewarden had so unceremoniously thrust into his lap? It must of course be reported. Here he was able to pause. *Must* it be reported? The data in the letter lacked any shred of supporting evidence—except perhaps the overwhelming evidence of a death which. . . . He lit a cigarette and whispered the words: "While the balance of his mind was disturbed." That at least was worth a grim smile! After all, the suicide of a political officer was not such an uncommon event; there had been that youth Greaves, in love with a cabaret-girl in Russia. . . . Somehow he still felt aggrieved at so malicious a betrayal of his friendship for the writer.

Very well. Suppose he simply burnt the letter, disposing with the weight of moral onus it bore? It could be done quite simply, in his own grate, with the aid of a safety-match. He could continue to behave as if no such revelation had ever been made—except for the fact that Nessim knew it had! No, he was trapped.

And here his sense of duty, like ill-fitting shoes, began to pinch him at every step. He thought of Justine and Nessim dancing together, silently, blindly, their dark faces turned away from each other, eyes half-closed. They had attained a new dimension in his view of them already—the unsentimental projection of figures in a primitive fresco. Presumably they also struggled with a sense of duty and responsibility—to whom? "To themselves, perhaps" he whispered sadly, shaking his head. He would never be able to meet Nessim eye to eye again.

It suddenly dawned on him. Up to now their personal relationship had been forced from any prejudicial cast by Nessim's tact—*and Pursewarden's existence*. The writer, in supplying the official link, had freed them in the personal lives. Never had the two men been forced to discuss anything remotely connected with official matters. Now they could not meet upon this happy ground. In this context too Pursewarden had traduced his freedom. As for Leila, perhaps here lay the key to her enigmatic silence, her inability to meet him face to face.

Sighing, he rang for Errol. "You'd better glance at this" he said. His Head of Chancery sat himself down and began to read the document greedily. He nodded slowly from time to time. Mountolive cleared his throat: "It seems pretty incoherent to me," he said, despising himself for so trying to cast a doubt upon the clear words, to influence Errol in a judgement which, in his own secret mind, he had already made. Errol read it twice slowly, and handed it back across the desk. "It seems pretty extraordinary" he said tentatively, respectfully. It was not his place to offer evaluations of the message. They must by rights come from his Chief. "It all seems a bit out of proportion" he added helpfully, feeling his way.

Mountolive said sombrely: "I'm afraid it is typical of Purse-warden. It makes me sorry that I never took up your original recommendations about him. I was wrong, it seems, and you were right about his suitability."

Errol's eye glinted with modest triumph. He said nothing, however, as he stared at Mountolive. "Of course," said the latter, "as you well know, Hosnani has been suspect for some time."

"I know, sir."

"But there is no *evidence* here to support what he says." He tapped the letter irritably twice. Errol sat back and breathed through his nose. "I don't know," he said vaguely. "It sounds pretty conclusive to me."

"I don't think" said Mountolive, "it would support a paper. Of course we'll report it to London as it stands. But I'm inclined not to give it to the Parquet to help them with their inquest. What do you say?"

Errol cradled his knees. A slow smile of cunning crept around his mouth. "It might be the best way of getting it to the Egyptians," he said softly, "and they might choose to act on it. Of course, it would obviate the diplomatic pressure we might have to bring if . . . later on, the whole thing came out in a more concrete form. I know Hosnani was a friend of yours, sir."

Mountolive felt himself colouring slightly. "In matters of business, a diplomat has no friends" he said stiffly, feeling that he spoke in the very accents of Pontius Pilate.

"Quite, sir." Errol gazed at him admiringly.

"Once Hosnani's guilt is established we shall have to act. But without supporting evidence we should find ourselves in a

189

weak position. With Memlik Pasha—you know he isn't very pro-British . . . I'm thinking. . . ."

"Yes, sir?"

Mountolive waited, drinking the air like a wild animal, scenting that Errol was beginning to approve his judgement. They sat silently in the dusk for a while, thinking. Then with a histrionic snap, the Ambassador switched on the desk-light and said decisively: "If you agree, we'll keep this out of Egyptian hands until we are better documented. London must have it. Classified of course. But not private persons, even next-of-kin. By the way, are you capable of undertaking the next-of-kin correspondence? I leave it to you to make up something." He felt a pang as he saw Liza Pursewarden's face rise before him.

"Yes. I have his file here. There is only a sister at the Imperial Institute for the Blind, I think, apart from his wife." Errol fussily consulted a green folder, but Mountolive said "Yes, yes. I know her." Errol stood up.

Mountolive added: "And I think in all fairness we should copy to Maskelyne in Jerusalem, don't you?"

"Most certainly, sir."

"And for the moment keep our own counsel?"

"Yes, sir."

"Thank you very much" said Mountolive with unusual warmth. He felt all of a sudden very old and frail. Indeed he felt so weak that he doubted if his limbs could carry him downstairs to the Residence. "That is all for the present." Errol took his leave, closing the door behind him with the gravity of a mute.

Mountolive telephoned to the buttery and ordered himself a glass of beef-tea and biscuits. He ate and drank ravenously, staring the while at the white mask and the manuscript of a novel. He felt both a deep disgust and a sense of enormous bereavement—he could not tell which lay uppermost. Unwittingly, too, Pursewarden had, he reflected, separated him forever from Leila. Yes, that also, and perhaps forever.

That night, however, he made his witty prepared speech (written by Errol) to the Alexandrian Chamber of Commerce, delighting the assembled bankers by his fluent French. The clapping swelled and expanded in the august banquet room of the Mohammed Ali Club. Nessim, seated at the opposite end of the long table, undertook the response with gravity and a calm address. Once or twice during the dinner Mountolive felt the dark eyes of his friend seeking his own, interrogating them, but he evaded them. A chasm now yawned between them which neither would know how to bridge. After dinner, he met Nessim briefly in the hall as he was putting on his coat. He suddenly felt the almost irresistible desire to refer to Purse-warden's death. The subject obtruded itself so starkly, stuck up jaggedly into the air between them. It shamed him as a physical deformity might; as if his handsome smile were disfigured by a missing front tooth. He said nothing and neither did Nessim. Nothing of what was going on beneath the surface showed in the elastic and capable manner of the two tall men who stood smoking by the front door, waiting for the car to arrive. But a new watchful, obdurate knowledge had been born between them. How strange that a few words scribbled on a piece of paper should make them enemies!

Then leaning back in his beflagged car, drawing softly on an excellent cigar, Mountolive felt his innermost soul become as dusty, as airless as an Egyptian tomb. It was strange too that side by side with these deeper preoccupations the shallower should coexist; he was delighted by the extent of his success in captivating the bankers! He had been undeniably brilliant. Discreetly circulated copies of his speech would, he knew, be printed verbatim in to-morrow's papers, illustrated by new photographs of himself. The Corps would be envious as usual. Why had nobody thought of making a public statement about the Gold Standard in this oblique fashion? He tried to keep his mind effervescent, solidly anchored to this level of self-congratulation, but it was useless. The Embassy would soon be moving back to its winter quarters. He had not seen Leila. Would he ever see her again?

Somewhere inside himself a barrier had collapsed, a dam had been broached. He had engaged upon a new conflict with himself which gave a new tautness to his features, a new purposeful rhythm to his walk.

That night he was visited by an excruciating attack of the earache with which he always celebrated his return home. This was the first time he had ever been attacked while he was outside the stockade of his mother's security, and the attack alarmed him. He tried ineffectually to doctor himself with the homely specific she always used, but he heated the salad oil too much by mistake and burnt himself severely in the process. He spent three restless days in bed after this incident, reading detective stories and pausing for long moments to stare at the whitewashed wall. It at least obviated his attendance at Pursewarden's cremation—he would have been sure to meet Nessim there. Among the many messages and presents which began to flow in when the news of his indisposition became known, was a splendid bunch of flowers from Nessim and Justine, wishing him a speedy recovery. As Alexandrians and friends, they could hardly do less!

He pondered deeply upon them during those long sleepless days and nights and for the first time he saw them, in the light of this new knowledge, as enigmas. They were puzzles now, and even their private moral relationship haunted him with a sense of something he had never properly understood, never clearly evaluated. Somehow his friendship for them had prevented him from thinking of them as people who might, like himself, be living on several different levels at once. As conspirators, as lovers—what was the key to the enigma? He could not guess.

But perhaps the clues that he sought lay further back in the past—further than either he or Pursewarden could see from a vantage-point in the present time.

There were many facts about Justine and Nessim which had not come to his knowledge—some of them critical for an understanding of their case. But in order to include them it is necessary once more to retrace our steps briefly to the period immediately before their marriage.

o   o   o   o   o

X

The blue Alexandrian dusk was not yet fully upon them. "But do you . . . how shall one say it? . . . Do you really *care* for her, Nessim? I know of course how you have been haunting her; and she knows what is in your mind."

Clea's golden head against the window remained steady, her gaze was fixed upon the chalk drawing she was doing. It was nearly finished; a few more of those swift, flowing strokes and she could release her subject. Nessim had put on a striped pullover to model for her. He lay upon her uncomfortable little sofa holding a guitar which he could not play, and frowning. "How do you spell love in Alexandria?" he said at last, softly. "That is the question. Sleeplessness, loneliness, *bonheur*, *chagrin* —I do not want to harm or annoy her, Clea. But I feel that somehow, somewhere, she must need me as I need her. Speak, Clea." He knew he was lying. Clea did not.

She shook her head doubtfully, still with her attention on the paper, and then shrugged her shoulders. "Loving you both as I do, who could wish for anything better? And I *have* spoken to her, as you asked me, tried to provoke her, probe her. It seems hopeless." Was this strictly true, she asked herself? She had too great a tendency to believe what people said.

"False pride?" he said sharply.

"She laughs hopelessly and," Clea imitated a gesture of hopelessness, "like that! I think she feels that she has all the clothes stripped off her back in the street by that book *Moeurs*. She thinks herself no longer able to bring anyone peace of mind! Or so she says."

"Who asks for that?"

"She thinks you would. Then of course, there is your social

position. And then she is, after all, a Jew. Put yourself in her place." Clea was silent for a moment. Then she added in the same abstracted tone: "If she needs you at all it is to use your fortune to help her search for the child. And she is too proud to do that. But . . . you have read *Moeurs*. Why repeat myself?"

"I have never read *Moeurs*" he said hotly, "and she knows that I never will. I have told her that. O Clea dear!" He sighed. This was another lie.

Clea paused, smiling, to consider his dark face. Then she continued, rubbing at the corner of the drawing with her thumb as she said: "*Chevalier sans peur*, etc. That is like you, Nessim. But is it wise to idealize us women so? You are a bit of a baby still, for an Alexandrian."

"I don't idealize; I know exactly how sad, mad or bad she is. Who does not? Her past and her present . . . they are known to everyone. It is just that I feel she would match perfectly my own. . . ."

"Your own what?"

"*Aridity*," he said surprisingly, rolling over, smiling and frowning at the same time. "Yes, I sometimes think I shall never be able to fall in love properly until after my mother dies —and she is still comparatively young. Speak, Clea!"

The blonde head shook slowly. Clea took a puff from the cigarette burning in the ashtray beside the easel and bent once more to the work in hand. "Well," said Nessim, "I shall see her myself this evening and make a serious attempt to make her understand."

"You do not say 'make her love'!"

"How could I?"

"If she *cannot* love, it would be dishonourable to pretend."

"I do not know whether I can yet either; we are both *âmes veuves* in a queer way, don't you see?"

"Oh, la, la!" said Clea, doubtfully but still smiling.

"Love may be for a time *incognito* with us," he said, frowning at the wall and setting his face. "But it is there. I must try to make her see.'' He bit his lip. ''Do I really present such an enigma?'' He really meant ''Do I succeed in deluding you?''

''Now you've moved,'' she said reproachfully; and then after a moment went on quietly: ''Yes. It is an enigma. Your passion sounds so *voulue*. A *besoin d'aimer* without a *besoin d'être aimé?* Damn!'' He had moved again. She stopped in vexation and was about to reprove him when she caught sight of the clock on the mantelpiece. ''It's time to go'' she said. ''You must not keep her waiting.''

''Good,'' he said sharply, and rising, stripped off the pull-over and donned his own well-cut coat, groping in the pocket for the keys of the car as he turned. Then, remembering, he brushed his dark hair back swiftly, impatiently, in the mirror, trying suddenly to imagine how he must look to Justine. ''I wish I could say exactly what I mean. Do you not believe in love-contracts for those whose souls aren't yet up to loving? A *tendresse* against an *amour-passion*, Clea? If she had parents I would have bought her from them unhesitatingly. If she had been thirteen she would have had nothing to say or feel, eh?''

''Thirteen!'' said Clea in disgust; she shuddered and pulled his coat down at the back for him. ''Perhaps,'' he went on ironically, ''unhappiness is a *diktat* for me. . . . What do you think?''

''But then you would believe in *passion*. You don't.''

''I do . . . but. . . .''

He gave his charming smile and made a tender hopeless gesture in the air, part resignation, part anger. ''Ah, you are no use,'' he said. ''We are all waiting for an education of sorts.''

''Go,'' said Clea, ''I'm sick of the subject. Kiss me first.''

The two friends embraced and she whispered: ''Good luck'' while Nessim said between his teeth ''I must stop this childish interrogation of you. It is absurd. I must do something decisive about her myself.'' He banged a doubled fist into the palm of his hand, and she was surprised at such unusual vehemence in one so reserved. ''Well,'' she said, with surprise opening her blue eyes, ''this is new!'' They both laughed.

He pressed her elbow and turning ran lightly down the darkening staircase to the street. The great car responded to his feather-deftness of touch on the controls; it bounded crying its klaxon-warnings, down Saad Zaghloul and across the tram-lines to roll down the slope towards the sea. He was talking to himself softly and rapidly in Arabic. In the gaunt lounge of the Cecil Hotel she would perhaps be waiting, gloved hands folded on her handbag, staring out through the windows upon which the sea crawled and sprawled, climbing and subsiding, across the screen of palms in the little municipal square which flapped and creaked like loose sails.

As he turned the corner, a procession was setting out raggedly for the upper town, its brilliant banners pelted now by a small rain mixed with spray from the harbour; everything flapped confusedly. Chanting and the noise of triangles sounded tentatively on the air. With an expression of annoyance he abandoned the car, locked it, and looked anxiously at his watch, ran the last hundred yards to the circular glass doors which would admit him upon the mouldering silence of the great lounge. He entered breathless but very much aware of himself. This siege of Justine had been going on for months now. How would it end—with victory or defeat?

He remembered Clea saying: "Such creatures are not human beings at all, I think. If they live, it is only inasmuch as they represent themselves in human form. But then, anyone possessed by a single ruling passion presents the same picture. For most of us, life is a *hobby*. But she seems like a tense and exhaustive pictorial representation of nature at its most superficial, its most powerful. She is possessed—and the possessed can neither learn nor be taught. It doesn't make her less lovely for all that it is death-propelled; but my dear Nessim—from what angle are you to accept her?"

He did not as yet know; they were sparring still, talking in different languages. This might go on forever, he thought despairingly.

They had met more than once, formally, almost like business partners to discuss the matter of this marriage with the detachment of Alexandrian brokers planning a cotton merger. But this is the way of the city.

With a gesture which he himself thought of as characteristic he had offered her a large sum of money saying: "Lest an inequality of fortune may make your decision difficult, I propose to make you a birthday present which will enable you to think of yourself as a wholly independent person—simply as a woman, Justine. This hateful stuff which creeps into everyone's thoughts in the city, poisoning everything! Let us be free of it before deciding anything."

But this had not answered; or rather had provoked only the insulting, uncomprehending question: "Is it that you really want to sleep with me? You may. O, I would do anything for you, Nessim." This disgusted and angered him. He had lost himself. There seemed no way forward along this line. Then suddenly, after a long moment of thought, he saw the truth like a flashing light. He whispered to himself with surprise: "But that is why I am not understood; I am not being really honest." He recognized that though he might have initially been swayed by his passion, he could think of no way to stake a claim on her attention, except, first, by the gift of money (ostensibly to "free" her but in fact only to try and bind her to him)—and then, as his desperation increased, he realized that there was nothing to be done except to place himself entirely at her mercy. In one sense it was madness—but he could think of no other way to create in her the sense of obligation on which every other tie could be built. In this way a child may sometimes endanger itself in order to canvass a mother's love and attention which it feels is denied to it.

"Look," he said in a new voice, full of new vibrations, and now he had turned very pale. "I want to be frank. I have no interest in *real life*." His lips trembled with his voice. "I am visualizing a relationship far closer in a way than anything passion could invent—a bond of a common belief." She wondered for a moment whether he had some strange new religion, whether this was what was meant. She waited with interest, amused yet disturbed to see how deeply moved he was. "I wish to make you a confidence now which, if betrayed, might mean irreparable harm to myself and my family; and indeed to the cause I am serving. I wish to put myself utterly in your power. Let us suppose we are both dead to love . . . I want to ask you to become part of a dangerous. . . ."

The strange thing was that as he began to talk thus, about what was nearest to his thoughts, she began to *care*, to really notice him as a man for the first time. For the first time he struck a responsive chord in her by a confession which was paradoxically very far from a confession of the heart. To her surprise, to her chagrin and to her delight, she realized that she was not being asked merely to share his bed—but his whole life, the monomania upon which it was built. Normally, it is only the artist who can offer this strange and selfless contract—but it is one which no woman worth the name can ever refuse. He was asking, not for her hand in marriage (here his lies had created the misunderstanding) but for her partnership in allegiance to his ruling *daimon*. It was in the strictest sense, the only meaning he could put upon the word "love". Slowly and quietly he began, passionately collecting his senses now that he had decided to tell her, marshalling his words, husbanding them. "You know, we all know, that our days are numbered since the French and the British have lost control in the Middle East. We, the foreign communities, with all we have built up, are being gradually engulfed by the Arab tide, the Moslem tide. Some of us are trying to work against it; Armenians, Copts, Jews, and Greeks here in Egypt, while others elsewhere are organizing themselves. Much of this work I have undertaken here. . . . To defend ourselves, that is all, defend our lives, defend the right to belong here only. You know this, everyone knows it. But to those who see a little further into history. . . ."

Here he smiled crookedly—an ugly smile with a trace of complacency in it. "Those who see further know this to be but a shadow-play; we will never maintain our place in this world except it be by virtue of a nation strong and civilized enough to dominate the whole area. The day of France and England is over—much as we love them. Who, then, can take their place?" He drew a deep breath and paused, then he squeezed his hands together between his knees, as if he were squeezing out the unuttered thought, slowly, luxuriously from a sponge.

He went on in a whisper: "There is only one nation which can determine the future of everything in the Middle East. Everything—and by a paradox, even the standard of living of the miserable Moslems themselves depends upon it, its power and resources. Have you understood me, Justine? Must I utter its name? Perhaps you are not interested in these things?" He gave her a glittering smile. Their eyes met. They sat staring at each other in the way that only those who are passionately in love can stare. He had never seen her so pale, so alert, with all her intelligence suddenly mobilized in her looks. "Must I say it?" he said, more sharply; and suddenly expelling her breath in a long sigh she shook her head and whispered the single word.

"Palestine."

There was a long silence during which he looked at her with a triumphant exultation. "I was not wrong," he said at last, and she suddenly knew what he meant: that his long-formulated judgement of her had not been at fault. "Yes, Justine, Palestine. If only the Jews can win their freedom, we can all be at ease. It is the only hope for us . . . the dispossessed *foreigners*." He uttered the word with a slight twist of bitterness. They both slowly lit cigarettes now with shaking fingers and blew the smoke out towards each other, enwrapped by a new atmosphere of peace, of understanding. "The whole of our fortune has gone into the struggle which is about to break out there" he said under his breath. "On that depends everything. Here, of course, we are doing other things which I will explain to you. The British and French help us, they see no harm. I am sorry for them. Their condition is pitiable because they have no longer the will to fight or even to think." His contempt was ferocious, yet full of controlled pity. "But with the Jews—there is something *young* there: the cockpit of Europe in these rotten marshes of a dying race." He paused and suddenly said in a sharp, twanging tone: "Justine." Slowly and thoughtfully, at the same moment they put out their hands to each other. Their cold fingers locked and squeezed hard. On the faces of both there was expressed an exultant determination of purpose, almost of terror!

His image had suddenly been metamorphosed. It was now lit with a new, a rather terrifying grandeur. As she smoked and watched him, she saw someone different in his place—an adventurer, a corsair, dealing with the lives and deaths of men; his power too, the power of his money, gave a sort of tragic back-cloth to the design. She realized now that he was not seeing her—the Justine thrown back by polished mirrors, or engraved in expensive clothes and fards—but something even closer than the chamber-mate of a passional life.

This was a Faustian compact he was offering her. There was something more surprising: for the first time she felt desire stir within her, in the loins of that discarded, pre-empted body which she regarded only as a pleasure-seeker, a mirror-reference to reality. There came over her an unexpected lust to sleep with him—no, with his plans, his dreams, his obsessions, his money, his death! It was as if she had only now understood the nature of the love he was offering her; it was his all, his only treasure, this pitiable political design so long and so tormentingly matured in his heart, that it had forced out every other impulse or wish. She felt suddenly as if her feelings had become caught up in some great cobweb, imprisoned by laws which lay beneath the level of her conscious will, her desires, the self-destructive flux and reflux of her human personality. Their

fingers were still locked, like a chord in music, drawing nour-
ishment from the strength transmitted by their bodies. Just to
hear him say: "Now my life is in your keeping," set her brain
on fire, and her heart began to beat heavily in her breasts. "I
must go now" she said, with a new terror—one that she had
never experienced before—"I really must go." She felt unsteady and faint, touched as she was by the coaxings of a power
stronger than any physical attraction could be. "Thank God"
he said under his breath, and again "O Thank God." Everything was decided at last.

But his own relief was mixed with terror. How had he managed at last to turn the key in the lock? By sacrificing to the
truth, by putting himself at her mercy. His unwisdom had
been the only course left open. He had been forced to take it.
Subconsciously he knew too, that oriental woman is not a sensualist in the European sense; there is nothing mawkish in her
constitution. Her true obsessions are power, politics and possessions—however much she might deny it. The sex ticks on in
the mind, but its motions are warmed by the kinetic brutali-
ties of money. In this response to a common field of action,
Justine was truer to herself than she had ever been, responding
as a flower responds to light. And it was now, while they
talked quietly and coldly, their heads bent towards each other
like flowers, that she could at last say, magnificently: "Ah,
Nessim, I never suspected that I should agree. How did you
know that I only exist for those who believe in me?"

He stared at her, thrilled and a little terrified, recognizing in
her the perfect submissiveness of the oriental spirit—the
absolute feminine submissiveness which is one of the strongest
forces in the world.

They went out to the car together and Justine suddenly felt
very weak, as if she had been carried far out of her depth and
abandoned in mid-ocean. "I don't know what more to say."

"Nothing. You must start living." The paradoxes of true
love are endless. She felt as if she had received a smack across

the face. She went into the nearest coffee-shop and ordered a cup of hot chocolate. She drank it with trembling hands. Then she combed her hair and made up her face. She knew her beauty was only an advertisement and kept it fresh with disdain.

It was some hours later, when he was sitting at his desk, that Nessim, after a long moment of thought, picked up the polished telephone and dialled Capodistria's number. "Da Capo," he said quietly, "you remember my plans for marrying Justine? All is well. We have a new ally. I want you to be the first to announce it to the committee. I think now they will show no more reservation about my not being a Jew—since I am to be married to one. What do you say?" He listened with impatience to the ironical congratulations of his friend. "It is impertinent," he said at last, coldly, "to imagine that I am not motivated by feelings as well as by designs. As an old friend I must warn you not to take that tone with me. My private life, my private feelings, are my own. If they happen to square with other considerations, so much the better. But do not do me the injustice of thinking me without honour. I love her." He felt quite sick as he said the words: sick with a sudden self-loathing. Yet the word was utterly exact—love!

Now he replaced the receiver slowly, as if it weighed a ton, and sat staring at his own reflection in the polished desk. He was telling himself: "It is all that I *am not* as a man which she thinks she can love. Had I no such plans to offer her, I might have pleaded with her for a century. What is the meaning of this little four-letter word we shake out of our minds like poker-dice—love?" His self-contempt almost choked him.

That night she arrived unexpectedly at the great house just as the clocks were chiming eleven. He was still up and dressed and sitting by the fire, sorting his papers. "You did not telephone?" he cried with delight, with surprise. "How wonderful!" She stood in grave silence at the door until the servant who had showed her in retired. Then she took a step forward letting her fur cape slide from her shoulders. They embraced passionately, silently. Then, turning her regard upon him in the firelight, that look at once terrified and exultant, she said: "Now at last I know you, Nessim Hosnani." Love is every sort of conspiracy. The power of riches and intrigue stirred within her now, the deputies of passion. Her face wore the brilliant look of innocence which comes only with conversion to a religious way of life! "I have come for your directions, for further instructions," she said. Nessim was transfigured. He ran upstairs to his little safe and brought down the great folders of correspondence—as if to show that he was honest, that his words could be verified there and then, on the spot. He was now revealing to her something which neither his mother nor his brother knew—the extent of his complicity in the Palestine conspiracy. They crouched down before the fire talking until nearly dawn.

"You will see from all this my immediate worries. You can deal with them. First the doubts and hesitations of the Jewish Committee. I want *you* to talk to them. They think that there is something questionable about a Copt supporting them while the local Jews are staying clear, afraid of losing their good name with the Egyptians. We must convince them, Justine. It will take more than a year at least to complete the arms build-up. Then, all this must be kept from our well-wishers here, the British and the French. I know they are busy trying to find out about me, my underground activities. As yet, I think they don't suspect. But among them all there are two people who particularly concern us. Darley's liaison with the little Melissa is one *point névralgique*; as I told you she was the mistress of old Cohen who died this year. He was our chief agent for arms shipments, and knew all about us. Did he tell her anything? I don't know. Another person even more equivocal is Pursewarden; he clearly belongs to the political agency of the Embassy. We are great friends and all that but . . . I am not sure what he suspects. We must if necessary reassure him, try and sell him community movement among the Copts! What else does he, might he, know or fear? You can help me here. Oh, Justine, I knew you would understand!" Her dark intent features, so composed in the firelight, were full of a new clarity, a new power. She nodded. In her hoarse voice she said "Thank you, Nessim Hosnani. I see now what I have to do."

Afterwards they locked the tall doors, put away the papers, and in the dead of night lay down before the fire in each other's arms, to make love with the passionate detachment of succubi. Savage and exultant as their kisses were, they were but the lucid illustrations of their human case. They had discovered each other's inmost weakness, the true site of love. And now at last there were no reserves and no inhibitions in Justine's mind, and what may seem wantonness in other terms was really the powerful coefficient of a fully realized abandonment to love itself—a form of true identity she had never shared with anyone else! The secret they shared made her free to act. And Nessim, foundering in her arms with his curiously soft—almost virginal—femininity, felt shaken and banged by her embrace like a rag doll. The nibbling of her lips reminded him of the white Arab mare he had owned as a child; confused memories flew up like flocks of coloured birds. He felt exhausted, on the point of tears, and yet irradiated by a tremendous gratitude and tenderness. In these magnificent kisses all his loneliness was expurgated. He had found someone to share his secret—a woman after his own special heart. Paradox within paradox!

As for her, it was as if she had rifled the treasury of his spiritual power symbolized so queerly in the terms of his possessions; the cold steel of rifles, the cold nipples of bombs and grenades which had been born from tungsten, gum arabic, jute, shipping, opals, herbs, silks and trees.

He felt her on top of him, and in the plunge of her loins he felt the desire to add to him—to fecundate his actions; and to fructify through these fatality-bearing instruments of his power, to give life to those death-burdening struggles of a truly barren woman. Her face was expressionless as a mask of Siva. It was neither ugly nor beautiful, but naked as power itself. It seemed coeval (this love) with the Faustian love of saints who had mastered the chilly art of seminal stoppage in order the more clearly to recognize themselves—for its blue fires conveyed not heat but cold to the body. But will and mind burned up as if they had been dipped in quicklime. It was a true sensuality with nothing of the civilized poisons about it to make it anodyne, palatable to a human society constructed upon a romantic idea of truth. Was it the less love for that? Paracelsus had described such relationships among the Caballi. In all this one may see the austere mindless primeval face of Aphrodite.

And all the time he was thinking to himself: "When all this is over, when I have found her lost child—by that time we shall be so close that there will never be any question of leaving me." The passion of their embraces came from *complicity*, from something deeper, more wicked, than the wayward temptings of the flesh or the mind. He had conquered her in offering her a married life which was both a pretence and yet at the same time informed by a purpose which might lead them both to *death!* This was all that sex could mean to her now! How thrilling, sexually thrilling, was the expectation of their death!

He drove her home in the first faint trembling light of dawn; waited to hear the lift climb slowly, painfully, to the third floor and return again. It stopped with a slight bounce before him and the light went out with a click. The personage had gone, but her perfume remained.

It was a perfume called *"Jamais de la Vie"*.

o   o   o   o   o

Throughout that summer and autumn the conspirators had worked together to mount entertainments of a scale seldom seen in the city. The big house was seldom quiet now for hours together. It was perpetually alive to the cool fern-like patterns of a quartet, or to the foundering plunge of saxophones crying to the night like cuckolds. The once cavernous and deserted kitchens were now full of the echoing bustle of servants preparing for a new feast or clearing up after one which had ended. In the city it was said that Nessim had deliberately set himself to launch Justine in society—as if the provincial splendours of Alexandria held any promise or charm to one who had become at heart a European, as he had. No, these planned assaults upon the society of the second capital were both exploratory and diversionary. They offered a backcloth against which the conspirators could move with a freedom necessary to their work. They worked indefatigably—and only when the pressure of things became too great stole short holidays in the little summer lodge which Nessim had christened "Justine's Summer Palace"; here they could read and write and bathe, and enjoy those friends who were closest to them—Clea and Amaril and Balthazar.

But always after these long evenings spent in a wilderness of conversation, a forest of plates and wine-bottles, they locked the doors, shot the great bolts themselves and turned sighing back to the staircase, leaving the sleepy domestics to begin the task of clearing up the *débris*; for the house must be completely set to rights by morning; they walked slowly arm in arm, pausing to kick off their shoes on the first landing and to smile at each other in the great mirror. Then, to quieten their minds, they would take a slow turn up and down the picture-gallery, with its splendid collection of Impressionists, talking upon neutral topics while Nessim's greedy eyes explored the great canvases slowly, mute testimony to the validity of private worlds and secret wishes.

So at last they came to those warm and beautifully furnished private bedrooms, adjoining one another, on the cool north side of the house. It was always the same; while Nessim lay down on the bed fully dressed, Justine lit the spirit-lamp to prepare the infusion of valerian which he always took to soothe his nerves before he slept. Here too she would set out the small card-table by the bed, and together they played a hand or two of cribbage or picquet as they talked, obsessively talked about the affairs which occupied their waking minds. At such times their dark, passionate faces glowed in the soft light with a sort of holiness conferred by secrecy, by the appetites of a shared will, by desires joined at the waist. To-night it was the same. As she dealt the first hand, the telephone by the bed rang. Nessim picked up the receiver, listened for a second, and then passed it to her without a word. Smiling, she raised her eyebrows in interrogation and her husband nodded. "Hullo," the hoarse voice counterfeited sleepiness, as if she had been woken from her bed. "Yes, my darling. Of course. No, I was awake. Yes, I am alone." Nessim quietly and methodically fanned out his hand and studied the cards without visible expression. The conversation ran stutteringly on and then the caller said good-night and rang off. Sighing, Justine replaced the receiver, and then made a slow gesture, as of someone removing soiled gloves, or of someone disembarrassing herself of a skein of wool. "It was poor Darley," she said, picking up her cards. Nessim raised his eyes for a moment, put down a card, and uttered a bid. As the game began, she started to talk again softly, as if to herself. "He is absolutely fascinated by the diaries. Remember? I used to copy out all Arnauti's notes for *Moeurs* in my own hand-writing when he broke his wrist. We had them bound up. All the parts which he did not use in the end. I have given them to

Darley as my diary." She depressed her cheeks in a sad smile. "He accepts them as mine, and says, not unnaturally, that I have a masculine mind! He also says my French is not very good—that would please Arnauti, wouldn't it?"

"I am sorry for him" said Nessim quietly, tenderly. "He is so good. One day I will be quite honest, explain everything to him."

"But I don't see your concern for the little Melissa" said Justine, again as if engaged in a private debate rather than a conversation. "I have tried to sound him in every way. He knows nothing. I am convinced that she knows nothing. Just because she was Cohen's mistress . . . I don't know."

Nessim laid down his cards and said: "I cannot get rid of a feeling she knows something. Cohen was a boastful and silly man and he certainly knew all that there was to know."

"But why should he tell her?"

"It is simply that after his death, whenever I ran across her, she would look at me in a new way—as if *in the light* of something she had heard about me, a piece of new knowledge. It's hard to describe."

They played in silence until the kettle began to whine. Then Justine put down her cards, went across to prepare the valerian. As he sipped it she went into the other room to divest herself of her jewellery. Sipping the cup, and staring reflectively at the wall, Nessim heard the small snap of her ear-rings as she plucked them off, and the small noise of the sleeping-tablets falling into a glass. She came back and sat down at the card-table.

"Then if you feared her, why did you not get her removed somehow?" He looked startled and she added: "I don't mean to harm her, but to get her sent away."

Nessim smiled. "I thought I would, but then when Darley fell in love with her, I . . . had a sympathy for him."

"There is no room for such ideas," she said curtly, and he nodded, almost humbly. "I know," he said. Justine dealt the cards once more, and once more they consulted their hands in silence.

"I am working now to get her sent away—by Darley himself. Amaril says that she is really seriously ill and has already recommended that she go to Jerusalem for special treatment. I have offered Darley the money. He is in a pitiable state of confusion. Very English. He is a good person, Nessim, though now he is very much afraid of you and invents all sorts of bogies with which to frighten himself. He makes me feel sad, he is so helpless."

"I know."

"But Melissa must go. I have told him so."

"Good." Then, in a totally different voice, raising his dark eyes to hers, he said: "What about Pursewarden?"

The question hung between them in the still air of the room, quivering like a compass needle. Then he slung his eyes once more to the cards in his hand. Justine's face took on a new expression, both bitter and haggard. She lit a cigarette carefully and said: "As I told you, he is someone quite out of the ordinary—*c'est un personnage*. It would be quite impossible to get a secret out of him. It's hard to describe."

She stared at him for a long time, studying those dark averted features with an expression of abstraction. "What I am trying to say is this: about the difference between them. Darley is so sentimental and so loyal to me that he constitutes no danger at all. Even if he came into the possession of information which might harm us, he would not use it, he would bury it. Not Pursewarden!" Now her eyes glittered. "He is somehow cold and clever and self-centred. Completely amoral— like an Egyptian! He would not deeply care if we died tomorrow. I simply cannot reach him. But potentially he is an enemy worth reckoning with."

He raised his eyes to her and they sat for a long moment staring sightlessly into each other's mind. His eyes were now full of a burning passionate sweetness like the eyes of some

210

strange noble bird of prey. He moistened his lips with his tongue but did not speak. He had been on the point of blurting out the words: "I am terrified that you may be falling in love with him." But a queer feeling of pudicity restrained him.

"Nessim."

"Yes."

She stubbed out her cigarette now and, deep in thought, rose to walk up and down the room, her hands hugged in her arm-pits. As always when she was thinking deeply, she moved in a strange, almost awkward way—a prowling walk which reminded him of some predatory animal. His eye had become vague now, and lustreless. He picked up the cards mechanically and shuffled them once, twice. Then he put them down and raised his palms to his burning cheeks.

At once she was at his side with her warm hand upon his brow. "You have a temperature again."

"I don't think so," he said rapidly, mechanically.

"Let me take it."

"No."

She sat down opposite him, leaning forward, and stared once more into his eyes. "Nessim, what has been happening? Your health . . . these temperatures, and you don't sleep?" He smiled wearily and pressed the back of her hand to his hot cheek.

"It is nothing," he said. "Just strain now that everything is coming to an end. Also having to tell Leila the whole truth. It has alarmed her to understand the full extent of our plans. Also it has made her relationship with Mountolive much harder. I think that is the reason she refused to see him at the Carnival meeting, remember? I had told her everything that morning. Never mind. Another six months and the whole build-up is complete. The rest is up to them. But of course Leila does not like the idea of going away. I knew she wouldn't. And then, I have other serious problems."

"What problems?"

But he shook his head, and getting up started to undress.

Once in bed he finished his valerian and lay, hands and feet folded like the effigy of a Crusader. Justine switched off the light and stood in the doorway in silence. At last she said: "Nessim. I am afraid that something is happening to you which I don't understand. These days . . . are you ill? Please speak to me!"

There was a long silence. Then she said: "How is all this going to turn out?"

He raised himself slightly on the pillows and stared at her. "By the autumn, when everything is ready, we shall have to take up new dispositions. It may mean a separation of perhaps a year, Justine. I want you to go there and stay there while it all happens. Leila must go to the farm in Kenya. There will certainly be sharp reactions here which I must stay to face."

"You talk in your sleep."

"I am exhausted" he cried shortly, angrily.

Justine stood still, motionless in silhouette, in the lighted doorway. "What about the others?" she asked softly, and once more he raised himself on the pillows to answer peevishly. "The only one who concerns us at the moment is Da Capo. He must be apparently killed, or must disappear, for he is very much compromised. I have not worked out the details properly. He wants me to claim his insurance, anyway, as he is completely in debt, ruined, so his disappearance would fit in. We will speak of this later. It should be comparatively easy to arrange."

She turned thoughtfully back into the lighted room and began to prepare for sleep. She could hear Nessim sighing and turning restlessly in the next room. In the great mirror she studied her own sorrowful, haunted face, stripping it of its colours, and combing her black hair luxuriously. Then she slipped naked between the sheets and snapped out the light, tumbling lightly, effortlessly into sleep in a matter of moments.

It was almost dawn when Nessim came barefoot into her room. She woke to feel his arms about her shoulders; he was

212

kneeling by the bed, shaken by a paroxysm which at first she took to be a fit of weeping. But he was trembling, as if with a fever, and his teeth were chattering. "What is it?" she began incoherently, but he put a hand over her mouth to silence her. "I simply must tell you why I have been acting so strangely. I cannot bear the strain any longer. Justine, I have been brought face to face with another problem. I am faced with the terrible possibility of having to do away with Narouz. That is why I have been feeling half-mad. He has got completely out of hand. And I don't know what to do. I don't know what to do!"

This conversation took place some little time before the un-expected suicide of Pursewarden in the Mount Vulture Hotel.

o   o   o   o   o

XII

But it was not only for Mountolive that all the dispositions on the chessboard had been abruptly altered now by Pursewarden's solitary act of cowardice—and the unexpected discovery which had supplied its motive, the mainspring of his death. Nessim too, so long self-deluded by the same dreams of a perfect finite action, free and heedless as the impulse of a directed will, now found himself, like his friend, a prey to the gravitational forces which lie inherent in the time-spring of our acts, making them spread, ramify and distort themselves; making them spread as a stain will spread upon a white ceiling. Indeed, now the masters were beginning to find that they were, after all, the servants of the very forces which they had set in play, and that nature is inherently ingovernable. They were soon to be drawn along ways not of their choosing, trapped in a magnetic field, as it were, by the same forces which unwind the tides at the moon's bidding, or propel the glittering forces of salmon up a crowded river—actions curving and swelling into futurity beyond the powers of mortals to harness or divert. Mountolive knew this, vaguely and uneasily, lying in bed watching the lazy spirals of smoke from his cigar rise to the blank ceiling; Nessim and Justine knew it with greater certainty, lying brow to cold brow, eyes wide open in the magnificent darkened bedroom, whispering to each other. Beyond the connivance of the will they knew it, and felt the portents gathering around them—the paradigms of powers unleashed which must fulfil themselves. But how? In what manner? That was not as yet completely clear.

Pursewarden, before lying down on that stale earthly bed beside the forgotten muttering images of Melissa or Justine—and whatever private memories besides—had telephoned to

Nessim in a new voice, full of a harsh resignation, charged with the approaching splendours of death. "It is a matter of life and death, as they say in books. Yes, please, come at once. There is a message for you in an appropriate place: the mirror." He rang off with a simple chuckle which frightened the alert, frozen man at the other end of the line; at once Nessim had divined the premonition of a possible disaster. On the mirror of that shabby hotel-room, among the quotations which belonged to the private workshop of the writer's life, he found the following words written in capitals with a wet shaving-stick:

NESSIM. COHEN PALESTINE ETC. ALL DISCOVERED AND REPORTED.

This was the message which he had all but managed to obliterate before there came the sound of voices in the hall and the furtive rapping at the panels of the door; before Balthazar and Justine had tiptoed softly into the room. But the words and the memory of that small parting chuckle (like a sound of some resurrected Pan) were burned forever into his mind. His expression was one of neuralgic vacancy as he repeated all these facts to Justine in later times for the exposure of the act itself had numbed him. It would be impossible to sleep, he had begun to see; it was a message which must be discussed at length, sifted, unravelled where they lay, motionless as the effigies upon Alexandrian tombs, side by side in the dark room, their open eyes staring into each other with the sightlessness of inhuman objects, mirrors made of quartz, dead stars. Hand in hand they sighed and murmured, and even as he whispered: "I told you it was Melissa. . . . The way she always looked at me. . . . I suspected it." The other troubling problems of the case interlocked and overlapped in his mind, the problem of Narouz among them.

He felt as a beleaguered knight must feel in the silence of a fortress who suddenly hears the clink of spades and mattocks, the noise of iron feet, and divines that the enemy sappers are burrowing inch by inch beneath the walls. What would Mountolive feel *bound* to do now, supposing he had been told? (Strange how the very phrase betrayed them both as having moved out of the orbit of human free will.) They were both *bound* now, tied like bondsmen to the unrolling action which illustrated the personal predispositions of neither. They had embarked on a free exercise of the will only to find themselves shackled, bricked up by the historical process. And a single turn of the kaleidoscope had brought it about. Pursewarden! The writer who was so fond of saying "People will realize one day that it is only the artist who can make things really *happen*; that is why society should be founded upon him." A *deus ex machina!* In his dying he had used them both like . . . a public convenience, as if to demonstrate the truth of his own aphorism! There would have been many other issues to take without separating them by the act of his death, and setting them at odds by the dispensation of a knowledge which could benefit neither! Now everything hung upon a hair—the thinnest terms of a new probability. Act, Mountolive would, but *if he must*; and his one word to Memlik Pasha would entrain new forces, new dangers. . . .

The city with its obsessive rhythms of death twanged round them in the darkness—the wail of tyres in empty squares, the scudding of liners, the piercing whaup of a tug in the inner harbour; he felt the dusty, deathward drift of the place as never before, settling year by year more firmly into the barren dunes of Mareotis. He turned his mind first this way and then that, like an hourglass; but it was always the same sand which sifted through it, the same questions which followed each other unanswerably at the same leaden pace. Before them stretched the potential of a disaster for which—even though they had evaluated the risk so thoroughly and objectively—they had summoned up no reserves of strength. It was strange. Yet Justine, savagely brooding with her brows drawn down and her knuckle against her teeth, seemed still unmoved, and his heart went out to her, for the dignity of her silence (the unmoved sibyl's eye) gave him the courage to think on, assess the dilemma. They must continue as if nothing had changed when, in fact, everything had changed. The knowledge of the fact that they must, expressionless as knights nailed into suits of armour, continue upon a predetermined course, constituted both a separation and a new, deeper bond; a more passionate comradeship, such as soldiers enjoy only upon the field of battle, aware that they have renounced all thought of human continuity in terms of love, family, friends, home—become servants of an iron will which exhibits itself in the mailed mask of duty. "We must prepare for every eventuality," he said, his lips dry from the cigarettes he had smoked, "and hold on until things are complete—around Christmas, I should say. We may have more time in hand than we imagine; indeed, nothing whatsoever may come of it all. Perhaps Mountolive has not been told." But then he added in a smaller voice, full of the weight of relization: "But if he has been, we shall know; his manner will show it at once."

He might suddenly find himself, at any street corner, face to face with a man armed with a pistol—in any dark corner of the town; or else he might find his food poisoned some day by some suborned servant. Against these eventualities he could at least react, by a study of them, by a close and careful attention to probabilities. Justine lay silent, with wide eyes. "And then," he said, "to-morrow I must speak to Narouz. He must be made to see."

Some weeks before he had walked into his office to find the grave, silver-haired Serapamoun sitting in the visitors' chair, quietly smoking a cigarette. He was by far the most influential and important of the Coptic cotton-kings, and had played a decisive role in supporting the community movement which Nessim had initiated. They were old friends though the older man was of another generation. His serene mild face and low voice carried the authority of an education and a poise which

217

spoke of Europe. His conversation had the quick pulse of a reflective mind. "Nessim," he said softly, "I am here as a representative of our committee, not just as myself. I have a rather disagreeable task to perform. May I speak to you frankly, without heat or rancour? We are very troubled."

Nessim closed and locked the door, unplugged his telephone and squeezed Serapamoun's shoulder affectionately as he passed behind his visitor's chair to reach his own. "I ask nothing better," he said. "Speak."

"Your brother, Narouz."

"Well, what of him?"

"Nessim, in starting this community movement you had no idea of initiating a *jehad*—a holy war of religion—or of doing anything subversive which might unsettle the Egyptian Government? Of course not. That is what we thought, and if we joined you it was from a belief in your convictions that the Copts should unite and seek a larger place in public affairs." He smoked in silence for a minute, lost in deep thought. Then he went on: "Our community patriotism in no way qualified our patriotism as Egyptians did it? We were glad to hear Narouz preach the truths of our religion and race, yes, very glad, for these things needed saying, needed *feeling*. But . . . you have not been to a meeting for nearly three months. Are you aware what a change has come about? Narouz has been so carried away by his own powers that he is saying things to-day which could seriously compromise us all. We are most alarmed. He is filled now with some sort of mission. His head is a jumble of strange fragments of knowledge, and when he preaches all sorts of things pour out of him in a torrent which would look bad on paper if they were to reach Memlik Pasha." Another long silence. Nessim found himself growing gradually pale with apprehension. Serapamoun continued in his low smoothly waxed voice. "To say that the Copts will find a place in the sun is one thing; but to say that they will sweep away the corrupt régime of the pashas who own ninety per cent of the land . . . to talk of taking over Egypt and setting it to rights. . . ."

"Does he?" stammered Nessim, and the grave man nodded.

"Yes. Thank God our meetings are still secret. At the last he started raving like someone *melboos* (possessed) and shouted that if it was necessary to achieve our ends he would arm the Bedouin. Can you improve on that?"

Nessim licked his dry lips. "I had no idea" he said.

"We are very troubled and concerned about the fate of the whole movement with such preaching. We are counting on you to act in some way. He should, my dear Nessim, be restrained; or at least given some understanding of our role. He is seeing too much of old Taor—he is always out there in the desert with her. I don't think she has any political ideas, but he gets religious fervour from these meetings with her. He spoke of her and said that they kneel together for hours in the sand, under the blazing sun, and pray together. 'I see her visions now and she sees mine.' That is what he said. Also, he has begun to drink very heavily. It is something which needs urgent attention."

"I shall see him at once," Nessim had said, and now, turning to stare once more into the dark, untroubled gaze of a Justine he knew to be much stronger than himself, he repeated the phrase softly, trying it with his mind as one might try the blade of a knife to test its keenness. He had put off the meeting on one pretext or another, though he knew that sooner or later it would have to be, he would have to assert himself over Narouz—but over a different Narouz to the one he had always known.

And now Pursewarden had clumsily intervened, interpolated his death and betrayal, to load him still more fully with the preoccupations with all that concerned affairs about which Narouz himself knew nothing; setting his fevered mind to run upon parallel tracks towards an infinity. . . . He had the sensation of things closing in upon him, of himself beginning slowly to suffocate under the weight of the cares he had himself invented. It had all begun to happen so suddenly—within a matter of weeks. Helplessness began to creep over him, for every decision now seemed no longer a product of his will but a response to pressures built up outside him; the exigencies of the historical process in which he himself was being sucked as if into a quicksand.

But if he could no longer control events, it was necessary that he should take control of himself, his own nerves. Sedatives had for weeks now taken the place of self-control, though they only exorcized the twitchings of the subconscious temporarily; pistol-practice, so useless and childish a training against assassination, offered little surcease. He was possessed, assailed by the dreams of his childhood, erupting now without reason or consequence, almost taking over his waking life. He consulted Balthazar, but was of course unable to let him share the true preoccupations which burdened him, so that his wily friend suggested that he should record the dreams whenever possible on paper, and this also was done. But psychic pressures are not lifted unless one faces them squarely and masters them, does battle with the perils of the quivering reason. . . .

He had put off the interview with Narouz until he should feel stronger and better able to endure it. Fortunately the meetings of the group were infrequent. But daily he felt less and less equal to confronting his brother and it was in fact Justine who, with a word spoken in season at last, drove him out to Karm Abu Girg. Holding the lapels of his coat she said slowly and distinctly: "I would offer to go out and kill him myself, if I did not know that it would separate us forever. But if you have decided that it must be done, I have the courage to give the orders for you." She did not mean it, of course. It was a trick to bring him to his senses and in a trice his mind cleared, the mist of his irresolution dissolved. These words, so terrible and yet so quietly spoken, with not even the pride of resolution in them, reawakened his passionate love for her, so that the tears almost started to his eyes. He gazed upon her like a religious fanatic gazing upon an ikon—and in truth her own features, sullen now and immobile, her smouldering eyes, were those of some ancient Byzantine painting.

"Justine," he said with trembling hands.

"Nessim," she said hoarsely, licking her dry lips, but with a barbaric resolution gleaming in her eyes. It was almost exultantly (for the impediment had gone) that he said: "I shall be going out this evening, never fear. Everything will be settled one way or the other." He was all of a sudden flooded with power, determined to bring his brother to his senses and avert the danger of a second compromising order to his people, the Copts.

Nor had the new resolute mood deserted him that afternoon when he set off in the great car, driving with speed and deliberation along the dusty causeways of the canals to where the horses for which he had telephoned would be waiting for him. He was positively eager to see his brother, now, to outface him, to reassert himself, restore himself in his own eyes. Ali the factor met him at the ford with the customary politeness which seemed comfortably to reaffirm this new mood of resolution. He was after all the elder son. The man had brought Narouz' own white Arab and they cantered along the edge of the canals at great speed, with their reflections racing beside them in the tumbled water. He had asked only if his brother were now at home and had received a taciturn admission of the fact that he was. They exchanged no further word on the ride. The violet light of dusk was already in the air and the earth-vapours were rising from the lake. The gnats rose into the eye of the dying sun in silver streams, to store the last memories of the warmth upon their wings. The birds were collecting their families. How peaceful it all seemed! The bats had begun to stitch and stitch slowly across the darker spaces. The *bats!*

The Hosnani house was already in cool violet half-darkness, tucked as it was under the shoulder of the low hillock, in the shadow of the little village whose tall white minaret blazed still in the sunset. He heard now the sullen crack of the whip as he dismounted, and caught a glimpse of the man standing upon the topmost balcony of the house, gazing intently down into the blue pool of the courtyard. It was Narouz: and yet somehow also not Narouz. Can a single gesture from someone with whom one is familiar reveal an interior transformation? The man with the whip, standing there, so intently peering into the sombre well of the courtyard, registered in his very stance a new, troubling flamboyance, an authority which did not belong, so to speak, to the repertoire of Narouz' remembered gestures. "He practises," said the factor softly, holding the bridle of the horse, "every evening now with his whip he practises upon the bats." Nessim suddenly had a feeling of incoherence. "The *bats?*" he repeated softly, under his breath. The man on the balcony—the Narouz of this hastily raised impression—gave a sudden chuckle and exclaimed in a hoarse voice: "Thirteen." Nessim threw back the doors and stood framed now against the outer light. He spoke upwards into the darkening sky in a quiet, almost conversational voice, casting it like a ventriloquist towards the cloaked figure which stood at the top of the staircase in silhouette, with the long whip coiled at its side, at rest. "Ya Narouz" he said, uttering the traditional greeting of their common childhood with affection.

"Ya Nessim" came the response after a pause, and then a long ebbing silence fell. Nessim, whose eyes had become accustomed to the dusk, now saw that the courtyard was full of the bodies of bats, like fragments of torn umbrella, some fluttering and crawling in puddles of their own blood, some lying still and torn up. So this was what Narouz did in the evenings— "practising upon the bats"! He stood for a while unsure of himself, unsure what to say next. The factor closed the great doors abruptly behind him, and at once he stood, black against the darkness now, staring up the stairway to where his unknown brother stood with a kind of watchful impenitent

222

awareness. A bat ripped across the light and he saw Narouz'
arm swing with an involuntary motion and then fall to the side
again; from his vantage point at the top of the stairway he
could shoot, so to speak, downwards upon his targets. Neither
said anything for a while; then a door opened with a creak,
throwing out a shaft of light across his path, and the factor
came out of the outhouse with a broom with which he started
to sweep up the fragments of fluttering bodies of Narouz's vic-
tims which littered the earthen floor of the courtyard. Narouz
leaned forward a little to watch him intently as he did so, and
when he had almost swept the pile of tattered bodies to the
door of the outhouse, said in a hoarse voice: "Thirteen, eh?"
    "Thirteen."
His voice gave Nessim a dull neuralgic thrill, for he sounded
drugged—the harsh authoritative voice of someone drunk on
hashish, perhaps, or opium; the voice of someone signalling
from a new orbit in an unknown universe. He drew his breath
slowly until his lungs were fully inflated and then spoke upwards once more to the figure on the stair. "Ya Narouz. I have
come to speak to you on a matter of great urgency."
    "Mount" said Narouz gruffly, in the voice of a sheepdog.
"I wait for you here, Nessim." The voice made many things
clear to Nessim, for never before had the voice of his brother
been completely free from a note of welcome, of joy even. At
any other time he would have run down the stairs in clumsy
welcome, taking them two at a time and calling out "Nessim,
how *good* you have come!" Nessim walked across the courtyard
and placed his hand upon the dusty wooden rail. "It is important" he said sharply, crisply, as if to establish his own importance in this tableau—the shadowy courtyard with the
solitary figure standing up against the sky in silhouette, holding
the long whip lightly, effortlessly, and watching him. Narouz
repeated the word "Mount" in a lower key, and suddenly sat
down putting his whip beside him on the top stair. It was the
first time, thought Nessim, that there had been no greeting for

him on his return to Karm Abu Girg. He walked up the steep stairs slowly, peering upwards.

It was much lighter on the first floor, and at the top of the second there was enough light to see his brother's face. Narouz sat quite still, in cloak and boots. His whip lay lightly coiled over the balustrade with its handle upon his knees. Beside him on the dusty wooden floor stood a half-empty bottle of gin. His chin was sunk upon his chest and he stared crookedly up under shaggy brows at the approaching stranger with an expression which combined truculence with a queer, irresolute sorrow. He was at his old trick of pressing his back teeth together and releasing them so that the cords of muscle at his temples expanded and contracted as if a heavy pulse were beating there. He watched his brother's slow ascent with this air of sombre self-divided uncertainty into which there crept from time to time the smouldering glow of an anger banked up, held under control. As Nessim reached the final landing and set foot upon the last flight of stairs, Narouz stirred and gave a sudden gargling bark—a sound such as one might make to a hound— and held out a hairy hand. Nessim paused and heard his brother say: "Stay there, Nessim" in a new and authoritative voice, but which contained no particular note of menace. He hesitated, leaning forward keenly the better to interpret this unfamiliar gesture—the square hand thrown out in an attitude almost of imprecation, fingers stretched, but not perfectly steady.

"You have been drinking" he said at last, quietly but with a profound ringing disgust. "Narouz, this is new for you." The shadow of a smile, as if of self-contempt, played upon the crooked lips of his brother. It broadened suddenly to a slow grin which displayed his hare-lip to the full: and then vanished, was swallowed up, as if abruptly recalled by a thought which it could not represent. Narouz now wore a new air of unsteady self-congratulation, of pride at once mawkish and dazed. "What do you wish from me?" he said hoarsely. "Say it here, Nessim. I am practising."

"Let us go indoors to speak privately."

Narouz shook his head slowly and after consideration said crisply:

"You can speak here."

"*Narouz*" cried Nessim sharply, stung by these unfamiliar responses, and in the voice one would use to awaken a sleeper, "*Please.*" The seated man at the head of the stairs stared up at him with the strange inflamed but sorrowful air and shook his head again. "I have spoken, Nessim" he said indistinctly. Nessim's voice broke, it was pitched so sharply against the silence of the courtyard. He said, almost pitifully now, "I simply must speak to you, do you understand?"

"Speak now, here. I am listening." This was indeed a new and unexpected personage, the man in the cloak. Nessim felt the colour rising in his cheeks. He climbed a couple of steps more and hissed assertively: "Narouz, I come from *them*. In God's name what have you been saying to them? The committee has become terrified by your words." He broke off and irresolutely waved the memorandum which Serapamoun had deposited with him, crying: "This . . . this paper is from them."

Narouz' eyes blazed up for a second with a maudlin pride made somehow regal by the outward thrust of his chin and a straightening of the huge shoulders. "My words, Nessim?" he growled, and then nodding: "And Taor's words. When the time comes we will know how to act. Nobody needs to fear. We are not dreamers."

"*Dreamers!*" cried Nessim with a gasp, almost beside himself now with apprehension and disgust and mortified to his very quick by this lack of conventional address in a younger brother. "You are the dreamers! Have I not explained a thousand times what we are trying to do . . . what we mean by all this? Peasant, idiot that you are. . . ." But these words which once might have lodged like goads in Narouz' mind seemed blunt, ineffectual. He tightened his mouth hard and made a slow cutting movement with his palm, cutting the air from left to right before his own body. "Words," he cried harshly. "I know you now, my brother." Nessim glanced wildly about him for a moment, as if to seek help, as if to seek some instrument heavy enough to drive the truth of what he had to say into the head of the seated man. A hysterical fury had beset him, a rage against this sottish figure which raised so uncomprehending a face to his pleas. He was trembling; he had certainly anticipated nothing like this when he set out from Alexandria with his resolution bright and his mind composed.

"Where is Leila?" he cried sharply, as if he might invoke her aid, and Narouz gave a short clicking chuckle. He raised his finger to his temple gravely and muttered: "In the summer-house, as you know. Why not go to her if you wish?" He chuckled again, and then added, nodding his head with an absurdly childish expression. "She is angry with *you*, now. For once it is with *you*, not with *me*. You have made her cry, Nessim." His lower lip trembled.

"Drunkard" hissed Nessim helplessly. Narouz' eyes flashed. He gave a single jarring laugh, a short bark, throwing his head right back. Then suddenly, without warning, the smile vanished and he put on once more his watchful, sorrowing expression. He licked his lips and whispered "Ya Nessim" under his breath, as if he were slowly recovering his sense of proportion. But Nessim, white with rage, was now almost beside himself with frustration. He stepped up the last few stairs and shook Narouz by the shoulder, almost shouting now: "Fool, you are putting us all in danger. Look at these, from Serapamoun. The committee will disband unless you stop talking like this. Do you understand? You are mad, Narouz. In God's name, Narouz, understand what I am saying. . . ." But the great head of his brother looked dazed now, beset by the flicker of contradictory expressions, like the lowered crest of a bull badgered beyond endurance. "Narouz, *listen* to me." The face that was slowly raised to Nessim's seemed to have grown larger and more vacant, the eyes more lustreless, yet full of the pain of a new sort of knowledge which owed little to the sterile revolutions of reason; it was full too of a kind of anger and incomprehension, confused and troubling, which was seeking expression. They stared angrily at each other. Nessim was white to the lips and panting, but his brother sat simply staring at him, his lips drawn back over his white teeth as if he were hypnotized.

"Do you hear me? Are you deaf?" Nessim shook, but with a motion of his broad shoulders Narouz shook off the importunate hand while his face began to flush. Nessim ran on, heedless, carried away by the burning preoccupations which poured out of him clothed in a torrent of reproaches. "You have put us all in danger, even Leila, even yourself, even Mountolive." Why should chance have led him to that fatal name? The utterance of it seemed to electrify Narouz and fill him with a new, almost triumphant desperation.

"Mountolive" he shouted the word in a deep groaning voice and ground his teeth together audibly; he seemed as if he were about to go berserk. Yet he did not move, though his hand moved involuntarily to the handle of the great whip which lay in his lap. "That British swine!" he brought out with a thunderous vehemence, almost spitting the words.

"Why do you say that?"

And then another transformation occurred with unexpected suddenness, for Narouz' whole body relaxed and subsided; he looked up with a sly air now, and said with a little chuckle, in a tone pitched barely above a whisper: "*You* sold our mother to him, Nessim. You knew it would cause our father's death."

This was too much. Nessim fell upon him, flailing at him with his doubled fists, uttering curse after guttural curse in Arabic. beating him. But his blows fell like chaff upon the huge body. Narouz did not move, did not make any attempt to avert or to respond to his brother's blows—here at least Nessim's seniority held. He could not bring himself to strike back at his elder brother. But sitting doubled up and chuckling

227

under the futile rain of blows, he repeated venomously over and over again the words: *"You sold our mother!"*

Nessim beat him until his own knuckles were bruised and aching. Narouz stooped under this febrile onslaught, bearing it with the same composed smile of maudlin bitterness, repeating the triumphant phrase over and over again in that thrilling whisper. At last Nessim shrieked *"Stop"* and himself desisted, falling against the rail of the balustrade and sinking under the weight of his own exhaustion down to the first landing. He was trembling all over. He shook his fist upwards at the dark seated figure and said incoherently "I shall go to Serapamoun myself. You will see who is master." Narouz gave a small contemptuous chuckle, but said nothing.

Putting his dishevelled clothes to rights, Nessim tottered down the stairway into the now darkened courtyard. His horse and Ali's had been tethered to the iron hitching post outside the great front door. As he mounted, still trembling and muttering, the factor raced out of the arches and unbolted the doors. Narouz was standing up now, visible only against the yellow light of the living-room. Flashes of incoherent rage still stormed Nessim's mind—and with them irresolution, for he realized that the mission he had set himself was far from completed, indeed, had gone awry. With some half-formulated idea of offering the silent figure another chance to open up a discussion with him or seek a *rapprochement*, he rode his horse into the courtyard and sat there, looking up into the darkness. Narouz stirred.

"Narouz," said Nessim softly, "I have told you once and for all now. You will see who is going to be master. It would be wise for you. . . ."

But the dark figure gave a bray of laughter.

"Master and servant" he cried contemptuously. "Yes, Nessim. We shall see. And now——" He leaned over the rail and in the darkness Nessim heard the great whip slither along the dry boards like a cobra and then lick the still twilight air of the courtyard. There was a crack and a snap like a giant mouse-trap closing, and the bundle of papers in his arm was flicked out peremptorily and scattered over the cobbles. Narouz laughed again, on a more hysterical note. Nessim felt the heat of the whipstroke on his hand though the lash had not touched him.

"Now go" cried Narouz, and once more the whip hissed in the air to explode menacingly behind the buttocks of his horse. Nessim rose in his stirrups and shaking his fist once more at his brother, cried "We shall see!"

But his voice sounded thin, choked by the imprecations which filled his mind. He drove his heels into the horse's flanks and twisted suddenly about to gallop abruptly out of the courtyard throwing up sparks from the stone threshold, bend-ing low in the saddle. He rode back to the ford now, where the car awaited, like a madman, his face distorted with rage; but as he rode his pulse slowed and his anger emptied itself into the loathsome disgust which flooded up into his mind in slow coils, like some venomous snake. Unexpected waves of remorse, too, began to invade him, for something had now been irrepar-ably damaged, irreparably broken, in the iron ceinture of the family relation. Dispossessed of the authority vested in the elder son by the feudal pattern of life, he felt all at once a prodigal, almost an orphan. In the heart of his rage there was also guilt; he felt unclean, as if he had debauched himself in this unexpected battle with one of his own kin. He drove slowly back to the city, feeling the luxurious tears of a new exhaustion, a new self-pity, rolling down his cheeks.

How strange it was that he had somehow, inexplicably, fore-seen this irreparable break with his brother—from the first discreet phrases of Serapamoun he had divined it and feared it. It raised once more the spectre of duties and responsibilities to causes which he himself had initiated and must now serve. Ideally, then, he should be prepared in such a crisis to disown Narouz, to depose Narouz, even if necessary to . . . him! (He slammed on the brakes of the car, brought it to a standstill,

229

and sat muttering. He had censored the thought in his mind, for the hundredth time. But the nature of the undertaking should be clear enough to anyone in a similar situation. He had never understood Narouz, he thought wistfully. But then, you do not have to understand someone in order to love them. His hold had not really been deep, founded in understanding: it had been conferred by the family conventions to which both belonged. And now the tie had suddenly snapped.) He struck the wheel of the car with aching palms and cried "I shall never harm him."

He threw in the clutch, repeating "Never" over and over again in his mind. Yet he knew this decision to be another weakness, for in it his love traduced his own ideal of duty. But here his *alter ego* came to his rescue with soothing formulations such as: "It is really not so serious. We shall, of course, have to disband the movement temporarily. Later I shall ask Serapamoun to start something similar. We can isolate and expel this . . . fanatic." He had never fully realized before how much he loved this hated brother whose mind had now become distended by dreams whose religious poetry conferred upon their Egypt a new, an ideal future. "We must seek to embody the frame of the eternal in nature here upon earth, in our hearts, in this very Egypt of ours." That is what Narouz had said, among so many other things which filled the fragmentary transcription which Serapamoun had ordered to be made. "We must wrestle here on earth against the secular injustice, and in our hearts against the injustice of a divinity which respects only man's struggle to possess his own soul." Were these simply the ravings of Taor, or were they part of a shared dream of which the ignorant fanatic had spoken? Other phrases, barbed with the magnificence of poetry, came into his mind. "To rule is to be ruled; but ruler and ruled must have a divine consciousness of their role, of their inheritance in the Divine. The mud of Egypt rises to choke our lungs, the lungs with which we cry to living God."

He had a sudden picture of that contorted face, the little gasping voice in which Narouz had, that first day of his possession, invoked the divine spirit to visit him with a declared truth. *"Meded! Meded!"* He shuddered. And then it slowly came upon him that in a paradoxical sort of way Narouz was right in his desire to inflame the sleeping will—for he saw the world, not so much as a political chessboard but as a pulse beating within a greater will which only the poetry of the psalms could invoke and body forth. To awaken not merely the impulses of the forebrain with its limited formulations, but the sleeping beauty underneath—the poetic consciousness which lay, coiled like a spring, in the heart of everyone. This thought frightened him not a little; for he suddenly saw that his brother might be a religious leader, but for the prevailing circumstances of time and place—*these*, at least, Nessim could judge. He was a prodigy of nature but his powers were to be deployed in a barren field which could never nourish them, which indeed would stifle them forever.

He reached the house, abandoned the car at the gate, and raced up the staircase, taking the steps three at a time. He had been suddenly assailed by one of the customary attacks of diarrhoea and vomiting which had become all too frequent in recent weeks. He brushed past Justine who lay wide-eyed upon the bed with the reading-lamp on and the piano-score of a concerto spread upon her breast. She did not stir, but smoked thoughtfully, saying only, under her breath, "You are back so soon." Nessim rushed into the bathroom, turning on the taps of the washbasin and the shower at the same time to drown his retching. Then he stripped his clothes off with disgust, like dirty bandages, and climbed under the hail of boiling water to wash away all the indignities which flooded his thoughts. He knew she would be listening thoughtfully, smoking thoughtfully, her motions as regular as a pendulum, waiting for him to speak, lying at length under the shelf of books with the mask smiling down ironically at her from the wall. Then the water

231

was turned off and she heard him scrubbing himself vigorously with a towel.

"Nessim" she called softly.

"It was a failure" he cried at once. "He is quite mad, Justine, I could get nothing out of him. It was ghastly."

Justine continued to smoke on silently, with her eyes fixed upon the curtains. The room was full of the scent of the pastels burning in the great rose-bowl by the telephone. She placed her score beside the bed. "Nessim" she said in the hoarse voice which he had come to love so much.

"Yes."

"I am thinking."

He came out at once, his hair wet and straggly, his feet bare, wearing the yellow silk dressing-gown, his hands thrust deep into the pockets, a lighted cigarette smouldering in the corner of his mouth. He walked slowly up and down at the foot of her bed. He said with an air of considered precision: "All this unease comes from my fear that we may have to do him harm. But, even if we are endangered by him, we must never harm him, *never*. I have told myself that. I have thought the whole thing out. It will seem a failure of duty, but we must be clear about it. Only then can I become calm again. Are you with me?"

He looked at her once more with longing, with the eyes of his imagination. She lay there, as if afloat upon the dark damascened bed-spread, her feet and hands crossed in the manner of an effigy, her dark eyes upon him. A lock of dark hair curled upon her forehead. She lay in the silence of a room which had housed (if walls have ears) their most secret deliberations, under a Tibetan mask with lighted eyeballs. Behind her gleamed the shelves of books which she had gathered though not all of which she had read. (She used their texts as omens for the future, riffling the pages to place her finger at hazard upon a quotation—"bibliomancy" the art is called.) Schopenhauer, Hume, Spengler, and oddly enough some novels, including three of Pursewarden's. Their polished bindings reflected the light of the candles. She cleared her throat, extinguished her cigarette, and said in a calm voice: "I can be resigned to whatever you say. At the moment, this weakness of yours is a danger to both of us. And besides, your health is troubling us all, Balthazar not least. Even unobservant people like Darley are beginning to notice. That is not good." Her voice was cold and toneless.

"Justine," his admiration overflowed. He came and sat down beside her on the bed, putting his arms around her to embrace her fiercely. His eyes glittered with a new elation, a new gratitude. "I am so weak," he said.

He extended himself beside her, put his arms behind his head, and lay silent, thinking. For a long time now they lay thus, silently side by side. At last she said:

"Darley came to dinner to-night and left just before you arrived. I heard from him that the Embassies will all be packing up next week to return to Cairo. Mountolive won't get back to Alexandria much before Christmas. This is also our chance to take a rest and recuperate our forces. I've told Selim that we are going out to Abu Sueir next week for a whole month. You must rest now, Nessim. We can swim and ride in the desert and think about nothing—nothing, do you hear? After a while I shall invite Darley to come and stay with us for a while so that you have someone to talk to apart from me. I know you like him and find him a pleasant companion. It will do us both good. From time to time I can come in here for a night and see what is happening . . . what do you say?"

Nessim groaned softly and turned his head. "Why?" she whispered softly, her lips turned away from him. "Why do you do that?"

He sighed deeply and said: "It is not what you think. You know how much I like him and how well we get on. It is only the pretence, the eternal play-acting one has to indulge in even with one's friends. If only we did not have to keep on acting a part, Justine."

But he saw that she was looking at him wide-eyed now, with an expression suggesting something that was close to horror or dismay. "Ah," she said thoughtfully, sorrowfully after a moment, closing her eyes, "ah, Nessim! Then I should not know who I was."

o   o   o   o   o

The two men sat in the warm conservatory, silently facing each other over the magnificent chessboard with its ivories—in perfect companionship. The set was a twenty-first birthday gift, from Mountolive's mother. As they sat, each occasionally mused aloud, absently. It wasn't conversation, but simply thinking aloud, a communion of minds which were really occupied by the grand strategy of chess: a by-product of friendship which was rooted in the fecund silences of the royal game. Balthazar spoke of Pursewarden. "It annoys me, his suicide. I feel I had somehow missed the point. I take it to have been an expression of contempt for the world, contempt for the conduct of the world."

Mountolive glanced up quickly. "No, no. A conflict between duty and affection." Then he added swiftly "But I can't tell you very much. When his sister comes, she will tell you more, perhaps, if she can." They were silent. Balthazar sighed and said "Truth naked and unashamed. That's a splendid phrase. But we always see her as she seems, never as she is. Each man has his own interpretation."

Another long silence. Balthazar *loquitur*, musingly, to himself. "Sometimes one is caught pretending to be God and learns a bitter lesson. Now I hated Dmitri Randidi, though not his lovely daughter; but just to humiliate him (I was disguised as a gipsy woman at the carnival ball), I told her fortune. Tomorrow, I said, she would have a life-experience which she must on no account miss—a man sitting in the ruined tower at Taposiris. 'You will not speak,' I said, 'but walk straight into his arms, your eyes closed. His name begins with an L, his family name with J.' (I had in fact already thought of a particularly hideous young man with these initials, and he was across the road at the Cervonis' ball. Colourless eyelashes, a snout, sandy hair.) I chuckled when she believed me. Having told her this prophecy—everyone believes the tale of a gipsy, and with my black face and hook nose I made a splendid gipsy —having arranged this, I went across the road and sought out L. J., telling him I had a message for him. I knew him to be superstitious. He did not recognize me. I told him of the part he should play. Malign, spiteful, I suppose. I only planned to annoy Randidi. And it all turned out as I had planned. For the lovely girl obeyed the gipsy and fell in love with this freckled toad with the red hair. A more unsuitable conjunction cannot be imagined. But that was the idea—to make Randidi hop! It did, yes, very much, and I was so pleased by my own cleverness. He of course forbade the marriage. The lovers—which *I* invented, *my* lovers—were separated. Then Gaby Randidi, the beautiful girl, took poison. You can imagine how clever I felt. This broke her father's health and the neurasthenia (never very far from the surface in the family) overwhelmed him at last. Last autumn he was found hanging from the trellis which supports the most famous grapevine in the city and from which. . . ."

In the silence which followed he could be heard to add the words: "It is only another story of our pitiless city. But check to your Queen, unless I am mistaken. . . ."

o   o   o   o   o

XIII

With the first thin effervescence of autumn rain Mountolive found himself back for the winter spell in Cairo with nothing of capital importance as yet decided in the field of policy; London was silent on the revelations contained in Pursewarden's farewell letter and apparently disposed rather to condole with a Chief of Mission whose subordinates proved of doubtful worth than to criticize him or subject the whole matter to any deep scrutiny. Perhaps the feeling was best expressed in the long and pompous letter in which Kenilworth felt disposed to discuss the tragedy, offering assurances that everyone "at the Office" was sad though not surprised. Pursewarden had always been considered rather *outré*, had he not? Apparently some such outcome had long been suspected. "His charm" wrote Kenilworth in the august prose style reserved for what was known as "a balanced appraisal", "could not disguise his aberrations. I do not need to dilate on the personal file which I showed you. *In Pace Requiescat*. But you have our sympathy for the loyal way in which you brushed aside these considerations to give him another chance with a Mission which had already found his manners insupportable, his views unsound." Mountolive squirmed as he read; yet his repugnance was irrationally mixed with a phantom relief for he saw, cowering behind these deliberations as it were, the shadows of Nessim and Justine, the outlaws.

If he had been reluctant to leave Alexandria, it was only because the unresolved problem of Leila nagged him still. He was afraid of the new thoughts he was forced to consider concerning her and her possible share in the conspiracy—if such it was—he felt like a criminal harbouring the guilt for some as yet undiscovered deed. Would it not be better to force his way in upon her—to arrive unannounced at Karm Abu Girg one day and coax the truth out of her? He could not do it. His nerve failed him at this point. He averted his mind from the ominous future and packed with many a sigh for his journey, planning to plunge once more into the tepid stream of his social activities in order to divert his mind.

For the first time now the aridities of his official duty seemed almost delightful, almost enticing. Time-killers and pain-killers at once, he followed out the prescribed round of entertainments with a concentration and attention that made them seem almost a narcotic. Never had he radiated such calculated charm, such attentiveness to considered trifles which turned them into social endearments. A whole colony of bores began to seek him out. It was a little time before people began to notice how much and in how short a time he had been aged, and to attribute the change to the unceasing round of pleasure into which he cast himself with such ravenous enthusiasm. What irony! His popularity expanded around him in waves. But now it began to seem to him that there was little enough behind the handsome indolent mask which he exposed to the world save a terror and uncertainty which were entirely new. Cut off in this way from Leila, he felt dispossessed, orphaned. All that remained was the bitter drug of duties to which he held desperately.

Waking in the morning to the sound of his curtains being drawn by the butler—slowly and reverently as one might slide back the curtains of Juliet's tomb—he would call for the papers and read them eagerly as he tackled a breakfast-tray loaded with the prescribed delicacies to which his life had made him accustomed. But already he was impatient for the tapping on the door which would herald the appearance of his young bearded third secretary, bringing him his appointments book and other impedimenta of his work. He would hope frantically that the day would be a full one, and felt almost anguish on those rare occasions when there were few engagements to be met. As he lay back on his pillows with controlled impatience Donkin would read the day's agenda in the manner of someone embarking on a formal recitation of the Creed. Dull as they always sounded, these official engagements, they rang in Mountolive's ear with a note of promise, a prescription for boredom and unease. He listened like an anxious voluptuary to the voice reciting: "There is a call on Rahad Pasha at eleven to deliver an *aide-mémoire* on investment by British subjects. Chancery have the data. Then Sir John and Lady Gilliatt are coming to lunch. Errol met the plane. Yes, we sent the flowers to the hotel for her. They will sign the book at eleven to-day. Their daughter is indisposed which rather mucked up the lunch-seating, but as you already had Haida Pasha and the American Minister, I took the liberty of popping in Errol and wife; the *placement* works out like this. I didn't need to consult protocol because Sir John is here on a private visit—this has been publicly announced in the Press." Laying down all the beautifully-typed memoranda on its stiff crested paper, Mountolive sighed and said "Is the new *chef* any good? You might send him to me later in my office. I know a favourite dish of the Gilliatts'."

Donkin nodded and scribbled a note before continuing in his toneless voice: "At six there is a cocktail party for Sir John at Haida's. You have accepted to dine at the Italian Embassy—a dinner in honour of Signor Maribor. It will be a tight fit."

"I shall change before," said Mountolive thoughtfully.

"There are also one or two notes here in your hand which I couldn't quite decipher, sir. One mentions the Scent Bazaar, Persian Lilac."

"Good, yes. I promised to take Lady Gilliatt. Arrange transport for the visit please, and let them know I am coming. After lunch—say, three-thirty."

"Then there is a note saying 'Luncheon gifts'."

"Aha, yes," said Mountolive, "I am becoming quite an

238

oriental. You see, Sir John may be most useful to us in London, at the Office, so I thought I would make his visit as memorable as possible, knowing his interests. Will you be good enough to go down to Karda in Suleiman Pasha and shop me a couple of those little copies of the Tel Al Aktar figurines, the coloured ones? I'd be most grateful. They are pretty toys. And see that they are wrapped with a card to put beside their plates? Thank you very much."

Once more alone he sipped his tea and committed himself mentally to the crowded day which he saw stretching before him, rich in the promise of distractions which would leave no room for the more troubling self-questionings. He bathed and dressed slowly, deliberately, concentrating his mind on a choice of clothes suitable for his mid-morning official call, tying his tie carefully in the mirror. "I shall soon have to change my life radically" he thought, "or it will become completely empty. How best should that be done?" Somewhere in the link of cause and effect he detected a hollow space which crystallized in his mind about the word "companionship". He repeated it aloud to himself in the mirror. Yes, there was where a lack lay. "I shall have to get myself a dog" he thought, somewhat pathetically, "to keep me company. It will be something to look after. I can take it for walks by the Nile." Then a sense of absurdity beset him and he smiled. Nevertheless, in the course of his customary tour of the Embassy offices that morning, he stuck his head into the Chancery and asked Errol very seriously what sort of dog would make a good house pet. They had a long and pleasurable discussion of the various breeds and decided that some sort of fox-terrier might be the most suitable pet for a bachelor. A fox-terrier! He repeated the words as he crossed the landing to visit the Service attachés, smiling at his own asininity. "What next!"

His secretary had neatly stacked his papers in their trays and placed the red despatch cases against the wall; the single bar of the electric fire kept the office at a tepid norm suitable for the routine work of the day. He settled to his telegrams with an exaggerated attention, and to the draft replies which had already been dictated by his team of juniors. He found himself chopping and changing phrases, inverting sentences here and there, adding marginalia; this was something new, for he had never had excessive zeal in the matter of official English and indeed dreaded the portentous circumlocutions which his own drafts had been forced to harbour when he himself had been a junior, under a Minister who fancied himself as a stylist—are there any exceptions in the Foreign Service? No. He had always been undemanding in this way, but now the forcible concentration with which he lived and worked had begun to bear fruit in a series of meddlesome pedantries which had begun mildly to irritate the diligent Errol and his staff. Though he knew this, nevertheless Mountolive persisted unshrinkingly; he criticized, quizzed and amended work which he knew to be well enough done already, working with the aid of the Unabridged Oxford Dictionary and a Skeat—for all the world like some mediaeval scholar splitting theological hairs. He would light a cheroot and smoke thoughtfully as he jotted and scored on the marbled minute-paper.

To-day at ten there came the customary welcome clinking of cups and saucers and Bohn, the Chancery Guard, presented himself somewhat precariously with the cup of Bovril and a plate of rusks to announce a welcome interval for refreshment. Mountolive relaxed in an armchair for a quarter of an hour as he sipped, staring heavily at the white wall with its group of neutral Japanese prints—the standard decoration chosen by the Ministry of Works for the offices of Ambassadors. In a little while it would be time to deal with the Palestine bag; already it was being sorted in the Archives Department—the heavy canvas ditty-bags lying about the floor with their mouths agape, the clerks sorting swiftly upon trestle tables, covered with green baize, the secretaries of the various departments waiting patiently outside the wooden pen each for her share of the spoils. . . . He felt a small premonitory unease this morning as he waited, for Maskelyne had not as yet shown any sign of life. He had not even acknowledged, let alone commented upon, Pursewarden's last letter. He wondered why.

There was a tap at the door, and Errol entered with his diffident ungainly walk, holding a bulky envelope impressively sealed and superscribed. "From Maskelyne, sir," he said, and Mountolive rose and stretched with an elaborate show of nonchalance. "Good Lord!" he said, weighing the parcel in his hand before handing it back to Errol. "So this came by pigeonpost, eh? Wonder what it can be? It looks like a novel, eh?"

"Yes, sir."

"Well, open it up, dear boy" (he had picked up a lot of avuncular tricks of speech from Sir Louis, he noted sadly; he must make a note to reform the habit before it was too late.)

Errol slit the huge envelope clumsily with the paper-knife. A fat memorandum and a bundle of photostats tumbled out on to the desk between them. Mountolive felt a small sense of shrinking as he recognized the spidery handwriting of the soldier upon the crowned notepaper of the covering letter. "What have we here?" he said, settling himself at his desk. "My dear Ambassador,"; the rest of the letter was faultlessly typed in Primer. As Errol turned over the neatly stapled photostats with a curious finger, reading a few words here and there, he whistled softly. Mountolive read:

My dear Ambassador,

I am sure you will be interested in the enclosed data, all of which has been recently unearthed by my department in the course of a series of widespread investigations here in Palestine.

I am able to supply a very large fragment of a detailed correspondence carried on over the last few years between Hosnani, the subject of my original *pended* paper, and the so-called Jewish Underground Fighters in Haifa and Jerusalem. One glance at it should convince any impartial person that my original appraisal of the gentleman in question erred on the side of moderation. The quantities of arms and ammunition detailed in the attached check-list are so considerable as to cause the Mandate authorities grave alarm. Everything is being done to locate and confiscate these large dumps, so far however with little success.

This of course raises once more, and far more urgently, the political question of how to deal with this gentleman. My original view, as you know, was that a timely word to the Egyptians would meet the case. I doubt if even Memlik Pasha would care to prejudice Anglo-Egyptian relations and Egypt's new-found freedom, by refusing to act if pressure were applied. Nor need we enquire too closely into the methods he might employ. Our hands would at least be clean. But obviously Hosnani must be stopped—and soon.

I am copying this paper to W.O. and F.O. The London copy leaves under flying seal with an Urgent Personal from the Commissioner to the F.S. urging action in these terms. Doubtless you will have a reaction from London before the end of the week.

Comment on the letter of Mr. Pursewarden which you copied to me seems superfluous at this stage. The enclosures to this Memorandum will be sufficient explanation. It is clear that he could not look his duty in the face.

I am, Sir, Your Most Obedient Servant,

Oliver Maskelyne, Brigadier.

The two men sighed simultaneously and looked at one another. "Well," said Errol at last, thumbing over the glossy photostats with a voluptuous finger. "At last we have proof positive." He was beaming with pleasure. Mountolive shook his head weakly and lit another cheroot. Errol said: "I've only flicked over the correspondence, sir, but each letter is signed Hosnani. They are all typescripts, of course. I expect you'll want to mull them over at leisure, so I'll retire for an hour until you need me. Is that all?"

Mountolive fingered the great wad of paper with nausea, with a sense of surfeit, and nodded speechlessly.

"Right," said Errol briskly and turned. As he reached the door, Mountolive found his voice, though to his own ears it sounded both husky and feeble. "Errol," he said, "there's only one thing; signal London to say that we have received Maskelyne's Memorandum and are *au courant*. Say we are standing by for instructions." Errol nodded and backed smiling into the passage. Mountolive settled to his desk and turned a vague and bilious eye upon the facsimiles. He read one or two of the letters slowly, almost uncomprehendingly, and was suddenly afflicted by a feeling of vertigo. He felt as if the walls of the room were slowly closing in upon him. He breathed deeply through his nose with his eyes fast closed. His fingers began involuntarily to drum softly upon the blotter, copying the syncopated rhythms of the Arab finger-drum, the broken-loined rhythms which one might hear any evening floating over the waters of the Nile from some distant boat. As he sat, softly tapping out this insidious dance measure of Egypt, with his eyes closed like a blind man, he asked himself over and over again: "Now what is to happen?"

But what could possibly happen?

"I should expect an action telegram this afternoon" he mumbled. This was where he found his duty so useful a prop. Despite his interior preoccupations, he allowed it to drag him along now, to drag his aberrant attention along like a dog on a lead. The morning was a relatively busy one. His lunch-party was an unqualified success, and the surprise visit to the Scent Bazaar afterwards confirmed his powers as a brilliant and thoughtful host. After it was over, he lay down for half an hour in his bedroom with the curtains drawn, sipping a cup of tea, and conducting the usual debate with himself which always began with the phrase: "Would I rather be a dunce than a fop—that is the question?" The very intensity of his self-contempt kept his mind off the issue concerned with Nessim

243

until six when the Chancery opened once more. He had a cold shower and changed before sauntering down from the Residence.

When he reached his office it was to find the desk-lamp burning and Errol seated in the armchair, smiling benignly and holding the pink telegram in his fingers. "It has just come in, sir" he said, passing it to his Chief as if it were a bouquet of flowers specially gathered for him. Mountolive cleared his throat loudly—attempting by the physical action to clear his mind and attention at the same time. He was afraid that his fingers might tremble as he held it, so he placed it elaborately on his blotter, thrust his hands into his trouser-pockets, and leaned down to study it, registering (he hoped) little beyond polite nonchalance. "It's pretty clear, sir" said Errol hopefully, as if to strike an echoing spark of enthusiasm from his Chief. But Mountolive read it slowly and thoughtfully twice before looking up. He suddenly wanted to go to the lavatory very much. "I must just do a pee" he said hastily, practically driving the younger man out of the door, "and I'll come down in a little while to discuss it. It seems clear enough, though. I shall have to act to-morrow. In a minute, eh?" Errol disappeared with an air of disappointment. Mountolive rushed to the toilet; his knees were shaking. Within a quarter of an hour, however, he had composed himself once more and was able to walk lightly down the staircase to where Errol's office was; he entered softly with the telegram in his hand. Errol sat at his desk; he had just put the telephone down and was smiling.

Mountolive handed over the pink telegram and sank into an armchair noticing with annoyance the litter of untidy personal objects on Errol's desk—a china ashtray in the likeness of a Sealyham terrier, a Bible, a pin-cushion, an expensive fountain-pen whose holder was embedded in a slab of green marble, a lead paperweight in the shape of a statue of Athene. . . . It was the sort of jumble one would find in an old lady's work-basket; but then, Errol was something of an old lady. He cleared his

244

throat. "Well, sir," said Errol, taking off his glasses, "I've been on to Protocol and said you would like an interview with the Foreign Minister to-morrow on a matter of great urgency. I suppose you'll wear uniform?"

"Uniform?" said Mountolive vaguely.

"The Egyptians are always impressed if one puts on a Tiger Tim."

"I see. Yes, I suppose so."

"They tend to judge the importance of what you have to say by the style in which you dress to say it. Donkin is always rubbing it into us and I expect it's true."

"It is, my dear boy." (There! The avuncular note again! Damn.)

"And I suppose you'll want to support the verbal side with a definitive *aide-mémoire*. You'll have to give them all the information to back up our contention, won't you sir?"

Mountolive nodded briskly. He had been submerged suddenly by a wave of hate for Nessim so unfamiliar that it surprised him. Once again, of course, he recognized the root of his anger—that he should be forced into such a position by his friend's indiscretion: forced to proceed against him. He had a sudden little series of mental images—Nessim fleeing the country, Nessim in Hadra Prison, Nessim in chains, Nessim poisoned at his lunch-table by a servant. . . . With the Egyptians one never knew where one was. Their ignorance was matched by an excess of zeal which might land one anywhere. He sighed.

"Of course I shall wear uniform" he said gravely.

"I'll draft the *aide-mémoire*."

"Very good."

"I should have a definite time for you within half an hour."

"Thank you. And I'd like to take Donkin with me. His Arabic is much better than mine and he can take minutes of the meeting so that London can have a telegram giving a full account of it. Will you send him up when he has seen the brief? Thank you."

For the rest of the morning he hung about in his office, turning over papers in a desultory fashion, forcing himself to work. At mid-day, the youthful bearded Donkin arrived with the typed *aide-mémoire* and the news that Mountolive's appointment was for nine the next morning. His small nervous features and watery eyes made him look more than ever a youthful figure, masquerading in a goatee. He accepted a cigarette and puffed it quickly, like a girl, not inhaling the smoke. "Well," said Mountolive with a smile, "your considered views on my brief, please. Errol has told you——?"

"Yes, sir."

"What do you think of this . . . vigorous official protest?"

Donkin drew a deep breath and said thoughtfully: "I doubt if you'll get any direct action at the moment, sir. The internal stresses and strains of the Government since the King's illness have put them all at sixes and sevens. They are all afraid of each other, all pulling different ways. I'm sure that Nur will agree and try hard to get Memlik to act on your paper . . . but. . . ." He drew his lips back thoughtfully about his cigarette. "I don't know. You know Memlik's record. He hates Britain."

Mountolive's spirits suddenly began to rise, despite himself. "Good Lord," he said, "I hadn't thought of it that way. But they simply can't ignore a protest in these terms. After all, my dear boy, the thing is practically a veiled threat."

"I know, sir."

"I really don't see *how* they could ignore it."

"Well, sir, the King's life is hanging by a hair at present. He might, for example, die to-night. He hasn't sat in Divan for nearly six months. Everyone is at jealousies nowadays, personal dislikes and rivalries have come very close to the surface, and with a vengeance. His death would completely alter things—and everyone knows it. Nur above all. By the way, sir, I hear that he is not on speaking terms with Memlik. There has been some serious trouble about the bribes which people have been paying Memlik."

"But Nur himself doesn't take bribes?"

Donkin smiled a small sardonic smile and shook his head slowly and doubtfully. "I don't know, sir," he said primly. "I suspect that they all do and all would. I may be wrong. But in Hosnani's shoes I should certainly manage to get a stay of action by a handsome bribe to Memlik. His susceptibility to a bribe is . . . almost legendary in Egypt."

Mountolive tried hard to frown angrily. "I hope you are wrong," he said. "Because H.M.G. are determined to get some action on this and so am I. Anyway, we'll see, shall we?"

Donkin was still pursuing some private thoughts in silence and gravity. He sat on for a moment smoking and then stood up. He said thoughtfully: "Errol said something which suggested that Hosnani knew we were up to his game. If that is so, why has he not cleared out? He must have a clear idea about our own line of attack, must he not? If he has not moved it must mean that he is confident of holding Memlik in check somehow. I am only thinking aloud, sir."

Mountolive stared at him for a long time with open eyes. He was trying hard to disperse a sudden and, it seemed to him, almost treacherous feeling of optimism. "Most interesting," he said at last. "I must confess I hadn't thought of it in those terms."

"I personally wouldn't take it to the Egyptians at all," said Donkin slyly. He was not averse to teasing his chief of Mission. "Though it is not my place to say so. I should think that Maskelyne has more ways than one of settling the issue. In my view we'd be better advised to leave diplomatic channels alone and simply pay to have Hosnani shot or poisoned. It would cost less than a hundred pounds."

"Well, thank you very much," said Mountolive feebly, his optimism giving place once more to the dark turmoil of half-rationalized emotions in which he seemed doomed to live perpetually. "Thank you, Donkin." (Donkin, he thought angrily, looked awfully like Lenin when he spoke of poison or the knife. It was easy for third secretaries to commit murder by proxy.) Left alone once more he paced his green carpet, balanced between conflicting emotions which were the shapes of hope and despair alternately. Whatever must follow was now irrevocable. He was committed to policies whose outcome, in human terms, was not to be judged. Surely there should be some philosophical resignation to be won from the knowledge? That night he stayed up late listening to his favourite music upon the huge gramophone and drinking rather more heavily than was his wont. From time to time he went across the room and sat at the Georgian writing-desk, with his pen poised above a sheet of crested notepaper.

"My dear Leila: At this moment it seems more necessary than ever that I should see you and I must ask you to overcome your. . . ."

But it was a failure. He crumpled up the letters and threw them regretfully into the wastepaper basket. Overcome her what? Was he beginning to hate Leila too, now? Somewhere, stirring in the hinterland of his consciousness was the thought, almost certain knowledge now, that it was she and not Nessim who had initiated these dreadful plans. She was the prime mover. Should he not tell Nur so? Should he not tell his own Government so? Was it not likely that Narouz, who was the man of action in the family, was even more deeply implicated in the conspiracy than Nessim himself? He sighed. What could any of them hope to gain from a successful Jewish insurrection? Mountolive believed too firmly in the English mystique to realize fully that anyone could have lost faith in it and the promise it might hold of future security, future stability.

No, the whole thing seemed to him simply a piece of gratuitous madness; a typical hare-brained business venture with a chance of large profits! How typical of Egypt! He stirred his own contempt slowly with the thought, as one might stir a mustard-pot. How typical of Egypt! Yet, strangely, how un-typical of Nessim!

Sleep was impossible that night. He slipped on a light over-coat, more as a disguise than anything, and went for a long walk by the river in order to settle his thoughts, feeling a fool-ish regretfulness that there was not a small dog to follow him and occupy his mind. He had slipped out of the servants' quarters, and the resplendent *kawass* and the two police guards were most surprised to see him re-enter the front gate at nearly two o'clock, walking on his own two legs as no Ambassador should ever be allowed to do. He gave them all a civil good-evening in Arabic and let himself into the Residence door with his key. Shed his coat and limped across the lighted hall still followed by an imaginary dog which left wet footprints every-where upon the polished parquet floors. . . .

On his way up to bed he found the now finished painting of himself by Clea standing forlornly against the wall on the first landing. He swore under his breath, for the thing had slipped his mind; he had been meaning to send it off to his mother for the past six weeks. He would make a special point of getting the Bag Room to deal with it to-morrow. They would perhaps have some qualms because of its size, he debated, but nevertheless: he would insist, in order to obviate the trouble of obtaining an export licence for a so-called "work of art". (It was certainly not that.) But ever since a German archaeologist had stolen a lot of Egyptian statuary and sold it to the Museums of Europe the Government had been very sensitive about letting works of art out of the country. They would certainly delay a licence for months while the whole thing was debated. No, the Bag Room must attend to it; his mother would be pleased. He thought of her with a sentimental pang, sitting reading by the fire in that snowbound landscape. He owed her a really long letter. But not now. "After all this is over" he said, and gave a small involun-tary shiver.

Once in bed he entered a narrow maze of shallow and un-refreshing dreams in which he floundered all night long—images of the great network of lakes with their swarming fish and clouds of wild birds, where once more the youthful figures of himself and Leila moved, spirited by the soft concussion of oars in water, to the punctuation of a single soft finger-drum across a violet night-scape; on the confines of the dream there moved another boat, in silhouette, with two figures in it—the brothers: both armed with long-barrelled rifles. Soon he would be overtaken; but warm in the circle of Leila's arms, as if he were Antony at Actium, he could hardly bring himself to feel fear. They did not speak, or at least, he heard no voices. As for himself, he felt only the messages passing to and from the woman in his arms—transmitted it seemed only by the ticking blood. They were past speech and reflection—the diminished figures of an unforgotten, unregretted past, infinitely dear now because irrecoverable. In the heart of the dream itself, he knew he was dreaming, and awoke with surprise and anguish to find tears upon the pillow. Breakfasting according to established custom, he suddenly felt as if he had a fever, but the thermometer refused to confirm his belief. So he rose reluctantly and presented himself in full fig, punctual upon the instant, to find Donkin nervously pacing the hall with the bundle of papers under his arm. "Well," said Mountolive, with a gesture vaguely indicating his rig, "here I am at last."

In the black car with its fluttering pennant they slid smoothly across the town to the Ministry where the timid and ape-like Egyptian waited for them full of uneasy solicitudes and alarms. He was visibly impressed by the dress uniform and by the fact that the two best Arabists of the British Mission had been detailed to call upon him. He gleamed and bowed, automatically playing the opening hand—an exchange of formal politenesses—with his customary practice. He was a small sad man with tin cuff-links and matted hair. His anxiety to please, to accommodate, was so great that he fell easily into postures of friendship, almost of mawkishness. His eyes watered easily. He pressed ceremonial coffee and Turkish delight upon them as if the gesture itself represented a confession of love almost. He mopped his brow continually, and gave his ingratiating pithe-canthropoid grimace. "Ah! Ambassador," he said sentimentally as the compliments gave place to business. "You know our language and our country well. We trust you." Paraphrased, his words meant: "You know our venality to be ineradicable, the mark of an ancient culture, therefore we do not feel ashamed in your presence."

Then he sat with his paws folded over his neat grey waist-coat, glum as a foetus in a bottle, as Mountolive delivered his strongly-worded protest and produced the monument to Mas-kelyne's industry. Nur listened, shaking his head doubtfully from time to time, his visage lengthening. When Mountolive had done, he said impulsively, standing up: "Of course. At once. At once." And then, as if plunged into doubt, unsteadily sat down once more and began to play with his cuff-links. Mountolive sighed as he stood up. "It is a disagreeable duty" he said, "but necessary. May I assure my Government that the matter will be prosecuted with speed?"

"With speed. With speed." The little man nodded twice and licked his lips; one had the impression that he did not quite understand the words he was using. "I shall see Memlik to-day" he added in lower tones. But the timbre of his voice had changed. He coughed and ate a sweetmeat, dusting the castor-sugar off his fingers with a silk handkerchief. "Yes," he said. If he was interested in the massive document lying before him it was (or so it seemed to Mountolive) only that the photostats intrigued him. He had not seen things like these before. They belonged to the great foreign worlds of science and illusion in which these Western peoples lived—worlds of great powers and responsibilities—out of which they sometimes descended, clad in magnificent uniforms, to make the lot of the simple Egyp-tians harder than it was at the best of times. "Yes. Yes. Yes," said Nur again, as if to give the conversation stability and depth, to give his visitor confidence in his good intentions.

Mountolive did not like it at all; the whole tone lacked

directness, purpose. The absurd sense of optimism rose once more in his breast and in order to punish himself for it (also because he was extremely conscientious) he stepped forward and pressed the matter forward another inch. "If you like, Nur, and if you expressly authorize me, I am prepared to lay the facts and recommendations before Memlik Pasha myself. Only speak." But here he was pressing upon the shallow, newly-grown skin of protocol and national feeling. "Cherished Sir," said Nur with a beseeching smile and the gesture of a beggar importuning a rich man, "that would be out of order. For the matter is an internal one. It would not be proper for me to agree."

And he was right there, reflected Mountolive, as they drove uneasily back to the Embassy; they could no longer give orders in Egypt as once the High Commission had been able to do. Donkin sat with a quizzical and reflective smile, studying his own fingers. The pennant on the car's radiator fluttered merrily, reminding Mountolive of the quivering burgee of Nessim's thirty-foot cutter as it slit the harbour waters. . . . "What did you make of it, Donkin?" he said, putting his arm on the elbow of the bearded youth.

"Frankly, sir, I doubted."

"So did I, really." Then he burst out: "But they will have to act, simply have to; I am not going to be put aside like this." (He was thinking: "London will make our lives a misery until I can give them some sort of satisfaction.") Hate for an image of Nessim whose features had somehow—as if by a trick of double-exposure—become merged with those of the saturnine Maskelyne, flooded him again. Crossing the hall he caught sight of his own face in the great pier-glass and was surprised to notice that it wore an expression of feeble petulance.

That day he found himself becoming more and more short-tempered with his staff and the Residence servants. He had begun to feel almost persecuted.

o   o   o   o   o

XIV

If Nessim had the temerity to laugh softly now to himself as he studied the invitation: if he propped the florid thing against his inkstand the better to study it, laughing softly and uneasily into the space before him; it was because he was thinking to himself:

"To say that a man is unscrupulous implies that he was born with inherent scruples which he now chooses to disregard. But does one visualize a man *born* patently conscienceless? A man *born* without a common habit of soul? (Memlik)."

Yes, it would be easy if he were legless, armless, blind, to visualize him; but a particular deficit of a glandular secretion, a missing portion of soul, that would make him rather a target for wonder, perhaps even commiseration. (Memlik). There were men whose feelings dispersed in spray—became as fine as if squeezed through an atomizer: those who had frozen them— "pins and needles of the heart"; there were others born without a sense of value—the morally colour-blind ones. The very powerful were often like that—men walking inside a dream-cloud of their actions which somehow lacked meaning to them. Was this also Memlik? Nessim felt all the passionate curiosity about the man which an entomologist might have for an unclassified specimen.

(Light a cigarette. Get up and walk about the room, pausing from time to time to read the invitation and laugh again silently. The relief kept displacing anxiety, the anxiety relief. He lifted the telephone and spoke to Justine quietly, with a smiling voice: "The Mountain has been to Mahomet." (Code for Mountolive and Nur.) "Yes, my dear. It is a relief to know for certain. All my toxicology and pistol-practice! It looks silly now, I know. This is the way I would have wanted it to happen;

253

but of course, one had to take precautions. Well, pressure is being put upon Mahomet, and he has delivered a small mouse in the form of an invitation to a *Wird*." He heard her laugh incredulously. "Please, my darling," he said, "obtain one of the finest Korans you can get and send it to the office. There are some old ones with ivory covers in the library collection. Yes, I shall take it to Cairo on Wednesday. He must certainly have his Koran." (Memlik). It was all very well to joke. The respite would only be a temporary one; but at least he need not for the moment fear poison or the stealthy figure lurking in an alley which *might* have. . . . No. The situation seemed not without a promise of fruitful delay.

To-day in the fifties the house of Memlik Pasha has become famous in the remotest capitals of the world chiefly because of the distinctive architecture of the Banks which bear their founder's name; and indeed their style has all the curious marks of this mysterious man's taste—for they are all built to the same grotesque pattern, a sort of travesty of an Egyptian tomb, adapted by a pupil of Corbusier! Irresistibly one is forced to stop short and wonder at their grim façades, whether one is walking in Rome or Rio. The squat pillars suggest a mammoth stricken by sudden elephantiasis, the grotesque survival, or per-haps revival, of something inherently macabre—a sort of Otto-man-Egyptian-Gothic? For all the world as if Euston Station had multiplied by binary fission! But by now the power of the man has gone out through these strange funnels into the world at large—all that power condensed and deployed from the small inlaid coffee-table upon which (if ever) he wrote, from the tat-tered yellow divan to which his lethargy held him tethered day by day. (For interviews of particular importance, he wore his tarbush and yellow suède gloves. In his hand he held a common market fly-whisk which his jeweller had embellished with a design in seed-pearls.) He never smiled. A Greek photographer who had once implored him in the name of art to do so had been unceremoniously carted out into the garden under the clicking palms and dealt twelve lashes to atone for his insult.

Perhaps the strange mixture of heredities had something to do with it; for his blood was haunted by an Albanian father and a Nubian mother, whose dreadful quarrels tormented his childhood sleep. He was an only son. This was perhaps how simple ferocity contrived to be matched against an apparent apathy, a whispering voice raised sometimes to a woman's pitch but employed without the use of gesture. Physically too, the long silky head-hair with its suggestion of kink, the nose and mouth carved flatly in dark Nubian sandstone and set in bas-relief upon a completely round Alpine head—they gave the show away. If indeed he had smiled he would have shown a half-circumference of nigger whiteness under nostrils flattened and expanded like rubber. His skin was full of dark beauty-spots, and of a colour much admired in Egypt—that of cigar-leaf. Depilatories such as *halawa* kept his body free from hair, even his hands and forearms. But his eyes were small and set in puckers, like twin cloves. They transmitted their uneasiness by an expression of perpetual drowsiness—the discoloured whites conveying a glaucous absence of mind—as if the soul inhabiting that great body were perpetually away on a private holiday. His lips too were very red, the underlip particularly so; and their contused-looking ripeness suggested: epilepsy?

How had he risen so swiftly? Stage by stage, through slow and arduous clerkships in the Commission (which had taught him his contempt for his masters) and lastly by nepotism. His methods were choice and studied. When Egypt became free, he surprised even his sponsors by gaining the Ministry of the Interior at a single bound. Only then did he tear off the disguise of mediocrity which he had been wearing all these years. He knew very well how to strike out echoes around his name with the whip—for he was now wielding it. The timorous soul of the Egyptian cries always for the whip. "O want easily supplied by one who has trained himself to see men and women as flies." So says the proverb. Within a matter of a year his name had become a dreaded one; it was rumoured that even the old King feared to cross him openly. And with his country's new-found freedom he himself was also magnificently free—at least with Egyptian Moslems. Europeans had still the right, by treaty, to submit their judicial problems or answer charges against them at Les Tribunaux Mixtes, European courts with European lawyers to prosecute or defend. But the Egyptian judicial system (if one could dare to call it that) was run directly by men of Memlik's stamp, the anachronistic survivals of a feudalism as terrible as it was meaningless. The age of the Cadi was far from over for them and Memlik acted with all the authority of someone with a Sultan's *firman* or dispensation in his hands. There was, in truth, nobody to gainsay him. He punished hard and often, without asking questions and often purely upon hearsay or the most remote suspicion. People disappeared silently, leaving no trace, and there was no court of appeal to heed their appeals—if they made any—or else they reappeared in civil life elegantly maimed or deftly blinded—and somehow curiously unwilling to discuss their misfortunes in public. ("Shall we see if he can sing?" Memlik was reputed to say; the reference was to the putting out of a canary's eyes with a red-hot wire—an operation much resorted to and alleged to make the bird sing more sweetly.)

An indolent yet clever man, he depended for his staff work upon Greeks and Armenians for the most part. He hardly ever visited his office in the Ministry but left its running to his minions, explaining and complaining that he was always besieged there by time-wasting petitioners. (In fact he feared that one day he might be assassinated there—for it was a vulnerable sort of place. It would have been easy, for example, to place a bomb in one of the unswept cupboards where the mice frolicked among the yellowing files. Hakim Effendi had put the idea into his head so that he himself could have a free play in the Ministry. Memlik knew this, but did not care.)

Instead he had set aside the old rambling house by the Nile

for his audiences. It was surrounded by a dense grove of palms
and orange-trees. The sacred river flowed outside his windows,
there was always something to see, to watch: feluccas plying up
or down-river, pleasure parties passing, an occasional motor-
boat. . . . Also it was too far for petitioners to come and bother
him about imprisoned relations. (Hakim shared the office
bribes anyway.) Here Memlik would only see people who were
relatively too important to dismiss: struggling upright into a
seated position on the yellow divan and placing his neat shoes
(with their pearl-grey spats) upon a damask footstool before
him, his right hand in his breast pocket, his left holding the
common market fly-whisk as if to confer an absolution with it.
The staff attending to his daily business transactions here consisted of an Armenian secretary (Cyril) and the little doll-like
Italian Rafael (by profession a barber and procurer) who kept
him company and sweetened the dullness of official work by
suggesting pleasures whose perversity might ignite a man who
appeared to have worn away every mental appetite save that for
money. I say that Memlik never smiled, but sometimes when
he was in a good humour, he stroked Rafael's hair thoughtfully
and placed his fingers over his mouth to silence his laughter.
This was when he was thinking deeply before lifting the receiver of the old-fashioned goose-necked telephone to have a
conversation with someone in that low voice, or to ring the
Central Prison for the pleasure of hearing the operator's obvious
alarm when he uttered his name. At this, Rafael particularly
would break into sycophantic giggles, laughing until the tears
ran down his face, stuffing a handkerchief into his mouth. But
Memlik did not smile. He depressed his cheeks slightly and
said: "Allah! you laugh." Such occasions were few and far
between.

Was he indeed as terrible as his reputation made him? The
truth will never be known. Legends collect easily around such a
personage because he belongs more to legend than to life.
("Once when he was threatened by impotence he went down

257

to the prison and ordered two girls to be flogged to death before his eyes while a third was obliged"—how picturesque are the poetical figures of the Prophet's tongue—"to refresh his lagging spirits." It was said that he personally witnessed every official execution, and that he trembled and spat continuously. Afterwards he called for a siphon of soda-water to quench his thirst. . . . But who shall ever know the truth of these legends?)

He was morbidly superstitious and incurably venal—and indeed was building an immense fortune upon bribery; yet how shall we add to the sum of this the fact of his inordinate religiosity—a fanatical zeal of observance which might have been puzzling in anyone who was not an Egyptian? This is where the quarrel with the pious Nur had arisen; for Memlik had established almost a court-form for the reception of bribes. His collection of Korans was a famous one. They were housed upstairs in a ramshackle gallery of the house. By now it was known far and wide that the polite form in which to approach him was to interleave a particularly cherished copy of the Holy Book with notes or other types of currency and (with an obeisance) to present him with a new addition to his great library. He would accept the gift and reply, with thanks, that he must repair at once upstairs to see if he already had a copy. On his return, the petitioner knew that he had succeeded if Memlik thanked him once more and said that he had put the book in his library; but if Memlik claimed to possess a copy already and handed back the book (albeit the money had inevitably been extracted) the petitioner knew that his plea had failed. It was this little social formula which Nur had characterized as "bringing discredit upon the Prophet"—and had so earned Memlik's quiet hate.

The long-elbowed conservatory in which he held his private Divan was also something of a puzzle. The coloured fanlights in cheap cathedral glass transformed visitors into harlequins, squirting green and scarlet and blue upon their faces and clothes as they walked across the long room to greet their host.

Outside the murky windows ran the cocoa-coloured river on whose further bank stood the British Embassy with its elegant gardens in which Mountolive wandered on the evenings when he found himself alone. The wall-length of Memlik's great reception-room was almost covered by two enormous and incongruous Victorian paintings by some forgotten master which, being too large and heavy to hang, stood upon the floor and gave something of the illusion of framed tapestries. But the subject-matter! In one, the Israelites crossed the Red Sea which was gracefully piled up on either side to admit their fearful passage; in the other a hirsute Moses struck a stage rock with a shepherd's crook. Somehow these attenuated Biblical subjects matched the rest of the furniture perfectly—the great Ottoman carpets and the stiff ugly-backed chairs covered in blue damask, the immense contorted brass chandelier with its circles of frosted electric light bulbs which shone night and day. On one side of the yellow divan stood a life-size bust of Fouché which took the eye of the petitioner at once by its incongruity. Once Memlik had been flattered by a French diplomat who had said: "You are regarded as the best Minister of Interior in modern history—indeed, since Fouché there has been no-one to equal you." The remark may have been barbed, but nevertheless it struck Memlik's fancy, and he at once ordered the bust from France. It looked faintly reproachful amidst all that Egyptian flummery, for the dust had settled thick upon it. The same diplomat had once described Memlik's reception room as a cross between an abandoned geological museum and a corner of the old Crystal Palace—and this also was apt though cruel.

All this detail Nessim's polite eye took in with many a hidden gleam of amusement as he stood in the doorway and heard his name announced. It appealed richly to him to be thus invited to share a prayer-meeting or *Wird* with the redoubtable Memlik. Nor were these functions uncommon, strange though it seems to relate, for Memlik frequently enjoyed these so-called "Nights of God" and his piety did not seem inconsistent with the rest of his mysterious character; he listened attentively, unwaveringly to the reciter, often until two or three in the morning, with the air of a hibernating snake. Sometimes he even joined in the conventional gasp "Allah" with which the company expressed its joy in some particularly felicitous passage of the Gospel. . . .

Nessim crossed the chamber with a light and lively walk, conventionally touching breast and lip, and seated himself before Memlik to express gratitude for an invitation which did him great honour. On the evening of his appearance there were nine or ten other guests only, and he felt certain that this was because Memlik wished to study him, if possible even to hold some private conversation with him. He carried the exquisite little Koran wrapped in soft tissue paper; he had carefully larded the pages with bank drafts negotiable in Switzerland. "O Pasha," he said softly, "I have heard of your legendary library and ask only the pleasure of a book-lover in offering you an addition to it." He laid his present down on the little table and accepted the coffee and sweetmeats which were placed before him. Memlik neither answered nor moved his position on the divan for a long moment, allowing him to sip his coffee, and then said negligently: "The host is honoured. These are my friends." He performed some rather perfunctory introductions to his other visitors who seemed rather an odd collection to gather together for a recitation of the Gospel; there was nobody here of any obvious standing in the society of Cairo, this much Nessim noticed. Indeed, he knew none of them though he was attentively polite to all. Then he permitted himself a few generalized comments on the beauty and appropriateness of the reception chamber and the high quality of the paintings against the wall. Memlik was not displeased by this and said lazily: "It is both my work-room and my reception-room. Here I live."

"I have often heard it described" said Nessim with his courtier's air, "by those lucky enough to visit you either for work or pleasure."

"My work" said Memlik with a glint "is done on Tuesdays only. For the rest of the week I take pleasure with my friends."

Nessim was not deaf to the menace in the words; Tuesday for the Moslem is the least favoured day for human undertakings, for he believes that on Tuesday God created all the unpleasant things. It is the day chosen for the execution of criminals; no man dares marry on a Tuesday for the proverb says: "Married on Tuesday, hanged on Tuesday." In the words of the Prophet: "On Tuesday God created darkness absolute."

"Happily," said the smiling Nessim, "to-day is Monday when God created the trees." And he led the conversation around to the lovely palm-trees which nodded outside the window: a conversational turn which broke the ice and won the admiration of the other visitors.

The wind changed now, and after half an hour of desultory talk, the sliding doors at the far end of the chamber were set aside to admit them to a banquet laid out upon two great tables. The room was decorated with magnificent flowers. Here at least over the expensive delicacies of Memlik's supper table, the hint of animation and friendship became a little more obvious. One or two people talked, and Memlik himself, though he ate nothing, moved slowly from group to group uttering laboured politenesses in a low voice. He came upon Nessim in a corner and said quite simply, indeed with an air of candour: "I wished particularly to see you, Hosnani."

"I am honoured, Memlik Pasha."

"I have seen you at receptions; but we have lacked common friends to present us to each other. Great regrets."

"Great regrets."

Memlik sighed and fanned himself with his fly-whisk, complaining that the night was hot. Then he said, in the tone of a man debating something with himself, hesitantly almost: "Sir, the Prophet has said that great power brings greater enemies. I know you are powerful."

"My power is insignificant, yet I have enemies."

"Great regrets."

"Indeed."

Memlik shifted his weight to his left leg and picked his teeth thoughtfully for a moment; then he went on.

"I think we shall understand each other perfectly soon."

Nessim bowed formally and remained silent while his host gazed speculatively at him, breathing slowly and evenly through his mouth. Memlik said: "When they wish to complain, they come to me, the very fountain-head of complaints. I find it wearisome, but sometimes I am forced to act on behalf of those who complain. You take my meaning?"

"Perfectly."

"At some moments, I am not bound to commit myself to particular action. But at others, I may be so bound. Therefore, Nessim Hosnani, the wise man removes the grounds for complaints."

Nessim bowed again gracefully and once more remained silent. It was useless to pursue the dialectics of their relative positions until he had obtained acceptance of his proffered gift. Memlik perhaps sensed this, for he sighed and moved away to another group of visitors. And presently the dinner ended and the company retired once more to the long reception-room. Now Nessim's pulse beat faster, for Memlik picked up the tissue-wrapped package and excused himself, saying "I must compare this with the books in my collection. The sheik of to-night—he of Imbabi—will come soon now. Seat yourselves and take your leisure. I will join you soon." He left the room. A desultory conversation began now, in which Nessim tried his best to take part though he realized that his heart was beating uncomfortably fast and his fingers felt shaky as they raised a cigarette to his lips. After a while, the doors were once more opened to admit an old blind sheik who had come to preside over this "Night Of God". The company surrounded him, shaking his hands and uttering compliments. And then Memlik entered abruptly and Nessim saw that his hands were empty: he uttered a prayer of thanksgiving under his breath and mopped his brow.

It did not take him long to compose himself once more. He was standing rather apart from the press of dark-coated gentlemen in whose midst stood the old blind preacher, his vacant, bewildered face turning from voice to voice with the air of some mechanical contrivance built to register sound-waves; his air of mild confusion suggested all the ghostly contentment of an absolute faith in something which was the more satisfying for not being fully apprehended by the reason. His hands were joined on his breast; he looked as shy as some ancient child, full of the kinetic beauty of a human being whose soul has become a votive object.

The pasha who entered once more made his slow way to Nessim's side, but by stages so delayed that it seemed to the latter he would never reach him. This slow progress was prolonged by compliments and an air of elaborate disinterestedness. At last he was there; at Nessim's elbow, his long clever fingers still holding the bejewelled fly-whisk. "Your gift is a choice one" the low voice said at last, with the faintest suggestion of honey in its tones. "It is most acceptable. Indeed, sir, your knowledge and discrimination are both legendary. To show surprise would betoken vulgar ignorance of the fact."

The formula which Memlik invariably used was so smooth and remarkably well-turned in Arabic that Nessim could not help looking surprised and pleased. It was a choice turn of speech such as only a really cultivated person would have used. He did not know that Memlik had carefully memorized it against such occasions. He bowed his head as one might to receive an accolade, but remained silent. Memlik flirted his fly-whisk for a moment, before adding in another tone: "Of course, there is only one thing. I have already spoken of the complaints which come to me, *effendi* mine. In all such cases I am bound sooner or later to investigate causes. Great regrets."

Nessim turned his smooth black eye upon the Egyptian and still smiling said in a low voice: "Sir, by the European Christmastide—a matter of months—there will be no further grounds for complaint." There was a silence.

"Then time is important" said Memlik reflectively.

"Time is the air we breathe, so says a proverb."

The pasha half turned now and, speaking as if to the company in general, added: "My collection has need of your most discriminating knowledge. I hope you may discover for me many other treasures of the Holy Word." Again Nessim bowed.

"As many as may be found acceptable, pasha."

"I am sorry we did not meet before. Great regrets."

"Great regrets."

But now he became the host again and turned aside. The wide circle of uncomfortable stiff-backed chairs had been almost filled by his other visitors. Nessim selected one at the end of the line as Memlik reached his yellow divan and climbed slowly upon it with the air of a swimmer reaching a raft in mid-ocean. He gave a signal and the servants came forward to remove the coffee-cups and sweetmeats; they brought with them a tall and elegant high-backed chair with carved arms and green upholstery which they set for the preacher a little to one side of the room. A guest rose and with mutterings of respect led the blind man to his seat. Retiring in good order the servants closed and bolted the tall doors at the end of the room. The *Wird* was about to begin. Memlik formally opened the proceedings with a quotation from Ghazzali the theologian—a surprising innovation for someone, like Nessim, whose picture of the man had been formed entirely from hearsay. "The only way," said Memlik "to become united with God is by constant intercourse with him." Having uttered the words he leaned back and closed his eyes, as if exhausted by the effort. But the phrase had the effect of a signal, for as the blind

264

preacher raised his scraggy neck and inhaled deeply before commencing, the company responded like one man. At once all cigarettes were extinguished, every leg was uncrossed, coat buttons formally done up, every negligent attitude of body and address corrected.

They waited now with emotion for that old voice, melodious and worn with age, to utter the opening strophes of the Holy Book, and there was nothing feigned in the adoring attention of the circle of venal faces. Some licked their lips and leaned forward eagerly, as if to take the phrases upon their lips; others lowered their heads and closed their eyes as if against a new experience in music. The old preacher sat with his waxen hands folded in his lap and uttered the first *sura*, full of the soft warm colouring of a familiar understanding, his voice a little shaky at first but gathering power and assurance from the silence as he proceeded. His eyes now were as wide and lustreless as a dead hare's. His listeners followed the notation of the verses as they fell from his lips with care and rapture, gradually seeking their way together out into the main stream of the poetry, like a school of fish following a leader by instinct out into the deep sea. Nessim's own constraint and unease gave place to a warmth about the heart, for he too loved the *suras*, and the old preacher had a magnificent speaking voice, although the tone was as yet furry and unaccentuated. But it was a "voice of the inmost heart"—his whole spiritual presence coursed like a blood-stream in the magnificent verses, filling them with his own ardour; and one could feel his audience tremble and respond, like the rigging of a ship in the wind. *"Allah!"* they sighed at every newly remembered felicity of phrasing, and these little gasps increased the confidence of the old voice with its sweet high register. "A voice whose melody is sweeter than charity" says the proverb. The recitation was a dramatic one and very varied in style, the preacher changing his tone to suit the substance of the words, now threatening, now pleading, now declaiming, now admonishing. It was no surprise that he

265

should be word-perfect, for in Egypt the blind preachers have a faculty for memorizing which is notorious, and moreover the whole length of the Koran is about two-thirds that of the New Testament. Nessim listened to him with tenderness and admiration, staring down upon the carpet, half-entranced by the ebb and flow of the poetry which distracted his mind from the tireless speculations he had been entertaining about Memlik's possible response to the pressures which Mountolive had been forced to bring upon him.

Between each *sura* there came a few moments of silence in which nobody stirred or uttered a word, but appeared sunk in contemplation of what had gone before. The preacher then sank his chin upon his breastbone as if to regain his strength and softly linked his fingers. Then once more he would look upwards towards the sightless light and declaim, and once more one felt the tension of the words as they sped through the attentive consciousness of his listeners. It was after midnight when the Koran reading was complete and some measure of relaxation came back to the audience as the old man embarked upon the stories of tradition; these were no longer listened to as if they were a part of music, but were followed with the active proverbial mind: for they were the dialectics of revelation—its ethic and application. The company responded to the changed tone by letting their expression brighten to the keenness of habitual workers in the world, bankers, students, or business men.

It was two o'clock before the evening ended and Memlik showed his guests to the front door where their cars awaited them, with a white dew upon their wheels and chromium surfaces. To Nessim he said in a quiet deliberate voice—a voice which went down to the heart of their relationship like some heavy plumb-line: "I will invite you again, sir, for as long as may be possible. But reflect." And with his finger he gently touched the coat-button of his guest as if to underline the remark.

Nessim thanked him and walked down the drive among the

266

palm-trees to where he had left the great car; his naked relief was by no means unmixed with doubt. He had at best, he reflected, gained a respite which did not fundamentally alter the enmity of the forces ranged against him. But even a respite was something to be grateful for; for how long though? It was at this stage impossible to judge.

Justine had not gone to bed. She was sitting in the lounge of Shepheards Hotel under the clock with an untouched Turkish coffee before her. She stood up eagerly as he passed through the swing doors with his usual gentle smile of welcome; she did not move but stared at him with a peculiar strained intensity—as if she were trying to decipher his feelings from his carriage. Then she relaxed and smiled with relief. "I'm so relieved! Thank God! I could see from your face as you came in." They embraced gently and he sank into a chair beside her whispering: "My goodness, I thought it would never end. I spent part of the time being rather anxious too. Did you dine alone?"

"Yes. I saw David."

"Mountolive?"

"He was at some big dinner. He bowed frigidly but did not stop to speak to me. But then, he had people with him, bankers or something."

Nessim ordered a coffee and as he drank it gave an account of his evening with Memlik. "It is clear," he said thoughtfully, "that the sort of pressure the British are bringing is based upon those files of correspondence they captured in Palestine. The Haifa office told Capodistria so. It would be a good angle to present these to Nur and press him to . . . take action." He drew a tiny gallows in pencil on the back of an envelope with a small fly-like victim hanging from it. "What I gathered from Memlik suggested that he can *delay* action but that the sort of pressure is too strong to ignore indefinitely; sooner or later he will be forced to satisfy Nur. I virtually told him that by Christmas I would be able . . . I would be out of the danger zone. His investigations would lead nowhere."

267

"*If* everything goes according to plan."

"Everything *will* go according to plan."

"Then what?"

"Then what!" Nessim stretched his long arms over his head, yawning, and nodded sideways at her. "We will take up new dispositions. Da Capo will disappear; you will go away. Leila will go down to Kenya for a long holiday together with Narouz. That is what!"

"And you?"

"I shall stay on a little while to keep things in place here. The Community needs me. There is a lot to be done politically still. Then I shall come to you and we can have a long holiday in Europe or anywhere you choose. . . ."

She was staring unsmilingly at him. "I am nervous" she said at last with a little shiver. "Nessim, let us drive by the Nile for an hour and collect our thoughts before we go to bed."

He was glad to indulge her, and for an hour the car nosed softly along the noble tree-lined roads of the Nile river-bank under the jacarandas, its engine purring, while they talked intermittently in low voices. "What worries me" she said, "is that you will have Memlik's hand upon your shoulder. How will you ever shake it off? If he has firm evidence against you, he will never relax his grip until you are squeezed dry."

"Either way," said Nessim quietly, "it would be bad for us. For if he proceeded with an open enquiry, you know very well that it would give the Government a chance to sequestrate our properties. I would rather satisfy his private cupidity as long as I can. Afterwards, we shall see. The main thing is to concentrate on this coming . . . battle."

As he uttered the word they were passing the brilliantly lighted gardens of the British Embassy. Justine gave a little start and plucked his sleeve, for she had caught sight of a slender pyjama-clad figure walking about the green lawns with an air of familiar distraction. "Mountolive" she said. Nessim looked sorrowfully across the gardens at his friend, suddenly

268

possessed by a temptation to stop the car and enter the gardens to surprise him. Such a gesture would have been in keeping with their behaviour towards each other—not three months before. What had happened to everything now? "He'll catch cold," said Justine; "he is barefooted. Holding a telegram."

Nessim increased speed and the car curved on down the avenue. "I expect" he said, "that he suffers from insomnia and wanted to cool his feet in the grass before trying to get to sleep. You often used to do that. Remember?"

"But the telegram?"

There was really no great mystery about the telegram which the sleepless Ambassador held in his hand and which he studied from time to time as he walked slowly about in his own demesne, smoking a cigar. Once a week he played a game of chess with Balthazar by telegram—an event which nowadays gave him great solace, and some of the refreshment which tired men of affairs draw from crossword puzzles. He did not see the great car as it purred on past the gardens and headed for the town.

o   o   o   o   o

XV

They were to stay like this for many weeks now, the actors: as if trapped once and for all in postures which might illustrate how incalculable a matter naked providence can be. To Mountolive, more than the others, came a disenchanting sense of his own professional inadequacy, his powerlessness to act now save as an instrument (no longer a factor), so strongly did he feel himself gripped by the gravitational field of politics. Private humours and impulses were alike disinherited, counting for nothing. Did Nessim also feel the mounting flavour of stagnation in everything, he wondered? He thought back bitterly and often to the casually spoken words of Sir Louis as he was combing his hair in the mirror. "The illusion that you are free to act!" He suffered from excruciating headaches now from time to time and his teeth began to give him trouble. For some reason or another he took the fancy that this was due to over-smoking and tried to abandon the habit unsuccessfully. The struggle with tobacco only increased his misery.

Yet if he himself were powerless, now, how much more so the others? Like the etiolated projections of a sick imagination, they seemed, drained of meaning, empty as suits of clothes; taking up emplacements in this colourless drama of contending wills. Nessim, Justine, Leila—they had an unsubstantial air now—as of dream-projections acting in a world populated by expressionless waxworks. It was difficult to feel that he owed them even love any longer. Leila's silence above all suggested, even more clearly, the guilt of her complicity.

Autumn drew to an end and still Nur could produce no proof of action. The life-lines which tied Mountolive's Mission to London became clogged with longer and longer telegrams full of the shrewish iterations of minds trying to influence the operation of what Mountolive now knew to be not merely chance, but in fact destiny. It was interesting, too, in a paradoxical sort of way, this first great lesson which his profession had to teach him; for outside the circumscribed area of his personal fears and hesitations, he watched the whole affair with a kind of absorbed attention, with almost a sense of dreadful admiration. But it was like some fretful mummy that he now presented himself to the gaze of Nur, almost ashamed of the splendours of that second-hand uniform, so clearly was it intended to admonish or threaten the Minister. The old man was full of a feverish desire to accommodate him; he was like a monkey jumping enthusiastically on the end of a chain. But what could he do? He made faces to match his transparent excuses. The investigations undertaken by Memlik were not as yet complete. It was essential to verify the truth. The threads were still being followed up. And so forth.

Mountolive did what he had never done before in his official life, colouring up and banging the dusty table between them with friendly exasperation. He adopted the countenance of a thunder-cloud and predicted a rupture of diplomatic relations. He went so far as to recommend Nur for a decoration . . . realizing that this was his last resort. But in vain.

The broad contemplative figure of Memlik squatted athwart the daylight, promising everything, performing nothing; immovable, imperturbable, and only faintly malign. Each was now pressing the other beyond the point of polite conciliation: Maskelyne and the High Commissioner were pressing London for action; London, full of moralizing grandeurs, pressed Mountolive; Mountolive pressed Nur, overwhelming the old man with a sense of his own ineffectuality, for he too was powerless to grapple with Memlik without the help of the King: and the King was ill, very ill. At the bottom of this pyramid sat the small figure of the Minister for Interior, with his priceless collection of Korans locked away in dusty cupboards.

Constrained nevertheless to keep up the diplomatic pressure, Mountolive was now irradiated by an appalling sense of futility as he sat (like some ageing *jeune premier*) and listened to the torrent of Nur's excuses, drinking the ceremonial coffee and prying into those ancient and imploring eyes. "But what more evidence do you need, Pasha, than the papers I brought you?" The Minister's hands spread wide, smoothing the air between them as if he were rubbing cold-cream into it; he exuded a conciliatory and apologetic affection, like an unguent. "He is going into the matter," he croaked helplessly. "There is more than one Hosnani, to begin with," he added in desperation. Backwards and forwards moved the tortoise's wrinkled head, regular as a pendulum. Mountolive groaned inside himself as he thought of those long telegrams following one another, endless as a tapeworm. Nessim had now, so to speak, wedged himself neatly in between his various adversaries, in a position where neither could reach him—for the time being. The game was in baulk.

Donkin alone derived a quizzical amusement from these exchanges—so characteristic of Egypt. His own affection for the Moslem had taught him to see clearly into his motives, to discern the play of childish cupidities underneath the histrionic silence of a Minister, under his facile promises. Even Mountolive's gathering hysteria in the face of these checks was amusing for a junior secretary. His Chief had become a puffy and petulant dignitary, under all this stress. Who could have believed such a change possible?

The observation that there was more than one Hosnani was a strange one, and it was a fruit of the prescient Rafael's thought as he quietly shaved his master one morning, according to custom; Memlik paid great attention to what the barber said—was he not a European? While the little barber shaved him in the morning they discussed the transactions of the day. Rafael was full of ideas and opinions, but he uttered them obliquely, simplifying them so that they presented themselves in readily understandable form. He knew that Memlik had been troubled by Nur's insistence, though he had not shown it; he knew, moreover, that Memlik would act only if the King recovered enough to grant Nur an audience. It was a matter of luck and time; meanwhile, why not pluck Hosnani as far as possible? It was only one of a dozen such matters which lay gathering dust (and perhaps bribes) while the King was ill.

One fine day His Majesty would feel much better under his new German doctors and would grant audience once again. He would send for Nur. That is the manner in which the matter would fall out. The next thing: the old goose-necked telephone by the yellow divan would tingle and the old man's voice (disguising its triumphant tone) would say, "I am Nur, speaking from the very Divan of the Very King, having received audience. That matter of which we spoke concerning the British Government. It must now be advanced and go forward. Give praise to God!"

"Give praise to God!" and from this point forward Memlik's hands would be tied. But for the moment he was still a free agent, free to express his contempt for the elder Minister by inaction.

"There are two brothers, Excellence," Rafael had said, putting on a story-book voice and casting an expression of gloomy maturity upon that little doll's face. "Two brothers Hosnani, not one, Excellence." He sighed as his white fingers took up small purses of Memlik's dark skin for the razor to work upon. He proceeded slowly, for to register an idea in a Moslem mind is like trying to paint a wall: one must wait for the first coat to dry (the first idea) before applying a second. "Of the two brothers, one is rich in land, and the other rich in money—he of the Koran. Of what good are lands to my Excellence? But one whose purse is fathomless. . . ." His tone suggested all the landless man's contempt for good ground.

"Well, well, but . . ." said Memlik with a slow, unemphatic impatience, yet without moving his lips under the kiss of the crisp razor. He was impatient for the theme to be developed. Rafael smiled and was silent for a moment. "Indeed," he said thoughtfully, "the papers you received from his Excellence were signed Hosnani—in the family name. Who is to say which brother signed them, which is guilty and which innocent? If you were wise in deed would you sacrifice a moneyed man to a landed one? I not, Excellence, I not."

"What would you do, my Rafael?"

"For people like the British it could be made to seem that the poor one was guilty, not the rich. I am only thinking aloud, Excellence, a small man among great affairs."

Memlik breathed quietly through his mouth, keeping his eyes shut. He was skilled in never showing surprise. Yet the thought, suspended idly in his mind, filled him with a reflective astonishment. In the last month he had received three additions to his library which had left in little doubt the comparative affluence of his client, the elder Hosnani. It was getting on for the Christian Christmastide. He pondered heavily. To satisfy both the British and his own cupidity. . . . That would be very clever!

Not eight hundred yards away from the chair in which Memlik sprawled, across the brown Nile water, sat Mountolive at his papers. On the polished desk before him lay the great florid invitation card which enjoined his participation in one of the great social events of the year—Nessim's annual duck-shoot on Lake Mareotis. He propped it against his inkwell in order to read it again with an expression of fugitive reproach.

But there was another communication of even greater importance; even after this long silence he recognized Leila's nervous handwriting on the lined envelope smelling of *chypre*. But inside it he found a page torn from an exercise book scrawled over with words and phrases set down anyhow, as if in great haste.

"David, I am going abroad, perhaps long perhaps short, I cannot tell; against my will. Nessim insists. But I must see you before I leave. I must take courage and meet you the evening before. Don't fail. I have something to ask, something to tell. 'This business'! I knew nothing about it till carnival I swear; now only you can save. . . ."

So the letter ran on pell-mell; Mountolive felt a queer mixture of feelings—an incoherent relief which somehow trembled on the edge of indignation. After all this time she would be waiting for him after dark near the *Auberge Bleue* in an old horse-drawn cab pulled back off the road among the palms! That plan was at least touched with something of her old fantasy. For some reason Nessim was not to know of this meeting— why should he disapprove? But the information that she at least had had no part in the conspiracies fostered by her son— that flooded him with relief and tenderness. And all this time he had been seeing Leila as a hostile extension of Nessim, had been training himself to hate her! "My poor Leila" he said aloud, holding the envelope to his nose to inhale the fragrance of *chypre*. He picked up the phone and spoke softly to Errol: "I suppose the whole Chancery has been invited to the Hosnani shoot? Yes? I agree, he has got rather a nerve at such a time. . . . I shall, of course, have to decline, but I would like you chaps to accept and apologize for me. To keep up a public appearance of normality merely. Will you then? Thank you very much. Now one more thing. I shall go up the evening before the shoot for private business and return the next day—we shall probably pass each other on the desert road. No, I'm *glad* you fellows have the chance. By all means, and good hunting."

The next ten days passed in a sort of dream, punctuated only by the intermittent stabbings of a reality which was no longer a drug, a dissipation which gagged his nerves; his duties were a torment of boredom. He felt immeasurably expended, used-up, as he confronted his face in the bathroom mirror, presenting it to the razor's edge with undisguised distaste. He had become quite noticeably grey now at the temples. From somewhere in the servants' quarters a radio burred and scratched out the

275

melody of an old song which had haunted a whole Alexandrian summer: "*Jamais de la vie*". He had come to loathe it now. This new epoch—a limbo filled with the dispersing fragments of habit, duty and circumstance—filled him with a gnawing impatience; underneath it all he was aware that he was gathering himself together for this long-awaited meeting with Leila. Somehow it would determine, not the physical tangible meaning of his return to Egypt so much as the psychic meaning of it in relation to his inner life. God! that was a clumsy way to put it —but how else could one express these things? It was a sort of barrier in himself which had to be crossed, a puberty of the feelings which had to be outgrown.

He drove up across the crackling desert in his pennoned car, rejoicing in the sweet whistle of its cooled engine, and the whickering of wind at the side-screens. It had been some time since he had been able to travel across the desert alone like this —it reminded him of older and happier journeys. Flying across the still white air with the speedometer hovering in the sixties, he hummed softly to himself, despite his distaste, the refrain:

> *Jamais de la vie,*
> *Jamais dans la nuit*
> *Quand ton coeur se démange de chagrin. . . .*

How long was it since he had caught himself singing like this? An age. It was not really happiness, but an overmastering relief of mind. Even the hateful song helped him to recover the lost image of an Alexandria he had once found charming. Would it, could it be so again?

It was already late afternoon by the time he reached the desert fringe and began the slow in-curving impulse which would lead him to the city's bristling outer slums. The sky was covered with clouds. A thunderstorm was breaking over Alexandria. To the east upon the icy green waters of the lake poured a rainstorm—flights of glittering needles pocking the waters; he could dimly hear the hush of rain above the whisper

276

of the car. He glimpsed the pearly city through the dark cloud-mat, its minarets poked up against the cloud bars of an early sunset; linen soaked in blood. A sea-wind chaffered and tugged at the sea-limits of the estuary. Higher still roamed packages of smoking, blood-stained cloud throwing down a strange radiance into the streets and squares of the white city. Rain was a rare and brief winter phenomenon in Alexandria. Presently the sea-wind would rise, alter inclination, and peel the sky clear in a matter of minutes, rolling up the heavy cumulus like a carpet. The glassy freshness of the winter sky would resume its light, polishing the city once more till it glittered against the desert like quartz, like some beautiful artifact. He was no longer impatient. Dusk was beginning to swallow the sunset. As he neared the ugly ribbons of cabins and warehouses by the outer harbour, his tyres began to smoke and seethe upon the wet tarmac, its heat now slaked by a light rain. Time to throttle down. . . .

He entered the penumbra of the storm slowly, marvelling at the light, at the horizon drawn back like a bow. Odd gleams of sunshine scattered rubies upon the battleships in the basin (squatting under their guns like horned toads). It was the ancient city again; he felt its pervading melancholy under the rain as he crossed it on his way to the Summer Residence. The brilliant unfamiliar lighting of the thunder-storm re-created it, giving it a spectral, story-book air—broken pavements made of tinfoil, snail-shells, cracked horn, mica; earth-brick buildings turned to the colour of ox-blood; the lovers wandering in Mohammed Ali Square, disoriented by the unfamiliar rain, disconsolate as untuned instruments; the clicking of violet trams along the sea-front among the tatting of palm-fronds. The desuetude of an ancient city whose streets were plastered with the wet blown dust of the surrounding desert. He felt it all anew, letting it extend panoramically in his consciousness—the moan of a liner edging out towards the sunset bar, or the trains which flowed like a torrent of diamonds towards the interior, their wheels chattering among the shingle ravines and the powder of temples long since abandoned and silted up. . . .

Mountolive saw it all now with a world weariness which he at last recognized as the stripe which maturity lays upon the shoulders of an adult—the stigma of the experiences which age one. The wind spouted in the harbour. The corridors of wet rigging swayed and shook like the foliage of some great tree. Now the tears were trickling down the windscreen under the diligent and noiseless wipers. . . . A little period in this strange contused darkness, fitfully lit by lightning, and then the wind would come—the magistral north wind, punching and squeezing the sea into its own characteristic plumage of white crests, knocking open the firmament until the faces of men and women once more reflected the open winter sky. He was in plenty of time.

He drove to the Summer Residence to make sure that the staff had been warned of his arrival; he intended to stay the night and return to Cairo on the morrow. He let himself into the front door with his own key, having pressed the bell, and stood listening for the shuffle of Ali. And as he heard the old man's step approaching, the north wind arrived with a roar, stiffening the windows in their frames, and the rain stopped abruptly, as if it had been turned off.

He had still an hour or so before the rendezvous: comfortable time in which to have a bath and change his clothes. To his own surprise, he felt perfectly at ease now, no longer tormented by doubts or elated by a sense of relief. He had put himself unreservedly in the hands of chance.

He ate a sandwich and drank two strong whiskies before setting out and letting the great car slide softly down the Grande Corniche towards the *Auberge Bleue* which lay towards the outskirts of the town, fringed by patches of dune and odd clusters of palm. The sky was clear again now and the white-caps were racing ashore to bang themselves in showers of spray upon the metal piers of Chatby. At the horizon's edge flickered the intermittent lightning still, but dimly. These faint gleams suggested perhaps the gun flashes of distant warships in a naval engagement.

He edged the car softly off the road and into the deserted car park of the Auberge, switching off the side-lamps as he did so. He sat for a moment, accustoming himself to the bluish dusk. The Auberge itself was empty—it was still too early for dancers and diners to throng its elegant floor and bars. Then he saw it. Just off the road, on the opposite side of the park, there was a bare patch of sand-dune with a few leaning palms. A gharry stood there. Its old-fashioned oil-lamps were alight and wallowed feebly like fireflies in the light sea-airs. There was a dim figure on the jarvey's box in a tarbush—apparently asleep.

He crossed the gravel with a light and joyous step, hearing it squeak under his shoes, and as he neared the gharry called, in a soft voice: "Leila!" He saw the silhouette of the driver turn against the sky and register attention; from inside the cab he heard a voice—Leila's voice—say something like: "Ah! David, so at last we meet. I have come all this way to tell you. . . ."

He leaned forward with a puzzled air, straining his eyes, but could not see more than the vague shape of someone in the far corner of the cab. "Get in," she cried imperiously. "Get in and we shall talk."

And it was here that a sense of unreality overtook Mountolive; he could not exactly fathom why. But he felt as one does in dreams when one walks without touching the ground, or else appears to rise deliberately through the air like a cork through water. His feelings, like antennae, were reaching out towards the dark figure, trying to gather and assess the meaning of these tumbling phrases and to analyse the queer sense of disorientation which they carried, buried in them, like a foreign intonation creeping into familiar voices; somewhere the whole context of his impressions foundered.

The thing was this: he did not quite recognize the voice. Or else, to put it another way, he could identify Leila but not quite believe in the evidence of his own ears. It was, so to speak, not the precious voice which, in his imagination, had lived on, inhabiting the remembered figure of Leila. She spoke now with a sort of gobbling inconsistency, an air of indiscretion, in a voice which had a slightly clipped edge on it. He supposed this to be the effect of excitement and who knows what other emotions? But . . . phrases which petered out, only to start again in the middle, phrases which lapsed and subsided in the very act of joining two thoughts? He frowned to himself in the darkness as he tried to analyse this curious unreal quality of distraction in the voice. It was not the voice that belonged to Leila—or was it? Presently, a hand fell upon his arm and he was able to study it eagerly in the puddle of soft light cast by the oil-lamp in the brass holder by the cabby's box. It was a chubby and unkempt little hand, with short, unpainted finger-nails and unpressed cuticles. "Leila—is it really you?" he asked almost involuntarily, still invaded by this sense of unreality, of disorientation; as of two dreams overlapping, displacing one another. "Get in" said the new voice of an invisible Leila.

As he obeyed and stepped forward into the swaying cab he smelt her strange confusion of scents on the night air—again a troubling departure from the accepted memory. But orange-water, mint, Eau de Cologne, and sesame; she smelt like some old Arab lady! And then he caught the dull taint of whisky. She too had had to string her nerves for the meeting with alcohol! Sympathy and indecision battled within him; the old image of the brilliant, resourceful and elegant Leila refused somewhere to fix itself in the new. He simply must see her face. As if she read his thoughts, she said: "So I came at last, *unveiled*, to meet you." He suddenly thought, bringing himself up with a start, "My God! I simply haven't stopped to think how old Leila might be!"

She made a small sign and the old jarvey in the tarbush drew his nag slowly back onto the lighted macadam of the Grande Corniche and set the gharry moving at walking pace. Here the sharp blue street-lamps came up one after the other to peer into the cab, and with the first of these intrusive gleams of light, Mountolive turned to gaze at the woman beside him. He could very dimly recognize her. He saw a plump and square-faced Egyptian lady of uncertain years, with a severely pock-marked face and eyes drawn grotesquely out of true by the antimony-pencil. They were the mutinous sad eyes of some clumsy cartoon creature: a cartoon of animals dressed up and acting as human beings. She had indeed been brave enough to unveil, this stranger who sat facing him, staring at him with the painted eye one sees in frescoes with a forlorn and pitiable look of appeal. She wore an air of unsteady audacity as she confronted her lover, though her lips trembled and her large jowls shook with every vibration of the solid rubber tyres on the road. They stared at each other for a full two seconds before the darkness swallowed the light again. Then he raised her hand to his lips. It was shaking like a leaf. In the momentary light he had seen her uncombed and straggly hair hanging down the back of her neck, her thoughtless and disordered black dress. Her whole appearance had a rakish and improvised air. And the dark skin, so cruelly botched and cicatriced by the smallpox, looked coarse as the skin of an elephant. *He did not recognize her at all!* "Leila!" he cried (it was almost a groan) pretending at last to identify and welcome the image of his lover (now dissolved or shattered forever) in this pitiable grotesque—a fattish Egyptian lady with all the marks of eccentricity and age written upon her appearance. Each time the lamps came up he looked again, and each time he saw himself confronting something like an animal cartoon figure—an elephant, say. He could hardly pay attention to her words, so intent was he upon his racing feelings and memories. "I knew we should meet again some day. I knew it." She pressed his hand, and again he tasted her breath, heavy with sesame and mint and whisky.

She was talking now and he listened uneasily, but with all the attention one gives to an unfamiliar language; and each time the street lamps came up to peer at them, he gazed at her anxiously—as if to see whether there had been any sudden and magical change in her appearance. And then he was visited by another thought: "What if I too have changed as much as she has—if indeed this is she?" What indeed? Sometime in the distant past they had exchanged images of one another like lockets; now his own had faded, changed. What might she see upon his face—traces of the feebleness which had overrun his youthful strength and purpose? He had now joined the ranks of those who compromise gracefully with life. Surely his ineffectuality, his unmanliness must be written all over his foolish, weak, good-looking face? He eyed her mournfully, with a pitiful eagerness to see whether she indeed really recognized him. He had forgotten that women will never surrender the image of their hearts' affections; no, she would remain forever blinded by the old love, refusing to let it be discountenanced by the new. "You have not changed by a day" said this unknown woman with the disagreeable perfume. "My beloved, my darling, my angel." Mountolive flushed in the darkness at such endearments coming from the lips of an unknown personage. And the known Leila? He suddenly realized that the precious image which had inhabited his heart for so long had now been dissolved, completely wiped out! He was suddenly face to face with the meaning of love and time. They had lost forever the power to fecundate each other's minds! He felt only self-pity and disgust where he should have felt love! And these feelings were simply not permissible. He swore at himself silently as they went up and down the dark causeway by the winter sea, like invalids taking the night air, their hands touching each other, in the old horse-drawn cab. She was talking faster, now, vaguely, jumping from topic to topic. Yet it all seemed an introduction to the central statement which she had come to make. She was to leave to-morrow evening: "Nessim's orders. Justine will come back from the lake and pick me up. We are disappearing together. At Kantara we'll separate and I shall go on to Kenya to the farm. Nessim won't say, can't say for how long as yet. I *had* to see you. I *had* to speak to you once. Not for myself—never for myself, my own heart. It was what I learned about Nessim at the carnival time. I was on the point of coming to meet you; but what he told me about Palestine! My blood ran cold. To do something against the British! How could I! Nessim must have been mad. I didn't come because I would not have known what to say to you, how to face you. But now you know all.''

She had begun to draw her breath sharply now, to hurry onward as if all this were introductory matter to her main speech. Then suddenly she came out with it. "The Egyptians will harm Nessim, and the British are trying to provoke them to do so. David, you must use your power to stop it. I am asking you to save my son. I am asking you to save him. You must listen, must help me. I have never asked you a favour before.''

The tear- and crayon-streaked cheeks made her look even more of a stranger in the street-lights. He began to stammer. She cried aloud: "I implore you to help" and suddenly, to his intense humiliation, began to moan and rock like an Arab, pleading with him. "*Leila!*" he cried. "*Stop it!*" But she swayed from side to side repeating the words "Only you can save him now" more, it seemed, to herself, than to anyone else. Then she showed some disposition to go down on her knees in the cab and kiss his feet. By this time Mountolive was trembling with anger and surprise and disgust. They were passing the Auberge for the tenth time. "Unless you stop at once" he cried angrily, but she wailed once more and he jumped awkwardly down into the road. It was hateful to have to end their interview like this. The cab drew to a halt. He said, feeling stupid, and in a voice which seemed to come from far away and to have no recognizable expression save a certain old-fashioned waspishness: "I cannot discuss an official matter with a private person." Could anything be more absurd than these words? He felt bitterly ashamed as he uttered them. "Leila, good-bye," he said hurriedly under his breath, and squeezed her hand once more before he turned. He took to his heels. He unlocked his car and climbed into it panting and overcome by a sense of ghastly folly. The cab moved off into the darkness. He watched it curve slowly along the Corniche and disappear. Then he lit a cigarette and started his engine. All of a sudden there seemed nowhere in particular to go. Every impulse, every desire had faltered and faded out.

After a long pause, he drove slowly and carefully back to the Summer Residence, talking to himself under his breath. The house was in darkness and he let himself in with his key. He walked from room to room switching on all the lights, feeling all of a sudden quite light-headed with loneliness; he could not accuse the servants of desertion since he had already told Ali that he would be dining out. But he walked up and down the drawing-room with his hands in his pockets for a long time. He smelt the damp unheated rooms around him; the blank re-proachful face of the clock told him that it was only just after nine. Abruptly, he went over to the cocktail cabinet and poured himself a very strong whisky and soda which he drank in one movement—gasping as if it were a dose of fruit salts. His mind was humming now like a high-tension wire. He supposed that he would have to go out and have some dinner by himself. But where? Suddenly the whole of Alexandria, the whole of Egypt, had become distasteful, burdensome, weari-some to his spirit.

He drank several more whiskies, enjoying the warmth they brought to his blood—so unused was he to spirits which usually he drank very sparingly. Leila had suddenly left him face to face with a reality which, he supposed, had always lain lurking behind the dusty tapestry of his romantic notions. In a sense, she had *been* Egypt, his own private Egypt of the mind; and now this old image had been husked, stripped bare. "It would be intemperate to drink any more" he told himself as he drained his glass. Yes, that was it! He had never been intem-

284

perate, never been natural, outward-going in his attitude to life. He had always hidden behind measure and compromise; and this defection had somehow lost him the picture of the Egypt which had nourished him for so long. Was it, then, all a lie?

He felt as if somewhere inside himself a dam were threatened, a barrier was on the point of giving way. It was with some idea of restoring this lost contact with the life of this embodied land that he hit upon the idea of doing something he had never done since his youth: he would go out and dine in the Arab quarter, humbly and simply, like a small clerk of the city, like a trades-man, a merchant. Somewhere in a small native restaurant he would eat a pigeon and some rice and a plate of sweetmeats; the food would sober and steady him while the surroundings would restore in him the sense of contact with reality. He could not remember ever having felt so tipsy and leaden-footed before. His thoughts were awash with inarticulate self-reproaches.

Still with this incoherent, half-rationalized desire in mind he suddenly went out to the hall cupboard to unearth the red felt tarbush which someone had left behind after a cocktail party last summer. He had suddenly remembered it. It lay among a litter of golf-clubs and stirrups and tennis racquets. He put it on with a chuckle. It transformed his appearance completely. Looking at himself unsteadily in the hall morror, he was quite surprised by the transformation: he was confront-ing not a distinguished foreign visitor to Egypt now, but—*un homme quelconque*: a Syrian business-man, a broker from Suez, an airline representative from Tel Aviv. Only one thing was necessary to lay claim to the Middle East properly—dark glasses, worn indoors, in winter! There was a pair of them in the top drawer of the writing desk.

He drove the car slowly down to the little square by Ramleh Station, quite absurdly pleased by his fancy dress, and eased it neatly into the car park by the Cecil Hotel; then he locked it and walked quietly off with the air of someone abandoning a lifetime's habit—walked with a new and quite delightful feeling of self-possession towards the Arab quarters of the town where he might find the dinner he sought. As he skirted the Corniche he had one moment of unpleasant fear and doubt— for he saw a familiar figure cross the road further down and walk towards him along the sea-wall. It was impossible to mistake Balthazar's characteristic prowling walk; Mountolive was overcome with a sheepish sense of shame, but he held his course. To his delight, Balthazar glanced once at him and looked away without recognizing his friend. They passed each other in a flash, and Mountolive expelled his breath loudly with relief; it was really odd the anonymity conferred by this ubiquitous red flower-pot of a hat, which so much altered the outlines of the human face. And the dark glasses! He chuckled quietly as he turned away from the sea-front, choosing the tangle of little lanes which might lead him towards the Arab bazaars and the eating houses round the commercial port.

Hereabouts it would be a hundred to one that he would ever be recognized—for few Europeans ever came into this part of the city. The quarter lying beyond the red lantern belt, populated by the small traders, money-lenders, coffee-speculators, ships' chandlers, smugglers; here in the open street one had the illusion of time spread out flat—so to speak—like the skin of an ox; the map of time which one could read from one end to the other, filling it in with known points of reference. This world of Moslem time stretched back to Othello and beyond— cafés sweet with the trilling of singing birds whose cages were full of mirrors to give them the illusion of company. The love-songs of birds to companions they imagined—which were only reflections of themselves! How heartbreakingly they sang, these illustrations of human love! Here too in the ghastly breath of the naphtha flares the old eunuchs sat at *trictrac*, smoking the long nargilehs which at every drawn breath loosed a musical bubble of sound like a dove's sob; the walls of the old cafés were stained by the sweat from the tarbushes

286

hanging on the pegs; their collections of coloured nargilehs were laid up in rows in a long rack, like muskets, for which each tobacco-drinker brought his cherished personal holder. Here too the diviners, cartomancers—or those who would deftly fill your palm with ink and for half a piastre scry the secrets of your inmost life. Here the pedlars carried magic loads of variegated and dissimilar objects of *vertu* from the thistle-soft carpets of Shiraz and Baluchistan to the playing cards of the Marseilles tarot; incense of the Hejaz, green beads against the evil eye, combs, seeds, mirrors for birdcages, spices, amulets and paper fans . . . the list was endless; and each, of course, carried in his private wallet—like a mediaeval pardoner—the fruit of the world's great pornographies in the form of handkerchiefs and post-cards on which were depicted, in every one of its pitiful variations, the one act we human beings most dream of and fear. Mysterious, underground, the everflowing river of sex, trickling easily through the feeble dams set up by our fretful legislation and the typical self-reproaches of the unpleasure-loving . . . the broad underground river flowing from Petronius to Frank Harris. (The drift and overlap of ideas in Mountolive's fuddled mind, rising and disappearing in pretty half-formulated figures, iridescent as soap-bubbles.) He was perfectly at his ease, now; he had come to terms with his unfamiliar state of befuddlement and no longer felt that he was drunk; it was simply that he had become inflated now by a sense of tremendous dignity and self-importance which gave him a grandiose deliberation of movement. He walked slowly, like a pregnant woman nearing term, drinking in the sights and sounds.

At long last he entered a small shop which took his fancy because of its flaring ovens from which great draughts of smoke settled in parcels about the room; the smell of thyme, roasting pigeon and rice gave him a sudden stab of hunger. There were only one or two other diners, hardly to be seen through the clouds of smoke. Mountolive sat down with the air of someone making a grudging concession to the law of gravity and ordered a meal in his excellent Arabic, though he still kept his dark glasses and tarbush on. It was clear now that he could pass easily for a Moslem. The café owner was a great bald Tartar-faced Turk who served his visitor at once and without comment. He also set up a tumbler beside Mountolive's plate and without uttering a word filled it to the brim with the colourless arak made from the mastic-tree which is called *mastika*. Mountolive choked and spluttered a bit over it, but he was highly delighted—for it was the first drink of the Levant he had ever tasted and he had forgotten its existence for years now. Forgetting also how strong it was, and overcome with nostalgia, he ordered himself a second glass to help him finish the excellent hot pilaff and the pigeon (so hot from the spit that he could hardly bear to pick it up with his fingers). But he was in the seventh heaven of delight now. He was on the way to recovering, to restoring the blurred image of an Egypt which the meeting with Leila had damaged or somehow stolen from him.

The street outside was full of the shivering of tambourines and the voices of children raised in a chanting sort of litany; they were going about the shops in groups, repeating the same little verse over and over again. After three repetitions he managed to disentangle the words. Of course!

> Lord of the shaken tree
> Of Man's extremity
> Keep thou our small leaves firm
> On branches free from harm
> For we thy little children be!

"Well I'm damned," he said, swallowing a fiery mouthful of arak and smiling as the meaning of the little processions became clear. There was a venerable old sheik sitting opposite by the window and smoking a long-shanked nargileh. He waved towards the din with his graceful old hand and cried: "Allah!

288

The noise of the children!" Mountolive smiled back at him and said: "Inform me if I err, sir, but it is for *El Sidr* they cry, is it not?" The old man's face lit up and he nodded, smiling his saintly smile. "You have guessed it truly, sir." Mountolive was pleased with himself and filled ever more deeply with nostalgia for those half-forgotten years. "To-night then," he said, "it must be mid-Shaaban and the Tree of Extremity is to be shaken. Is that not so?"

Once more a delighted nod. "Who knows," said the old sheik, "but that both our names may be written on the falling leaves?" He puffed softly and contentedly, like a toy train. "Allah's will be done."

The belief is that on the eve of mid-Shaaban the Lote Tree of Paradise is shaken, and the falling leaves of the tree bear the names of all who will die in the coming year. This is called the Tree of Extremity in some texts. Mountolive was so pleased by the identification of the little song that he called for a final glass of arak which he drank standing up as he paid his reckoning. The old sheik abandoned his pipe and came slowly towards him through the smoke. He said: "Effendi mine, I understand your purpose here. What you seek will be revealed to you by me." He placed two brown fingers on Mountolive's wrist, speaking modestly and softly, as one who had secrets to impart. His face had all the candour and purity of some desert saint. Mountolive was delighted by him. "Honoured sheik," he said, "divulge your sense, then, to an unworthy Syrian visitor." The old man bowed twice, looked circumspectly round the place, and then said: "Be good enough to follow me, honoured sir." He kept his two fingers on Mountolive's wrist as a blind man might. They stepped into the street together; Mountolive's romantic heart was beating wildly—was he now to be vouchsafed some mystical vision of religious truth? He had so often heard stories of the bazaars and the religious men who lurked there, waiting to fulfil secret missions on behalf of that unseen world, the numinous, carefully guarded world of the hermetic doctors. They walked in a soft cloud of unknowing with the silent sheik swaying and recovering himself at every few paces and smiling a maudlin smile of beatitude. They passed together at this slow pace through the dark streets—now turned by the night to long shadowy tunnels or shapeless caverns, still dimly echoing to muffled bagpipe music or skirmishing voices muted by thick walls and barred windows.

Mountolive's heightened sense of wonder responded to the beauty and mystery of this luminous township of shadows carved here and there into recognizable features by a single naphtha lamp or an electric bulb hanging from a frail stalk, rocking in the wind. They turned at last down a long street spanned with coloured banners and thence into a courtyard which was completely dark where the earth smelt vaguely of the stale of camels and jasmine. A house loomed up, set within thick walls; one caught a glimpse of its silhouette on the sky. They entered a sort of rambling barrack of a place passing through a tall door which was standing ajar, and plunged into a darkness still more absolute. Stood breathing for half a second in silence. Mountolive felt rather than saw the worm-eaten staircases which climbed the walls to the abandoned upper floors, heard the chirrup and scramble of the rats in the deserted galleries, together with something else—a sound vaguely reminiscent of human beings, but in what context he could not quite remember. They shuffled slowly down a long corridor upon woodwork so rotten that it racked and swayed under their feet, and here, in a doorway of some sort, the old sheik said kindly: "That our simple satisfactions should not be less than those of your homeland, effendi mine, I have brought you here." He added in a whisper, "Attend me here a moment, if you will." Mountolive felt the fingers leave his wrist and the breath of the door closing at his shoulder. He stayed in composed and trustful silence for a moment or two.

Then all at once the darkness was so complete that the light, when it did come, gave him the momentary illusion of something taking place very far away, in the sky. As if someone had opened and closed a furnace-door in Heaven. It was only the spark of a match. But in the soft yellow flap he saw that he was standing in a gaunt high chamber with shattered and defaced walls covered in *graffiti* and the imprint of dark palms—signs which guard the superstitious against the evil eye. It was empty save for an enormous broken sofa which lay in the centre of the floor, like a sarcophagus. A single window with all the panes of glass broken was slowly printing the bluer darkness of the starry sky upon his sight. He stared at the flapping, foundering light, and again heard the rats chirping and the other curious susurrus composed of whispers and chuckles and the movement of bare feet on boards. . . . Suddenly he thought of a girls' dormitory at a school: and as if invented by the very thought itself, through the open door at the end of the room trooped a crowd of small figures dressed in white soiled robes, like defeated angels. He had stumbled into a house of child prostitutes, he realized with a sudden spasm of disgust and pity. Their little faces were heavily painted, their hair scragged up in ribbons and plaits. They wore green beads against the evil eye. Such little creatures as one has seen incised on Greek vases —floating out of tombs and charnel houses with the sad air of malefactors fleeing from justice. It was the foremost of the group who carried the light—a twist of string burning in a saucer of olive oil. She stooped to place this feeble will-o-the-wisp on the floor in the corner and at once the long spiky shadows of these children sprawled on the ceiling like an army of frustrated wills. "No, by Allah" said Mountolive hoarsely, and turned to grope at the closed door. There was a wooden latch with no means of opening it on his side. He put his face to a hole in the panel and called softly "O sheik, where are you?" The little figures had advanced and surrounded him now, murmuring the pitiable obscenities and endearments of their trade in the voices of heartbroken angels; he felt their warm nimble fingers on his shoulders, picking at the sleeves of his coat. "O

sheik," he called again, shrinking up, "it was not for this."
But there was a silence beyond the door. He felt the children's
sharp arms twining round his waist like lianas in a tropical
jungle, their sharp little fingers prying for the buttons of his
coat. He shook them off and turned his pale face to them,
making a half-articulate sound of protest. And now someone
inadvertently kicked over the saucer with its floating wick and
in the darkness he felt the tension of anxiety sweep through
them like a fire through brushwood. His protests had made
them fear the loss of a lucrative client. Anxiety, anger and a
certain note of terror was in their voices now as they spoke to
him, wheedling and half-threatening; heaven only knew what
punishments might attend them if he escaped! They began to
struggle, to attack him; he felt the concussion of their starved
little bodies as they piled round him, panting and breathless
with importunity, but determined that he should not retreat.
Fingers roved over him like ants—indeed, he had a sudden
memory, buried from somewhere back in his remembered
reading, of a man staked down upon the burning sand over a
nest of white ants which would soon pick the flesh from his
very bones.

"No," he cried incoherently again; some absurd inhibition
prevented him from striking out, distributing a series of brutal
cuffs which alone might have freed him. (The smallest were so
very small.) They had his arms now, and were climbing on his
back—absurd memories intruded of pillow fights in a dark dormitory at school. He banged wildly on the door with his elbow,
and they redoubled their entreaties in whining voices. Their
breath was as hot as wood-smoke. "O Effendi, patron of the
poor, remedy for our affliction. . . ." Mountolive groaned and
struggled, but felt himself gradually being borne to the
ground; gradually felt his befuddled knees giving way under
this assault which had gathered a triumphant fury now.

"No!" he cried in an anguished voice, and a chorus of voices
answered "Yes. Yes, by Allah!" They smelt like a herd of goats

292

as they swarmed upon him. The giggles, the obscene whispers, the cajoleries and curses mounted up to his brain. He felt as if he were going to faint.

Then suddenly everything cleared—as if a curtain had been drawn aside—to reveal him sitting beside his mother in front of a roaring fire with a picture-book open on his knee. She was reading aloud and he was trying to follow the words as she pronounced them; but his attention was always drawn away to the large colour-plate which depicted Gulliver when he had fallen into the hands of the little people of Lilliput. It was fascinating in its careful detail. The heavy-limbed hero lay where he had fallen, secured by a veritable cobweb of guy-ropes which had been wound around him pinioning him to the ground while the ant-people roved all over his huge body securing and pegging more and more guy-ropes against which every struggle of the colossus would be in vain. There was a malign scientific accuracy about it all: wrists, ankles and neck pinioned against movement; tent-pegs driven between the fingers of his huge hand to hold each individual finger down. His pigtails were neatly coiled about tiny spars which had been driven into the ground beside him. Even the tails of his surtout were skilfully pinned to the ground through the folds. He lay there staring into the sky with expressionless wonder, his blue eyes wide open, his lips pursed. The army of Lilliputians wandered all over him with wheel-barrows and pegs and more rope; their attitudes suggested a feverish ant-like frenzy of capture. And all the time Gulliver lay there on the green grass of Lilliput, in a valley full of microscopic flowers, like a captive balloon. . . .

He found himself (though he had no idea how he had finally escaped) leaning upon the icy stone embankment of the Corniche with the dawn sea beneath him, rolling its slow swell up the stone piers, gushing softly into the conduits. He could remember only running in dazed fashion down twisted streets in darkness and stumbling across the road and onto the sea-front. A pale rinsed dawn was breaking across the long sea-swell and a light sea-wind brought him the smell of tar and the sticky dampness of salt. He felt like some merchant sailor cast up helpless in a foreign port at the other end of the world. His pockets had been turned inside out like sleeves. He was clad in a torn shirt and trousers. His expensive studs and cuff-links and tie-pin had gone, his wallet had vanished. He felt deathly sick. But as he gradually came to his senses he realized where he was from the glimpse of the Goharri Mosque as it stood up to take the light of dawn among its clumps of palms. Soon the blind muezzins would be coming out like ancient tortoises to recite the dawn-praise of the only living God. It was perhaps a quarter of a mile to where he had left the car. Denuded now of his tarbush and dark glasses, he felt as if he had been stripped naked. He started off at a painful trot along the stony embankments, glad that there was nobody about to recognize him. The deserted square outside the Hotel was just waking to life with the first tram. It clicked away towards Mazarita, empty. The keys to his car had also disappeared and he now had the ignominious task of breaking the door-catch with a spanner which he took from the boot—terrified all the time that a policeman might come and question or perhaps even arrest him on suspicion. He was seething with self-contempt and disgust and he had a splitting headache. At last he broke the door and drove off wildly—fortunately, the chauffeur's keys were in the car—in the direction of Rushdi through the deserted streets. His latch-key too had disappeared in the mêlée and he was forced to burst open one of the window-catches in the drawing-room in order to get into the house. He thought at first that he would spend the morning asleep in bed after he had bathed and changed his clothes, but standing under the hot shower he realized that he was too troubled in mind; his thoughts buzzed like a swarm of bees and would not let him rest. He decided suddenly that he would leave the house and return to Cairo before even the servants were up. He felt that he could not face them.

He changed his clothes furtively, gathered his belongings together, and set off across the town towards the desert road, leaving the city hurriedly like a common thief. He had come to a decision in his own mind. He would ask for a posting to some other country. He would waste no more time upon this Egypt of deceptions and squalor, this betraying landscape which turned emotions and memories to dust, which beggared friendship and destroyed love. He did not even think of Leila now; to-night she would be gone across the border. But already it was as if she had never existed.

There was plenty of petrol in the tank for the ride back. As he turned through the last curves of the road outside the town he looked back once, with a shudder of disgust, at the pearly mirage of minarets rising from the smoke of the lake, the dawn mist. A train pealed somewhere, far away. He turned on the radio of the car at full blast to drown his thoughts as he sped along the silver desert highway to the winter capital. From every side, like startled hares, his thoughts broke out to run alongside the whirling car in a frenzy of terror. He had, he realized, reached a new frontier in himself; life was going to be something completely different from now on. He had been in some sort of bondage all this time; now the links had snapped. He heard the soft hushing of strings and the familiar voice of the city breaking in upon him once again with its perverted languors, its ancient wisdoms and terrors.

> Jamais de la vie,
> Jamais dans ton lit
> Quand ton coeur se démange de chagrin. . . .

With an oath he snapped the radio shut, choked the voice, and drove frowning into the sunlight as it ebbed along the shadowy flanks of the dunes.

He made very good time and drew up before the Embassy to find Errol and Donkin loading the latter's old touring car with all the impedimenta of professional hunters—gun-cases and cartridge bags, binoculars and thermos flasks. He walked slowly and shamefacedly towards them. They both greeted him cheerfully. They were due to start for Alexandria at midday. Donkin was excited and blithe. The newspapers that morning had carried reports that the King had made a good recovery and that audiences were to be granted at the week-end. "Now, sir," said Donkin, "is Nur's chance to make Memlik act. You'll see." Mountolive nodded dully; the news fell flatly on his ear, toneless and colourless and without presage. He no longer cared what was going to happen. His decision to ask for a transfer of post seemed to have absolved him in a curious way from any further personal responsibility as regards his own feelings.

He walked moodily into the Residence and ordered his breakfast tray to be brought into the drawing-room. He felt irritable and abstracted. He rang for his despatch box to see what personal mail there might be. There was nothing of great interest: a long chatty letter from Sir Louis who was happily sunning himself in Nice; it was full of amusing and convivial gossip about mutual friends. And of course the inevitable anecdote of a famous *raconteur* to round off the letter: "I hope, dear boy, that the uniform still fits you. I thought of you last week when I met Claudel, the French poet who was also an Ambassador, for he told me an engaging anecdote about *his* uniform. It was while he was serving in Japan. Out for a walk one day, he turned round to see that the whole residence was a sheet of flame and blazing merrily; his family was with him so he did not need to fear for *their* safety. But his manuscripts, his priceless collection of books and letters—they were all in the burning house. He hurried back in a state of great alarm. It was clear that the house would be burned to the ground. As he reached the garden he saw a small stately figure walking towards him—the Japanese butler. He walked slowly and circumspectly towards the Ambassador with his arms held out before him like a sleepwalker; over them was laid the dress uniform of the poet. The butler said proudly and sedately: 'There is no cause for alarm, sir. I have saved the only valuable object.' And the half-finished play, and the poems lying upstairs on the burning desk? I suddenly thought of you, I don't know why."

He read on sighing and smiling sadly and enviously; what would he not give to be retired in Nice at this moment? There was a letter from his mother, a few bills from his London tradesmen, a note from his broker, and a short letter from Pursewarden's sister. . . . Nothing of any real importance.

There was a knock and Donkin appeared. He looked somewhat crestfallen. "The M.F.A.," he said, "have been on the line with a message from Nur's office to say that he will be seeing the King at the weekend. But . . . Gabr hinted that our case is not supported by Memlik's own investigations."

"What does he mean by that?"

"He says, in effect, that we have got the wrong Hosnani. The real culprit is a brother of his who lives on a farm somewhere outside Alexandria."

"Narouz" said Mountolive with astonishment and incredulity.

"Yes. Well apparently he——"

They both burst out laughing with exasperation. "Honestly" said Mountolive, banging his fist into his palm, "the Egyptians really are incredible. Now how on earth have they arrived at such a conclusion? One is simply baffled."

"Nevertheless, that is Memlik's case. I thought you'd like to know, sir. Errol and I are just off to Alex. There isn't anything else, is there?"

Mountolive shook his head. Donkin closed the door softly behind him. "So now they are going to turn on Narouz. What a muddle of conflicting policies and diversions." He sank despairingly into a chair and frowned at his own fingers for a long moment before pouring himself out another cup of tea. He felt incapable now of thought, of making the smallest decision. He would write to Kenilworth and the Foreign

Secretary this very morning about his transfer. It was something he should have considered long since. He sighed heavily.

There came another and more diffident rap at the door. "Come in" he called wearily. It opened and a dispirited-looking sausage-dog waddled into the room followed by Angela Errol who said, in a tone of strident heartiness not untouched by a sort of aggressive archness, "Forgive the intrusion, but I came on *behalf* of the Chancery *wives*. We thought you seemed rather *lonely* so we decided to put our *heads* together. *Fluke* is the result." Dog and man looked at each other in a dazed and distrustful silence for a moment. Mountolive struggled for words. He had always loathed sausage-dogs with legs so short that they appeared to flop along like toads rather than walk. Fluke was such an animal, already panting and slavering from its exertions. It sat down at last and, as if to express once and for all its disenchantment with the whole sum of canine existence, delivered itself of a retromingent puddle on the beautiful Shiraz. "Isn't he jolly?" cried the wife of the Head of Chancery. It cost Mountolive something of an effort to smile, to appear to be overcome with pleasure, to express the appropriate thanks due to a gesture so thoughtful. He was wild with vexation. "He looks charming" he said, smiling his handsome smile, "really charming. I am most awfully grateful, Angela. It was a kind thought." The dog yawned lazily. "Then I shall *tell* the wives that the *gift* has met with *approval*," she said briskly, and moved towards the door. "They will be *delighted*. There is *no* companionship like that of a dog, is there?" Mountolive shook his head seriously. "None," he said. He tried to look as if he meant it.

As the door closed behind her he sat down once more and raised his cup of tea to his lips as he stared unwinkingly and with distaste into the dog's lustreless eyes. The clock chimed softly on the mantelpiece. It was time to be going to the office. There was much to be done. He had promised to finish the definitive economic report in time for this week's bag. He must bully the bag room about that portrait of himself. He must. . . .

Yet he sat on looking at the dispirited little creature on the mat and feeling suddenly as if he had been engulfed in a tidal wave of human contumely—so appropriately expressed by his admirers in this unwanted gift. He was to be *garde malade*, a male nurse to a short-legged lap dog. Was this now the only way left of exorcizing his sadness. . . ? He sighed, and sighing pressed the bell. . . .

o   o   o   o   o

XVI

The day of his death was like any other winter day at Karm Abu Girg; or if it was different it was only in one small and puzzling detail, the significance of which did not strike him at first: the servants suddenly ebbing away to leave him alone in the house. All night long now he lay in troubled sleep among the luxuriant growths of his own fantasy, dense as a tropical vegetation; only waking from time to time to be comforted by the soft whewing of the cranes flying overhead in the darkness. It was full winter and the great bird migrations had begun. The long vitreous expanses of the lake had begun to fill up with their winged visitants like some great terminus. All night long one could hear the flights come in—the thick whirring of mallard-wings or the metallic *kraonk kraonk* of high-flying geese as they bracketed the winter moon. Among the thickets of reed and sedge, in places polished to black or viper-green by the occasional clinging frosts, you could hear the chuckling and gnatting of royal duck. The old house with its mildewed walls where the scorpions and fleas hibernated among the dusty interstices of the earth-brick felt very empty and desolate to him now that Leila had gone. He marched defiantly about it, making as much noise as he could with his boots, shouting at the dogs, cracking his whip across the courtyard. The little toy figures with windmill arms which lined the walls against the ubiquitous evil eye, worked unceasingly, flurried by the winter winds. Their tiny celluloid propellers made a furry sound as they revolved which was somehow comforting.

Nessim had pleaded hard with him to accompany Leila and Justine but he had refused—and indeed behaved like a bear though he knew in truth that without his mother the loneliness

300

of the house would be hard to support. He had locked himself into the egg-incubators, and to his brother's feverish knocking and shouting had opposed a bitter silence. There had been no way of explaining things to Nessim. He would not emerge even when Leila came to plead with him—for fear that his resolve might weaken under her importunities. He had crouched there in silence with his back against the wall, his fist crammed into his mouth to stifle the noiseless sobbing—how heavy was the guilt one bore for filial disobedience! They had abandoned him at last. He heard the horses clatter out of the courtyard. He was alone.

Then after that a whole month of silence before he heard his brother's voice on the telephone. Narouz had walked all day long in a forest of his own heart-beats, attending to the work of the land with a concentrated fury of purpose, galloping along the slow-moving river of his inheritance on horseback, his reflection flying beside him: always with the great whip coiled at his saddle-bow. He felt immeasurably aged now—and yet, at one and the same time, as new to the world as a foetus hanging from the birth-cord. The land, *his* land, now brown and greasy as an old wineskin under the rain, compelled him. It was all he had left now to care for—trees bruised by frost, sand poisoned by desert salt, water-pans stocked with fish and geese; and silences all day except for the sighing and the groaning of the water-wheels with their eternal message ("Alexander has asses' ears") carried away by the winds to the further corners of the land, to pollinate history once more with the infectious memory of the soldier-god; or the suck and pluck of the black "fore-head-smasher" buffalo wallowing in the ooze of the dykes. And then at night the haunting plural syllables of the duck deploying in darkness, calling to one another in anxiety or content—travellers' codes. Screens of mist, low-lying clouds through which the dawns and sunsets burst with unexampled splendour each one the end of a world, a dying into amethyst and nacre.

Normally, this would be the hunter's season which he loved, brisk with great wood-fires and roving gun-dogs: time for the dousing of boots with bear's fat, for the tuning in of the long punt-guns, the sorting out of shot, the painting of decoys. . . . This year he had not even the heart to join in the great annual duck-shoot given by Nessim. He felt cut off, in a different world. He wore the bitter revengeful face of a communicant refused absolution. He could no longer exorcize his sadness privately with a dog and gun; he thought only of Taor now, and the dreams he shared with her—the fierce possessive recognition of his dedicated role *here*, among his own lands, and in the whole of Egypt. . . . These confusing dreams interlinked, over-lapped, intersected—like so many tributaries of the great river itself. Even Leila's love threatened them now—was like some brilliant parasite ivy which strangles the growth of a tree. He thought vaguely and without contempt of his brother still there in the city—(he was not to leave until later)—moving among people as insubstantial as waxworks, the painted society women of Alexandria. If he thought at all of his love for Clea it was for a love left now like some shining coin, forgotten in a beggar's pocket. . . . Thus, galloping in savage exultation along moss-green wharves and embankments of the estuary with its rotting palms fretted by the wind, thus he lived.

Once last week Ali had reported the presence of unknown men upon the land, but he had not given the matter a thought. Often a stray Bedouin took a short cut across the plantations or a stranger rode through the property bound for the road to the city. He was more interested when Nessim telephoned to say that he would be visiting Karm Abu Girg with Balthazar who wished to investigate reports of a new species of duck which had been seen on the lake. (From the roof of the house one could sweep the whole estuary with a powerful glass.)

This indeed was what he was doing now, at this very moment. Tree by tree, reed-patch by reed-patch, turning a patient and curious eye upon the land through his ancient telescope. It lay, mysterious, unpeopled and silent in the light of the dawn. He intended to spend the whole day out there among the plantations in order to avoid, if possible, seeing his brother. But now the defection of the servants was puzzling, and indeed, inexplicable. Usually when he woke he roared for Ali who brought him a large copper can with a long spout full of hot water and sluiced him down as he stood in the battered Victorian hip-bath, gasping and hissing. But to-day? The courtyard was silent, and the room in which Ali slept was locked. The key hung in its place upon the nail outside. There was not a soul about.

With sudden quick strides he climbed to the balcony for his telescope and then mounted the outer wooden staircase to the roof to stand among the turrets of the dovecots and scan the Hosnani lands. A long patient scrutiny revealed nothing out of the ordinary. He grunted and snapped the glass shut. He would have to fend for himself to-day. He climbed down from his perch and taking the old leather game-bag made his way to the kitchens to fill it with food. Here he found coffee simmering and some pans set to heat upon the charcoal fire, but no trace of the cooks. Grumbling, he helped himself to a snag of bread which he munched while he assembled some food for lunch. Then an idea struck him. In the courtyard, his shrill angry whistle would normally have brought the gun-dogs growling and fawning about his boots from wherever they had taken refuge from the cold; but to-day the empty echo of his own whistle was all that the wind threw back to him. Had Ali perhaps taken them out on some excursion of his own? It did not seem likely. He whistled again more loudly and waited, his feet set squarely apart in his jackboots, his hands upon his hips. There was no answer. He went round to the stables and found his horse. Everything was perfectly normal here. He saddled and bridled it and led it round to the hitching-post. Then he went upstairs for his whip. As he coiled it, another thought struck him. He turned into the living-room and took a revolver from the writing-desk, checking it to see that the chambers were primed. He stuck this in his belt.

Then he set out, riding softly and circumspectly towards the east, for he proposed first of all to make an exploratory circuit of the land before plunging into the dense green plantations where he wished to spend the day. It was crisp weather, rapidly clearing, the marsh-mist full of evanescent shapes and contours but rising fast. Horse and rider moved with smooth deftness along the familiar ways. He reached the desert fringe in half an hour, having seen nothing untoward though he looked about him carefully under his bushy brows. On the soft ground the horse's hooves made little noise. In the eastern corner of the plantation, he halted for a good ten minutes, combing the landscape once more with his telescope. And once more there was nothing of particular importance. He neglected none of the smaller signs which might indicate a foreign visitation, tracks in the desert, footmarks on the soft embankment by the ferry. The sun was rising slowly but the land slept in its thinning mist. At one place he dismounted to check the depth-pumps, listening to their sullen heart-beats with pleasure, greasing a lever here and there. Then he remounted and turned his horse's head towards the denser groves of the plantations with their cherished Tripoli olives and acacia, their humus-giving belts of juniper, the wind-breaks of rattling Indian corn. He was still on the alert, however, and rode in short swift spurts, reining in every now and again to listen for a full minute. Nothing but the distant gabble of birds, the slither of flamingo-wings on the lake-water, the melodious horns of teal or the splendour (as of a tuba in full pomp) of honking geese. All familiar, all known. He was still puzzled but not ill at ease.

He made his way at last to the great *nubk* tree standing up starkly in its clearing, its great trophied branches dripping with condensing mist. Here, long ago, he had stood and prayed with Mountolive under the holy branches, still heavy with their curious human fruitage; everywhere blossomed the *ex votos* of the faithful in strips of coloured cloth, calico, beads. They were tied to every branch and twig and leaf so that it looked like some giant Christmas tree. Here he dismounted to take some cuttings which he wrapped and stowed carefully. Then he straightened up for he had heard the sounds of movement in the green glades around him. Difficult to identify, to isolate— slither of a body among the leaves, or perhaps a pack-saddle catching in a branch as horse and rider moved swiftly out of ambush? He listened and gave a small spicy chuckle, as if at some remembered private joke. He was sorry for anyone coming to molest him in such a place—every glade and ride of which he knew by memory. Here he was on his own ground—the master.

He ran back to his horse with his curious bandy-legged stride, but noiselessly. He mounted and rode slowly out of the shadow of the great branches in order to give his long whip a wide margin for wrist-play and to cover the only two entrances to the plantation. His adversaries, if such there were, would have to come upon him down one of two paths. He had his back to the tree and its great stockade of thorns. He gave a small clicking laugh of pleasure as he sat there attentively, his head on one side like a listening gun-dog; he moved the coils of his whip softly and voluptuously along the ground, drawing circles with them, curling them in the grass like a snake. . . . It would probably turn out to be a false alarm—Ali coming to apologize for his neglect that morning? At any rate, his master's posture of readiness would frighten him, for he had seen the whip in action before. . . . The noise again. A water-rat plopped into the channel and swam quickly away. Among the bushes on two sides of the ride he could see indistinct movements. He sat, as immobile as an equestrian statue, his pistol grasped lightly in the left hand, his whip lying slightly behind him, his arm carved in the position of a fisherman about to make a long cast. So he waited, smiling. His patience was endless.

The sound of distant shooting upon the lake was a common-place among the vocabulary of lake-sounds; it belonged to the music of the gulls, visitants from the seashore, and the other water-birds which thronged the reed-haunted lagoons. When the big shoots were on the ripple of thirty guns in action at one and the same time flowed tidelessly out into the air of Mareotis like a cadenza. Habit taught one gradually to differentiate be-tween the various sounds and to recognize them—and Nessim too had spent his childhood here with a gun. He could tell the difference between the deep *tang* of a punt gun aimed at high-flying geese and the flat biff of a twelve-bore. The two men were standing by their horses at the ferry when it came, a small puckering of the air merely, falling upon the ear-drum in a patter: raindrops sliding from an oar, the drip of a tap in an old house, were hardly less in volume. But it was certainly shoot-ing. Balthazar turned his head and gazed out over the lake. "That sounded pistolish" he said; Nessim smiled and shook his head. "Small calibre rifle, I should say. A poacher after sitting duck?" But there were more shots than could be accommodated at one time in the magazine of either weapon. They mounted, a little puzzled that the horses had been sent for them but that Ali had disappeared. He had tied the animals to the hitching-post of the ferry, commending them to the care of the ferryman, and vanished in the mist.

They rode briskly down the embankments side by side. The sun was up now and the whole surface of the lake was rising into the sky like the floor of a theatre, pouring upwards with the mist; here and there reality was withered by mirages, land-scapes hanging in the sky upside down or else four or five superimposed on each other with the effect of a multiple ex-posure. The first indication of anything amiss was a figure dressed in white robes which fled into the mist—an unheard-of action in that peaceful country. Who would fly from two horsemen on the Karm Abu Girg road? A vagabond? They stopped in bemused wonder. "I thought I heard shouts" said

306

Nessim at last in a small constrained voice, "towards the house." As if both were stimulated by the same simultaneous anxiety, they pushed their horses into a brisk gallop, heading them for the house.

A horse, Narouz' horse, now riderless, stood trembling outside the open gates of the manor house. It had been shot through the lips—a profusely-bleeding graze which gave it a weird bloody smile. It whinnied softly as they came up. Before they had time to dismount there came shouts from the palm-grove and a flying figure burst through the trees waving to them. It was Ali. He pointed down among the plantations and shouted the name of Narouz. The name, so full of omens for Nessim, had a curiously obituary ring already, though he was not as yet dead. "By the Holy Tree" shouted Ali, and both men drove their heels into their horses' flanks and crashed into the plantation as fast as they could go.

He was lying on the grass underneath the *nubk* tree with his head and neck supported by it, an angle which cocked his face forward so that he appeared to be studying the pistol-wounds in his own body. His eyes alone were movable, but they could only reach up to the knee of his rescuers; and the pain had winced them from the normal periwinkle blue to the dull blue of plumbago. His whip had got coiled round his body in some manner, probably when he fell from the saddle. Balthazar dismounted and walked slowly and deliberately over to him, making the little clucking noise he always made with his tongue; it sounded sympathetic, but it was in fact a reproof to his own curiosity, to the elation with which one part of his professional mind responded to human tragedy. It always seemed to him that he had no right to be so interested. *Tsck, tsck.* Nessim was very pale and very calm but he did not approach the fallen figure of his brother. Yet it had for him a dreadful magnetism—it was as if Balthazar were laying some tremendously powerful explosive which might go off and kill them both. He was merely helping by holding the horse.

307

Narouz said in a small peevish voice—the voice of a feverish child which can count on its illness for the indulgence it seeks —something unexpected. "I want to see Clea." It ran smoothly off his tongue, as if he had been rehearsing the one phrase in his mind for centuries. He licked his lips and repeated it more slowly. It seemed from Balthazar's angle of vision that a smile settled upon his lips, but he recognized that the contraction was a grimace of pain. He hunted swiftly for the old pair of surgical scissors which he had brought to use upon the soft wire duck-seals and slit the vest of Narouz stiffly from North to South. At this Nessim drew nearer and together they looked down upon the shaggy and powerful body on which the blue and bloodless bullet-holes had sunk like knots in an oak. But they were many, very many. Balthazar made his characteristic little gesture of uncertainty which parodied a Chinaman shaking hands with himself.

Other people had now entered the clearing. Thinking became easier. They had brought an enormous purple curtain with which to carry him back to the house. And now, in some strange way, the place was full of servants. They had ebbed back like a tide. The air was dark with their concern. Narouz ground his teeth and groaned as they lifted him to the great purple cloak and bore him back, like a wounded stag, through the plantations. Once as he neared the house, he said in the same clear child's voice: "To see Clea," and then subsided into a feverish silence punctuated by occasional quivering sighs.

The servants were saying: "Praise be to God that the doctor is here! All will be well with him!"

Balthazar felt Nessim's eyes turned upon him. He shook his head gravely and hopelessly and repeated his clucking sound softly. It was a matter of hours, of minutes, of seconds. So they reached the house like some grotesque religious procession bearing the body of the younger son. Softly mewing and sobbing, but with hope and faith in his recovery, the women gazed down upon the jutting head and the sprawled body in the purple curtain which swelled under his weight like a sail. Nessim gave directions, uttering small words like "Gently here," and "Slowly at the corner." So they gradually got him back to the gaunt bedroom from which he had sallied forth that morning. While Balthazar busied himself, breaking open a packet of medical supplies which were kept in a cupboard against lake-accidents, hunting for a hypodermic needle and a phial of morphia. Small croaks and groans were now issuing from the mouth of Narouz. His eyes were closed. He could not hear the dim conversation which Nessim, in another corner of the house, was having with Clea on the telephone.

"But he is dying, Clea."

Clea made an inarticulate moaning noise of protest. "What can I do, Nessim? He is nothing to me, never was, never will be. O it is so *disgusting*—please do not make me come, Nessim."

"Of course not. I simply thought as he is dying——"

"But if you think I should I will feel obliged to."

"I think nothing. He has not long to live, Clea."

"I hear from your voice that I must come. O Nessim, how disgusting that people should love without consent! Will you send the car or shall I telephone Selim? My flesh quails on my bones."

"Thank you Clea," said Nessim shortly and with sadly downcast head; for some reason the word "disgusting" had wounded him. He walked slowly back to the bedroom, noticing on the way that the courtyard was thronged with people—not only the house servants but many new curious visitors. Calamity draws people as an open wound draws flies, Nessim thought. Narouz was in a doze. They sat for a while talking in whispers. "Then he must really die?" asked Nessim sadly, "without his mother?" It seemed to him an added burden of guilt that it was through his agency that Leila had been forced to leave. "Alone like this." Balthazar made a grimace of impatience. "It is amazing he's alive at all still," he said. "And there is absolutely nothing. . . ." Slowly and gravely Balthazar shook that dark intelligent head. Nessim stood up and said: "Then I should tell them that there is no hope of recovery. They will want to prepare for his death."

"Do as you wish."

"I must send for Tobias the priest. He must have the last sacraments—the Holy Eucharist. The servants will know the truth from him."

"Act as seems good to you" said Balthazar dryly, and the tall figure of his friend slipped down the staircase into the courtyard to give instructions. A rider was to be despatched at once to the priest with instructions to consecrate the holy elements in the church and then come post-haste to Karm Abu Girg to administer the last sacraments to Narouz. As this intelligence went abroad there went up a great sigh of dreadful expectancy and the faces of the servants lengthened with dread. "And the doctor?" they cried in tones of anguish. "And the doctor?"

Balthazar smiled grimly as he sat on the chair beside the dying man. He repeated to himself softly, under his breath, "And the doctor?" What a mockery! He placed his cool palm on Narouz' forehead for a moment, with an air of certitude and resignation. A high temperature, a dozen bullet-holes. . . . "And the doctor?"

Musing upon the futility of human affairs and the dreadful accidents to which life exposed the least distrustful, the most innocent of creatures, he lit a cigarette and went out onto the balcony. A hundred eager glances sought his, imploring him by the power of his magic to restore the patient to health. He frowned heavily at one and all. If he had been able to resort to the old-fashioned magic of the Egyptian fables, of the New Testament, he would gladly have told Narouz to rise. But . . . "And the doctor?"

Despite the internal haemorrhages, the drumming of the pulses in his ears, the fever and pain, the patient was only resting—in a sense—husbanding his energies for the appearance of Clea. He mistook the little flutter of voices and foot-steps upon the staircase which heralded the appearance of the priest. His eyelashes fluttered and then sank down again, ex-hausted to hear the fat voice of the goose-shaped young man with the greasy face and the air of just having dined on sucking-pig. He returned to his own remote watchfulness, content that Tobias should treat him as insensible, as dead even, pro-vided he could husband a small share of his dying space for the blonde image—intractable and remote as ever now to his mind —yet an image which might respond to all this hoarded suffer-ing. Even from pity. He was swollen with desire, distended like a pregnant woman. When you are in love you know that love is a beggar, shameless as a beggar; and the responses of merely human pity can console one where love is absent by a false travesty of an imagined happiness. Yet the day dragged on and still she did not come. The anxiety of the house deepened with his own. And Balthazar, whose intuition had guessed rightly the cause of his patience, was tempted by the thought: "I could imitate Clea's voice—would he know? I could soothe him with a few words spoken in her voice." He was a ventriloquist and mimic of the first order. But to the first voice a second replied: "No. One must not interfere with a destiny however bitter by introducing lies. He must die as he was meant to." And the first voice said bitterly: "Then why morphia, why the comforts of religion, and not the solace of a desired human voice imitated, the pressure of a hand imitated? You could easily do this." But he shook his dark head at himself and said "No" with bitter obstinacy, as he listened to the unpleasant voice of the priest reading passages of scripture upon the bal-cony, his voice mixing with the murmuring and shuffling of the human beings in the courtyard below. Was not the evangel all that the imitation of Clea's voice might have been? He kissed his patient's brow slowly, sadly as he reflected.

Narouz began to feel the tuggings of the Underworld, the five wild dogs of the sense pulling ever more heavily upon the leash. He opposed to them the forces of his mighty will, playing for time, waiting for the only human revelation he could expect —voice and odour of a girl who had become embalmed by his senses, entombed like some precious image. He could hear the nerves ticking away in their spirals of pain, the oxygen bubbles rising ever more slowly to explode in his blood. He knew that he was running out of funds, running out of time. The slowly gathering weight of a paralysis was settling over his mind, the narcotic of pain.

Nessim went away to the telephone again. He was wax pale now, with a hectic spot of pink in each cheek, and he spoke with the high sweet hysterical voice of his mother. Clea had already started for Karm Abu Girg, but it seemed that a part of the road had been washed away by a broken dyke. Selim doubted whether she could get through to the ferry that evening.

There now began a tremendous struggle in the breast of Narouz—a struggle to maintain an equilibrium between the forces battling within him. His musculature contracted in heavy bunches with the effort of waiting; his veins bunched out, polished to ebony with the strain, controlled by his will. He ground his teeth savagely together like a wild boar as he felt himself foundering. And Balthazar sat like an effigy, one hand upon his brow and the other fiercely holding the contorted muscles of his wrist. He whispered in Arabic: "Rest, my darling. Easily, my loved one." His sadness gave him complete mastery of himself, complete calm. Truth is so bitter that the knowledge of it confers a kind of luxury.

So it went for a while. Then lastly there burst from the hairy throat of the dying man a single tremendous word, the name of Clea, utttered in the cavernous voice of a wounded lion: a voice which combined anger, reproof and an overwhelming sadness in its sudden roar. So nude a word, her name, as simple as "God" or "Mother"—yet it sounded as if upon the lips of some dying conqueror, some lost king, conscious of the body and breath dissolving within him. The name of Clea sounded through the whole house, drenched by the splendour of his anguish, silencing the little knots of whispering servants and visitors, setting back the ears of the hunting dogs, making them crouch and fawn: ringing in Nessim's mind with a new and terrifying bitterness too deep for tears. And as this great cry slowly faded, the intelligence of his death dawned upon them with a new and crushing weight—like the pressure of some great tomb door closing upon hope.

Immobile, ageless as pain itself, sat the defeated effigy of the doctor at the bedside of pain. He was thinking to himself, full of the bright light of intellection: "A phrase like 'out of the jaws of death' might mean something like that cry of Narouz', its bravery. Or 'out of the jaws of Hell'. It must mean the hell of a private mind. No, we can do nothing."

The great voice thinned softly into the burring comb-and-paper sound of a long death-rattle, fading into the buzz of a fly caught in some remote spider's web.

And now Nessim gave a single sweet sob out there on the balcony—the noise that a bamboo stem makes when it is plucked from the stalk. And like the formal opening bars of some great symphony this small sob was echoed below in the darkness, passed from lip to lip, heart to heart. Their sobs lighted one another—as candles take a light from one another—an orchestral fulfilment of the precious theme of sorrow, and a long quivering ragged moan came up out of the empty well to climb upwards towards the darkening sky, a long hushing sigh which mingled with the hushing of the rain upon Lake Mareotis. The death of Narouz had begun to be borne. Balthazar with lowered head was quoting softly to himself in Greek the lines:

> Now the sorrow of the knowledge of parting
> Moves like wind in the rigging of the ship
> Of the man's death, figurehead of the white body,
> The sails of the soul being filled
> By the Ghost of the Breath, replete and eternal.

313

It was the signal for a release, for now the inescapably terrible scenes of a Coptic wake were to be enacted in the house, scenes charged with an ancient terror and abandon.

Death had brought the women into their kingdom, and made them free to deliver each her inheritance of sorrow. They crept forward in a body, gathering speed as they mounted the staircases, their faces rapt and transfigured now as they uttered the first terrible screaming. Their fingers were turned into hooks now, tearing at their own flesh, their breasts, their cheeks, with a lustful abandon as they moved swiftly up the staircase. They were uttering that curious and thrilling ululation which is called the *zagreet*, their tongues rippling on their palates like mandolines. An ear-splitting chorus of tongue-trills in various keys.

The old house echoed to the shrieks of these harpies as they took possession of it and invaded the room of death to circle round the silent corpse, still repeating the blood-curdling signal of death, full of an unbearable animal abandon. They began the dances of ritual grief while Nessim and Balthazar sat silent upon their chairs, their heads sunk upon their breasts, their hands clasped—the very picture of human failure. They allowed these fierce quivering screams to pierce them to the very quick of their beings. Only submission now to the ritual of this ancient sorrow was permissible: and sorrow had become an orgiastic frenzy which bordered on madness. The women were dancing now as they circled the body, striking their breasts and howling, but dancing in the slow measured figures of a dance recaptured from long-forgotten friezes upon the tombs of the ancient world. They moved and swayed, quivering from throat to ankles, and they twisted and turned calling upon the dead man to rise. "Rise, my despair! Rise, my death! Rise, my golden one, my death, my camel, my protector! O beloved body full of seed, arise!" And then the ghastly ululations torn from their throats, the bitter tears streaming from their torn minds. Round and round they moved, hypnotized by their own lamentations, infecting the whole house with their sorrow while from the dark courtyard below came the deeper, darker hum of their menfolk sobbing as they touched hands in consolation and repeated, to comfort one another:*"Ma-a-lesh! let it be forgiven! Nothing avails our grief!"*

So the sorrow multiplied and proliferated. From everywhere now the women came in numbers. Some had already put on the dress of ritual mourning—the dirty coverings of dark blue cotton. They had smeared their faces with indigo and rubbed ash from the fires into their black loosened tresses. They now answered the shrieks of their sisters above with their own, baring their glittering teeth, and climbed the stairs, poured into the upper rooms with the ruthlessness of demons. Room by room, with a systematic frenzy, they attacked the old house, pausing only to utter the same terrifying screams as they set about their work.

Bedsteads, cupboards, sofas were propelled out upon the balcony and hurled from there into the courtyard. At each new crash a fresh fever of screaming—the long bubbling *zagreet*— would break out and be answered from every corner of the house. Now the mirrors were shivered into a thousand fragments, the pictures turned back to front, the carpets reversed. All the china and glass in the house—save for the ceremonial black coffee set which was kept for funerals—was now broken up, trampled on, shivered to atoms. It was all swept into a great mound on the balcony. Everything that might suggest the order and continuity of earthly life, domestic, personal or social, must be discarded now and obliterated. The systematic destruction of the memory of death itself in plates, pictures, ornaments or clothes. . . . The house was completely wrecked now, and everything that remained had been covered in black drapes.

Meanwhile, down below a great coloured tent had been pitched, a marquee, in which visiting mourners would come and sit through the whole of the "Night of Loneliness" drinking coffee in silence from the black cups and listening to the deep thrilling moaning up above which swelled up from time to time into a new outbreak of screaming or the noise of a woman fainting, or rolling on the ground in a seizure. Nothing must be spared to make this great man's funeral successful.

Other mourners too had now begun to appear, both personal and professional, so to speak; those who had a personal stake in the funeral of a friend came to spend the night in the coloured marquee under the brilliant light. But there were others, the professional mourners of the surrounding villages for whom death was something like a public competition in the poetry of mourning; they came on foot, in carts, on camel-back. And as each entered the gate of the house she set up a long shivering cry, like an orgasm, that stirred the griefs of the other mourners anew, so that they responded from every corner of the house— the low sobbing notes gradually swelling into a blood-curdling and sustained tongue-trill that pierced the nerves.

These professional mourners brought with them all the wild poetry of their caste, of memories loaded with years of death-practice. They were often young and beautiful. They were singers. They carried with them the ritual drums and tambourines to which they danced and which they used to punctuate their own grief and stimulate the flagging griefs of those who had already been in action. "Praise the inmate of the House" they cried proudly as with superb and calculated slowness they began their slow dance about the body, turning and twisting in an ecstasy of pity as they recited eulogies couched in the finest poetic Arabic upon Narouz. They praised his character, his rectitude, his beauty, his riches. And these long perfectly turned strophes were punctuated by the sobs and groans of the audience, both above and below; so vulnerable to poetry, even the old men seated on the stiff-backed chairs in the tent below, found their throats tightening until a dry sob broke from their lips and they hung their heads, whispering "Ma-a-lesh."

316

Among them, Mohammed Shebab, the old schoolmaster and friend of the Hosnanis, had pride of place. He was dressed in his best and even wore a pair of ancient pearl spats with a new scarlet tarbush. The memory of forgotten evenings which he had spent on the balcony of the old house listening to music with Nessim and Narouz, gossiping to Leila, smote him now with pain which was not feigned. And since the people of the Delta often use a wake as an excuse to discharge private griefs in communal mourning, he too found himself thinking of his dead sister and sobbing, and he turned to the servant, pressing money into his hand as he said: "Ask Alam the singer to sing the recitative of the Image of Women once more, please. I wish to mourn it through again." And as the great poem began, he leaned back luxuriously, swollen with the refreshment of a sorrow which would achieve catharsis thus in poetry. There were others too who asked for their favourite laments to be sung, offering the singers the requisite payment. In this way the whole grief of the countryside was refunded once again into living, purged of bitterness, reconquered by the living through the dead image of Narouz.

Until morning now it would be kept up, the strange circling dances, the ripple and shiver of tambourines, the tongue-trilling screams, and the slow pulse of the dirges with their magnificent plumage of metaphor and image—poetry of the death-house. Some were early overcome with exhaustion and several among the house-servants had fainted from hysteria after two hours of singing thus; the professional keeners, however, knew their own strength and behaved like the ritual performers they were. When overcome by excess of grief or by a long burst of screams, they would sink to the floor and take a short rest, sometimes even smoking a cigarette. Then they would once more join the circle of dancers, refreshed.

Presently, however, when the first long passion of grief had been expressed, Nessim sent for the priests who would add the light of tall bloodless candles and the noise of the psalms to the

317

sound of water and sponge—for the body must be washed. They came at last. The body-washers were the two beadles of the little Coptic Church—ignorant louts both. Here a hideous altercation broke out, for the dead man's clothes are the perquisites of the layer-out, and the beadles could find nothing in Narouz' shabby wardrobe which seemed an adequate recompense for the trouble. A few old cloaks and boots, a torn nightshirt, and a small embroidered cap which dated from his circumcision—that was all Narouz owned. Nor would the beadles accept money—that would have been unlucky. Nessim began to rage, but they stood there obstinate as mules, refusing to wash Narouz without the ritual payment. Finally both Nessim and Balthazar were obliged to get out of their own suits in order to make them over to the beadles as payment. They put on the tattered old clothes of Narouz with a shiver of dread— cloaks which hung down like a graduate's gown upon their tall figures. But somehow the ceremony must be completed, so that he could be taken to the church at dawn for burial—or else the ceremonial mourners might keep up the performance for days and nights together: in the olden times such mourning lasted forty days! Nessim also ordered the coffin to be made, and the singing was punctuated all night by the sound of hammers and saws in the wheelwright's yard hard by. Nessim himself was completely exhausted by now, and dozed fitfully on a chair, being woken from time to time by a burst of keening or by some personal problem which remained to be solved and which was submitted to his arbitration by the servants of the house.

Sounds of chanting, rosy flickering of candle-light, swish of sponges and the scratching of a razor upon dead flesh. The experience gave no pain now, but an unearthly numbness of spirits. The sound of water trickling and of sponges crushing softly upon the body of his brother, seemed part of an entirely new fabric of thought and emotion. The groans of the washers as they turned him over; the thump of the body on the table as it turned over. The soft thump of a hare's dead body

318

when it is thrown onto a kitchen table. . . . He shuddered.

Narouz at last, washed and oiled and sprinkled with rosemary and thyme, lay at ease in his rough coffin clad in the shroud which he, like every Copt, had preserved against this moment; a shroud made of white flax which had been dipped in the River Jordan. He had no jewels or rich costumes to take to the grave with him, but Balthazar coiled the great blood-stained whip and placed it under his pillow. (The next morning the servants were to carry in the body of a wretch whose whole face had been pulped by the blows of this singular weapon; he had run, it seems, screaming and unrecognizable, across the plantation to fall insensible in a dyke and drown. So thoroughly had the whip done its work that he was unidentifiable.)

The first part of the work was now complete and it only remained to wait for dawn. Once more the mourners were admitted to the room of death where Narouz lay, once more they resumed their passionate dancing and drumming. Balthazar took his leave now, for there was nothing more he could do to help. The two men crossed the courtyard slowly, arm in arm, leaning on each other as if exhausted.

"If you meet Clea at the ferry, take her back" said Nessim.

"Of course I will."

They shook hands slowly and embraced each other. Then Nessim turned back, yawning and shivering, into the house. He sat dozing on a chair. It would be three days before the house could be purged of sadness and the soul of Narouz "sent away" by the priestly rituals. First would come the long straggling procession with the torches and banners in the early dawn, before the mist rose, the women with faces blackened now like furies, tearing their hair. The deacons chanting "Remember me O Lord when Thou hast come to Thy Kingdom" in deep thrilling voices. Then on the cold floor of the church the sods raining down on Narouz' pale face and the voices reciting "From dust to dust", and the rolling periods of the evangel singing him away to heaven. Squeak of the brass screws as the lid went down. All this he saw, foreshadowed in his mind as he drowsed upon the stiff-backed chair beside the rough-hewn coffin. Of what, he wondered, could Narouz be dreaming now, with the great whip coiled beneath his pillow?

o o o o o